A MULLIGAN
FOR
BOBBY JOBE

A MULLIGAN
FOR
BOBBY JOBE

BOB CULLEN

HarperCollins*Publishers*

HarperCollins books may be purchased for educational, business, or sales promotional use. For information please write: Special Markets Department, HarperCollins Publishers, Inc., 10 East 53rd Street, New York, NY 10022.

FIRST EDITION

Designed by Jackie McKee

Cullen, Robert, 1949–
    A Mulligan for Bobby Jobe / by Bob Cullen—1st ed.
      p. cm.
    ISBN 0-06-018554-6
      1. Golfers—Fiction. 2. Golf—Tournaments—Fiction. 3. Lightning—Fiction.
      4. Caddies—Fiction. 5. Blind—Fiction. I. Title.

    PS3553.U297 M85 2001
    813′.54—dc21

                                        00-050636

00 01 02 03 04 ❖ RRD 10 9 8 7 6 5 4 3 2 1

For Rafe Sagalyn—agent, muse, and friend

A MULLIGAN
FOR
BOBBY JOBE

1

▼

We were leading the PGA Championship by two strokes when he started seeing all the wrong stuff.

I read that sentence now and I know it's a cliché. Caddies say "we" until the player messes up. Then it's "he."

I was a caddie. That's how I thought.

The fifteenth hole on the West Course at Oak Valley Country Club is a long, dogleg right par four, 463 yards, with a fairway that slopes from right to left. Palmer took a triple there one of the years he blew the PGA.

It's got an elevated tee and the grass was wet because of an earlier thunderstorm. I damn near slipped and fell flat on my face as I humped Bobby's bag up the slope. He was five paces ahead and he didn't notice.

What he did notice, unfortunately, was a blonde in a peach-colored shirt and shorts who was standing just the other side of the ropes along the right side of the tee. She was the kind of woman you often see around golf tournaments and golfers. Everything matches—the clothes, the lipstick, the shades, the shoes, the toenail polish. They're not teenyboppers anymore, maybe got a first marriage behind them, but they're fighting time in a gym and they got the sleek little butt to prove it. This one did. Her name was Lane, or Blaine, or something—one of those family names that rich girls often get instead of something common like Jane or Peggy. I think Bobby met her at one of the pretournament cocktail parties. I don't know if he'd gotten to her at that point but her body language was saying she'd sure as hell give it up for a PGA champion.

I could've walked up behind him, plucked him on the sleeve, and said, "Bobby, you're in the last round of the P-G-goddam-A and you're in the lead and you've just got to play four solid holes to win the thing and there's fifteen thousand people watching you to say nothing of the little guy from CBS with the minicam and the microphone right behind us and you're technically still married and so why don't you start thinking with your head instead of your dick and play some golf?"

But I didn't. Wouldn't've done any good.

He'd've just gotten ticked off and said something like, "Greyhound, why don't you shut the hell up and go clean the grooves on my seven-iron?"

So I just stood there and watched Leonard up ahead of us sweat out his club selection. First he took a long-iron, then a five-wood, then a wedge, and then he reached down and plucked some grass and watched it flutter straight down. Wind didn't matter anyway. The only thing that mattered was I couldn't see Leonard's ankles, the rough was so high. The smart play was to chop it out of there with a wedge. Leonard is a smart player; he did. Then Faxon, who was twenty yards longer than Leonard, had to hit.

I wiped the sweat off my forehead with the towel I used to clean Bobby's golf balls and took a little Powerade from the big canister by the side of the tee and cut it with water. Stuff tastes terrible, but it was a hot day.

"I don't know how you manage in this humidity with that big bag," said the lady who was walking with us, keeping score. She was an older woman name of Florence, with steel-gray hair that was somehow still dry despite the muggy air. Her skin had that kind of slightly loose, slightly wrinkled nutty brown texture that you see on women of a certain age who play a lot of golf. But you could tell she'd been pretty once, so I flirted with her.

"I treat my body like a temple," I said.

She had the grace to laugh. She could probably smell the beer and the hamburger grease coming out my pores. I was twenty-eight years old at that time, but my insides felt like fifty-eight.

Finally, Faxon hit up toward the green, turned the corner of the dogleg, and disappeared. Bobby strolled back to the bag. I looked down the fairway—a tight little ribbon of crosshatched emerald flanked by thick, forest-green rough. Spectators and oak trees lined the hole on both sides, and the low, gray-black clouds overhead completed the frame. But I was looking at the two bunkers on the inside corner of the dogleg, 280 yards out, and thinking, Let's stay out of those; and let's stay out of the rough.

I fingered Bobby's three-wood and pulled it halfway out of the bag.

He had a nice little cut shot with the three-wood that went about 260 yards and that's what I wanted him to hit, short of the bunkers, out of the rough. Leave us a smooth four-iron up to the green and two putts. You're leading by two at the PGA with four to play, pars are like found money.

But Bobby said, "Gimme the driver."

It was Blaine or Lane or whoever she was, that was for sure. The long drive is the big penis of golf and Bobby wanted to show her his.

I almost argued with him, tried to talk him into the three-wood. But I didn't. I'd learned a long time before that it didn't help. Bobby would've taken the driver anyway. Then he'd've stood up to the ball and thought, Jesus. Greyhound doesn't think I can hit this club. That's not what you want your player thinking on his backswing.

So I said, "Good. Shade it a little left of center." I handed him the club.

And damned if he didn't just kill it. It rose straight up against those gray-black clouds, up over the tops of the oaks, and just stayed there.

"Serve dinner and show a movie before that one lands," I murmured to him, just loud enough for him to hear me, in that moment before the screams and cheers of the crowd washed over us. In the last few holes of a big championship the crowd is part of it. You feel their excitement. You jazz them up with a big shot. They jazz you up with a big roar. The ball soared out over the bunkers, faded just a little and bounced to a stop in the middle of the fairway, maybe 330 yards from the tee.

Bobby finished posing the way he liked to do as he watched a good shot. Then he half turned and flipped the driver toward the bag. "Don't show me a club till I tell you what I want to hit," he said. He turned his back on me and strolled off toward the fairway.

He was arrogant. But when you hit the ball 300-plus yards down the middle in the final round of a major, not too many people are going to begrudge you a little ego. It still ticked me off. The three-wood was the right club to hit off that tee.

After I put the driver back in the bag I had to kind of jog a little to try to catch up. No one looks good moving fast with a touring pro's bag on his back. You're like one of those wretched native bearers in a Tarzan movie. And my legs are short and a little bowed. A few people laughed as I hustled after Bobby.

Most people think that was why my nickname out on the Tour was

Greyhound, because my legs were short and I moved slow. That wasn't the reason, but I never bothered to correct people who thought it was. I didn't like the damn name no matter how I got it.

Montgomerie, who did hit three-wood, was seventy yards back of us, so we had some time while we waited for our next shot. The gallery around the hole was getting thicker than a mine owner's belly. I could see people running through the trees from other holes, striving to get a glimpse of the next PGA champion.

And I could see the green up ahead, long and narrow with two tiers. The year he made 7 here, Snead had hit into a left-hand bunker, then Blue Angeled his explosion into a bunker on the other side. I set the bag down a couple of yards to the right of the ball and paced off the distance to the closest sprinkler head. I pulled out my yardage book and the pin sheet and did the arithmetic, going over it twice to make sure I had it right. We had 116 yards to the front edge, 142 to the pin, and another 4 to the back edge.

Bobby was standing there with his hands on his hips and before I could give him the numbers, he kind of leered at me.

"Nice set, huh?" he asked me, so quiet only I could hear it. "You figure they're real?"

"Dammit, Bobby . . . ," I started in.

"I hope they're real," he said. "I hate those damn airbags."

It's a good thing Ken Venturi's never learned to read lips. I've watched the tape of the tournament and at that moment, Bobby was on camera and Kenny was telling people he was talking to his caddie about where he wanted to place his approach shot.

I wanted to chew Bobby out, but I didn't. For one, he wasn't paying me to chew him out. For another, who can say what's the right thing to think about in Bobby's situation? If some guy wins the PGA and lets it be known that he walked down the last few fairways thinking about tits, half the golfing members of the Fellowship of Christian Athletes will be out there the next week undressing spectators in their minds.

So I just said to him, "Okay, you got Joe Montana to the front and Walter Payton to the middle."

Bobby was a big football fan. Sometimes, just to try to loosen him up a little bit, I'd use old football players' numbers to indicate yardage; Joe

Montana wore number 16 and Walter Payton was 34. I hoped that if I got him thinking about what number Walter Payton wore, he'd forget to ask me why I was giving him the yardage to the middle of the green instead of to the pin.

He didn't. "Gale Sayers to the pin?" he asked.

"Ronnie Lott," I told him.

He had no business thinking about the pin. It was set toward the back of the green, way back. Shooting for the pin brought a little pot bunker behind the green into range. We didn't want to go there. But maybe in the back of his primitive little brain he was thinking of what Blaine or Lane might do for another birdie. Or maybe, way the hell in the back, he was thinking of a way to blow it. He'd've punched my lights out if I'd suggested he was tanking it. And he wasn't tanking, if by tanking you mean blowing it on purpose. But there've always been guys in golf who've managed to find ways to come up dumb when they most need to come up smart. It can't always be accidental.

Montgomerie played it safe to the middle of the green and it was our turn. "Gimme the nine," he said. The nine-iron is his 140-yard club.

If he'd asked me first, I'd've told him I thought a wedge was the play. But he didn't. And, again, I didn't want to argue with him, didn't want to mess up his confidence. So I handed him the club. "Hit it close," I said.

Bobby hit it close all right—close to an old guy with a big belly and a cigar who was sitting in one of those little folding chairs behind the green. He made a beautiful swing—too beautiful—and just pured it. The ball lit on the very back edge of the green, took a big hop, and half buried in the little bunker.

"Shit," Bobby yelled, and Venturi wouldn't've had to read lips to know what he said. You could hear it all over the golf course. He turned to me, his face red underneath his Callaway visor. "Wrong fucking yardage, Greyhound," he snarled at me, like it was my fault.

I didn't say anything. Just put my head down and walked up to the green. A caddie's got to take some abuse. It's part of the job.

Bobby made a pretty good shot from the bunker, but he had a downhill lie and the ball was half-plugged. He had as much chance of stopping it near the pin as he'd have of wedging one off the floor of his kitchen and stopping it on the breakfast table. It trickled slowly down to the front like a tear trickling down a kid's cheek. He was lucky to get down in two putts and make a bogey.

I got next to him as we walked to the sixteenth tee and took a look at his face. He was scowling, but his color was closer to normal.

"No big deal," I said. "We're still one up. You're hitting the ball great."

He didn't say anything. Bobby had some history to get around. He'd played four years on the Tour. He'd made a lot of money. But he hadn't won. He'd lost leads early and he'd lost leads late but he'd always found a way to lose them. Now every writer in the media center was thinking that he was going to find some way to blow it again. And so were the people in the gallery. Instead of whooping and hollering and telling Bobby to go get 'em, they were quiet. It was like watching a bad movie where you figure out the ending twenty minutes in and then you have to sit there for another hour and watch while it unfolds.

He stepped out on the tee at No. 16, par five, 570 yards, with a creek running all the way down the left side and curling around the green. We had to wait because Faxon was standing in the fairway about 300 yards out, getting ready to go for the green in two. Reachable par fives can be the toughest holes on the back nine of a major, not because they're so difficult, but because you always have to wait to hit your tee shot. Bobby pulled a seven-iron out of the bag and started doing something I've never seen anyone else do—bouncing a ball off the clubface without looking at it. You've seen Tiger do it in the commercials, but Tiger uses a wedge, and he looks. Bobby was staring down the fairway and the ball just kept bouncing, click-click-click off the face of the iron. Bobby has always had remarkable hands.

THE FIRST TIME I EVER SAW BOBBY HE WAS WINNING MONEY WITH THOSE hands in a beer joint outside of Orlando, where we were both playing on a Class D circuit called the Walter Hagen Tour. The Hagen Tour was for the most marginal of professional tournament golfers, mostly guys like me who were never going to get inside the ropes on the Tour unless we became cops—or caddies. Basically, on the Hagen Tour you bet the field you could win. You anted up a $250 entry fee and played two rounds. The purse came out of the entry fees, after the tour organizer, an old club pro named Hoffenberg, deducted what it cost him to rent the course and cover his own salary. If you played real well on the Hagen Tour for a month, you could break even.

To survive, you had to have a sponsor or you had to hustle and there weren't any sponsors lining up to back me. So I hustled. I had a swing that looked like a beach chair unfolding anyway. And I had a beat-up old golf bag with a clear plastic sleeve sewn into the side. Instead of having my name embroidered on the bag, like a real pro, I had it printed on a piece of stiff paper I could slip in and out of that plastic sleeve. When the tourist season came, I'd pull my name out of the sleeve and go looking for guys with no suntans and expensive golf clubs. It wasn't hard to find 'em and it wasn't hard to convince 'em I was a 12 handicapper just like them. I wasn't proud of it, but I will say that I never wrung anyone dry. I'd keep it close until the last hole or two and I never took anyone for more than a few hundred bucks.

Then I'd put my name back on my bag and go try to be a golf pro, blowing my winnings on Hagen Tour entry fees. I didn't hit the ball all that straight but I putted worse.

Once in a while some kid who was waiting for the Tour Qualifying School would spend a few weeks on the Hagen Tour before moving on. That was Bobby Jobe. He was out of the University of Georgia. He was supposed to be the next Fran Tarkenton, but he hurt his knees. Never played golf seriously till he was nearly through with college.

But he could play. First round he played on the Hagen Tour he shot something like 63. That night I was sitting around with a couple of other Hagen Tour lifers, trying to forget the fact that we'd never shot 63 and never would and here he'd done it in maybe his second year of serious golf. He walks in and takes a seat at the bar and the next thing I see, he's betting some guy a hundred dollars that he can drain six shot glasses full of Scotch and then juggle the glasses through the jukebox rendition of "Margaritaville" without dropping any. And, of course, he did, grinning that damn arrogant grin of his the whole time. He was never movie-star handsome. But he had a mess of hair the color of the prairie around Fort Worth, clear brown eyes, and a swagger in everything he did. He made an impression.

Before the night was out, I told him if he was looking for a caddie at Q-School, I was available. We made it through Q-School easy, and his first tournament was out in Palm Springs, the Bob Hope. I didn't have enough money to fly out. I had to take the bus, a Greyhound bus, and when I got into Indio I had to call him to come pick me up at the bus station in his courtesy car. That's why he started calling me Greyhound and why I've always hated the name. It reminds me of being poor.

FAXON HIT HIS SHOT TOWARD THE GREEN. WE COULDN'T SEE IT LAND, BUT the gallery's roar told us it was on, maybe close. We knew Faxon was just a shot back. If he made birdie, we'd be tied.

Bobby didn't react. He just kept bouncing that ball off his iron and staring at the pot bunker in the middle of the fairway.

That bunker, 275 yards out from the tee box, was the defining characteristic of No. 16. If you wanted to, you could hit a three-wood or an iron short of the bunker, but then you couldn't hope to reach the green in two shots. You could play to the left or the right, but that meant you were aiming for only half a fairway. Or you could try to hit over it, which is what Bobby had done the first three rounds. If you hit the bunker, though, you might need need both hands to count your strokes on.

The breeze kicked up the way it often does before a thunderstorm, turning up the leaves on the maple and oak trees around the tee, showing their gray undersides, fluttering the sleeve on Bobby's blue-and-white striped shirt. It was right in our face.

Montgomerie hit his usual dead-straight three-wood and it stopped about twenty yards short of the sand, right in the middle. But he was three strokes behind and what he did didn't matter to us. It was Bobby and Faxon.

Bobby stepped back to the bag and laid a hand over the top of it. Just to kind of hint at what I was thinking, I reached down and snatched a handful of grass off the tee and let it flutter from my fingers. It blew back against the PGA logo across the chest of my caddie bib.

"Whaddaya think?" he asked. It was a bad sign. Some guys routinely ask their caddie for club advice before they make their selection. Bobby only did when his instincts shrugged their shoulders and told him, "Don't look at us."

"Three-wood," I said. "Put it in the fairway, hit a two-iron, knock the wedge stiff. We'll get a birdie with your putter."

He didn't say yes or no. "Wouldn't you know the wind would come up after Faxon hit?" he said. He said it loud enough so that Montgomerie heard. So did Jello McKay, who was carrying Montgomerie's bag that week. Montgomerie's eyes widened slightly. He's thrown enough pity parties for himself to recognize what Bobby was doing.

Bobby sighed. "Gotta try for the birdie, 'Hound. I think I can carry it." He pulled the driver out of the bag.

I wanted to say, "Bobby, you can't think you can carry it over. You gotta know you're gonna carry it." I wanted to ask him if he wanted to blow it, if he was afraid to win. I didn't. I just watched.

Bobby made a pretty good swing, but a little quick. The wind seemed to freshen just as he hit it.

"Get up," Bobby said. So did about ten thousand other people.

I don't talk to golf balls much and I could see right away it wouldn't do much good with this one. It headed for that bunker like one of those laser-guided bombs, caught the lip and disappeared. The crowd let out a soft little "ooh."

Bobby watched it for a minute, then glared at me. "You had to tell me to hit three-wood," he snapped. "You knew I'd wind up hitting driver!"

I suddenly didn't want to take any more crap from him. "If you don't want to know what I think, don't ask," I snapped. "Why don't you quit being an asshole and play some golf?"

I still couldn't tell you exactly why I lost it like that. I mean, obviously, the guy's in the process of pissing away a win that would've been worth about sixty grand to me, since the caddie generally gets ten percent of a winner's purse. But it wasn't the money—or, at least, it wasn't only the money. I was just fed up with working so hard to help get Bobby into a position to win, to change both our lives, and then seeing him blow it because he didn't have the guts of a goldfish.

A few guys out on the Tour might've responded positively to hearing that, the way some kids will stop crying and whining if you give them a little smack across the mouth. Not Bobby. For a minute he looked surprised. Then his face kind of twisted like I was a mouse he'd woke up and found in his bed. I knew then that I'd crossed a line.

Jello McKay was looking almost as upset as Bobby, and as we walked down the fairway, he sidled over toward me. Jello was an old black guy, a freelancer. He'd work for one guy for a month, then another for a few weeks. Not many black guys have regular bags anymore. He was working for Montgomerie that week because Montgomerie's regular guy was sick back in London. I guess Jello had taken a lot more crap in his day than I'd ever had to take from Bobby Jobe, because he looked at me pretty sternly.

"Calm down, young man. This ain't the time for arguing," he said.

I should've listened to him. I just nodded.

The bunker was a nasty one, a little pit with walls about six feet high and barely enough room inside to take a club back. We were nearly three hundred yards from the pin. It was going to take a damn good shot just to get it out of there, let alone advance it far enough to have a prayer of reaching the green in three. Just then another roar came from around the green. Faxon was in the hole and we had to try to gauge the noise level to figure out how many strokes it had taken him.

"Not loud enough for an eagle," Bobby said. "But I think he made birdie."

"Probably," I said.

I could barely look at him, I was so angry.

"I think I can get the sand wedge out of here," Bobby said.

He had a lob wedge in the bag with more loft than his sand wedge. But I knew what he was thinking. His lob wedge wouldn't carry more than seventy yards. He needed to hit it a little longer to have a good shot at the green and a chance to save par.

"Go for it," I said. I handed him the club.

He almost pulled the shot off. He caught it clean and he got it up in the air. But the damn ball caught the lip and rolled right back toward his feet. He had to hop out of the way to avoid a penalty stroke. He looked like a guy putting out the garbage dodging a raccoon who jumps out from behind the cans.

Someone in the gallery tittered behind us. I could see the PGA guy out of the corner of my eye, wondering if maybe the ball hadn't brushed over Bobby's shoes.

Bobby turned pale for a moment, then purple like an unripe blackberry. I don't think he was as mad about seeing his lead slip away as he was embarrassed to look like a Sunday hacker on national television.

And of course he took it out on me.

"Yeah, Bobby, you can get a sand wedge out of there. Go for it," he snarled. "Greyhound, you're the biggest waste of white skin I've seen in my goddam life."

I didn't have any trouble hearing him. On the other side of the bunker, out of the corner of my eye, I could see that Peter Kostis from CBS had heard it, too. His mouth was open. Florence the scorekeeping lady heard it. She gasped.

But I asked him anyway. "What'd you say?"

Bobby didn't even have the guts to own up to it. "I said gimme the lob wedge."

At that point I wanted him to leave a few more shots in the bunker. I try not to be a racist, though I guess I am. I try to treat everyone the same and I try not to say anything that'll offend someone. But where I come from, what Bobby said to me was cause enough for a fistfight. I couldn't tolerate it. For the moment, I just handed him the club and took the sand wedge back, wiped it off and stuck it in the bag real hard. But I knew I was going to have to quit when the tournament was over. I was sick to death of taking crap from Bobby Jobe.

Bobby took a couple of deep breaths, tried to compose himself. And though he caught a little sand, he managed to hit the lob wedge out of the bunker, pushing it maybe fifty yards closer to the green.

Then he started singing under his breath. "They're writing winner's checks," he sang. "But not for me."

Only I could hear it.

It was part of his routine when he choked. He liked to sing something to irritate me, to rub my nose in the fact that he was going to choke away a lot of money, a piece of which would've been mine. Most times he sang "I Fall to Pieces." He knew that got to me because I revered Patsy Cline. This time it was a song Ella Fitzgerald had done because he knew I'd inherited a taste for Ella from my mother. Bobby thought it was like dressing a monkey in a tuxedo for me to like an Ella Fitzgerald song. When he was feeling particularly mean and miserable, he'd sing a snatch of "But Not for Me." It wasn't like Bobby knew anything about music and was mocking my taste. His favorite singer was Dolly Parton, and his next-favorite would've been whoever had the next-biggest rack. He was just mean when things went wrong.

"Jesus," I said. "Can't you pretend you're trying to win this thing? And can't we leave Ella Fitzgerald out of this?"

"Shut up, Greyhound," he said. "Get the yardage."

I paced off the distance from the nearest sprinkler head and I didn't bother to encode it in football players' numbers. "Two-twenty-seven front, two-forty-three pin," I told him.

He didn't really have a club for the shot. Because he carried a lob wedge, he didn't have a one-iron or a fairway wood shorter than his three-wood. The three-wood was too much club.

"Gotta be the 2-iron," I said. He just nodded.

I gave him the club. He couldn't seem to get his feet settled when he addressed the ball. He backed off once, then squirmed into position again. He waggled. He looked at the distant green. He waggled again. He looked up one more time and I could tell that what he was seeing wasn't the pin. It was the creek. And he swung.

It was an ugly swing, one I'd seen before. When Bobby choked, he usually swung too hard, closed the face, and snapped the ball left. He hit a duck hook that practically quacked. It dove into the creek about thirty yards shy of the green.

The crowd let out another punched-in-the-gut moan. Montgomerie turned away. It wasn't something he wanted to watch.

Bobby seemed strangely listless. He watched the ball sink out of sight and tossed the club toward the bag. "Nice clubbing, 'Hound," he said. "You're fired."

I didn't think. I just reacted.

"Fine, Bobby," I said mildly. "Carry your own damn bag in."

And I dropped the bag on the ground, letting the clubs rattle. I pulled the caddie bib over my head and dropped it on top of the bag. I knocked my hat off doing it. I smoothed my soaking wet hair down, picked up the hat and put it back on, and walked toward the ropes.

Jello McKay intercepted me. He grabbed my elbow.

"Don't do this, young man," he said quietly. "I heard what he said. It doesn't matter. You stay with the bag. Wanna quit, quit later."

It was good advice. But Jello seemed to me then a sorry figure with curly gray hair matted down under a cap, his shirt and his big belly wet with sweat. I understood that for all that he'd no doubt put up with in his life and his looping, he'd never done what I was doing.

"Thanks, Jello," I said. "But I don't care."

I walked off. When I ducked under the ropes, people parted for me like I had the measles. I could hear whispering and buzzing; my ears felt hot. When I looked back, Bobby was staring at me, hands on his hips. Our eyes caught one another. I thought he looked more forlorn than mad, like maybe he'd like to do the last twenty minutes over.

But I lived by the code that there are no do-overs in golf or anything else. People sometimes pretended there were. They'd take mulligans on the first tee till they'd be happy with one. But they didn't fool me. I knew that first ball is the only one that counts.

So I couldn't go back.

I felt both lost and free as I walked away.

I know what happened to Bobby on the last few holes only by what I read in the papers and saw on tape. He drafted some kid out of the gallery to carry his bag. He dropped next to the creek, hit a sloppy pitch, and wound up taking 9 on the hole. And he bogeyed one of the last two. He finished tied for tenth.

I RETREATED TO THE LITTLE TENT THAT THE PGA SO GENEROUSLY PROVIDES to shelter caddies from the sun and rain, the kind of sideless tent they pitch over gravesites. They had a few folding chairs there and I sat a while, got myself a beer from one of the concession stands, and sat some more. A few of the guys patted me on the back and told me they'd have done the same thing, but they were obviously lying. Most of them stayed away from me. Off in the distance I could hear the applause as the last groups finished and they presented the trophy.

My head was down and I saw a pair of beat-up running shoes coming my way and smelled smoke from a cheap cigar. I looked up and saw Ken Alyda from the AP.

"Got a minute, Greyhound?" he asked me.

I usually didn't talk to reporters. No smart caddie does. It can only get you in trouble like it got Mike Cowan in trouble with Tiger Woods. But I knew Alyda a little. He was a gangly, ugly old guy with a rough complex-

ion and just a frizzy fringe of gray hair around his head, but he was one of
the reporters who got out of the media center and its free buffet and actually walked around the golf course to see what was going on. Besides, I
wasn't caddying for anyone anymore. So I said, yeah, I had a minute. He
asked me what happened out there. I told him the truth. He wrote some
notes in the pad he was carrying.

When I was finished, Alyda shook his head.

"That Jobe," he said. "A million-dollar swing and a ten-cent head."

I didn't argue with him.

"So what're you going to do now?" Alyda asked. "Any chance you'll
get back together with him?"

I snorted. "About the same chance you and I got of starring in
Cameron Diaz's next movie."

Cameron Diaz is my favorite actress, even though she was putting a
pretty lousy swing on the ball in the driving-range scene in *There's
Something About Mary.*

Alyda smiled. "You'll get another bag," he said.

We both knew he was just trying to be polite. "After I do that movie,"
I said.

Alyda nodded. "Where you going now?"

I'd been thinking about that. I had a little condo in Orlando, a one-bed-
room near the airport, but I'd sublet it to a guy who was trying his luck on
the Hagen Tour. I couldn't go back there without paying rent to someone.

I'd been staying mostly away from home since I finished high school.
Partly it was because of the girl I was in love with in high school. She married someone else while I was in the army. She'd lived at home, but my
mother had just written and told me she'd moved to Roanoke with her
husband and kids. In the same letter, my mother had written me that her
superintendent had quit. So I had a couple of reasons to visit her. I figured
it would be just temporary, till the stink of my quitting on Bobby wore off
and I figured out how to get back on the Tour.

"I think I might go home for a little while," I said to Alyda. "My mother
runs a little nine-hole course back there. She could use some help."

Alyda nodded. "Your home's in Virginia, right?"

I nodded, surprised he knew. "Allegheny Gap," I said.

"That's the course your father built?"

Alyda couldn't have surprised me more if he'd told me about the little tiger tattoo I had on my butt for a while when I was in the service.

"How'd you know that?"

Alyda put the cigar back in his mouth and chewed a little. "I been out here a long time, Greyhound," he said. "I knew your father back when he was on the Tour. He told me once about the course he was building. How is he?"

I was still a little flustered, so I told Alyda the truth. "I don't know," I said. "He took off when I was thirteen. Haven't heard from him since."

Alyda stuffed his notebook in his back pocket and exhaled a cloud of smoke. "Sorry to hear that," he said. I thought about asking what else he remembered about Clayton Mote. I didn't. My mother hadn't raised me to talk about private matters with strangers. I just nodded. He shifted on his feet, uncomfortable. Then he told me he had to run and file his story. We shook hands and he left.

A rumble of thunder got me out of my chair. I stepped outside the little tent and looked around. Nearly everyone was gone. The concessionaires were banging things together, breaking down their stands. A couple of black guys in coveralls were walking around with sacks and sticks, poking at scraps of paper with a needle mounted in the end of the stick.

It was getting very dark. The clouds I'd seen earlier had massed and thickened. The air had that pregnant feel to it. The sky looked black and purple, with a faint yellow haze underneath it. Off in the distance, I could see the line of rain. Judging by the wind, it would be over the golf course in maybe five minutes.

I had to catch the shuttle bus between the course and a shopping center five miles away where the caddies assembled to ride to work. I headed for the bus stop, which was over by the practice range. The leaves in the trees above me were starting to rustle the way they do before it rains. I picked up my pace.

But above that rustling sound I heard something else—the whoosh that a club shaft makes when a good player swings and the solid thwack you hear when he makes contact with a ball. That sound, more than anything else, tells you a shot is good, because you only hear it when the clubface meets the ball flush on the sweet spot and the ball flattens out for an instant before it flies away.

In fact, it's my opinion that good golfers all have a distinctive sound print they make when they hit the ball, a combination of whoosh and thwack that marks them and them alone, the way some unique combination of scents marks a dog's territory.

I knew that sound. I'd heard it often enough to have it engraved in my inner ear. It was Bobby's.

I was in the drive heading for the parking lot. A grass berm separated me from the practice tee. I climbed it.

There was only one player out there, standing next to a loose pile of those fresh Titleists that the pros hit for practice. It was Bobby. His bag lay on the ground nearby. He was swinging his two-iron, checking his backswing, trying to figure out how he'd got into position to snap it. It was getting black around the edges of the encroaching storm cell, but I could make out a white towel set ten paces in front of one of the distant blue flags 250 yards from the tee. I knew immediately what Bobby was doing. He was hitting the shot he'd butchered on the sixteenth hole.

More thunder rumbled, and then lightning flashed. It looked to be a mile away. The wind picked up to a gale, blowing dust and bits of turf over the tee. The first few fat, warm drops of rain started to fall.

I thought about leaving, but I couldn't.

A guy in a blue PGA blazer trotted out of the clubhouse to the practice tee just as Bobby launched another shot. The ball started low and rose gradually, hanging white and bright in the sky against those black-and-purple clouds, picking up and reflecting the little bit of late sunlight that was filtering through the incoming storm. Then it curved gently from right to left and came down maybe five paces short of the towel. It bounced twice, softly, then stuck.

The PGA guy had stopped moving while the ball was in flight, impressed by the purity of Bobby's swing. But then he moved forward and grabbed Bobby's right arm. Bobby shook him off and raked another ball into place, setting it up on the back edge of the divots line he was making as he hit the ball.

The man in the blue blazer stepped forward again. I couldn't hear what he was saying, because the wind had shifted. But I could see him pointing to the sky and it was clear that he was telling Bobby it was dangerous to stay out there.

It was also clear Bobby wasn't in a mood to listen. Bobby didn't practice all that much. I can't remember the number of times he told me to show up at the course at seven so he could hit balls for a couple of hours before he teed off, and then he strolled in at eight-thirty, having decided he needed rest more than practice. But there were times, generally right after he'd lost a lead, when he'd get obsessed with working some kink out of his swing. This was one of them. Of course, he should've been thinking of ways to work the kink out of his brain.

He took a practice swing that nearly clipped the ear off the PGA guy. The guy shrugged elaborately and trotted back to where he came from.

The rain started to come down harder, though it was evident that the worst of it, the downpour, was still a few minutes away. I wanted to head for the bus, but I also had half a notion to walk out there and stand behind Bobby for old time's sake, maybe clean the grooves on that two-iron one more time, maybe say good-bye. He had a ten-cent head, just like Ken Alyda had said. He was nasty mean. But he'd given me the chance to hang around the best golfers in the world for four years and get paid for doing it. That was something.

He swung again, taking the club back nice and slow and lazy-looking, like he didn't want to do more than bunt the ball down the range. Then the power uncoiled and before you could even see what happened his body unwound and the club came down and he was standing there in his follow-through position, his shoulders 180 degrees from where they were at the top of his backswing, and the ball was just crushed.

This one had less draw than the one before. It flew a little lower. It screamed off the range like an arrow and before it was halfway to its target I knew that Bobby had pured it. It needed to draw in just a fraction and it did. It took one little skippy bounce and landed smack on the towel. There it rested.

I didn't know whether to clap or to cry. Bobby held his follow-through position for a moment, then raised both arms toward that black, lowering sky in triumph, the club held high above him. The rain was pelting his face now and he was saying something I couldn't quite make out, saying it to the sky. It didn't look like a prayer. The wind gusted and I saw it blow his visor off.

I didn't see the lightning bolt. You see lightning bolts, the jagged kind, from a distance. When it comes down nearly on top of you, all you see is a quick, general flash, like a strobe popping in your face. But I do remember seeing Bobby's club light up first, just for an instant, before everything disappeared in the general glare.

I felt a concussive kind of blast. It knocked me over, flat on my back. The electricity in the air made the hairs on my head stand straight up. I may have been unconscious for a minute or two. I know that when I got up, Bobby was stretched out on the ground next to that pile of Titleists, writhing on his back. It was raining harder, really pouring. The PGA guy had come out of the clubhouse again and was sprinting toward Bobby.

I ran toward him, too, but I couldn't move very fast. I was dizzy. I smelled a strange kind of electrical stench, like a short circuit smells, acrid and unsettling.

When I got there, the PGA guy was crouched over Bobby, holding his head up, keeping his mouth open. The skin on his face was all red and swollen and blistered. The hair at the top of his head, the hair where his eyebrows used to be—it was gone. His eyes were nearly swollen shut; they were just slits. But he was breathing, moaning softly.

I stood over him and that blistered, swollen face turned straight toward mine.

"Bobby, you okay?" the PGA guy yelled.

"Who's that?" Bobby croaked out.

Without answering, the PGA guy turned around and called out in the general direction of the clubhouse for someone to send the ambulance.

Bobby's head rotated around, trying to locate the source of the voice. He couldn't. There was nothing behind those scorched eyelids but ashes.

2

▼

I VISITED HIM ONCE IN THE HOSPITAL. THE TOP HALF OF HIS HEAD WAS wrapped in bandages like a mummy's and I guess he was under pretty heavy sedation. I managed to say that I was sorry for what had happened to him and I was sorry I'd walked off and left his bag. I told him I was sure his eyes would get better, even though I didn't think they would. I'd seen what happened to them. I had a wan hope that he would say he was sorry for what he'd said and done, too, that he'd settle accounts and leave things even. But he didn't.

He sat halfway up, propping himself on his elbows. His voice, when he started to talk, was raspy and low, like the lightning had scorched his throat as well as his eyes. This is what he said: "Fuck you, Greyhound. If it weren't for you, this wouldn't've happened to me. Go straight to fucking hell and rot there."

Anyone else, I'd've just told him where to shove it and walked away. But I was making allowances for Bobby's condition. So I started to sweet-talk him a little. He didn't mean that, I said.

That only upset him.

"Fuck you!" he started to yell, his voice cracking under the strain. "Go to hell! Go to hell!"

Bobby was always one of your more eloquent and articulate athletes.

The ruckus he raised caused the nurses to come running into the room. They shoved me out the door and I left.

He never paid me for my last week's work, but I figured he had enough problems and he was out of my life, anyway. I didn't forget what he'd said to me, though. That sort of thing stays with you.

Jello McKay, it turned out, had been right about one thing. No one wanted to hire a caddie who'd walk off, even if he'd walked off from a certified jerk. I phoned every pro I heard had fired his caddie. I wrote letters to the ones who got through Q-School in the fall. I went out to California in January to see if someone was looking for a looper on the West Coast swing. No one would hire me. Most of 'em talked to me like I had some kind of disease. I don't guess they actually thought I'd caused the lightning to hit Bobby in the eyes. But a lot of pro golfers don't even like to be around troubles and failure. They know it can't really rub off on them, but why take chances? Making money on the Tour is hard enough when everything's going right. So my temporary stay at home started to look ominously longer. And, of course, the more it looked like I couldn't go back on the Tour, the more I wanted to be out there.

Eight long months passed. Spring came. It was time for the Masters and I was watching it on the television set that hangs over the little snack bar at the Eadon Branch Golf Course, the one my father had built and my mother owned. Watching the Masters was like going to church on Easter, something you just had to do. But usually I didn't like to watch much golf on TV. It made me miss the Tour too much and it made me feel like maybe I never would get out of Allegheny Gap.

Allegheny Gap is a good place for making you restless. It isn't much, just a coal-mining town on the eastern side of the mountains in southwest Virginia, hugging both sides of the bottomland around the Gaulor River. It's big enough for a McDonald's and a Wal-Mart, and a courthouse. A couple of thousand clapboard houses that used to be owned by the mines, a neighborhood called The Heights where the doctors and lawyers and bankers live, one movie theater, one high school with a big football field, a few gas stations, and that's about it. When coal prices are good, there's a little money around. When coal prices fall, when miners get laid off, half the town goes to the hills to hunt small game and half the rest goes to bed hungry.

Eadon Branch G.C. is in a cramped little valley a mile outside of town, tucked in between Eadon Mountain and the county airstrip. I can remember when I was very young that the mountain and the smaller hills around it were all velvety green with trees in the summer and blazing red and yellow in the fall. But that was before the coal companies got hold of them and stripped them and left the hillsides a mess of brown gashes the size of aircraft carriers. The feds make them plant something when they leave, but not much grows on scarred land—a few scrubby pines and some weeds, maybe, but not the hickory and ash and oak and maple trees that were there before. They won't come back in my lifetime. And I can remember when Eadon Branch had fish in it—brook trout, mostly. They're gone, too. The water looks clear, but it's full of acids and poisons that leach out of the mines. We were having a tough time growing good turf grass on the golf course, especially down by the water.

The course was as important in the world of golf as Allegheny Gap was in the world—not very. My father had drawn up plans for 18 holes, but he only built nine. The rest were just fading orange ribbons wrapped around trees higher up the slope, trees my father would've had logged to make room for his fairways if he hadn't gone away. Still, even with just nine holes and turf that could get patchy, it was a layout that was better than it looked. The greens were small and tricky—you thought that all putts should break away from the mountain, but Clayton Mote had put the holes in unpredictable places. He'd laid out a reachable par five to start you off, but then he had doglegs left and doglegs right, a long par four with the stream down the left side, and a par three over a little pond. He had a short, tight hole with trees on both sides and a wide-open par four where you could blast away with the driver. The layout was a little weird—when you left the fourth green you had to circle around the ninth to get to the fifth tee. But from the back tees, par 36 was a fine score. He'd set the course record the spring he left—31. The best I'd ever done was 35. When my mother managed to collect the money, we charged nine dollars for nine holes and fifteen dollars to go around twice, so it was a bargain, too.

We had a one-room clubhouse built of whitewashed cinder blocks with a peaked tin roof. It sat on a knoll a couple of hundred yards from the road and looked down on No. 1, going away, and No. 9, coming in. The clubhouse had a few racks of shirts and hats, a couple of sets of new clubs for anyone who wasn't smart enough to buy 'em for less at Wal-Mart, a Formica lunch counter, a cash register, and three tables where some of the old guys, retired miners, spent their time playing gin rummy for nickels and dimes. The walls had some posters my mother got years ago from a Wilson rep—Sam Snead promoting a line of clubs that Sam never really used and the company didn't make anymore. The only thing new in the place was the television and satellite dish that my mother bought so she could watch the soaps on slow afternoons. Eudora handled the cash and the lunch counter. She took in the greens fees, cooked the hot dogs, and put together the pimento cheese sandwiches. I handled everything else. Eudora'd told me I was the pro, but that was a joke. No one took lessons. We didn't have the money to hire an experienced superintendent, so I did that job. And I had to be the starter, too, or else half the players would've sneaked on. I spent my days busting my butt to keep the place going and my nights thinking of ways I could help my mother replace me.

This was a Saturday afternoon, and the early-morning guys had all gone off and finished, and the handful of players who'd try to get in nine after the first shift ended in the mines hadn't gotten there yet. I was sitting at the counter, working through a can of Miller, having a pimento cheese sandwich, and telling a couple of regulars, Conrad Williams and J. R. Neill, about shots I'd seen Tiger hit during practice rounds at Augusta, back before his disk problems started. Since I'd caddied on the Tour, people in Allegheny Gap tended to think of me as an expert on golf and I have to admit I didn't mind occasionally playing the part. The third round of the tournament was about half over, but we weren't paying close attention.

"Henry, you're on TV!" Eudora said.

Eudora is a pretty sophisticated lady for a town like Allegheny Gap. She wears skirts and dresses and she buys Lancome perfume. She could've gone to college and she traveled a fair amount before I was born. But it was still hot stuff to her when someone she knew got on TV. She grabbed the remote and raised the volume.

"Hey, that is you, Henry," J. R. confirmed. He was almost as impressed as Eudora.

I was eager to see myself. I'd had the back of my head on *Sports Center* a lot when I was on the Tour with Bobby, but the past eight months I'd felt pretty anonymous.

It was tape of last year's PGA, the sixteenth hole in the final round, and I watched Bobby hit into that pot bunker and then stay in it. It was damned unpleasant to see again, and I stuffed the last of the pimento cheese sandwich into my mouth and reached for a Moon Pie in the little rack of candy and cakes Eudora kept by the cash register. She gently slapped my hand away.

"You don't need that," she said softly. Both of us were paying more attention to the TV than to what we were doing.

"Oh, come on, Eudora," I started to complain.

"Hush up," Conrad said. "This is interesting."

He meant the TV, not whether my mother was going to stop treating me like a ten-year-old and let me have a damn Moon Pie. Eudora worried that if I let myself get too fat I wouldn't be able to find a wife and settle down. When I was eighteen, she was scared to death I'd marry my high school flame, Peggy Shiflett, and stay in Allegheny Gap forever. Ten years later—after Peggy'd long since married someone else and I finally came back home—she was scared to death I wouldn't marry someone and stay in Allegheny Gap forever. She's a good mother but she's not 100 percent logical. And it ticked me off that she and everyone else in the town assumed that I'd had my chance to get out, blown it, and was home to stay.

On the TV, the scene switched to a shot of Bobby Jobe in a hospital in Nashville, wearing golf clothes and big Oakley sunglasses. It was a little strange seeing him on TV without his Callaway hat. The company had always paid him a bonus if he got himself interviewed with that hat on and he'd've worn it in the shower if he had to to collect that money. I figured it meant that his Callaway contract had expired. He looked a little thinner, I thought, but strong, not frail. The swagger was still in his walk, even though he was walking a half step behind a pretty girl with a frizzy mane of flame-red hair and fair skin. He had his hand on her elbow. She was his rehab instructor, Jim Nantz said.

I'll bet, I thought. Even blind, Bobby Jobe would have a good-looking woman at his side.

Now Bobby was sitting somewhere and the camera was full in his face—you could see the camera and the spotlight reflected in his Oakleys—and he was telling Nantz how much he appreciated all the cards and letters from golf fans all over the world, how they made it easier to accept that he had to get on with his life.

"I bet he's going to say, 'The Lord does these things for a purpose,'" I told Eudora.

"The Lord does these things for a purpose," Bobby said on the screen. "Right now, I'm trying to figure out what his purpose was." He grinned a little.

Bobby was always big on getting Jesus into his TV interviews.

"You've had a rough year in many ways," Nantz was saying. "You've had a divorce."

Bobby nodded. I was sorry to hear that he and Paula had gone ahead and made their separation final. I'd always liked Paula. She'd treated me nice and she'd tried to be a good influence on Bobby. I'd been hoping that maybe they'd get back together after the accident.

"That was in the works long before the accident and it was all my fault," Bobby said.

Well, I thought, at least he told the truth about that.

Nantz asked him what he intended to do after his rehab was over. Bobby said he hoped to start a career as a motivational speaker.

I snorted. There were only two things I'd ever seen motivate Bobby. One was money and the other was women. I could just imagine the motivational speech he'd give: "Get rich, folks! And after you're rich, chase pussy!"

Now Nantz was talking about Bobby's rehab program, how he was working on something called facial vision. The camera cut to a shot of Bobby and his rehab instructor. He was wearing gym shorts and a T-shirt and those Oakleys and he was standing in a room where a couple of dozen pieces of masonite were dangling from the ceiling, hanging down to about waist level. Bobby's job was to walk slowly, shuffling his feet, trying to detect the location of the masonite panels and walk around them. The blind can learn to navigate independently if they can pick up the echoes that bounce off walls and things, Nantz said. Bobby apparently still had some things to learn, because he bumped into a few of the panels before the camera cut back to Nantz and Ken Venturi in the booth at No. 18.

"A courageous man," Nantz said.

"A real tragic story," Venturi said, nodding.

"But we have a story of a different kind unfolding here," Nantz said, and it was back to golf coverage.

The door from the first tee burst open just then and Raymond Vickers stuck his head inside just long enough to yell, "Incoming!"

"Hot damn," J. R. said. He and Conrad hustled outside, looking for their drivers. I got ready to follow them.

"Henry, you've got to stop letting them do this," Eudora said. "The insurance man said we're not covered for it."

I turned and looked at her and I was suddenly struck by how old she was getting. Eudora was only eighteen when she had me—six months after the wedding—and I'd always known she was the prettiest mother in all the classes I was in, right through high school. Whatever good features I have—thick brown hair, blue eyes, a good, strong chin—come from her. And I remember that when I was a boy, she was always ready to have a little fun. I remember her taking me to the county fair every summer, all dressed up and eager to plunk down a quarter at every carny's booth on the midway. But her life certainly hadn't turned out the way she'd planned, and I'd noticed more and more since I got home how cautious and close to dry she was getting.

"It's all right, Eudora," I said. I patted her hand. "You know we can't hit anything."

She just frowned, picked up the remote, and switched the channel from CBS and the Masters to American Movie Classics. Every time Eudora felt unhappy about something, she blamed golf.

I picked up a demo driver, a discontinued TaylorMade the sales rep had given us for nothing, and hustled out the door toward the golf course. Eadon Branch didn't have a real practice range, but it did have a wide strip of weedy grass next to the first hole, with a lesson tee at the top. My father, I guess, had figured he'd be doing some teaching, so he'd built it there. We used it mainly for the junior clinics we held on Fridays in the summertime—and for shooting at airplanes.

Shooting at airplanes was a tradition at Eadon Branch that I am told by J. R. Neill was started by my father. The way the wind blows most of the time in the Gaulor Valley, small planes coming into the county airstrip fly right over the golf course. The knoll where the clubhouse sits looks out over the flight path. What you see mostly are company planes carrying coal executives in from Richmond or Pittsburgh or wherever.

This plane was a little single-engine Cessna, and it was almost over the third green when I got there. J. R., Conrad, Raymond and a couple of other guys were already teed up. I grabbed a ball—a beat-up old Top-Flite—from the milk crate on the tee where I kept found golf balls. I stuck it on a tee and put it in the ground. Before I could straighten up, J. R. Neill had hit.

J. R. has a bad left arm, permanently bent from an old mine accident, so his swing is a little cramped, and he's always too anxious and hits too soon. This ball was pathetic, a low semi-skull job that could only have hit the Cessna if it was parked on the ground a hundred and fifty yards off the tee.

"Damn, that was close," J. R. yelled, which is what he's been yelling since Eadon Branch golfers started shooting at planes.

Conrad and Raymond and the others fired away before I could get set up properly. Their shots were about as good as J. R.'s. I tried to take my time, but the plane was just about right in front of me when I drew the club back.

I knew that I wasn't going to hit it. No one ever had. The planes looked a lot closer than they were. You'd have to hit a drive that was a hundred feet up in the air nearly three hundred yards off the tee just to have a chance. But I liked to hit a good shot when I fired at planes, liked being considered the guy with the best chance to hit one.

I was too rushed. I swayed back instead of turning, lost my balance a little, and pulled up as I was coming through the hitting area. Instead of a line drive over the wall in left center, I hit a pop-up behind third base. The plane descended blithely toward the airstrip and disappeared from our view behind a copse of pines.

"Oh, you scared him with that one, Henry," J. R. said. He was being sarcastic.

"Yeah, he's changing course and flying back to Roanoke," Conrad joined in. Conrad always took his cues from J. R.

I just scowled and took a couple of practice swings, the way Bobby Jobe did when he mishit a shot, so his last muscle memory would be of a good swing.

"I think you missed by the most, Henry," J. R. said. That meant I had to go down the hill off the practice tee and pick up the golf balls, a house rule I had established thinking that I would never be the one to have to do it. I could've argued that J. R. missed by more than I did, but J. R. was fifty-seven years old, which is old for a man in Allegheny Gap, and it was a hot day so I picked up the milk crate and walked down the knoll to shag the balls.

I was sweating pretty good by the time I came back up the slope to the tee, thinking that Eudora was right when she tried to get me to stop eating so many Moon Pies. The guys had all gone back inside to watch the Masters, and there was a lone figure standing there, waiting—a woman. She could've been twenty-five or thirty-five. It was hard to tell. She was wearing a New York Mets hat that barely stayed on the curly red hair that blasted out of her head in thick, shiny bunches. It was the color of flame—deep orange in some spots, nearly yellow in others, nearly brown in some, depending on how the light struck her. She was thin, pale, kind of tall, maybe two inches taller than me, almost gawky. She had a little pink lipstick on a wide mouth that seemed like it would hold a good smile. She had freckles, faded jeans and a red plaid shirt with no sleeves, and some kind of sandals on her feet. I couldn't see her eyes because of her sunglasses—the cheap kind you can get for $4.95 at Sheetz gas stations. But I thought she might've been pretty. Look at her from one angle and she looked like a Raggedy Ann doll. From just a slightly different angle, she looked like Angie Everhart, who, if Tour caddies were in charge of *Sports Illustrated*, would have been on the cover of the swimsuit issue many times by now. That was how she was—hard to pin down.

She took a step toward me as I climbed up onto the lesson tee and said, "Are you Greyhound?"

And then I recognized her. She was the girl I'd just seen on television with Bobby Jobe—the rehab instructor.

I didn't know why, but I felt irritated. "No," I said. "I'm not."

That kind of brought her up short. She looked around. "This is the Eadon Branch Golf Course?" She pronounced it "Ee-don."

"Nope," I told her. It's traditional in Allegheny Gap to be a little rude to outsiders, especially outsiders in New York hats with New York accents, but this was more than just the traditional local rudeness. I didn't know why I resented her right off, but I did.

"But the sign on the road says Eadon Branch Golf Course," she said stubbornly.

"It's pronounced Ay-don," I told her.

She flushed a little and winced and I realized that I'd been nasty to her. Sometimes, if brains were dynamite, I wouldn't have enough to blow my nose.

"And did I mispronounce 'Greyhound,' too?" she asked, letting some irritation show.

I felt ashamed of myself for making things hard on her. "No," I told her. "But my name's Henry. Henry Mote."

I stuck out my hand. She took it. She had long, thin fingers. She told me her name: Angela Murphy.

"I work with Bobby Jobe, Mr. Mote," she said. I could tell by the way she said, "Mr. Mote" that she was frosted. I have such a winning way with women.

"I know."

That surprised her. "How do you know?"

"Well, for one, Bobby would've told you my name was Greyhound. And two, I just saw you on TV."

She didn't say anything you'd expect, like how long was she on TV or how she looked or whether we'd happened to tape it. She just nodded and then looked over my shoulder toward the valley and the golf course.

It was a good time of day and time of year to look at it. The sun was getting a little lower behind Eadon Mountain and the shadows cast by the hickory trees and the pines were sharp and cool. Eadon Branch glistened in the light and the pond looked clear and blue. The turf on the course was fresh and green because we were still having cool nights and the summer goose grass and the brown patch funguses hadn't set in. A couple of purple martins that build their nest every spring on the lintel over the cart barn door were skimming low along the ninth fairway looking for whatever it is they feed on—beetles, I think. A few birds were chirping and the sky was blue, mottled with a few mackerel-skin clouds.

"It's a beautiful course," she said.

I knew right away she couldn't be much of a golfer, because if she was she'd have known that the Augusta National and Cypress Point are beautiful courses. Next to them, Eadon Branch was homely.

"Just a country goat track, " I said.

She looked at me. "And you're just like Bobby described you."

"And how's that?"

"Ornery," she said, but she smiled and she had a smile that could take the sting out of anything.

"Bobby'll make you ornery if you're with him very long," I said. "He's got a knack for it."

"So I've noticed," she said, and she smiled again and I felt like we at least had something in common. "You have to get past that facade with him, Mr. Mote."

Now I felt like she was teasing me with the "Mr. Mote" business. I wished I'd just said yes when she asked me if I was Greyhound.

I might've said I didn't think there was anything to Bobby except facade, but I didn't. Women have always seen something in him that I didn't.

I put the milk crate down by the lesson tee and figured I'd better not make her stand there in the sun all afternoon. I didn't want to take her inside and have to introduce her to Eudora and Conrad and J. R. and them, so I pointed to a little bench we have under an elm tree by the first tee and we sat down. She pushed her sunglasses off her nose and propped them on the bill of her cap the way Annika Sorenstam does. She had blue eyes and soft, fine eyebrows. They were almost a kid's eyes, kind of wide and innocent and trusting, except that behind them there was something altogether different, something tough. There was a little film of sweat on her forehead and the hair that poked out under the brim of the cap looked a little wet and curly, so I got her a cup of water from the canister we keep by the tee.

"So how is Bobby?"

"Not good," she said.

"He looked all right on TV."

"Physically, he's doing well," she said. She sipped the water. "His injuries from the accident have healed, except for his eyes. He's working out in a gym a couple of hours every day."

"I could see he was in shape. So what's the matter?"

I could guess, of course. I didn't think I'd be too thrilled if I was blind.

"He's depressed. He needs golf," she said. She gestured with her hand, taking in the view of the course and the surrounding hills. "He needs all this."

"So take him out to a course," I said. "Let him smell it. Let him hear the birds chirp. I bet his hearing and his smell have gotten better."

She sighed and I realized I'd said the wrong thing again. "No," she told me. "Blind people don't hear or smell better. They just pay more attention to what they hear and smell."

"Okay," I said.

"He needs more than that," she explained. "He needs to get back to doing what he used to do. When an adult is blinded, his future usually depends on getting back to his old job. If he's a lawyer, he's got to get people to read to him and learn to practice law without his sight. If he's a teacher, he's got to learn to teach without seeing his students."

"And if he's a truck driver?" I asked. "What's he going to do then?"

It was a nasty question. I was sorry I asked it the minute the words were out of my mouth.

She didn't answer right away, but I could tell I'd frosted her again.

"He needs your help," she said, very clipped. "He needs to play golf."

"And he sent you here to get me to help him get back to playing golf? Blind?"

She shook her head. "No. He doesn't know I've come here."

I saw her then in a new way. She was being truthful; I was sure of that. I know guile, and there was none in her. She was all zeal, all afire to transform at least something in the world. And she loved Bobby. I admired her for the zeal and almost forgave her for the love. She just happened to know nothing about what she was talking about.

"You just came here on your own because you think this is what he should do."

She nodded solemnly. "I know it."

"Did Bobby tell you what he said to me the last time we saw each other?"

"No. What was it?"

"Not important," I said. "He just told you I was ornery?"

She nodded.

I didn't want to tell her she was crazy. She was too sweet.

"Miss Murphy," I said, "have you ever played golf?"

She shook her head. "My family wasn't exactly the country club sort."

"But you've seen it on TV."

She nodded.

I teed up a ball and handed her the TaylorMade I'd used to shoot at the Cessna. I pointed to a blue flag stuck in the ground about 200 yards out from where we were standing, listing to the right.

"Hit this ball to that flag," I told her. I thought I knew what was going to happen. I thought she'd top the ball, hit a little foozle that dribbled off the front of the tee. That's what beginners usually do.

She couldn't even do that. She grabbed the club with her hands set about four inches apart. Then she got more awkward. She swayed back with crooked arms, rared up, and swung hard. The clubhead hit the dirt about six inches behind the ball. When it did she jerked back instinctively and pulled the clubhead a foot off the ground as it passed over the ball. A clod of dirt flew about twenty yards down the range. The ball, perhaps influenced by the breeze she'd made, fell off the tee and came to rest against it. Her total distance was about an inch.

She glared at me.

"Now try it with your eyes closed," I said.

She was so frosted she could've been sold from a Good Humor truck.

"I'm not very coordinated physically and I can't play golf," she said. "Bobby can, Mr. Mote."

"Bobby could," I corrected her. "Look, Miss Murphy, I didn't mean to embarrass you there. I just wanted you to realize how hard it is to hit a golf ball. Multiply that by ten and you have how hard it is to hit a golf ball good enough to win tournaments. And do it blind? I don't have enough fingers and toes to do the multiplying to tell you how hard that would be."

Her jaw set and she sat down on the bench next to me. "You may know golf. But you don't know what blind people are capable of."

She was right about that. I tried a different argument. "Has Bobby been hitting any balls?"

"No," she admitted.

"Why not?"

She showed some frustration in her face. "Because he doesn't think it's possible. He thinks like you."

"Well, there you go," I said.

"But blind people can play golf!" She was adamant. "There's even a blind golf championship!"

"Sure," I said. "I know they play. And they're lucky if they break a hundred."

"You're wrong," she said. "There's a blind golfer in New Orleans named Pat Browne. He shoots in the seventies."

Even if that was true, shooting somewhere in the 70s will make your wallet real thin real fast in professional golf. But she didn't understand that. I looked for a way to explain to her how Bobby felt.

"Look. Suppose you were a piano player, one of the best piano players in the world. And you got in a wreck and they had to amputate your hands. And then someone told you it was still possible to play 'Chopsticks' with your toes. Would you be interested?"

"But you don't play golf with your eyes," she said.

"You can't play without them," I answered.

"You'd be his eyes," she said.

I shook my head. "I might be able to line him up. But how's he going to hit the ball if he can't see it? And even if he does manage to hit it, there are dozens of little shots that are all touch and judgment. Like, say, you got a forty-foot downhill putt on a slick green, like at Augusta. You gotta see the hole. You gotta see the slope. He'll never be able to do it."

She wouldn't give up. "Won't you come to Nashville for a couple of days and try? Help me talk him into it?"

I didn't want to go. Even if I'd loved the guy, I don't think I'd've wanted to do it. I didn't want to be tangled up with Bobby if some guy called from the Tour, looking for me to caddie for him. I damn sure didn't want to watch another woman waste her time on Bobby Jobe. And besides, he'd flat told me to go to hell.

So I said no. I told her I couldn't leave my responsibilities at Eadon Branch, which was true enough. If I left for a few days my so-called assistant superintendent, Hayden Pritchett, might turn the golf course into a fungus farm.

She drew in a breath. "Mr. Mote, I'll level with you," she said.

Most of the time, when someone says that to you, it means they're about to tell you the biggest lie they can think of. But I didn't think she was. So I nodded, let her know I was still listening.

"I'm not just thinking of Bobby. I'm thinking of all blind people."

I didn't get it. "Okay," I said.

"They need heroes, Mr. Mote. They need someone to show the rest of the world what the blind can do. They need people to inspire them. Bobby can be one of those people."

I knew for sure then that she wasn't lying. Who'd make up that kind of crap? She was an honest do-gooder, a crusader. You see that sort every once in a while around Allegheny Gap. Usually they've seen a movie about Bloody Harlan County, over in Kentucky, and they're in town to organize the miners. Angela had that same kind of look in her eyes.

I was about to say no again when the door to the clubhouse opened and Eudora walked out carrying a couple of iced teas in tall cups. Her skirt billowed a little in the breeze off the course. Eudora always dressed that way during the day, never wore pants or shorts. Always a skirt, as if she was just stopping by the course to help out before she took off for a luncheon at the women's club. It was clear to me that she'd recognized Angela from the television and figured she was some kind of celebrity, because Eudora hadn't carried drinks out to anyone on the first tee before.

I introduced them.

"I saw you on television. Won't you come inside where it's a little cooler?" Eudora asked Angela. That was stretching it a little. We had a fan in the clubhouse. The air conditioner in the front window hadn't worked for two years.

Angela politely declined. Eudora asked her what brought her to Allegheny Gap. Eudora was normally hospitable enough, but she seemed to be going overboard in this case. I noticed that she'd fixed her hair and makeup a little and gotten rid of the apron she normally wore behind the lunch counter. I figured that new faces don't show up that often in Allegheny Gap and pretty faces even less often called on Eudora's only child.

But Eudora's smile faded as Angela told her that she wanted to talk me into going to Nashville to work with Bobby Jobe.

"Oh, we couldn't spare Henry," she said very firmly. "Even if he wanted to go off and do that work again."

She knew very well I wanted to do that work again and that I wasn't going to be staying at Eadon Branch. I'd told her a dozen times. But Eudora had a way of not listening to things she didn't want to hear.

Angela seemed to realize that even if she could charm me into changing my mind, she wasn't going to budge Eudora. She got a sad look in her
eyes and shrugged her shoulders. "All right," she said. "I can't argue with
a mother. I'm sorry to have troubled you."

She extended her hand coolly. I shook it, feeling kind of selfish, like I
remember feeling as a kid when they passed the basket at church and I
decided to keep my only quarter for myself, like you want to do the right
thing but you can't afford it. Or just can't bring yourself to do it. Angela,
I knew, was the sort of kid who'd have tossed her last quarter right in
there.

"I'm sorry you came all this way," I told her.

"Won't you stay for supper?" Eudora asked, all hospitable again.

Angela shook her head. "I'd like to, but it's a long drive back to
Nashville. If I leave now, I can make it before it gets too late."

I was sorry she was going, but I couldn't think of anything to say that
might make her want to stay. That's usually the way I am with women.
When I need to talk to them, the words won't come. After they're gone, I
can always think of lots of smart things I should've said.

So I just walked quietly with her to the parking lot on the other side
of the clubhouse, where she'd parked a beat-up old green Toyota with
New York plates still on it. I told her to say hello to Bobby, though I was
pretty sure she wouldn't, since she'd come to see me without telling him.
And I watched the dust plume kick up as she started to drive off toward
the highway.

Ornery was one thing, but I didn't like feeling nasty. You had to try to
help a blind man. Even if blind golf was a dumb idea and even if it was
Bobby Jobe who told me to go to hell.

"Wait!" I yelled.

She stopped the car. I walked up to her.

"I can't leave Eadon Branch right now," I said, "but if you can get him
here, I'll do what I can. As long as I don't have an offer from the Tour."

She gave me one of those smiles again, all teeth and joy and promise.

"Thank you, Mr. Mote," she said. And that's all. She drove off.

3

▼

A FEW DAYS LATER EUDORA TOLD ME TO FIND SOMEONE TO COVER FOR us on Sunday afternoon. We were having Jimmy Edmisten and his family to lunch.

Jimmy Edmisten was the cornerstone of the economy in Allegheny Gap. He owned the Chevy-GMC dealership. Starting from about the time you were fourteen, you couldn't avoid hearing his slogan: "Come see Jimmy's Jimmies!" That's because there were only two radio stations, one country and one rock, and Jimmy's ads were all over both of them. Unless you were deaf, you knew where a young man could get himself a truck with very little money down.

Not that it was hard to persuade the boys in Allegheny Gap they needed trucks. With a truck, you could take girls out. With a truck, you could go hunting. With a truck, you could ride around town after a Hilltoppers' football game with the horn blaring. With a truck, you could head to McDonald's when you were hungry. With a truck, you had friends. With a truck, you were a man. Without one, you weren't.

For a boy in Allegheny Gap, buying a truck at Jimmy's was like going out alone on the prairie and killing a buffalo was for a young Indian. As soon as you could after your sixteenth birthday, you dragged your father or mother down to the dealership, plunked down everything you had, and signed up to make payments for the next four years. You started to drive. Then you figured out that you really couldn't afford the payments with what you made stocking shelves at Wal-Mart evenings and week-ends. Rather than lose the truck, you dropped out of school and went to work in the mines on the second shift for twelve dollars an hour. And since the truck gave you the chance to take a girl someplace where her parents couldn't see you—quite often the fourth green at the Eadon Branch Golf Course—you often found yourself getting married and becoming a father at about the same time. And, boom, there was your life. Truck, mine, wife, baby.

And it all began with Jimmy's Jimmies.

I'd managed to avoid signing my life away at Jimmy's only through luck. For one thing, Clayton Mote left behind an old blue Ford pickup when he took off. It was starting to rust by the time I got old enough to drive, but I managed to get it started and keep it running. We still used it at the golf course. For another, Peggy Shiflett didn't give it up until after she dumped me.

At the time, I didn't appreciate the favor she was doing me.

Of course, I knew Jimmy Edmisten even though I didn't buy a truck from him. It was hard not to know him. He was president of the Kiwanis and got himself elected to the state legislature a few times. He owned pieces of several mines and one of the radio stations. He was head of the Hilltopper Club. His son, Jimmy Jr., was in my class. Jimmy was there when I played Little League baseball; I was the catcher and Junior was the pitcher. He was there when I played high school football; I was the left guard and Junior was the quarterback. I used to think that maybe Junior was the quarterback because his father was head of the booster club or something like that. I see now that he played quarterback because he believed he was destined to be quarterback. I played left guard because I thought that was where I belonged.

I mostly got along with Jimmy Sr. He was a tough, tightly wired little guy with wavy gray hair. He wore suits everywhere and usually had a flower in his lapel, the only flower you'd see someone wearing all year in Allegheny Gap outside of weddings and proms. He'd come into the locker room after a game and lead the team in a prayer and slap your back and congratulate you. You'd never see his tough side unless, say, you'd let a tackle for the other team get in and sack Junior. Then he'd say something like, "We're going to block some people next week, huh Henry?" And the hand on your back would clamp down and you felt like you damn well better not let anyone sack his son the next week.

I knew that Eudora had been seeing Jimmy a little. Jimmy was a widower. His wife had died during the time I was out on Tour. And two people can't keep company in Allegheny Gap without everyone knowing about it, especially if one of them is as rich as Jimmy Edmisten.

But since I'd been back, I'd been trying hard to keep some distance between myself and Eudora. I was way too old to be living with my mother, so I didn't move back into my room at home, which was a one-story brick house across the highway. I lived in the superintendent's quarters that Clayton Mote had put in over the barn where he kept the mowers and the tractor and stored the seed and fertilizer. It wasn't much—just a room with a shower and a hot plate. At night, if I wanted to watch television, I had to go to the clubhouse. I didn't mind. And since I didn't want Eudora watching over everything I did, I went out of my way not to watch what she was doing. We saw each other during the day at the golf course, and we had dinner together a couple of nights a week. That was it.

So when she told me Jimmy Edmisten and his family were coming to Sunday lunch, it was a shock. A Sunday meal with families invited is a serious matter. It suggests commitment. I knew Eudora was eligible. She'd written me three or four years before, to tell me she'd finally gotten a divorce from Clayton Mote. I'd figured at that time that she must've wanted her freedom for some reason, but I hadn't figured it in relation to a specific person, particularly not to Jimmy Edmisten.

"You serious about him?" I asked her that morning when she showed up, briefly, to remind me to be there at three o'clock.

"You put on your coat and tie," she told me.

That was serious.

Jimmy arrived promptly, driving up in a gray Cadillac that looked big enough to hold a basketball game between the windshield and the hood ornament. It looked like it was going to dock with the house as it moved slowly up the driveway, crunching pinecones and pushing up a little dust.

Peeking out the front window while Eudora attended to something in the kitchen, I could see he had Junior and Junior's wife, Kellee, with him. Junior was working by that time as the general manager of the GMC dealership. Kellee was busy being good-looking. They were dressed like they'd just come out of church at Easter, right down to the white carnation Jimmy wore in his lapel. Kellee, Miss Warmerdam County of 1989, was wearing enough eye shadow and mascara to do the chorus line at Caesar's Palace, I thought, but I reminded myself to be nice.

They came in and we said our awkward hellos, as if Junior and I were dear old friends who each hadn't known the other was in town for the past nine months. Junior, I noticed with some satisfaction, was looking like the guy in the television commercials who should've tried Rogaine before it was too late. He must've gotten his hairline from his mother.

I had a tense, brittle moment while they were sitting on the couch and I suddenly saw my mother's house through their eyes. I could see threadbare patches in the rug and the spot on the wall where my father's picture, taken at the U.S. Open years ago, used to hang. I could see the nicks in the furniture and stain on the couch where I'd once dropped a pizza and the patch on the ceiling where the roof leaked a few years ago. I could see the big TV and the Binion's casino ashtrays Eudora liked to buy on the one vacation she treated herself to each year—a flight to Vegas and a week playing high-low Omaha. I could sense how small the room seemed and I realized that Eudora had bought nothing new for the house in the time since my father left.

But I put those thoughts out of my mind and asked everyone what they'd like to drink, trying to be a good host.

"Do you have Sweet'n Low?" Kellee asked.

I was sure I could find some.

"Ice tea, then, please," she said.

I nodded. "Junior, how about you? Something stronger?"

Junior flushed and Kellee looked annoyed.

"He doesn't drink," Kellee answered for him. "Anymore."

"Iced tea'll be fine," Junior said.

"Make it three," Jimmy added.

I could've used a Jack Daniel's right about then and so could Eudora. But I wanted to do right by Eudora and I contented myself with slipping a shot of it into the glasses of iced tea destined for her and me. I brought the drinks out and passed them out. Eudora smiled sweetly when she tasted hers.

She was wearing a new dress, a soft, flowery thing with puffy sleeves that wasn't really her style. She looked best in black. She fussed around, passing out deviled eggs and cheese and crackers and listening attentively while Jimmy explained why he'd been certain all along that the Japanese could never compete with General Motors in the long run.

It was, he said, because they couldn't think originally.

Eudora looked uncomfortable, like one of the eggs might've been bad. She's too smart to advertise it, but Eudora doesn't exactly share what I would call the widespread view in Allegheny Gap that there must be something wrong with any group that doesn't drive pickup trucks, work in the coal business, have white skin, and carry a Bible to church on Sunday morning. I would call it the widespread view except that Eudora always taught me not to generalize about people.

I didn't say anything. I was saved by the bell—the one on Eudora's stove. It rang to announce that the main course, a roast lamb, was ready. I volunteered to go into the kitchen and carve it and serve it.

When I came back out, my iced tea a little fresher, Jimmy and his family were already seated. Eudora asked me to say the blessing.

I didn't think I could remember it. "Well," I said, "I think I should defer to our guest for that."

Jimmy was willing.

"Let us join hands," he intoned. He reached out to his left toward me, and Kellee stuck a cool, bony little hand out to the right. I clasped them and bowed my head.

"Dear Lord," Jimmy said, "thank you for thy bounty, which we are about to receive . . ."

"A—" I started to say. But Jimmy cut me off before I could get out the "—men."

"Thank you for thy other blessings, O Lord," Jimmy went on, his head bowed, his brow furrowed. "Thank you for the love in this room and thank you for the opportunity to unite these two families."

I looked up, trying to catch Eudora's eye. She didn't raise her head or state any objections.

Then it was time to say "Amen" and pass the lamb and potatoes. I couldn't help myself. I had to do something. The thought of being united with the Edmisten family made me feel about like Bobby Jobe looking at that brook on the sixteenth hole. A little antsy.

"Thank you for that fine blessing," I said as deferentially as I could to

Jimmy. "It reminded me of someone. Can't think of his name, but I've seen him on TV . . ."

"Jerry Falwell," Kellee said, before Jimmy could answer. "Daddy Edmisten loves Jerry Falwell. Has all his books and tapes."

I peeked at Eudora out of the corner of my eye. I knew she had no use for Jerry Falwell. She didn't look too happy.

"He's your favorite, Mr. Edmisten?" I asked.

"I'm very partial to his views," Jimmy allowed.

"It's been a cool spring this year, hasn't it?" Eudora broke in. She looked distressed.

"Sure," I said. "And damp. Going to have fungus problems on the golf course later this summer."

Then I thought that maybe fungus wasn't a good thing to talk about over food. So I asked about their golf games. They didn't play, thought it was frivolous. They liked stock-car racing and hunting.

I asked about the football team at Virginia Tech, where Junior had gone to college. He didn't follow it anymore, Junior said. Too many black players on the team. All dating white girls, Kellee added.

Eudora kept looking grimmer and grimmer as the conversation dragged on. She pushed a piece of potato back and forth across her plate, but it was plain she'd lost her appetite.

So I asked Jimmy how things were going at the dealership and that brought the first smile of the afternoon to his face.

"Going great," Jimmy said. "Just great." And he gave a quick, mean-ingful glance to Eudora as he smeared a little more mint jelly on the last of his lamb.

"Fact is, Henry, we're looking to add to our sales staff. Could be a natural spot for you. We'd like to have you." He paused. "Wouldn't we, Junior?"

Junior looked less than thrilled, but he nodded.

"Reunion of the old Hilltoppers," Jimmy said.

Suddenly, I had the feeling of being a lost child in a storm, a feeling that my fate was about to be determined by forces I neither controlled nor understood. Eudora was looking at me half apologetically, half curiously. It was clear that she was in on this.

To be honest, I could understand why Eudora was worried about me.

But I knew one thing. I would rather go work in a mine than go work for Junior Edmisten and his father.

"Well, thank you, Mr. Edmisten," I said. "But I'm still planning to get back on Tour. And in the meantime, I like what I'm doing at Eadon Branch."

Whereupon Jimmy positively glared at Eudora, who blushed, and mumbled something about clearing the table. She got up and went into the kitchen. Jimmy roused himself and cleared his own plate. I grabbed Kellee's, mine, and Junior's and followed him into the kitchen. Jimmy was standing, hands on hips, behind Eudora. Eudora was piling dishes in the sink and running water over them.

"Would you excuse us for a moment?" Eudora asked me.

I left.

Junior, Kellee, and I sat at the dining room table, trying not to look as if we were eavesdropping on the conversation in the kitchen. We could hear murmuring, but we couldn't make anything out.

For Kellee, it must have been too awkward to stand. She smiled brightly at me, trying to figure out how poise and pep would carry her through this like they'd carried her through the Miss Warmerdam County pageant.

"So who's your favorite evangelist, Henry?" she asked.

"Jimmy Swaggart," I said.

Kellee's forehead wrinkled. Sarcasm was beyond her powers of comprehension.

Before I had to explain, Jimmy Edmisten came out of the kitchen. He looked mad, like he looked the night we lost a playoff game to Bath County High when Junior fumbled on their six-yard line. Eudora trailed behind him. Her eyes were glittering.

"Thank you, Eudora. Under the circumstances, I don't think we'll stay for dessert."

Kellee looked baffled. Junior didn't bother to hide his relief.

"Henry," Jimmy nodded to me as they walked out.

Eudora closed the door behind them, walked back to the table, and started clearing the other dishes. A tear rolled out of her eye and down one cheek. I gave her a hug and she clung to me in a way she hadn't ever done before, sobbing. She separated from me, took a deep breath, and resumed clearing the table.

"That didn't exactly go according to plan," she said.

"What was the plan?"

She sat down at the table and I sat next to her. She started kneading her fingers in front of her. "The plan was that Jimmy and I were going to announce our engagement," she said. "I told him in the kitchen I couldn't go through with it."

I thought of a lot of things. I thought about my father and then I thought about how relieved I was not to face the prospect of Christmas with the Edmistens every year. And then I thought of Eudora, alone all these years, and of the likelihood that anyone else half as well off or half as respectable would ask her to marry him. I started to understand why she'd wanted me to get out of Allegheny Gap when I was eighteen and wanted to keep me when I was twenty-eight. It wasn't that I was ten years older. It was that she was.

"I'm sorry, Eudora," I said, and I meant it. "I hope it wasn't anything I said that . . ."

She shook her head. "No, it wasn't. Although I'm sure you had only evil intentions when you got him talking about that idiot Jerry Falwell."

"If I'd known . . ."

She waved a hand. "You did me a favor," she said. "Made me see him as he is. I should have known a few weeks ago. We went to Vegas together and all he wanted to do was watch Siegfried and Roy."

I'd thought she'd gone to Vegas alone.

"You spent a week in Vegas together," I said, like a disapproving parent. "You never talked about that sort of thing?"

Eudora smiled thinly. "I guess we had basically a physical thing."

That thought was enough to start the lamb bleating in my gut.

"And me selling trucks for Jimmy and Junior? Was that part of the plan?"

She nodded.

"I thought you wanted me to keep working at the golf course."

Eudora looked very weary. "There's something you need to know, Henry," she said. "In a year or so, I don't think there's going to be a golf course anymore."

Some of my earliest memories were of the chainsaws and bulldozers that built the course, of my father with a sheaf of rolled-up paper on which he'd sketched the holes. Much as I wanted to get away from it, Eadon Branch was as fundamental to my world as heartache was to Patsy Cline's.

"Why? What do you mean?"

"There's a loan." Eudora sighed. "I took it out a few years ago. The course was losing money but I thought things would get better. I needed it to buy new carts, rebuild the greens, remember? There's a balloon payment due July first next year. I can't pay it. The course is still losing money."

"How much is it?"

"Two hundred fifty thousand dollars."

That was about 225,000 more than I'd managed to save.

"The thing is," Eudora went on, "that Jimmy thinks the land is worth a lot more if you sell it to a mine company and let 'em strip it. He's had geologists in. There's coal under there."

"So if you got married, you were going to sell it for a coal mine."

"He was going to buy it."

"How much?"

"Five hundred thousand."

"Probably worth twice that."

She nodded.

"But Henry, you see, I need to have something in the bank. I'm not getting any younger."

I knew it would mortify Eudora to have to ask someone for a job. Her parents had been quality in Allegheny Gap. Her dad owned a hardware store and a sporting goods store. Like I said, she could've gone to college, if she hadn't met Clayton Mote and had me. I'd always figured that the money her parents had left her was substantial, but now Eudora was saying it was all gone.

The work in Allegheny Gap for women like Eudora was telemarketing. A company that answered the phones for catalogs had a big operation on the other side of town. It paid just above minimum wage. I figured it was about as attractive to Eudora as mining was to me.

"Can't you get the bank to reschedule the loan? They do it all the time for Russia and Mexico."

"Jimmy's chairman of the loan committee. I don't think he'll be too sympathetic. I'll have to declare bankruptcy. The course'll be auctioned off."

I could imagine what Jimmy would have to pay for it under those circumstances. He'd probably wind up considering that this day had been profitable for him.

I walked to the window and poked at the sheer white curtains Eudora had there. I looked out toward Eadon Branch. From there, I could see just the fifth fairway and the upper half of the clubhouse. A man and a boy were walking down the fifth hole, pulling their clubs behind them on handcarts.

Eudora came over and kissed me on the cheek and tried to hold me the way she had when I was a boy and something sad happened. It wasn't quite the same, since I was now bigger than her. But I appreciated the gesture and the smell of Lancome and mint jelly mixed together. She went off to finish clearing the table, and I told her I would do the dishes. But I stayed at the window.

Suddenly, the course seemed different to me, like a girl who starts looking a whole lot better when you see her out with someone else. Why is it we never appreciate what we have until we lose it?

A Wal-Mart truck rolled slowly up the hill from the course, heading out of town, lumbering. It hid the rest of the road for a minute or two, and the window trembled slightly in front of my nose. It was only when it passed that I saw the beat-up green Toyota with the New York tags making its way toward us. It was going slowly, slower than the truck, as if the driver was looking for something. It slowed even more as it neared the house, stopped in the road, then turned into our driveway.

The car surprised me. I'd thought about Angela Murphy in the days since she'd left. It's not as if I was constantly meeting so many new and attractive women in Allegheny Gap that I'd forget one. But I'd figured she wouldn't be back. That was because I felt like I knew Bobby Jobe and I knew Bobby wouldn't be interested in playing golf anymore. He'd always been vain about how he looked on the course, about the way he swung and dressed. I couldn't imagine him wanting to play blind. But there were two people in the car and the man in the passenger seat was wearing Oakleys.

"We've got company, Eudora," I said.

"Jimmy?"

"No. I believe it's Bobby Jobe."

She came to the window and we both peered out like villagers in a Frankenstein movie.

Angela got out of the car. I half expected her to go around to the passenger side and open Bobby's door for him, but she didn't. She just stood there and let him get out. He was wearing a sport shirt with buttons down the front and a button-down collar, which looked a little odd on him. I was used to seeing him only in golf shirts. Slowly, cautiously, Bobby moved around the car, trailing a hand on the fenders and trunk until he came up behind Angela. The swagger I'd seen in his TV appearance must've been an act, because he looked tentative and hesitant, like you might if you had to walk across a dark room with a hole in the floor. Angela said something to him and he took her elbow. If I hadn't known it was Bobby Jobe, I'm not sure I'd have recognized him. His body hadn't changed except for his eyes. But his appearance sure had.

I went to the front door and opened it, then stood on the concrete slab we called the porch.

Angela was leading him up the walk. She was wearing shorts. Her knees were knocked, which I guess is what had made her seem a little gawky when I first saw her. She wore a pink gingham top and that same New York Mets hat.

"Steps," she said softly to Bobby. "Three steps."

She stumbled a little on the second step and for a second I thought Bobby was going to lose his balance. But he didn't. And even though she had the eyes and he didn't, he grabbed her elbow and pulled her up the last step, righted her, and deposited her on the top.

She was awfully awkward. It was no wonder she couldn't drive a golf ball. It was all she could do to walk up stairs.

"Hello, Bobby," I said. "Hello, Miss Murphy."

He stood, kind of disoriented, turning his head a little. I imagined what he could sense: the flagstones under his feet, the smell of the pines in our yard, maybe the smell of tar and oil from the highway. And then the sound of my voice, coming to him from out of a void.

"Greyhound?"

"That's right," I said. "How are you, Bobby?"

I figured he'd stick his hand out and wait for me to grab it, but he didn't.

"Geez, Angela," he said. "You brought me all this way to see Grey-hound?"

His tone was weary and sad, rather than petulant. But he could still piss me off.

"You're just as charming as ever, Bobby," I said.

Bobby looked a little perplexed by that. He shrugged. "Thanks," he said.

That was one of the ways Bobby was obtuse. Like Kellee Edmisten, he didn't get sarcasm. Small-town beauty queens have a lot in common with small-town jocks.

"Angela has this damned idea that I should play golf again and you can help me," Bobby said.

I waited for a moment for him to apologize for what he'd said to me the last time I'd seen him, in the hospital. He didn't. I imagined he'd forgotten it. Maybe he'd been doped up when he said it. More likely, he was just like a lot of other jocks who figure they don't have to be nice to people. I could've reminded him of it, but I was one of those people who let the jocks get away with it.

"So she told me," I replied.

"I've told her it wasn't gonna work and I didn't want to do it. So today she puts me in the car and just says we're going for a drive. I didn't know where."

Angela was looking like a six-year-old getting ready to shoot the moon in Hearts. I looked at her with a new wariness.

Eudora came out of the door behind me and started right in scolding me. "Henry, why haven't you invited these people in? It's Angela, right? And you must be Bobby Jobe."

I managed to make the introductions that had to be made and Bobby managed to be reasonably polite to Eudora. Eudora said she just happened to have some cake and coffee ready. Angela said she was starving.

So there we were at the recently cleared dining table, ready to entertain still more guests and begin yet another round of witty, inspired conversation. Two lovely parties in one day would be a Mote family record. We'd be on the society page of the *Warmerdam County Weekly News*.

It was hard not to notice that Angela had to help Bobby get started in just about everything. She guided him to the table. She put his hands on the fork and on the plate with his slice of cake. She whispered to him what was on it. Eudora and I pretended we weren't watching and listening.

But then she let Bobby do for himself. He had to poke around at the cake till he found it, then hack at it till he managed to cut himself off a piece.

"How'd you know Angela?" Bobby asked Eudora as soon as he'd managed to sip a little coffee.

"Why, she was here just last week," Eudora said.

"You were?" Bobby demanded.

"I was," Angela confirmed. Evidently, she'd told me the truth when she said she hadn't told Bobby she was coming that time. She didn't seem the least embarrassed about it.

"Angela, how many times do I have to explain to you that this is just not going to happen? You've gotta forget it! I'll work on facial vision with you till I'm black and blue. But not this."

Angela's jaw set a little. "You hired me to help you with your rehabilitation. If you want to be rehabilitated, you have to play golf. You're a golfer."

"I told her I thought it was a bad idea, Bobby," I said. I hated to agree with him, but he was right on this one.

"You said you'd help if Bobby came here, Mr. Mote," Angela reminded me.

"You didn't tell me you were going to kidnap him," I pointed out.

"Henry!" Eudora scolded me. "This poor girl wants to help Bobby. You ought to be thanking her, not accusing her of things."

She turned to Angela. "Henry's always been a little grouchy. I think golf causes it. His father was the same way." Angela smiled at her, glad to have an ally.

"I think he's really a good person underneath, though, Mrs. Mote. He must get that from you."

Now Eudora beamed.

"Actually," I said, "This gruff, ornery exterior is just a facade covering a tough, prickly interior."

"Got that right, Greyhound," Bobby said.

"And you can call me Henry," I said to Bobby. "Now that you're not paying me. Or would you rather I call you Bat?"

"Bat?" Bobby asked.

"As in 'blind as a . . .'" Angela filled him in.

"Still quick on the uptake, Bobby," I said. He glowered, I think. A lot of his face was covered up by those Oakleys.

"Isn't it neat," Angela said, "the way warmth and love overflow from our hearts when old friends are reunited?"

I looked at her, just making sure she was being sarcastic. Sometimes with women it's hard to tell. And Angela had such an innocent face, porcelain skin and faint freckles. Or maybe I just thought she did. It dawned on me that if I didn't get Bobby out to hit some golf balls, she'd probably leave, and I didn't want her to leave.

"Sorry," I told her. "I know you were trying to do a good deed. Bobby, what do you say we go over to the course, make Miss Murphy happy. No one'll see, 'cept her."

"Sorry, Greyhound," Bobby said. "Not gonna happen."

"Bobby," Angela said, "I'll make you a proposition. Either you go over to that golf course with us, or I drive off and you can take the bus back to Nashville. What'll it be?"

"You wouldn't do that," he said, but I could hear a little tremor in his voice and I could tell that just the suggestion that she might leave him terrified Bobby. He was that dependent on her.

"Try me," she said.

He gave in, but not gracefully. "All right," he said. "What the hell. We'll go take a look at Greyhound's golf course."

He said it as if he was talking about the busted Lionel train set Eudora had kept somewhere up in the attic.

"Why don't you use Mr. Mote's arm?" Angela suggested to Bobby. I figured she meant that Bobby would put a light hand on my elbow the way he did to hers when she was leading him.

"Think you can handle it, Greyhound?" Bobby said. Angela put his hand on my right elbow.

I didn't say anything. I just guided him right into the doorjamb.

"Ouch," he said, rubbing his nose.

"The name's Henry," I said.

I looked at Angela. She didn't seem to mind what I'd done. I guess rehabilitation is a complex process.

So we drove off in Angela's car, me in the front seat, Bobby in back, Angela driving. We pulled into the gravel parking lot at the course and Bobby started sniffing, almost like a dog will sniff when he's trying to pick up a scent, poking his nose in one direction and another.

Seeing him do it made me sniff a little, too. I was aware, suddenly, of things I'd long ago stopped noticing—the smell of the oil in the spot where J. R. Neill's crankcase leaked; the smell of the wind filtering through the pines behind the ninth green; the smell of the grass clippings where Hayden tossed 'em, in a copse of trees on the other side of the green; the smell of honeysuckle in a thicket next to the clubhouse. Farther away, I even thought I could smell the heavy, fetid odor of Eadon Branch carrying its load of silt and algae and God knew what mine residues down to the Gaulor River.

And I could hear things, too, hear them the way Bobby might hear them. I could hear the low sound of a truck leaving town half a mile away, its gears grinding as it climbed a hill. The sound bounced off the side of Eadon Mountain. I could hear someone teeing off on No. 1 on the other side of the clubhouse. Whoever it was hadn't hit a very good shot because it didn't make that pure click you get when someone hits the ball flush on the clubface. And a second later the word "mullicant" drifted over the clubhouse and into our ears.

"What's 'mullicant'?" Bobby asked me.

"It's just what people here've always called mulligans," I said. "There's a sign by the first tee. 'No mullicants.' I guess whoever put it up couldn't spell."

"Maybe it means, 'You can't take a mulligan,'" Bobby said.

"People do anyway," I told him.

Bobby smiled for the first time since he'd got to Allegheny Gap.

He had my elbow again, so I walked him down to the ninth green, which was empty. I felt the different surfaces under my feet: hard dirt in the parking lot, loose, bumpy stones at the border, thick grass around the collar of the green, then bent grass cut to five-sixteenths of an inch on the green itself.

"Know where we are now?" I said.

"I'd say it's a green," Bobby said. "And I'd say you got fungus problems with it."

"Damn," I said. "You can tell that with your feet?"

"Nah," Bobby said, smirking. "I just guessed. Figured if you were the greenskeeper I'd probably be right."

I wanted to ask him if he knew how much the Monsanto people were asking for fungicide in this part of Virginia, the kind the Homestead bought by the truckload. But I let it go. Blind or not, there were things Bobby'd never been able to see and never would.

We walked around the clubhouse to the lesson tee, only I didn't call it that because I figured Bobby would only mock the idea that someone might actually pay me to give him a lesson. I told him we were on the practice range.

He listened for a minute. "Where're the other people practicing?" he asked.

"Not many customers this time Sunday afternoon," I said.

It was already getting on close to five o'clock. The sun was low enough to start casting shadows over the fairways and to glint on the little riffles in Eadon Branch as it wound its way through the course, but still high enough to make your cheeks feel warm. The breeze was like a mother's kiss. The sky was pure blue and big. You could see some of the diehards down on the fifth green in a group of six. Someone missed a putt, and their hoots and whistles drifted up to the tee. I wished then that Bobby could take it all in, see it the way I saw it.

"Someone made a birdie," Bobby said. He'd been listening.

"Or missed a bogey putt, more likely," I said. "Big money game down there. Six-pack a hole."

Then something truly amazing happened. A tear trickled down from behind those Oakleys. I'd never seen Bobby cry before, not even when he blew a four-shot lead with two holes to go at the Heritage one year. Get mad, curse, throw clubs, say terrible things to me, all of that. But never cry.

It made me feel terrible, made me feel for the first time how much he'd lost.

Angela, I could see, understood very well what was going on, understood why Bobby'd been trying so hard to avoid this moment. I guess she'd seen this grief with other blind people. I figured she'd wanted it to happen, maybe the way a doctor has to twist a broken bone to set it, even though it hurts the patient something awful.

She patted him on the shoulder and stroked his arm. "You want to bat a few balls now?" she asked softly.

"It's hit," Bobby corrected her. "Bat is in baseball."

"Hit some balls, then," she said.

He nodded. But his shoulders were drooping and his head was down. He was moving like a whipped dog. I didn't think it was the right time to put a golf club in his hands, but I didn't say anything. Angela had gotten him this far. It was up to her.

She told me how she'd seen blind golfers hitting balls in a film. My job would be to make sure Bobby was lined up properly, to help him grip the club right, and then set the clubhead directly behind the ball. Then I was to step away. Bobby would swing.

I pulled the seven-iron from my bag and poked the handle into Bobby's hand; he grabbed it. He kept the grip in his left hand and ran his right hand slowly up the shaft and over the hosel to the clubface, feeling with his fingers. I saw him trace the numeral 7 on the sole, feel the cavity behind the clubface, work his fingers over the Callaway trademark on the back of the clubhead.

I teed a practice ball the way Bobby had teed them on par-three holes, so close to the grass that the ball was almost sitting down in it. I took the clubface and set it down behind the ball.

"Now take your stance," I told him. I held the clubface steady while he arranged himself.

I could tell he wasn't into it. His posture was all wrong, shoulders hunched, weight on his toes, as if he was leaning on the club instead of getting ready to swing it.

"Straighten up a little," I said.

"I am straight," he replied.

All right, I thought. Let him hit it this way.

I stood up behind him and took a couple of steps back. "Okay," I said. "You're aimed downrange. Your clubhead is on the ball. Feel it?"

He pressed forward a little bit with his hands, nudging at the ball ever so gently. He took his usual two waggles and swung.

I half expected to see his usual seven-iron shot, to hear that crisp sound of flush contact, to watch the ball power up against the sky like it was shot from a cannon.

He shanked it. The ball hit the hosel of the club and skittered off to the right, banging against the bench at the first tee and landing with a small thump on the lesson tee again. It settled about five yards behind us.

If I'd seen some customer hit a ball like that I'd've had to work hard to not laugh at him. But I didn't feel like laughing. I'd really been hoping Bobby would stripe the ball.

"Shanked it, didn't I? I could feel it in my hands." He sounded defeated and disgusted.

"Yeah," I said. "But it was about the purest shank I ever saw."

He scowled, flipped the club in my general direction, and turned toward the last place he'd heard Angela's voice.

"Okay?" he asked. "Satisfied?"

"Wait a minute, Bobby," I said. "I think I know why you didn't hit that one good."

I was thinking of his waggles.

"So do I," Bobby snapped. "I couldn't see the goddamn thing."

Before I could answer, a ball came down in the vicinity of the ninth green. Then another and a third. Each one made a light thump as it hit the ground.

Bobby, of course, heard them. "What's going on? Where're those balls coming from?"

I looked down the ninth fairway. There was no one there, but then I saw J. R., Conrad, Raymond, Joe Dill, Mel Lang, and a couple of other guys thrashing through the woods that separate the ninth from the fifth.

"It's just some guys playing cross-country golf," I explained to Bobby. "Cross-country's a two-hole course—down to the fifth green and from the sixth tee back to the ninth hole. Gotta go over a lot of trees. They're not supposed to, but we generally let 'em late in the day if it's not busy."

"And they're coming up this way?"

"Yeah. Not many guys can hit an iron high enough to carry over the trees and far enough to reach the green. So they'll have little pitch shots."

"Try that shot again, Bobby," Angela said.

Bobby shook his head. "No way. Not with those guys watching. Not ever."

"Boy, this'll make a helluva story for your motivational speech—if at first you don't succeed, give up," I said. I was trying to goad him because I thought it might be possible now that I'd seen him try it.

We stood there as the guys came up. Two of them were in a cart and the others were walking. They were all drinking beer and having a fine time. Two of them made their chip shots up to the green, but before Raymond would make his, we heard the distant sound of an airplane.

"Incoming!" J. R. yelled.

"Incoming!" Conrad whooped.

I looked east to where planes usually approach. There was a twin engine a mile or so out and another, just a speck in the sky, a mile or so behind it.

"Two of 'em," I said.

"Two of what incoming?" Bobby asked.

So I told him about the county airstrip and shooting golf balls at planes. As I explained it, J. R. and Conrad and Raymond and Joe and Mel were scrambling up the slope to the lesson tee, getting ready to fire. They looked for a moment at Bobby and Angela. They didn't recognize him. Without his Callaway hat and his golf shirts, he didn't look like a golf pro. It was like seeing Payne Stewart before he died when he was playing a Tuesday practice round wearing long pants and a baseball hat like everyone else. Without his goofy hats and knickers, he looked like just another golf pro.

"Two planes?" Angela asked.

"Must be a mine up for sale," I said. "They're bringing in engineers and geologists to have a look at it Monday morning."

The first plane was gliding downward now, making its approach. You could see the sun glinting off the props and the red stripe down the fuselage. J. R. hit a little early, maybe thinking unkind thoughts about the people who bought and sold mines. His shot was on the ground before the plane even passed over the first fairway. He didn't even bother to say that it was close.

The other guys swung a few seconds later, but their results weren't much better. Bobby stood there listening to the drone of the airplane propellers and the sound of the clubs striking balls. Not one had that solid click you hear when someone puts the sweet spot on a ball. They all sounded a little tinny, like hitting the edge of a drum.

"No one hit it, I imagine," Bobby said.

"Shoot at the next plane, Bobby," Angela said.

Bobby hesitated for a moment. I remembered how he used to love to play games on the practice tee with the other pros. They used to fire at the little tractors that collect range balls, each betting fifty bucks the other couldn't hit it.

"Just like hitting a range tractor, Bobby," I said.

He said all right.

I gave him my TaylorMade driver, the demo club. It had a stiff shaft and an eight-degree face, just like Bobby's Callaway, but the head was a little heavier. I didn't know if that mattered. It would have a year before, when Bobby was still on the Tour. But I figured his feel was probably too rusty to tell.

This time, after I teed the ball, I grabbed Bobby by the shoulders and put him into position, making sure his feet were aligned right and his shoulders and hips were where they needed to be. Then I squatted down and set the clubhead.

"Don't waggle," I said. "If you waggle it, you lose the clubhead position."

"Well, I've always waggled," Bobby objected.

"You mean you used to always waggle," I told him. I was very firm.

I looked over to the east. The second plane was getting larger now. It was only a single-engine job, maybe four passengers. The lower-ranking guys, I imagined.

"I hear it," Bobby said. "When do I swing?"

"I'll tell you," I replied, trying to make my voice calm and steady. "We're going to hit a little power fade and cut it right into the fuselage, okay?"

"Okay." Bobby's posture looked good. But I could see he was nervous because of the way he wrapped and unwrapped his hands on the grip.

I stepped back. I looked at the plane. "Count of three take it back. One. Two. Three."

Bobby drew the club back low and slow, like he was playing the third hole Thursday morning, nice and relaxed. He coiled, hesitated for a microsecond at the top, and then the magic happened. All that power and energy somehow flowed into his downswing, and again it was so fast you couldn't see it happen. But I heard his whoosh, and his thwack, the sounds I hadn't heard since that night on the practice tee at Oak Valley. I knew he'd pured it. The ball zipped out of there.

It would be a neat story, I guess, to say that Bobby became the first man ever to hit a plane off the lesson tee at Eadon Branch.

He didn't.

He hit it over the damn plane. For the longest time I thought for sure he would bounce it off the fuselage. The ball started low and kept rising, rising, getting small in a hurry. And I could see that the timing was perfect. It was like watching one of those submarine movies where the torpedo and the ship are on the sonar screen, getting closer and closer and you know they're going to converge.

But this ball kept rising and the plane dropped down a touch. The ball passed directly over the cockpit.

"Holy shit," J. R. said.

"Holy shit," Conrad repeated.

"Sorry, Bobby," I said. "I overclubbed you."

4

▼

THAT NEAR MISS CHANGED BOBBY JOBE. IT SHOWED HIM THE POWER AND the promise he still had. As Angela said, with that smile that hinted at joys we had yet to dream of, "It's still inside you, Bobby. You just have to let it out."

He wanted to let it out. He wanted it the way he wanted women. That one shot was like a sniff of cocaine to a reformed addict. It was intoxicating.

Of course, I knew one shot didn't mean that much. I sure didn't think it meant Bobby could play tournament golf again. But I was willing to work with Bobby because I'd also had a little vision after I saw him hit that ball.

I figured that even if he couldn't play tournament golf again, there was a good chance he could make some money doing exhibitions. I could get a piece of that. Plus, I figured that some of the exhibitions would be held in conjunction with tournaments on the Tour. People would see that I'd stuck with Bobby after all. And I'd be around, maybe, when some good player fired his caddie and was looking for a replacement. Half of getting a job as a caddie is being in the right place at the right time.

And I figured that once Bobby got going and started making money again, I could suggest a little investment for him: Eadon Branch. That would save the place for Eudora and keep her occupied. At the same time, it would free me to get out of Allegheny Gap.

I knew it wouldn't be easy. Angela thought he just had to let it out. Angela didn't know golf. Golf is hard. It's hard if you've got your eyes. I knew it was not going to be like getting back on a bicycle.

•   •   •

WHEN BOBBY AND I GOT TOGETHER ON THE LESSON TEE AT EIGHT O'CLOCK
the next morning, I started to feel like I'd been too optimistic. He had on
a yellow golf shirt I'd given him with "Eadon Branch G.C." embroidered
on the left side, and an Eadon Branch cap. It was a cool, bright morning,
with a little dew still sparkling on the ninth fairway and long shadows cast
by the pines and poplars along the first. Bobby looked like a golfer and
Eadon Branch looked like a golf course.

I heard the sound of clubs clattering and turned around. Angela was
coming down from the parking lot and she had a surprise with her—
Bobby's clubs, in his big pro bag with the white script "Callaway" on the
black leather and his name imprinted right above the ball pocket. Except
she hadn't had it balanced and the clubs had all just fallen out in the grass.
I hustled up to her and grabbed the bag, then stuffed the clubs in, one by
one, in order. I liked the way the irons lined up when they were in order.

"Thank you, Mr. Mote," she said formally. She was still in the Good
Humor mode with me—frozen. "I didn't quite have the hang of carrying
it and moving. I'm such a klutz."

"Don't say that, Miss Murphy," I said. "Us klutzes'll take offense."

She had the grace to laugh.

I shouldered the bag. I'd forgotten how heavy it was—about forty
pounds. Bobby carried everything from sunscreen to rain pants. It didn't
feel good to be hefting it again. It felt like I'd grown a hump. But I was
enough caught up in the moment not to mind. That's one of the things
about golf. No matter how often it's smacked you in the face, golf on every
new day dares you to hope.

I set it down in front of Bobby and told him to put his hands on it. He did.

"Clubs," he said, a little dubiously, as he fingered the clubheads.

Then he touched the bulldog clubhead cover, for the University of
Georgia, that he used on his driver. He fingered it for a second. "My
clubs!" he yelped. His hands were all over that bag for a while, tracing the
script on the outside, tracing his name.

"I think he's glad to see them, Mr. Mote," Angela said. She was
pleased with herself.

"How'd you get them?" Bobby asked her.

"Asked Paula for them," she said.

"You knew I'd do this, didn't you?"

"Yes," she said. Nothing more. I believed she had known. I didn't know how she'd known, but she knew. Knew I'd be helping him, too. Knew it even though Bobby hadn't bothered to take the clubs when he moved out of his and Paula's house.

Bobby looked at me, or, rather, turned his head toward me. Sometimes when he was standing still and didn't need any help, I'd forget he couldn't see.

"Henry, what kind of shoes is she wearing?"

She was wearing sandals, same as the day before. Same shorts, same knock knees, same New York Mets hat, but a T-shirt this time that said she was a friend of the Bronx Zoo. Her toenails were painted pink.

"Hippie shoes," I said.

"Well, you go in there and tell Eudora I'm buying you some golf shoes," Bobby told her. "You can't be hanging around a golf course in hippie shoes."

I half expected her to tell him where to stick his golf shoes. She didn't. She just smiled and went into the clubhouse. I still couldn't figure out women and Bobby Jobe.

Bobby and I got down to practice. We both knew it couldn't be like it was before. Back then, I'd stand behind Bobby on the practice range, cleaning clubs after he used them, tossing him balls when he teed them up to practice with his driver, telling him "good shot" when I thought he needed to hear it. It was the easiest part of my job, the part I liked the best. The bag was on the ground, not on my back. Bobby wasn't going to get upset if he missed one. There was time to socialize with the players and the other caddies.

But that was when Bobby could see.

"We've got to get you lined up," I said.

That meant putting his feet in the right position. So I squatted down and grabbed his shinbones just below the knee and half prodded, half pulled him until the line between his toes was parallel to the line from the ball to the target, that broken-down old flag I had out there at the two-hundred-yard mark.

I must've pushed Bobby when he expected to be pulled, because he damn near fell over on top of me. He caught himself by jamming a hand into my shoulder and I nearly fell over backwards. It looked like he was trying to stick his knee through my windpipe.

"Uh, Henry, I'm not sure this is going to work," he said.

My mouth was pressed against his right leg.

"I think you may be right."

"And I'm damn sure not going to do it in public," he added.

"Wouldn't do my image a lot of good, either," I said, and slithered out from under him.

I tried standing behind him and adjusting his shoulders, but that left his feet misaligned. I tried telling him to move his feet a few inches forward or backward, but it was like teaching an elephant to dance. You could get a foot to move, but you couldn't expect precision. And we needed precision. If a golfer's body isn't aligned right, a good swing isn't going to help him.

Finally, I had an idea. I was going to have to hand him a club anyway. So why not use it to get him lined up? I pulled his wedge and pointed it out in front of me about thigh high, along a line parallel to and slightly left of the line I wanted the ball to take. I told Bobby to step forward until he could feel the shaft snug against both thighs when he was in Hogan's shooting-stick posture. He did.

And there it was. He was aligned.

Then we had to figure out how to put the club in his hands right. Bobby tried fingering the clubhead and then sliding his hands down the shaft to the grip. But when he did that, he was usually off by a few degrees when he set the clubhead down and I placed it behind the ball. Then I'd twist the clubhead so it was square to the target line, but that would foul up the rest of Bobby's alignment. Balls flew left and balls flew right but they never flew straight.

Angela walked out of the pro shop with Eudora. They stood there watching us for a moment, Angela in her new golf shoes. They were Nikes.

"Wow," I said. "You look just like Tiger Woods in those shoes except he's a black male and you're not."

"Thank you, Mr. Mote," she said. "For trying your best to be complimentary."

Eudora looked a little saddened by the hostility between Angela and me. I considered explaining to her that it wasn't my fault I'd been raised not to know how to be charming to a woman. But I decided against it. No point in having all of the women in my life mad at me.

"Henry, I'm going to the Seven-Eleven to buy some tickets," she said. "Angela's going to keep an eye on the shop." Powerball was one of Eudora's gambling vices. She knew the odds were like a jillion to one against winning, but she liked the action.

I rolled my eyes. "What's it up to now?" I said.

"Four million," she said.

"Great," I said. "Our money problems are over."

"You're so cynical, Mr. Mote," Angela said. "Eudora, let me get a dollar. Buy one for me."

"With pleasure, Angela," Eudora said, looking at me triumphantly as if to say, "See?" They went inside together.

Bobby was just standing there, looking bemused and happy to be out in the sun. Of course, all he had to do was stand there and chip the ball. I did the squatting, the pushing, the prodding and the fixing. I teed the balls so he'd have a good lie every time. It was not even nine o'clock and there was already sweat dripping off the bill of my cap, dripping steadily like a leaky faucet into the mess of clover and rye and clipped crabgrass on the lesson tee. Except we called the crabgrass Bermuda.

"Better watch out, Henry," he said. "Eudora may write you out of her will."

"Then I'd have to do something degrading, like caddie for a blind golfer," I said.

We got back to work on the grip problem and finally worked out a compromise. I set the clubhead behind the ball, while Bobby kept the shaft loosely in his hands. When I told him it was right, he tightened his grip. That helped, a little. But he still sprayed his shots and he still hit about one in five of them fatter than Roseanne Barr. And this was just little chips and pitches. I didn't want to know what he'd do with full swings and bad lies.

He'd hit a little pitch and I'd describe it to him. "Low, right, about fifty yards." Or "high, left, about seventy yards." But only rarely did I tell him what he wanted to hear, which was "straight, high, sixty yards."

"Damn," he'd say when I told him a shot had strayed. But he didn't complain and he didn't give up. He had more work ethic than I'd seen before. Then again, he'd had other things to do before.

After a couple of hours he suggested we go to work on putting, which I had figured was going to be the downfall of any attempt to play serious golf. You can hit full shots just by swinging well and letting the ball get in the way of the club. But I just didn't see how a player without eyes could react to the hole the way a good putter does. And since putting largely determines how well good players score, I couldn't imagine a blind golfer scoring well.

Bobby'd always hated to practice putting. He'd say putting was something you either had or didn't have on a given day. The truth was he didn't get a kick out of putting the way he did out of flushing a ball on the range and watching it fly. So he didn't bother. He was a pretty good natural putter, so by and large he got away with it.

"I figure we got to start with two-footers," Bobby said. "I gotta be able to make those."

I found a flat spot on the practice green and gave him a straight two-footer, a little uphill. We lined it up and I got the club in his hands, squatting down behind and peering over the alignment stripe on top of the blade. He missed the cup by a few inches and rolled it three feet past.

"Close," I said.

"How close?"

I didn't want to tell him. "Not close enough," I replied.

Bobby got annoyed. "Damn it, Henry, if you're going to be my eyes, you've got to be my eyes. Now what happened?"

"You missed by three inches on the right side and pushed it three feet past."

"Thank you," he said. He paused. "Pretty lousy putt, huh?"

"Never seen you putt worse without big money on the line," I said.

Bobby ignored the insult. "Try it again," he said.

And we did. He made the third, and the fourth. He wanted to make ten in a row before he moved back to three feet. He'd get up to six, or seven. Then he'd miss.

Angela came out with a couple of cups of lemonade. Then she spelled me for a while. My knees were aching.

Angela was a lot more descriptive than I had been. "Okay, Bobby, it's a beautiful little strip of green turf Mr. Mote's grown for us here, smooth and satiny," she said. "The hole's got some kind of white sleeve inside it. It's nice and big. Your ball says 'Titleist,' with a little number two on it. Your putter says 'Odyssey.' It's a very literary club. The little lines on the putter point right to the cup. It's two feet away. Just needs a nice, smooth swing."

He rolled it in. I could hear the rattle of the ball at the bottom of the hole.

"Hear that, Bobby? Sound of success. Make it for me again." She put another ball in front of the putter blade and went through the whole description again. Bobby made it again. He made his first five putts with Angela.

I could see what she'd done. She'd given him a picture for his mind. He'd responded to it.

So we backed it up to three feet and I took over. I did my best to make a picture for Bobby. I pretended I was a radio announcer. And he got better at putting. After a day or two, he'd got to where he could make maybe seven out of ten three-footers. A pro has to be able to make at least nine out of ten, unless we're talking slippery putts on sideslopes like they have at Augusta or Oakmont.

We spent hours on that green. I made marks in the grass with chalk and then I'd pace off a distance from the mark—say, twenty feet. Bobby would putt from there. Angela would stand beside the mark and call out the distance. If he got it within a foot of the mark, she'd hoot and holler. If he ran it by, she'd tell him how much. "Twenty-three feet!" "Twenty-four feet." After about twenty hours of that, Bobby had a pretty good touch.

WE DID SOMETHING SIMILAR WITH THE IRONS. I GOT ONE OF THOSE NEW distance-measuring binoculars down at Wal-Mart, and we set flags out from the lesson tee at twenty-five-yard intervals. Bobby would hit his irons and he'd try to say how far the ball was going to travel before it hit the ground. He might, for instance, be hitting an eight-iron, and he'd say, "one fifty-five" if he thought he'd caught it right. Angela was down on the range shagging the balls, and she'd call back the actual distance.

I could see that Angela had been right. Bobby needed golf. Once he got clubs in his hands, Bobby started to work harder than I'd ever seen him work at anything. He'd show up at eight in the morning and they'd already have been to the gym, stretching and lifting weights. He'd hit balls or practice putting until dark, as long as Angela or I was willing to stand behind him and line him up and get the club square and in his hands. I guess it beat taking Braille lessons.

When I wasn't available, when I had to deal with something in the shop or some weed problem out on the course, or just when my knees and back needed a rest, Angela and Bobby would go somewhere and work on that facial vision thing. He'd shuffle slowly around the parking lot, or the shop, trying to make sound from his feet bounce off the cars or the stock shelves, trying to use the sound to avoid the obstacles. When things were noisy or crowded, they'd go off into the woods by the fifth fairway and do it—the facial vision thing, I mean. Then it would be back to the range and hitting more balls. At night, they'd head back to the Econo Lodge, where they were staying, and I'd fall into bed in my room over the equipment barn, exhausted.

No matter how tired I was, though, I'd lie there a moment and think about my plans, think about the right time to ask Bobby for an investment. I figured each time I squatted behind him and lined his club up was another favor he owed me. I'm a greedy person. It's another one of my many character flaws.

The trouble was, the time just never seemed exactly right, because the longer and harder we worked, the more frustrated we got. Except for Angela, who didn't seem to know how to be frustrated. Bobby got to a certain point, a point where he was hitting some good shots on the range and the putting green—not all that consistently, but often enough to make us see possibilities. Late one Wednesday afternoon, about two weeks into this process, we decided it was time to take it out to the course.

That's when the frustration set in. Bobby, Angela, and I walked onto the first tee. No one else was around; Eadon Branch doesn't get too much Wednesday afternoon play. Not many doctors in Allegheny Gap, and the ones there are all work now for some HMO that runs 'em like coal miners.

"Okay, Bobby," I said. "We got a birdie hole to start off. Straightaway par five, four-eighty-five. Tee shot's a little downhill. We're on top of a knoll. The sky is blue and the grass is green. Got some big old oak trees just leafing up down the left side, but plenty of room. There's a little bunker down the right side, but it's only two-forty to carry it. No trouble for you. We just need a plain-vanilla tee shot, right down the sprinkler heads."

Eadon Branch didn't actually have sprinkler heads, or a sprinkling system for that matter. But Bobby wouldn't know that.

I got him set up, got the club square, and stepped back.

Bobby wound up, slid his hips when he should have uncoiled, and sliced it halfway to the West Virginia line.

"A little right," I said. "Nice and long, though."

"Don't try to bullshit me, Henry!" Bobby snapped. "I sliced the crap out of it."

I could tell two things from his reaction. One was that he'd cared a whole lot more about that tee shot than I had. I'd looked at it as just an extension of the practice we'd been doing. He looked at it as the first real golf shot since his accident. Cutting that first one so bad made him feel like a kid who sticks his hand in a candy bag and finds a dog turd. Except the kid can blame someone else. The golfer can't.

I was glad he was ticked, though. Showed he was into it.

And I could tell that I was going to have to stop patronizing him. There was a temptation to do that. If he hit his tee shot into the practice range, I was inclined to just pretend it was in the rough right off the fairway, let him think it was a pretty good shot. Then I'd lead him to it and let him hit the next shot with some confidence.

But in just the couple of weeks we'd been working, Bobby had developed his sensitivity. He could tell a lot about the way a ball went from the sound as it left the clubhead, from the way his hands felt at impact, from the balance and rhythm he felt, or didn't feel, in his body. It was not that he didn't have those feelings before. He just hadn't paid a lot of attention to them.

"Okay," I said. "You hit a bad shot. About two-eighty, but it started right of the bunkers on the right side and kept getting right. It's over in the range somewhere, barely on the property. Take a mullicant."

Bobby didn't smile. "No fucking mulligans," he said. "Or mullicants. This is golf."

I could see Angela out of the corner of my eye. She'd been watching this without saying anything, but now she was nodding at me, telling me silently to go along with whatever Bobby wanted.

That's what a caddie does anyway.

So I wiped off the driver and put the head cover back on, shouldered the bag, and touched his elbow so he knew where I was and could put a hand on the back end of the bag.

"Okay. Let's go find it," I said. And we set out.

"Going downhill a bit," I told him. He eased in behind me and we got down the slope to the fairway without any trouble. From a distance, someone in the clubhouse might've thought we were just a regular golfer and his caddie.

Then we veered off right, through the light rough and then into the heavy grass at the end of the cleared area below the lesson tee. I'd always figured that Clayton Mote had cleared that piece of land to someday be his eighteenth hole, a long par four headed back up the hill to the clubhouse. I didn't know for sure because he didn't leave behind any drawings or plans. But I'd think about him whenever I was down there.

"God, are we on a golf course or a farm?" Bobby asked. The ground under his feet was getting hummocky and the grass was ankle high. Hayden didn't bother to cut this area very often. No one who played Eadon Branch could hit it this far.

"I'll tell you if I see any cows," I said.

"Damn, I hit that thing off the world," Bobby moaned.

Surprisingly enough, I found it without much trouble. It was nestled down in the grass, but it was on top of a little muffin of ground. I said, "Here it is," and Bobby stopped. Angela, walking behind, was just watching quietly, saying nothing.

I looked over the situation. We were maybe fifty yards away from the fairway, with some young spruce trees in our way. I couldn't see the green. There was a thick stand of mature oaks and pines in the way and I didn't think Bobby could hit over it, not with a club that would carry the ball two hundred yards to the green, not with that lie.

I described this to him and said, "I think we gotta just wedge it back to the fairway, then hit the third onto the green."

"Can't go for it?"

"No way," I said.

Bobby nodded glumly. He always hated laying up on a par five.

So we went through the routine. It was, of course, tougher than it had been on the lesson tee. The ball was above his feet and he hadn't practiced that kind of shot.

Once he was lined up, Bobby swung. He dipped and swayed. He buried the clubhead an inch or so behind the ball, tearing out an enormous chunk of grass and dirt. The ball floated out about twenty feet and settled in an even worse position, on the downslope of another hummock, buried in thick grass.

"Shit! Fat!" Bobby groaned.

"Well, there's good news and there's bad news," I said. "The bad news is you can't move that much dirt around here without getting a permit from the Bureau of Mines."

Bobby scowled. "Very funny, Greyhound," he said. "What's the good news?"

"The good news is I think I see gold at the bottom of your divot," I said.

Angela laughed, but Bobby just got angrier.

"I'm not ready yet," he announced. "Let's go back to work on the practice tee."

Angela nodded again, so I said okay and picked up the ball.

We went back to work. This time, we spent more time on drives and we set up on the sideslopes next to the tee and practiced some from those lies. He hit some good balls. Just before dark, we played the first hole again. But it wasn't much better. Bobby snapped his drive and made 7.

"I know you can play in the dark, Bobby," I said, "but I can't caddie. Let's get after it again tomorrow."

And we did. Bobby was out there again at eight o'clock the next morning, and the next. We practiced for hours, more hours in two days than he used to put in in a month on the Tour. He and Angela worked on his other rehab program back at the motel—I didn't want to ask what all else they did back there. It wasn't my business and I didn't like thinking about it.

We played the first hole a few more times. But he could never put two decent swings together. He bogeyed it and double bogeyed it. He refused to go on till he'd at least parred it and we never got to the second tee.

I tried everything I could think of. One time two middle-aged women were playing the hole, approaching the green when we stepped onto the tee. One of them owned the nail salon in town. The other worked nights at East Coast Communications, the telemarketing mill on the other side of town. Either one would be lucky to break 90 for nine holes. They were both out for exercise and they both needed it. Their bottoms were as broad as a bovine's.

"They're gorgeous, Bobby," I said. "Slender, long legs. Tight little butts twitching. Short shorts. Tube tops. One with short, curly black hair and the other long and blonde. Just hit it straight down toward them, nice and long, and I'll tell you what they look like when they bend over to mark their balls on the green."

Bobby took a cramped, tight swing and foozled the ball, topped it so bad it dribbled forty yards and stopped in the rough, not even making the fairway.

The sounds and the feeling in his hands told him what had happened. He started to slam the club into the ground. In the old days, he'd've probably done just that and snapped the head off. But in the old days the Callaway rep would've been there to give him a new club. He remembered that just in time and pulled the clubhead back a little. It thumped the ground, but it didn't break.

I wanted to tell him his life would be a whole lot easier if he could learn to laugh at himself, but I didn't bother. That was like telling me I could've been a star halfback if I was bigger and faster.

"Damn, Henry," he growled. "Don't talk to me about women. I never could hit it too good with a hard"—he remembered Angela's presence and stifled the rest of it.

"In a state of distraction," I offered.

"Yeah," he said. "That's it. Distraction."

Angela just shook her head.

"It's okay," I said. "It wouldn't be a good long-term strategy anyway. 'Less you could join the LPGA Tour."

"It's in me," he said. "I know it's in me. I just can't seem to get it out."

"We've all been there," I told him. It was true, but lame. Everyone knows that about golf.

He wanted to practice some more, but I looked at my watch. It was half past three.

"Can't do it, Bobby," I said. "Got my junior clinic coming in."

"Your junior clinic?"

"Yeah, first of the season."

"You run a junior clinic?"

I flushed, a little angry at the doubt I heard in his voice and a little embarrassed.

"Yeah," I said. "You want to stay and teach 'em how to top the ball?"

He didn't say anything.

"I didn't know you had a junior clinic, Mr. Mote," Angela said. She sounded interested.

I'd been getting along a little better with Angela. We were still pretty formal and stiff with each other and I knew she hadn't forgotten the rude way I'd treated her. But I didn't feel the temperature drop every time she was around. I think she respected the work I'd put in with Bobby. I know I respected the work she was doing. If I ever needed rehabilitation, I'd've wanted Angela to do it. She was infinitely patient with Bobby, demanding of him, yet encouraging. Her presence had a way of gentling him and prodding him at the same time.

"Yeah, well, when I came home last summer the guy who's the head of the Boys' and Girls' Club suggested it. Since he's a cop, I kinda felt it would be smart to do it. They got radar on the roads around here."

"I understand," Angela said. "Good luck."

I didn't know if she meant with the kids or with not getting tickets. She and Bobby went off toward the trees near the fifth tee to work on his facial vision.

Right on time, the police van drove up. Gilmore Clevinger, the night dispatcher and bulwark of the Allegheny Gap Rescue Squad, was behind the wheel. He got out, wearing his white uniform coveralls.

"Hey, Henry," he said. "Just got four for you. The rest'd rather play basketball."

The kids were coming out the sliding passenger door—a girl and three boys, all of whom looked to be about eleven years old. One of the boys was a black kid, which surprised me. I thought I knew all the black families in Allegheny Gap—there were only three or four. None of them had a boy this age as far as I knew. So I introduced myself to him first.

"I'm Michael," he said. The kid had a T-shirt on with a picture of the Chicago skyline that said "Windy City," I figured maybe he was visiting relatives in Allegheny Gap.

"I bet you're named for Michael Jordan," I replied, trying to be friendly.

He gave me a scornful look. "Nah, I'm named for my father."

"Okay," I said, and I decided not to poke into how the other three kids—Peter, Kimberly, and George—got their names.

But I was annoyed with myself for being such a racist. I didn't want Michael to get the idea that golf wouldn't welcome him.

So when I took them into the clubhouse, I let him pick first in the barrel of old clubs I'd sawed down during the winter. He grabbed the biggest one he could find, a beat-up old Founder's Club driver. Then the other kids picked, and we went back outside. I carried my boom box, the one I had in my room over the cart barn, under my arm. They stared at it curiously.

Most golf teachers start off by making kids learn the proper grip. That was the way Clayton Mote had taught me, to the degree that he did. When I was about eight years old and he was home for a week between tournaments, I told him I wanted to learn to play golf. He found an old shaft someone had broken off and he gave it to me. He showed me the interlocking grip, because my fingers were so small. He himself used an overlapping grip.

"Your grip is the most important fundamental in golf," he told me. "I want you to carry that shaft around with you, gripping it just that way. Keep doing it till it feels like the most natural thing in the world."

He showed me how to flex the shaft in my hands to check and see if I had the right grip pressure. Then he went off for another month out on Tour.

I'm not very disciplined. I got bored carrying a busted shaft around and pretty soon baseball season rolled around and I started to play second base. I lost the shaft. When Clayton Mote came home again for another week's rest, he asked me to get it and show him my grip. I had to admit that I'd lost it. I remember how ashamed I was. He didn't say anything. He just glared. I never asked him for another golf lesson, and he never offered me one.

I didn't think the grip was the right way to start a kid. Caddying for Bobby and hanging around golf courses a lot, I'd been able to see a lot of clinics, a lot of lessons. The best teacher I'd ever run across was a round-bellied old guy named Gene Hilen from a municipal course in Kentucky somewhere who gave a clinic at Horseshoe Bend in Cincinnati the first year they held the PGA there. He started the kids out skipping rocks, and that's what I intended to do with these kids.

"I know you want to start hitting balls right away," I said, "but there are a couple of moves you need to learn first. I'm going to teach you the first one down at the pond in front of the fourth green."

The kids looked mystified; Michael looked downright scornful. When I set out down the hill from the first tee, though, they followed me. When I cut left toward the fourth green, they were still there.

Clayton Mote had built the fourth at Eadon Branch around a pond left by a farmer who owned the land before it was a golf course. There was a little cement dam across the brook and the water backed up to make a pond maybe forty yards across. Clayton just added a tee and a green. Over the years, without hogs wallowing on them, the banks had greened up pretty nicely and some willow trees and lily pads had taken root. Although the acids from the mines up on Eadon Mountain kept the water from supporting fish, it was the prettiest place on the golf course. It was nothing, of course, that the people at Augusta wouldn't have ripped up and built over.

I led the kids to a little pile of flat rocks I'd been building up for a month or two. Every time I found one, I'd slip it in my pocket and when I was around No. 4, I'd toss it into the pile. I had a few dozen rocks. I'd been expecting more kids.

"Anyone know how to skip a rock?" I asked.

The kid named George raised his hand. He was a homely child, with a dirty face, a dirtier Virginia Tech hat on, jeans, and a sweatshirt that proclaimed North Wilkesboro, North Carolina, the moonshine capital of the world.

I handed George a rock and told him to have at it. He flung it sidearm and he did pretty well. It skipped twice before it sank. Then Michael tried, and then Peter, and finally, Kimberly.

I know it's not acceptable to say this, but Kimberly threw like a girl. So

I worked with her and let the boys have a contest to see who could get the most bounces out of a rock. Peter won with six. It took Kimberly a bunch of tries to get one to skip once. She just wasn't used to throwing things. But I'll say this for her. She was a gritty little girl with a chin that didn't quit. She paid attention and she kept trying.

Finally, I told them to stop and picked up a rock and flung it myself and got it to skip a few times. "The reason I wanted you all to do that," I said, "is that the movement you make when you hit a golf ball is very similar to the movement you make when you skip a rock. In fact, they're pretty much the same. So when we get clubs in our hands and I tell you to 'fire your right side,' I want you to remember skipping rocks and make the same kind of move."

To be honest, I'd half expected that the kids would break out in smiles when I told them this and congratulate me for my cleverness. But they just looked puzzled.

"Any questions?" I said.

Michael raised his hand. "Yeah. Do you really have golf balls?"

"Yeah," I said.

"And you're gonna let us hit 'em?"

"Yeah," I said. "I promise. I'm not asking you to skip rocks because I don't have golf balls for you to hit."

Michael nodded, appeased for the moment.

Out of the corner of my eye, I saw Angela and Bobby. They were standing at the edge of the trees on the side of the pond. Angela was whispering something to Bobby. I figured the sounds of the kids and the skipping rocks must've caught their attention. I suddenly felt stupid and self-conscious. Angela was a teacher and Bobby was a professional golfer and they both knew I wasn't qualified to teach golf or anything else for that matter.

But I was in it too deep to stop. I slid one of my Patsy Cline CDs in the box and turned it on. That tinkly piano laid down the melody and the Jordanaires laid down a soft background bass line and then Patsy's voice floated over the pond. "Crazy for feeling so lonely."

"Argh," George, said. He stuck a finger in his mouth and pretended to be throwing up.

I guessed they weren't Patsy Cline fans.

"Any of you kids know how to dance?"

"Not to this shit," Peter said. Michael and George giggled appreciatively at his sharp wit. Only Kimberly hung on to a neutral face.

"Well, I could tell you about Patsy Cline, but I'll save that for a rainy day," I said. "The main thing is the rhythm in this song. Hear it?"

The boys giggled again. I was this close to losing them.

"Now I want to see if you can shift your feet back and forth to that rhythm," I said. And I demonstrated, there on the bank of the pond. I shifted my weight slowly left, then slowly right. I guess I must've looked like an old woman doing the hula.

"You crazy all right," Michael sneered.

I wanted them to get this, so I ignored Michael and grabbed Kimberly by the hands. "Come on, Kim," I said. "You can do this." And I shifted back and forth in front of her until I felt not just crazy, but like a complete idiot. Kimberly looked like she wanted to try it, but she wasn't about to risk a year's worth of teasing on the school bus from Michael, George, and Peter. I dropped her hands, my face flushed. I was wondering whether we had a basketball somewhere in the shed, thinking that maybe I could keep them busy playing basketball until Gilmore Clevinger came to pick them up.

Then I heard Angela's voice behind me, saying to Michael, "You look like a dancer, Windy City. How 'bout trying it with me?"

She and Bobby must've come up behind us from the other side of the pond.

I wasn't as surprised as Michael was. Here was this white woman, grown up and just this side of beautiful, stepping in front of him and daring him to dance, trailed by this other reasonably hefty white guy in dark glasses who for all he knew might've been fixing to pound the crap out of him if he did dance.

But Angela just kind of smiled at him and did that gentling thing she did and took his hand and in a second or two, she and Michael were really dancing, shifting and swaying in unison. Then Kimberly and I started doing it, and then Angela switched to Peter, and finally to George. She had those boys charmed. They were all three dancing with her, all three with stupid grins on their faces. She showed more rhythm in those sixty seconds or so than she'd shown in the previous weeks.

I was dumb with gratitude, but I knew better than to get greedy. So as soon as the song ended, I switched the music off and declared victory.

"Okay," I said. "You've all got the rhythm you need to play golf. Now it's time to start hitting golf balls." Then I introduced them to Angela and Bobby. I didn't tell them who Bobby was, and they didn't know.

We started walking back to the lesson tee and I got up on Angela's left side. Bobby was walking along on her right elbow.

But before I could thank her, I heard whispering among the boys behind me and then George ran up and plucked at my sleeve. "Hey, Mr. Mote," he said, "Where's the passion pit?"

Michael and Peter, who'd obviously put George up to asking the question, exploded in laughter. Kimberly giggled nervously. Angela and Bobby just looked puzzled.

Truth was, it was right in front of us. Nearly every night when the weather was warm, I could lie in bed and hear the tires of pickup trucks driven by Allegheny Gap kids coasting down the dirt service road that led from the Eadon Branch parking lot to the prime boondocking spot in the willows by the pond fronting the fourth green. Nearly every summer morning, we'd pick beer cans and condom wrappers out of the grass around the pond.

It'd been going on since the course was built, and the chances were not too bad that George or Peter or Kimberly had been conceived right where we were standing. The pond by the fourth green at Eadon Branch was tightly linked to the cycle of life in Allegheny Gap, right along with the mines and Jimmy Edmisten's truck showroom.

"I don't know what you mean, George," I said.

I knew I sounded stiff and stupid. If Angela hadn't been around, I probably would've suggested he ask his mother. But it didn't seem like a fit reply for her ears. I didn't know anything about Angela's personal life except that she was with Bobby. But she didn't seem like the sort of girl who'd ever go off boondocking on a moonlit golf course.

Bobby, however, had no such compunction. He flashed his lecher's grin for the first time since he'd arrived in Allegheny Gap, the kind of grin he'd always have when he were waiting out a backup on a par three somewhere, checking out the babes in the gallery while we pretended to gauge the wind, throwing bits of grass in the air.

"You know, Henry," he cackled. "The passion pit. Golf course where I grew up in Dalton, it was next to the eighteenth green."

"Well, we don't have that here," I said, sounding grumpy.

"No passion at all, Coach?" Angela asked me, cocking an eyebrow. And that was all she said, but you could read a lot into that eyebrow.

She'd been telling Bobby to think of me not as a caddie, but as a coach. That was the term blind golfers used. That was the first time she'd called me "Coach," though. I wasn't sure whether I liked it, though I was certain it was better than "Mr. Mote."

"No," I said. "We don't have an eighteenth hole."

She kind of smiled, like she was getting ready to challenge me on it, but she didn't. I walked a little faster till I got to the lesson tee. The rest of them straggled along behind me.

When I had the kids gathered around me, I picked up a club and started to show them the grip and the stance. Then I had an idea.

"We've got a professional here who can demonstrate this a lot better than I can," I said. "Bobby, would you?"

And Bobby, like I'd figured, was glad to be asked. In fact, he was so glad that he forgot he needed to have someone help him walk. He strode forward, toward my voice, reaching out to take the club. And he walked right into the ball washer, groin first.

It must've hurt like, well, like a kick in the nuts. He yelped and then he was staggering around the tee, bent half over, clutching his balls like he was trying to hold them on, muttering things I didn't want the kids to repeat to Gilmore Clevinger or their parents.

George, Michael, and Peter, of course, thought this was the most hilarious thing they'd seen since the last episode of *South Park*. They started chuckling, and then they laughed out loud. From their point of view, I guess it was pretty funny. I'd've laughed, too, if I hadn't known why it happened and if I hadn't seen how horrified Angela was and if I hadn't seen the look on Bobby's face. It was pain, but frustration pain more than physical pain. It wasn't funny.

He straightened up, finally, and the kids slowly stopped laughing as he looked at them. I could see the anger on his face, but he didn't cuss them out. His face gradually relaxed.

"That's an optional part of the golf swing," I said, opening my mouth before I thought about what I was going to say. "You don't have to do that on every shot."

Angela smiled. Bobby didn't.

"Sorry," I said to Bobby.

He didn't acknowledge the apology, just said, "Whyn't you give me a driver, Henry?"

I put my club in his hands, and I showed the kids his grip and his stance. Then I had him swing in slow motion, and I showed them how he shifted his weight from the right side to the left and how he fired his right side.

Michael raised his hand.

"Is he blind?"

"Whattaya think, kid, I walk into ball washers 'cause I like it?" Bobby snapped.

"Yes, Michael, he is," I said.

"Then how come he knows how to play golf?"

"Ask him," I said.

Bobby didn't wait for a question. "You don't have to see to play golf," he said. "You can see in your mind's eye. And you can tell your body how to hit the ball."

"Yeah, right," George said.

"Show us," Kimberly suggested.

So I teed a ball up and got Bobby lined up, and he hit one of his better shots, a dart that bore out of there straight and drew in a little before it came down.

The kids were impressed.

"If I can do it blind," Bobby said, "Think how easy it's going to be for you guys."

I blinked. He was getting into it.

I teed up practice balls for the four of them, and they started hitting them. Of course, none of them could produce a shot remotely like what Bobby'd hit, but the three boys at least got the ball off the ground.

Kimberly was a problem. Whatever talent the girl had, she was effectively stifling it. She clenched the club in her hands. She stood frozen over the ball for the longest time, and you could see her lips moving as she reviewed what she'd heard. Then she drew the club back, but she was too tight to turn. She rared back and came down at the ball like she was killing a snake. She made some major divots, but she didn't hit the ball.

I did what I could with her. I got her to relax her grip until her knuckles were pink again—actually, hers were a kind of muddy brown that day. I got her to waggle her shoulders. Nothing helped.

"I'm trying, Mr. Mote," she said. "I'm thinking about shifting my weight and I'm thinking about firing the right side. I just can't do it. I'm not very good at sports." She sounded a half an inch away from tears.

Bobby was listening to the sounds of clubs and balls, and he heard that. He walked over in front of Kimberly, guiding himself by the sound of her voice.

"Sweetheart," he said in a soft voice. "I know you can do this. Henry's taught you what you need to know. Your body knows what to do. You just have to stop thinking about it and relax. It's only a game."

He might as well have told Kimberly to take a couple of steps and jump over the clubhouse.

"How can I relax if I can't do it?"

Bobby considered that a moment. Then he had a thought. "When you eat, do you think about how your hand's going to get the food into your mouth?"

"No."

"But you do it. You do it without thinking about it."

"Well, I've been eating all my life."

"You can do this golf swing, too," Bobby insisted. "The same way. If you relax and let yourself do it."

"I doubt it," Kimberly said.

"Let's try something," Bobby told her.

It was odd to watch him, because the way his head was set, it looked like he was talking to someone a foot taller than Kimberly, but I could tell he was concentrating on her, focused in a way I had never seen before.

"You get yourself set up the way Henry showed you."

She did.

"Okay," he said. "Now pick out a target."

"Try that brown patch of ground out there," I said. I pointed to a bare spot about a hundred yards out.

"Okay," Kim said, nodding.

"Now think about the ball going to the target."

Kim stood there.

"Can you see it?" Bobby asked her.

"I can see it."

"Okay. Now look at the target."

Kim looked downrange.

"Look at the ball."

She turned her head back.

"Swing."

She swung, and this time she had some rhythm and the clubhead caught the ball and knocked it down the range, ten yards over the bare spot she'd been aiming at.

"I did it!" she squealed. She nearly jumped up and down, she was so pleased with herself.

Bobby beamed.

"Thanks," she said to him. He looked happier than I could remember seeing him on a golf course.

Something occurred to me. "How'd you know to tell her that?" I asked him. You could never tell Bobby something flat out if you wanted him to accept it. You had to nudge him toward it.

It took Bobby a second to reply. "I knew it, but I'd forgotten it," he said. "That's the way I used to think when I was playing well. That's the way I've got to think again."

5

▼

RELAXATION AND TRUST BECAME OUR NEW SLOGANS. THEY WEREN'T A magic cure. Magic cures in golf tend to last about three holes, or until there's some pressure. Then they leave you with a messed-up swing and a lost ball. Real progress comes slowly and painfully, a fraction of a stroke at a time.

That's the kind of progress I thought we were making over the next week. Bobby worked on his game like a coal miner getting paid by the ton. We changed his routine. We started having him run his hand down along my arm to the grass and put his fingers just behind the ball so he could have a better idea of the lie he had. He tried to keep that picture in his mind. I tried to do better at filling in Bobby's picture. I gave him not just the yardage I wanted him to hit but also the trajectory, the flight path. Most important, Bobby tried to loosen up. I started to see his lips move a little before he swung, and I tried to figure out what he was saying to himself. I think it was "let it happen." That's one definition of relaxing. You let it happen instead of trying to make it happen.

Back when he was a touring pro, Bobby'd basically tried to do just the opposite. He didn't practice all that much and he tried too hard when he was playing. I couldn't help but think that if he'd had this attitude when he was playing, things might've happened differently. He might've been in the media center telling the writers how he'd won the PGA rather than being out on the practice tee in a thunderstorm.

He got pretty good at the little games we played, like the pitching drill with Angela calling out the distances. We had a putting drill where we dropped four balls on the practice green and then putted each to a different hole. We got the first one in the hole with our second putt, then hit it toward the second hole. When we'd hole those two out, we putted them toward the third hole, and so on. The idea was to complete this circuit without three-putting. Bobby got to where he could do it on the first try most of the time. Of course, by then he knew the practice green like you know your own bed. Every dip and curve was familiar.

But it still wasn't working on the golf course. We still hadn't seen the second tee. Bobby could feel the difference in his mind when we tried to play the first hole. "I can't free it up and let it go," he told me. "Once I know we're actually playing, my mind changes."

Then two things happened—cross-country golf and Paula Jobe.

J. R. Neill got us into cross-country golf. He and Conrad and Raymond and some of their friends from the Pittston mine came out late on a Friday afternoon. We'd had rain a little earlier that day, so the course was pretty much empty. Angela was down at Eudora's house, doing laundry for herself and Bobby. She had to sort his socks and things for him, put the colors together right. Bobby and I were working on the putting green when J. R. walked up.

"Okay with you if we play a little cross-country?" J. R. asked me.

It was okay with me.

"You and Bobby like to play?" he asked.

I looked at Bobby. "How about it?"

"What's cross-country?" He'd forgotten that J. R. and the boys were playing it that first Sunday at Eadon Branch, before he almost hit the airplane.

"Well," J. R. explained, "it's sorta like ordinary golf only you play, say, from the first tee to the seventh hole as fast as you can. That's what we're starting with today. And you drink a lotta beer."

We were both sick to death of putting drills. "Sounds good," Bobby said. "What are the stakes?"

"More beer," J. R. said.

"Sounds better," Bobby said, grinning.

There were six of us when we teed off. The first five all hit the standard tee shot for this particular cross-country golf route, which was a five- or six-iron over the pond to the front of the fourth tee. A couple of them hit in the pond; J. R. and two others made it over. But I figured I had me a stud horse for this game, and when Bobby's turn came, I handed him the driver and I pointed him toward the ninth fairway. He was going to have to hit it high and carry it about 250 yards, because there was a row of sycamore and ash trees lining the ninth fairway that J. R. and his crowd had no chance of driving over. But I didn't tell Bobby about the trees. I just told him to hit a high, smooth draw and I teed the ball a smidgen higher than usual.

"See it and let it happen" were the last words I said to him, and I could see his lips move a little, telling himself the same thing.

He did. He found a swing somewhere in the vault of his brain that I hadn't seen in a long time. He hit himself a comet, a thing of beauty. It cleared the row of trees by about twenty feet, still on the rise, and disappeared down the middle of the ninth fairway. There's something almost miraculous about that kind of shot, almost otherwordly. It's just so perfect. Watching it made me feel good. It's no accident that Tiger Woods and John Daly are the two biggest draws on the Tour. It's because they hit it so long, and people love to watch a ball get crushed.

"Dinner and a movie, kid," I told Bobby. I laughed out loud.

Bobby knew it was launched from the feeling in his hands and his body, but he wasn't sure about the direction.

"On target?" he asked.

"Piped it," I said, still grinning. I wished he could've seen it.

"Shit," J. R. said in a fake whine. "You guys been sandbagging?"

"Nah," I told him. "But playing for your beer is a powerful incentive."

We grabbed a cart, advanced ourselves a couple of Millers from J. R.'s cooler, and took off after the others. The ones that'd cleared the pond had to hit six and seven-irons over the trees to the front of the ninth green, so we were a stroke to the good.

The next shot was a toughy. A big swath of woods separated the ninth fairway from the sixth, which was in turn separated by some towering trees from the seventh. The longer you chose to carry it over the woods onto the sixth, the shorter your final iron to the green at seven would be. Bobby bent over and checked the lie with his fingertips. I gave him the five-iron and he ripped it, clearing the trees and landing on the sixth fairway just a wedge from home. Raymond tried to hit the same club in the same direction, left it ten yards deep in the woods, and never found it.

J. R. Neill and Billy Prescott were the only ones left alive, and they played safe, hitting short irons over short carries, keeping the ball in play. Bobby's third shot, a wedge, covered the flag and wound up thirty feet past the hole. J. R. and Billy reached the green in five, but they were inside Bobby's ball, each maybe fifteen feet away.

J. R. knew Bobby would have to putt three or four times for him or Billy to halve the hole and keep the beer score square. If one tied, all tied. Otherwise, a hole winner got a beer from everyone. I guess he was feeling a little irritated with himself for underestimating Bobby and not getting a handicap stroke or two. And J. R. always was the type to say anything he could think of to rattle an opponent. He hated to give beers away.

"Okay, blind boy, let's see if you can putt," he said, not very kindly.

Bobby raised the beer to his lips and poured it down his throat like he was a sinner and the beer was grace. Then he belched loudly. "Care to press?" he invited J. R. That would double the beers at stake and make things more interesting.

"You got it, blind boy," J. R. said.

I could sense something in Bobby that I hadn't sensed in a long time, since the time he ripped that drive on the fifteenth hole at the PGA. His juices were flowing, but he was still patient and calm, enjoying himself. It's the kind of confidence only someone with a gift like Bobby's can feel. I've never had it in anything. You could almost call it cruel, because he was toying with J. R. the way a kid might pull the wings off a firefly.

I walked him carefully along a line parallel to his putt's. It was a downhill, left-to-right breaker, about as fast as they come at Eadon Branch. The ball came down off a terrace and kept breaking back toward the pond at four.

I lined Bobby up with the blade of the putter aimed about four feet left of the hole. "Twenty-footer," I told him, figuring that if he hit it hard enough to move the ball twenty feet on a flat green, it would cover thirty-five feet downhill. Bobby shifted his feet around and I figured he was trying to get another feel for the slope with his feet. "Feel it and go," I told him. "Twenty feet."

He drew the putter back short and made a long, smooth, accelerating stroke. I thought for a moment he hadn't put enough pace on it, because the ball slowed down just before the edge of the terrace. But it got there, and it picked up speed down the slope and damn near went in the hole, missing by a couple of inches on the high side. It rolled about two feet past.

"Whoo," I said as the ball missed.

"What happened?" Bobby demanded.

"I should've told you nineteen and a half feet," I said. "Went by about a ball and a half on the high side. Got a two-footer."

"Damn," Bobby said. "I thought I'd made it."

I loved hearing that. It meant he had a picture of a hole in his mind and of the stroke that would get the ball there, and he'd made the stroke he wanted.

J. R. and Billy putted, almost on the same line. Billy got a good read off J. R.'s putt and he sank his, putting him in at six. Bobby needed to sink his putt to win two six-packs.

"Short putts," J. R. said, needling Bobby, "must be tough if you can't see the hole."

"Judging by you, J. R., I'd say they're tougher when you *can* see it," Bobby said. Hoots arose from the other golfers, now gathered around the green in their carts.

We lined up the next putt. It was going to break, but if he hit it firm and just left of center, it was not going to break outside the hole. It was a delicate putt, the kind that causes putter shafts to get wrapped around tree trunks.

"Three feet," I said, adding one foot to the distance. "Straight in." I lined him up center-left, aimed at a bit of brown grass on the edge of the hole. Bobby rolled it right in. Never a doubt, you could say, except that it would be a lie.

"We're drinking," I said after the ball stopped rattling in the hole.

Those two six-packs meant almost as much to me as the biggest check I ever got on the Tour, which was five thousand dollars after Bobby finished second at Doral. I'd say they meant more, but I'm not that sentimental. One thing, though: I'd worked harder for them than I ever had for money.

J. R., Conrad, Raymond, and the guys looked a little like they'd been fleeced by some woman.

"What's the next hole?" Bobby asked. He was juiced.

"Well, we usually play to the ninth green from here," J. R. said.

"Let the beers ride?" Bobby asked.

"You got it, blind boy," J.R . said.

Bobby hit another great tee shot off the eighth tee, and then he listened to J. R.'s shot. His wasn't bad, but it was an amateur's shot. Bobby's was a pro shot.

"Something wrong with that club, J. R.? With the acute hearing I got after I lost my sight, I'd say it sounds a little cracked," Bobby said innocently.

J. R. pulled the clubhead up toward his face and started examining it before he realized what Bobby was doing to him. J. R. had been the number one needler at Eadon Branch, but he'd just become number two. He managed to smile about it—barely.

We drove off. Birds were chirping and the late afternoon sun was warm on our faces. Bobby was smiling, staring into the blackness around him.

"God," he said. "You know I never appreciated the way a golf course smelled. Outside of a woman when she's naked and horny, I think it's the best damn smell in the world."

I'd been wanting since the first day to ask him about that, to ask him how he perceived things.

"What's your sense of the place? Is it like being in a dark room?"

"Not really," Bobby said. He reached down, groping, till he found his Miller in the can holder on the dashboard of the cart. He took a sip. "It's more like being in a submarine, you know, in one of those movies. I can't see out. But I got other ways of knowing what's around me, just like the submarine guys do. Like I can hear wind in the trees, if the cart's stopped, so I know where they are. I can hear the birds chirp and I can hear a woodpecker from a mile away. I can smell the difference between the fairway, when it's been cut, and the rough. I can tell you from my feet how firm the greens are. I can feel the sun on my face. I just can't see the light."

I nodded. He seemed very mellow and I figured it was as good a time as I was likely to have to talk to him about investing.

"I think you're starting to like it around here," I started in.

"Great place," Bobby nodded agreeably. "You're lucky to have it, Coach."

It seemed like the right moment to try out my investment idea.

"Well, as a matter of fact, we could use a partner," I said. "Eudora made a bad business decision and we got a quarter-million-dollar loan coming due. We could sell you a big piece of the place for a quarter million."

Bobby whistled. Then he clacked his tongue against the roof of his mouth. "Coach, I'd like to help you. This'd be a great place for me," he said.

I could sense the turndown coming, but I didn't stop him, partly because I was surprised he'd called me "Coach." Angela had used that word, but Bobby never had. I slowed the cart by his ball, which was down near the sixth green.

"But I don't have that much money," he said.

I stopped the cart and looked at him. His face was hard to read behind those Oakleys, but I thought he must be lying. I couldn't tell you exactly how much money Bobby'd made since he'd been on Tour, but his official earnings were $2,733,457.67. I figured he'd made about that much more on the side, from Callaway and Titleist and the other endorsement deals he had.

"If you don't want to invest, you don't have to, Bobby," I said.

He put his hand on my shoulder and looked somewhere in the direction of my left ear. "Coach, I'm telling you the truth. I haven't got it."

I was confounded. "Where'd it go?" He shrugged.

"Paula and Robby got most of it. I agreed to that before the accident." Robby was his little boy.

"Couldn't you change it after—?"

He shook his head violently. "Didn't want to," he said. "She deserves it. He deserves it. Hospital got a lot of what was left. Few bad investments. Prosperous agent. That sort of thing."

"You're broke?"

He smiled. "Not quite. Got a fish and chips restaurant that loses money. Got enough to pay Angela till the end of the year. By then I'd better be rehabbed."

Bobby was feeling apologetic. "Coach, I'm sorrier than I can be about it. You been working hard and I know I haven't been paying you, and I know I've been imposing on you. I'm going to make it good for you. I just don't know exactly how yet."

I felt sorry for him, so I told him I believed him. "I know you will, Bobby, but you don't have to worry about it. I'm glad to help," I said, and I realized, somewhat to my surprise, that it was the truth.

But I was also a little dazed. I'd been so sure that Bobby would buy a piece of Eadon Branch I'd started to wonder about the clothes I ought to pack when I left town. I was so distracted I almost ran over Bobby's golf ball.

Golf is a weird game. You'd think that with Bobby thinking about money and me thinking about staying in Eadon Branch and going to work in a mine, the game would be harder. Instead, it got easier. Maybe it was because the conversation reminded us that none of the other problems in our lives seemed even close to solvable. Next to them, how hard could golf be?

He smacked a three-wood through the opening over the seventh tee and the sixth green and on down the ninth fairway. Then he hit a two-iron a little shy of 250 yards to the ninth green. He was on the green two strokes ahead of the nearest competitor, Conrad. Conrad, I think, was closing his eyes as he swung, imitating Bobby. Another two putts, and we'd won again.

"We got ourselves a case, Coach," Bobby said. A couple of the guys slapped him on the back, and J. R. said the payoff could be collected that night at Gully's.

"What's Gully's?" Bobby asked.

I didn't answer because of what I saw coming down toward the green from the clubhouse. It was Angela and Paula Jobe and Bobby's little boy, Robby.

LIKE I SAID, I'D ALWAYS LIKED PAULA JOBE. SOME PLAYERS' WIVES TREAT THEIR husbands' caddies like shit, especially if they're the ones who keep the family books and write the checks. They hate that if a player wins a tournament, his caddie gets 10 percent. They don't think a caddie's work for a week can be worth fifty or sixty thousand dollars. They don't understand that part of what keeps caddies out there is the knowledge that there is a partnership and that if they can help their players win, they'll finally make enough to pay for the long hours of work and the abuse they suffered along the way. Some wives are just snotty and see caddies as beneath them. And some just resent the time their husbands spend at the golf course and they associate the caddie with that.

Paula wasn't like that. Of course, she never had to write me any check for 10 percent of a winner's purse. But she was always friendly in the years before Robby was born, when she used to spend a lot of time on the Tour. If anything, she appreciated my presence. "When he's with you, I know what he's up to," she once told me. She knew, I figured, that when Bobby wasn't with her and wasn't with me, he was most likely off chasing. But she never did what some wives have been known to do, which is try to enlist the caddie as a spy. She just treated me very decent.

She was blonde, of course. Bobby was always partial to blondes. If she wasn't the homecoming queen at Georgia, I sure wouldn't mind seeing the girl who beat her out. She seemed to have a year-round tan, and she liked good clothes and jewelry the way a lot of players' wives do. I'd seen her once in a while at the end of a day of shopping, when she came back to pick Bobby up in his courtesy car. The woman could shop. But she wasn't an airhead. She had a sly little sense of humor and she used to read a lot. Whenever I'd see her on the course, she'd have a book in the bag she carried, and if there was a delay, as like as not she'd pull it out and spend the time reading. Hardcover books, too, not those paperback romances.

The one thing I couldn't figure out was, if she was a good, smart, pretty woman, why'd she marry Bobby Jobe? I guess you could ask the same question about a lot of women, though.

Paula walked out on the green, wearing a coordinated slacks and sweater outfit that looked like it was made of equal parts butter and cashmere, and said hello, Bobby. She put the little boy on the ground and I expected to see him run to Bobby. But the kid held back, kind of half hiding behind his mother's leg. There was an awkward second, and then Paula picked the boy up and pushed him into Bobby's arms. He let Bobby give him a hug, but his head was swiveled back toward Paula. It was painful to watch. Bobby, you could tell, was trying to see his son with his hands, running them up and down the boy's body, checking out how much he'd grown, hefting him for weight, tracing the shape of his cheeks and the length of his hair and all the while telling him how good it was to see him and how daddy'd missed him.

And while this was going on, Paula unexpectedly walked up to me and gave me a big, warm hug. She smelled good and she felt light, almost birdlike. Her shoulder blades were sharp and she'd gotten thinner since I last saw her.

"Greyhound, it's so good to see you," she said in my ear. "When I heard Bobby was up here working with you it was the best news in months."

She was maybe the one person I didn't mind calling me Greyhound.

"How'd you hear?" I asked.

"Angela," Paula said.

"Angela called you?"

"Uh-huh."

Paula looked like she didn't understand why I found that surprising. I just hadn't thought Angela would be friendly with Bobby's ex, or want her around.

Bobby navigated slowly toward us, drawn by the sound of Paula's voice. He had Robby in his arms. "This is such a nice surprise," he said in Paula's general direction.

Paula seemed a little strained in his company. "Angela told me you were making good progress and I hated to make you leave for a few days so you could have your visitation this weekend. So Robby and I decided to take a trip, didn't we, Robby?"

The boy nodded and stretched out his chubby arms. He wanted to be back with his mother. Paula stepped forward and took him, but it was awkward. She seemed to want to take him without touching Bobby.

"Thanks," Bobby mumbled. "Thanks, Paula. I owe you one."

Bobby'd always been real cocky in Paula's presence, had a negligent sort of charm that somehow seemed of a piece with his negligent, natural golf swing. That charm was all gone. He looked awkward, uncertain. Losing your eyes can change you in a lot of ways, I figured. So can losing a marriage.

J. R. Neill walked by just then, lugging his cooler on his right shoulder, making his way toward the parking lot. He came up to me. "Nine o'clock at Gully's if you want that beer, Henry," he said.

"What's Gully's?" Bobby wanted to know again.

"Gully's is the entertainment capital of southwest Warmerdam County," I said. "It's where the beautiful people in Allegheny Gap go to drink, throw up, stomp around, and call it dancing. And it's where beer bets at Eadon Branch normally get paid off."

"Sounds like such fun," Paula said. I think she was kidding.

"Well, I can't do it tonight," Bobby said. "Gotta be with Robby. Whyn't you take Paula and Angela, Coach? They can have my beers. Robby and me've got some records to listen to and some songs to sing. And we gotta get to McDonald's for dinner. Want a Happy Meal, Robby?"

Robby didn't say anything, but he nodded.

"Henry can go with us," Bobby said. "It'll be guys' night out."

So I wound up putting Robby and Bobby and Robby's kid seat— Paula insisted on that—in Clayton's old pickup truck. We drove to McDonald's while Angela and Paula went back to the motel to rest up for their big night at Gully's. The evening was shaping up as the highlight of my social season.

It was tough to watch Bobby and his boy. Playing golf, Bobby and I could control some things. I could make sure he set up right, make sure he had the right club, tell him how the putts would break. But I didn't know how to help him be a father to his son. Paula had equipped us with a diaper bag and I had assured her I could help Bobby out if we needed to change Robby. I was terrified that Robby would make me prove it. The Mote family didn't have such a great record in the paternity department.

"Thanks for doing this, Coach. I get visitation one weekend a month," Bobby explained to me as we headed out of the parking lot and turned toward town. "I gotta take advantage of it. Gotta spend every minute with my boy."

The lights in the Wal-Mart parking lot were coming on. It was dusk and the sky in the west had an orange tint. Dusk was a pretty time in Allegheny Gap. The fading light worked for the hills and ridges above us the way candlelight works for an aging woman, hiding and softening the scars and slashes left by the strip mine operators.

Robby started to cry before we'd gone a mile from Eadon Branch. He seemed like a sweet, docile kid, but when he saw his mother through the rear window he almost lost it, even though she told him six or seven times that she was not going to be far away. Gradually, his little face tightened up and when he passed Jimmy Edmisten's GMC place, he started to cry. Just wailed.

"Maybe he doesn't like Jimmy Edmisten," I said. "Or probably he just doesn't like strangers."

I was talking about myself, of course. Bobby didn't hear it that way.

"I'm no stranger, Robby," he said to the boy. "I'm your Daddy!"

I made up my mind right there if I ever had kids I would never get a divorce. 'Course, I've made up my mind about a lot of things. I've passed drunks puking in a parking lot and made up my mind never to drink beer again.

But Bobby was about as sad-looking as I'd ever seen him.

"Happy Meal, Robby, Happy Meal," Bobby babbled.

Robby cried louder.

"'S'okay," Bobby crooned, trying to calm him.

Robby started to cough and cry at the same time. Bobby reached out, I guess trying to pat his head. He poked Robby near the eye instead. Robby started to scream and for a moment I thought he was having an asthma attack or something. He started to gasp, like he couldn't get any air into his lungs before he cried it out.

That was it for Bobby's repertoire of soothing gestures. He knew more ways of hitting bunker shots than he did of being nice to the kid. He got all stern with him, grabbing the boy's little hands and raising his voice. "Hush, Robby," he commanded. "Hush or no Happy Meal!"

I knew that approach would never work. It had never worked with me. Robby kept crying.

So I stopped the car about three blocks shy of McDonald's, just yanked it over to the side of the road and parked.

"We there?" Bobby asked. He could tell we hadn't entered a parking lot.

"Not quite," I said. I unbuckled Robby's seat belt and pulled him from the car seat. I handed him to Bobby.

I didn't have to tell him to hug him. Bobby did it, and after a minute or so, Robby started to calm down. He was still whimpering, but I put the truck in gear and drove slowly on.

The sight of the golden arches calmed Robby down the rest of the way. Shows the way television ads have trained us, I guess. Plus, the kid was hungry. So was I.

It was past the usual Allegheny Gap dinner hour and the rush was starting to slack off when we walked in. Bobby had Robby cradled in his left arm and his right hand on my left elbow. I held the door open for them.

Bobby started sniffing like a spaniel seeking a scent, poking his nose in the air.

"This place look clean to you, Coach?" he whispered to me.

It looked like an ordinary McDonald's. Four kids with pimply faces and funny red hats were serving customers. Another kid, a girl with a figure like a bowling ball, was filling drive-through orders. There was a little puddle of white milk shake on the floor by the counter, but it hadn't congealed so I didn't imagine it'd been there long.

"It's fine, Bobby," I said. Bobby nodded, uncertain but unable to contradict me, either.

Robby got a Happy Meal and milk. Bobby and I got Big Macs and Cokes and we split an order of fries. We grabbed a table by the window and I got us a kid's seat for Robby.

I slid the french fries in front of Bobby. He reached out with his left hand to ascertain where Robby was, then put a fry in his right hand and fed it to him. The boy took it from his father's hand and stuffed it in his mouth. He looked a lot happier than he had in the car. Guess that's why they call it a Happy Meal.

"Is there a toy, Coach?" Bobby asked after he'd fed Robby half the potatoes. There was—some kind of plastic knight mounted on a horse. I gave it to Bobby and he fingered it, but he must've missed the sword the knight had in his hand.

"Look, Robby, a cowboy!" he said, and he gave it to the boy. "Giddyup!"

I couldn't bring myself to correct him. Maybe the kid would grow up someday and flunk the SATs because he didn't know the difference between a knight and a cowboy, but Bobby was trying hard.

Then I wondered if Clayton Mote might've wanted to be a good father at some time, but, like Bobby, couldn't figure out how to pull it off.

Robby played with the toy long enough to give Bobby a chance to grab his Big Mac and take a bite. He spilled a big glob of ketchup on his shirt. I waited until I saw some ketchup dribbling down Robby's chin, then I wiped both of them off at the same time.

"Thanks, Coach," he said. "Did I look stupid?"

I told him no, he hadn't.

"You know," he said, "I live in fear of the day when it's Robby has to do that. Wipe food off my shirt."

"I don't think he'll mind," I said. And I didn't.

"Coach," Bobby said, "I got another favor to ask you."

"Sure."

"Well," he whispered, as if Robby was not to overhear, "I wonder if when you're out with Paula and Angela tonight you could just kind of ask Paula how she's doing?"

"Sure," I said.

He nodded, hesitated, then went on.

"Ask her if she's still seeing the dentist."

"The dentist?"

"She took up with a dentist after the divorce. He moved in. But the last time I called and left a message, her machine didn't say, 'We're not here.' She said, 'I can't come to the phone right now.'"

I told him I would find out what I could.

Bobby nodded, then wrinkled his nose. He started to laugh.

"What's so funny?"

"Well, you know that hypersensitive smell that blind people have?"

I knew that was a myth, but I played along. "Yeah," I said.

"Well, it just told me that you need to help me change Robby's diaper."

BY THE TIME I GOT ROBBY AND HIS FATHER AND MYSELF CLEANED UP AND dropped them off at the Econo Lodge, it was nearly nine o'clock. Angela and Paula were ready.

Paula was wearing the same clothes she'd had on at the golf course, but Angela had changed. She had on a loose, flowery skirt, mainly black, and a severe, plain white blouse. It was as if she hadn't been able to decide whether to dress up or not and finally compromised in the middle.

"You ladies ready?" I said. "Been a while since I took two beautiful women into Gully's." I was feeling a little full of myself for some reason. I think it must've been the way Bobby had finally put it together on the course that afternoon.

Paula gave me a big smile and took my arm. "Oh, come on, Greyhound, I bet you have the women in this town lined up to go out with you," she said.

"Yeah, but I get so bored with that," I said. "They're just after my body."

Angela didn't say anything. She seemed a little distracted. I figured she must be uncomfortable around Paula.

In the truck, Paula sat in the middle and Angela rode shotgun. When we got to Gully's the parking lot was filling up and the little mobile sign outside said, "Midnight Rodeo, Fri–Sat."

"They're going to have a rodeo here tonight?" Angela asked.

"No," I told her. "I believe that's the name of the band."

It was. They were starting to play the "Watermelon Crawl" when we walked in. Gully's was a big old cavernous place with a couple of pool tables, a couple of bars, and a central dance floor. There was a painting of the Western desert—cactuses and tumbleweeds and such—on the cinder block wall behind the bandstand and the whole place kind of glowed from the neon beer signs hanging on the walls. You could get any kind of beer you wanted in Gully's, as long as it wasn't imported or a microbrew.

J. R. Neill had seats set aside for us at a big table in the corner under a Coors sign with the "r" burnt out. "Pour from the pitcher," J. R. shouted. "There's lots more."

I poured a few beers. Angela watched what was going on on the dance floor, watching the way the line moved and slowed and moved again in unison. "They really dance," she said. "You said they just stomped around. But they don't. They're not faking it."

Paula nodded. "Don't know what you're doing out there, you could cause a collision."

Angela stared some more.

"Where's your cowboy hat? And your boots? And your big belt buckle?" Paula demanded of me.

Most of the regulars at Gully's, when they come in to dance, dress up like kids playing cowboys. I've never been able to figure out why, except that the costume seems to go with the dance.

"If I'd wanted to be a cowboy," I said, "I'd've moved to New Mexico or someplace."

J. R. and his wife came off the dance floor. "So why aren't you dancing?" J. R. asked me, like he'd come to school and found me goofing off instead of working on my spelling.

"Well," I said, groping a little. "You can't fake this dancing."

"Shoot," J. R. said. "What've you taken all them lessons for, then?"

"Lessons?" Paula laughed. "You been sandbagging us, Greyhound?"

Well, in fact, they give lessons free at Gully's on Monday and Tuesday nights and I'd come in a few times—all right, a lot of times—but mainly to see if any interesting women would show up to take lessons, which never seemed to happen. I guess that was my fault. I figured if they showed up to take lessons at Gully's, they might be as desperate as I was, and I believe in never getting involved with a woman who's got as many troubles as you have.

"I've had a few lessons," I said to Paula.

"Well then, you have to teach me," she said.

The band struck up "I Like My Women a Little on the Trashy Side."

"Hot damn," Paula said. "I'm feeling trashy."

So we got up and danced. I set myself up behind her and breathed in the jonquil smell of her hair and took both her hands and led her. It was maybe the first time in my life I'd danced with someone who felt graceful, who made me feel graceful, even though she was a little taller than me. The instructors I'd worked with had known the steps, but they made me feel awkward. Paula dipped when she was supposed to dip, kicked when she was supposed to kick, and twirled when she was supposed to twirl. At first I could see her watching some of the other dancers out of the corner of her eye, but she never watched, waited, and reacted. She seemed to sense what they, or I, were going to do before they did it, the way a really good boxer sees a punch coming before it gets thrown. She never missed a beat and she laughed all the time and told me I was a great dancer. With her, I almost was.

How could Bobby have fooled around on a woman like that?

"I've missed seeing you, Paula," I said to her once we had the steps down and were just stepping and circling and feeling sophisticated. "You were always my favorite member of the Jobe family."

She laughed. "If I'd known you could dance this well, Greyhound, you'd've seen a lot more of me. You're good!"

That puffed me up a little bit, though once I thought about it, I wondered why she'd been so surprised that I could dance. I guess if you only see a man trudging along with a bag on his shoulder, you don't see all that he can do.

"You miss the Tour?" I asked her.

Before she could answer, "I Like My Women a Little on the Trashy Side" ended and they started right into an old Patsy song, "Faded Love." It's a slow, melancholy song that starts with a single violin and talks about the pleasures of the past. It seemed appropriate. We kept on dancing, very grave and dignified, with me still holding her from behind. •

"Not much," she said. She was talking back over her shoulder, into my ear. "I sure don't miss the traveling and the hotels. I don't miss sitting somewhere and wondering where Bobby was. Sometimes I miss the feeling I had when we were first starting out and it was a big adventure we were on together." She was quiet for a moment as she twirled away from me and then back into my arms.

"I miss that a lot," she said.

"So what's your life like now?" I asked her, wondering how I could get around to asking her about what Bobby wanted to know. It wasn't that I wanted to spy for him. I was curious myself. I wanted Paula to be happy. She deserved it.

"It's mostly Robby," she said. "I'll stay home with him for a couple of more years and then I'm going to teach. High school history."

"Any, uh, men in your life? Besides Robby?"

Her eyes narrowed. "Did Bobby ask you to ask me that?"

My face got hot. I swayed and dipped and kicked as the girl from Midnight Rodeo covering Patsy's song confessed that with every heartbeat, she still thought of you.

Paula was angry or upset, or something. I could tell. Her body had gotten rigid in my arms and my rhythm left me. I stepped into her Achilles tendon and nearly hurt her.

"Sorry, Paula," I said.

"Oh, I don't blame you," she said. "But you tell him it's none of his damn business." She hadn't even noticed, I thought, that I'd stepped on her.

The girl singing Patsy's song brought it down the way Patsy had, though she didn't get anywhere near as much into the last "luh-huve," as Patsy had.

It seemed like a good time to sit down. Angela was alone at the table, looking a little like a wallflower. Someone, I could see, had emptied one pitcher and gotten halfway through another while Paula and I were dancing.

"I've got to go," Paula said. "I want to check on Robby. Was that a taxicab I saw parked outside?"

In fact, Stevie Tolliver, who owned Allegheny Gap's taxi, generally set up shop at Gully's on weekends, making a living taking drunks home. I knew I should've taken Paula back anyway. It was the gentlemanly thing to do. But I knew if I offered to do that, Angela would probably say she wanted to go back, too. I didn't want that.

"Yeah," I said. "Stevie's taxi'll run you over."

Paula leaned over and kissed me on the cheek. Then she whispered in my ear. "Thanks for the dance, Greyhound. Take care of Bobby, okay?"

Angela watched her go. I half expected her to say I should take her back myself. She didn't.

"You really can dance, Mr. Mote," she said. "I was watching you."

She was sagging a little, like her bones had gotten rubbery, and she may have had a few more beers than she was used to.

I suddenly felt like I'd better catch up. I poured myself a fresh beer and emptied the rest of the pitcher into her cup.

Angela was different somehow in this place, or I was seeing her different. It was probably the way she was dressed. The women in Gully's tend to go all out in their own fashion. A lot of them wear special dancing outfits with boots or something. Or if they wear jeans and a T-shirt, it's a T-shirt that shows off the parts they think are most showable. Their makeup is just so. But Angela looked a little lost in this atmosphere with no makeup and clothes that seemed like she hadn't been sure if she'd be dancing or teaching school. When I'd seen her with Bobby, she'd been the guide helping the blind, wise and competent and inspiring. She'd had more energy than a puppy dog. Now she seemed a little blind herself, a little hesitant.

"Like to try a dance?" I said.

She shook her head. "I can't dance."

"You danced pretty good with little Michael the other day."

She smiled a little at the memory, without showing any teeth, like she was replaying the tape in her mind and finding it enjoyable. "That was great," she said. "But it wasn't really dancing."

"I bet you could learn."

She just shook her head and sipped her beer, peering into the glass. "I'm a klutz. And I'm not very good at drinking beer, Mr. Mote," she said. "Can't hold it too well. Gotta learn."

"Why would you want to learn, Miss Murphy?" I asked her.

She didn't look good. Normally, Angela had an enthusiasm that buoyed her, kept her floating atop waves that would wash over me. Not this night.

"You shouldn't call me Miss Murphy," she said.

"You shouldn't call me Mr. Mote."

"No, it's not that," she said. Her voice was blurry. "It's that I've been married."

That surprised me. Not that she'd been married. But that she'd get divorced.

"You been married, Mr.—Henry?"

I was glad she was finally calling me that.

"Came a little close, once, but no," I said.

"What happened?"

The truth of the matter was that when I lived in Florida I'd been involved with a woman named Nancy. She was a librarian. I'd told her I'd graduated Virginia Tech. I'd told her I was a professional golfer, when all I was was a hustler. We'd talked about getting married, but then I started caddying for Bobby. I just couldn't tell her the truth about myself, about my education, about why being a caddie was a good job for me. So I made up a reason to break up with her. Said I'd be traveling too much and didn't want to be tied down. She cried a little. I didn't.

"Oh, you know, I wasn't really good enough for her," I said.

It was the truth, or part of it.

She looked at me kind of hard, like she didn't believe me. But she didn't say anything.

"What about you?" I asked.

"He ran around," she said.

Some men are like that. They get a good woman like Angela and they can't help looking for someone else. It's stupid, but it happens.

"Some guys are idiots," I said, thinking of Bobby.

She gave me that smile, real quick. "Thanks, Henry," she said.

"You're welcome, Angela," I replied.

She swallowed some more beer, nearly gagged on it, and I started to worry about how much she was drinking.

"I seem to have a knack for picking out inappropriate men, don't I?" she said.

I figured she was talking about Bobby.

I nodded. "You're not the first person that Bobby's done that to," I said.

She shook her head. "Bobby didn't do anything," she said.

"He's got that . . ." I stopped, searching for the word.

"Charisma," she said.

"Yeah. Like Kennedy had."

She nodded. "For a guy that can't short his own shocks, he's as charismatic as they come."

I laughed. She got a little indignant. "Was that funny?"

"Well, you kind of said, 'short his shocks.' "

She smiled at herself, hung her head for a second, then raised it. "I'm a helluva woman, huh? Can't dance, can't drink, can't . . ."

I didn't want her to go on. I reached out and took her hand and moved it toward her lips to close them. She let me hold it.

Behind us, Midnight Rodeo started playing "Crazy." They liked Patsy. Angela heard it and started to laugh. "There's something to this country music," she said. "It plucks the right strings, doesn't it?"

I stood up, still holding her hand. "Come on," I said. "We can take care of your first problem. I'll teach you to dance."

And I did. She felt so light in my arms, like those filmy white curtains Eudora has that blow in the slightest breeze. There was almost no scent to her. Her hands barely touched mine. She was hesitant and gawky at first, but she started to pick up the basic shuffle, and then we started to move around the floor, her with a pleased little smile on her face.

"You're doing great," I told her. "How come you said you couldn't dance?"

"I didn't think I could," she said.

"Why not?"

"No one ever asked me."

"No one?"

She shrugged. "Almost. For a long time I went to girls' schools."

I found that an insufficient explanation, but I let it go. We shuffled a little more and then attempted a modest little twirl. She pulled it off and grinned like she'd just been hired to dance in the movies.

"How come you decided to teach blind people?" I asked her.

"Why do you think?"

"Religious?" I figured that with a name like Murphy she was probably Catholic and that she'd gone to Catholic girls' schools.

She wrinkled her nose. "No. Not since I was about fifteen."

"Why, then?"

She craned her neck a little bit to look at me. "I believe in second chances," she said. "I believe in third chances. I just like giving people chances."

I was beguiled. "That's what golf does," I said. "It gives you a new chance every day. Every swing."

She smiled. "And is that why you became a caddie, Henry?"

There were a lot of things I could've told her, but the one that came to mind was this:

"Listen to the music," I said.

She did, with a kind of very serious, very deliberate bewilderment on her face.

"Hear the piano?" I asked her.

She listened some more, nodded, and smiled again. The piano accompaniment in "Crazy" is great, understated, melodic, especially if there's a real piano. Midnight Rodeo had an electric keyboard, but the guy playing it was doing a passable job of imitating the arrangement on Patsy's recording.

"Most people don't notice the piano," I said. "They just hear Patsy. But if I could do anything in music, I'd like to be playing piano for Patsy Cline. When she was alive, I mean."

"Never wanted to make your own records?" she asked.

"Nah," I told her. "Wouldn't be me. Wouldn't feel comfortable."

The song ended and the tune changed. "It's a sixteen-stepper," I told Angela. "Want to try it?"

"What's a sixteen-stepper?"

So I demonstrated the sixteen steps, backing and forthing, heeling and toeing, kicking and twirling. I couldn't believe I was willing to do that sort of thing in public. Before that night, I never would have been.

But Angela smiled and shook her head. "I don't think so. I think I'd better call it a night. Too many steps. Too much beer."

I took her back to the motel. She sat properly on the other side of the seat, close to the open window, letting the air flow over her face. She seemed content. I was very conscious of the expanse of vinyl between us.

"I love the way Eadon Mountain looks at night," she said. "Like an angel watching over the town."

"I don't think that's the way an angel looks," I said.

We pulled into the lot at the Econo Lodge and she directed me toward her room. When I stopped the truck, she opened her door before I could get out and open it for her.

"Don't get out, Henry," she said. She walked around the front of the truck and up to the window on my side. She put her hand on the rearview mirror and propped herself a bit.

"Thanks for teaching me to dance," she said. And she leaned in the window, kissed me on the left cheek. Before I could do anything, she was out of the window and gone.

"You're welcome," I told her, and I watched her let herself into her room, which was number 131.

I didn't know what to make of that kiss. It was sweet, but I didn't get the feeling she meant anything more by it. At least, I figured, she wasn't mad at me anymore. That was something.

BOBBY SHOWED UP AT EADON BRANCH BEFORE EIGHT THE NEXT MORNING. Paula, Angela, and Robby came with him, Paula pushing Robby in a stroller, Angela looking a little peaked. I noticed something new. Bobby walked on his own, not touching anyone's elbow. I couldn't tell for sure how he did it, whether it was memory, or facial vision, or maybe listening to the sound of the wheels on Robby's stroller and following that sound. Probably it was some of all three. But he was navigating on his own, without a guide, without a cane. He stepped over the logs at the bottom of the parking lot that keep cars with failed brakes from rolling into the course. He skirted the clubhouse and walked around the trunk of the big elm that shades the first tee. If you hadn't known him, you might've thought he was just someone who walked a little slow and didn't pick up his feet too well.

I walked toward him and said hello, as I'd taken to doing, so he'd know I was there. Bobby homed in on my voice. He stepped right to my side.

"I want to play, Coach. Dreamed about it all night. I'm ready."

It was Saturday morning, and a fine one. The morning dew had burned off early, the sky was a cloudless blue, the leaves were out on the trees, and wildflowers were blooming in the woods. The course was at its best, except that a pair of foxes had decided to dig a home for themselves in the bunker next to the green at No. 8. Saturday mornings were our busiest time, especially prime Saturday mornings in early May, and we had a line of people waiting to tee off.

But it wasn't the line that worried me, really. I ran the course. I could send off whoever I wanted. The feeling I had was more like the one I used to get in school right before an exam, the urge to postpone a reckoning.

"I can't get you off right now, Bobby. I got foursomes out on the course and people lined up waiting. You sure you can't wait till later in the day?"

Bobby frowned. He reached for his wallet, opened it, and held it out to me. "Take nine dollars," he said.

"What do you mean, 'Take nine dollars'?"

"Well, I can't count it for myself," Bobby said.

I knew that. I was offended by him offering me money to play.

"I'm just a regular customer. Put me on line and tell me when you have a slot available and when you can caddie for me, Coach."

"You're really up for it, aren't you?"

Bobby nodded. "Coach, I had a dream. I was playing, playing good. I think I can play even better than I used to."

That set me back a bit. "How you figure that?"

Bobby answered like a missionary invited to explain the Gospel. "Well, when I used to screw up, it was usually because I'd see a bunker or a pond or some OB stakes and I'd think, 'Don't hit it there.' I'd get tense. I didn't let the good swing inside me come out. Now, you tell me, 'Hit this eight iron-a hundred and fifty-five with a little fade,' and I can just click on a picture in my mind—a nice big green, pin in the middle, no trouble anywhere. Like calling up a slide in a slide projector. Then I relax, and then I hit it there. The good swing comes out. I can be better 'cause I *can't* see."

"Uh-huh," I said.

Bobby lowered his voice. "And, Coach," he said, nearly whispering. "I want Robby to see me play."

So I said, "Okay, Bobby, I got a threesome coming up next. I'll see if we can go off with them, if you don't mind company."

"No problem," Bobby said. "Glad to do it."

The threesome was a group of guys who worked the night shift at Wal-Mart—Leo Grabowski, Jimmy Settles, and a guy I hadn't seen before named Peter. They all wore denim Wal-Mart hats. Leo and Jimmy were regulars who struggled to get around Eadon Branch in less than fifty strokes. But they were easy guys to play with, quiet and amiable.

"Sure," Leo said when I asked him if it was all right to add Bobby to their group. "You got him ready to play a round, huh? We been wondering when that would happen."

Of course, I'd known that it was no secret in Allegheny Gap that Bobby was at Eadon Branch, practicing. I hadn't realized people were talking about it.

So that was the foursome—Leo, Jimmy, and Peter humping their own bags and me carrying Bobby's. Angela, Paula, and Robby in his stroller were our gallery.

The other three hit their usual fades and foozles off the tee and then it was Bobby's turn. "Point me down the sprinkler heads, Coach," he said. I did, and we went through the routine of getting the clubface lined up and getting his grip on it. It was habit by then, like shifting gears in the truck. We didn't have to think about it. I stepped back once he was ready, and I could tell he was looking at that slide show between his ears. Then he swung, taking the club back low and slow, a full coil, a slow start to the downswing. The power kicked in.

For the first time playing that hole, he pured it. The ball soared over the horizon line, hung there for a while, drew in a little ,and then blew on down the fairway, way past the bunker. Then he hit a four-iron that covered the flag and wound up six feet away. He sank the putt for an eagle three.

"Feels good, Coach," he said, grinning a little.

Leo Grabowski, finishing up his seven after Bobby's putt went in, said, "So that's the secret! Where can I get me a blindfold?"

I don't think Bobby heard him. Bobby was off somewhere in his own mind, a little like a horse ready to run, but calmer, more serene. The only voices he was hearing were mine and Robby's. Mine I think he heard more like a computer taking in input. Robby's I know he heard because whenever Robby said something, like "mama," Bobby would address him. "That's right, Robby," he'd say. "Your mommy's here." But he was oblivious to everything else.

So for the first time we got to the second tee. "Jerry Rice front, Reggie White pin," I said, just like in the old days. There was a bunker left and the pin was cut to that side of the green, so I told him to draw an easy six-iron into it.

"Point me five yards right of the stick," Bobby said. I did. His ball drew a little, but not enough, and our birdie putt rolled six inches past. Bobby was getting very precise with his putting distances.

When he sank his par putt, I heard some clapping from behind us, and I turned around. There were half a dozen people there, guys who'd been waiting on line to tee off. They'd decided to watch Bobby play instead. I hoped they'd paid their greens fees before they did.

If Bobby heard the clapping, he gave me no sign of it. He just put his hand on the end of the bag, waiting for me to guide him to the next tee.

We played the next six in a trance. He birdied four with a seven-iron over the pond. He birdied eight. He parred the rest, hitting every green. Bobby was four under on the ninth tee. And I started thinking of Clayton Mote's record of five under. I'd been there when he set it, caddying for him.

But I didn't tell Bobby about it. That's not the sort of thing you want to tell a player when he's going good.

I thought for just a second about giving him a three-wood or an iron off the tee, making it impossible for him to reach the green in two. But I didn't. I gave him the driver. The groove he was in, it was the right club for hitting down a fairway half as wide as No. 9's.

But he didn't hit this driver well. He pushed it a little and rolled in through the dogleg and under some pines that line the right side of the hole. We found the ball. That was never a question, given the number of spectators we had helping us look. But it was resting in long, stringy grass under a tree. The lowest branch looked like it might constrict Bobby's swing.

I filled Bobby in on the situation—somewhat. I helped him bend down and touch the grass behind the ball. I had him reach up with a club to touch the overhanging branch and get a feel for where it was. And I gave him the yardage, 220 to the front and 225 to the hole. I didn't mention Eadon Branch, which ran in front of the green. Bobby'd said he didn't want to know about hazards.

"Ball's sitting up okay," Bobby said. "I can get a three-iron on it. Let's go for it."

It was an idiotic play. In any serious competition, I'd've told him to punch a seven-iron out of there a hundred yards or so and go for the green with his third shot. I'd've told him to do that in this case, too, except that in the back of my mind, I didn't want him to tie Clayton Mote's record. If he hit it into Eadon Branch, the record was out of reach.

I know. I was working for Bobby. And my father deserted me when I was thirteen. But for some reason, I didn't want Bobby to have that record. It was one of the last threads connecting me to my father, and I didn't want to cut it. So I gave Bobby the three-iron. If a caddie ever wanted to help a gambler fix a golf tournament against his own player, all he'd usually have to do is wait till the player got excited and set to make a mental blunder, then not talk him out of it.

"Need to hit a nice low power fade," I said. I aimed him at the left edge of the green.

Bobby took a practice half-swing to check to make sure the branch wasn't going to catch the club. It just squeezed under it, brushing some pine needles as it did. "Tight," Bobby said.

"You got room," I told him.

I stepped back and he swung.

He muscled the club through the gunch and somehow managed to put the clubface on the ball and squeeze it. The ball flew out of it low and hot and for a second I thought it would plow directly into the stream. But then something strange happened. It seemed to kick on the afterburners and rise when it should've been starting down. It soared over Eadon Branch and landed on the front of the green, rolled a little right and stopped about twenty feet from the hole. Now the applause behind us was loud and insistent, and Bobby turned toward it, touched a finger to his cap, and smiled. Angela was beaming. So was Paula. Robby was asleep in his stroller, but I didn't tell Bobby that.

It was not till we were on the bridge crossing the stream that Bobby told me he had known about the water. "We played over it yesterday, remember?" he asked. "Glad you didn't remind me of it, though."

The sun was beaming down now, and I had a film of sweat on my forehead. The sound of my footsteps, thunking on the wooden planks of the bridge, brought me back to other bridges and other eagle putts we'd had—the thirteenth at Augusta one year, when the azaleas were blazing around us and the grass looked like God had planted every blade. There's a sense of anticipation at that moment, a sense that you're stepping onto the dance floor and it's party time. You just know in this situation something good is going to happen, that the worst outcome is a birdie and that there could be an eagle that'll set everyone yelling. It's the jauntiest feeling I know.

I was still not sure I wanted Bobby to sink the putt and make eagle. But I did my job. It was a speed putt, along the side of a slope, but I'd had the putt myself before and I gave him the line. It was just a question of whether he hit it right.

Sometimes there are putts, long putts even, that you can tell are going in from the minute they hit the putter blade. You know as much, I think, by the sound of a true stroke and the way the ball hugs the ground and starts rolling right away as by the line it takes. This was one of them. I knew it as soon as Bobby hit it. I had time to think, "Damn, Clayton Mote's record is gone," before I saw it dive right into the center of the hole for the eagle.

Angela and Paula and Leo Grabowski and Jimmy Settles and Peter all swarmed around, pumping our hands and the spectators applauded and I guess when Angela saw the tear in my eye and saw me wipe it away, she thought it was a tear of joy.

No one knew what the course record was except me and Eudora.

6
▼

THE MOST DANGEROUS TIME IN GOLF IS WHEN YOU THINK YOU'VE GOT IT figured out.

For instance, it rained in the early evening right after Bobby Jobe broke Clayton Mote's course record. The bunker next to the third green filled up like a swimming pool. All we needed was a springboard and we could have had the damn Olympic diving trials at Eadon Branch. I'd spent the better part of a week in February digging that bunker out and lining the drain with a new felt cover that was guaranteed to keep sand from clogging the pipe. I thought I had that problem licked. Turned out the foxes dug down and stole the felt and used it for their dens. I phoned the company that sold me the thing and they told me they weren't responsible for damage done by wild animals and suggested I call on some hunters to kill off the foxes. I said, yeah, that's all I need is the local hunters thinking that I wanted them out on the course looking for things to shoot at. So I swallowed the three hundred bucks I'd paid for the guaranteed drain cover and started offering the regulars free lessons on how to hit the mud wedge.

Then some pythium fungus broke out about two months before it should've been a problem and instead of disking the fairways the way I wanted to the following Monday, I had to call the Monsanto man for an emergency shipment of fungicide, which ate up all of Saturday's greens fees. It couldn't be helped. If you let pythium get started, it can take over a golf course. I'd been so damn certain that it wouldn't be warm or humid enough for pythium till August and now my maintenance schedule and budget were both screwed up and the golf course had gone from being damn near perfect to being barely playable in forty-eight hours.

As I say, you have to be your most careful in golf right when you think you've got every reason to be confident.

Of course, Bobby loved being confident. When he was hitting it good, he saw no reason why he couldn't keep hitting it that way forever. So I wasn't too surprised when Bobby decided he just had to rush off and play a real tournament.

He and Angela came out to the fifth fairway to find me. I was trying to fix the spray attachment on the tractor so Hayden could lay down the fungicide. Hayden hadn't cleaned the sprayer out properly after he last applied liquid fertilizer, and the stuff had hardened inside a valve. I was scraping away with a pocket knife, thinking that if I got any of it on my fingers and then inadvertently touched my mouth, future generations of Motes might have fins where their hands ought to be. I wasn't exactly in my sunniest mood, but it wasn't just the clogged valve. I kept thinking about Clayton Mote. I had this idea that wherever he was, if he was alive, he'd want to know that someone had broken his record and that I'd been the caddie.

"What do you think of the Captain Dick Grand Strand Classic?" Bobby asked me.

"Is it a rum punch or a condom, or what?" I replied. Then I flushed, remembering Angela. Sometimes I'm so suave.

"Sorry, Angela," I said.

"It's all right," she replied. "What's a condom, Mr. Mote?"

Bobby snickered. I laughed, too, but it was a struggle.

Angela was another thing I'd been wrong to think I'd figured out. Back when we left Gully's, I figured she was going to be my buddy now that we'd broken the ice. But it was like she didn't want to remember that evening. She was back to working hard with Bobby and being polite and cool toward me.

"It's a tournament, Coach," Bobby said. "They said they'd give me a sponsor's exemption."

"Funny, I didn't hear Venturi say anything about the Captain Strand Grand Dick Classic during the Masters telecast," I said. I guess I was still a little flustered.

Bobby seemed hurt that I was making fun of his tournament. "Uh, that's Captain Dick Grand Strand Classic. It's on the Cooters Tour, down in Myrtle Beach. This week."

"Why can't we go down to Orlando and play something on the Hagen Tour?"

"I thought of that," Bobby said. "For old times' sake. But they haven't got anything going this week."

The Cooters Tour is somewhere between the Masters and a driving range in the world of professional golf. It has real tournaments, with real golfers, but they are about as far from the PGA Tour as Eadon Branch is from Pebble Beach. The sponsors throw in a little money, but most of the purse comes from the players' entry fees. The title sponsor, as they like to say in golf nowadays, is the Cooters restaurant chain, which gives the whole thing a raunchy aura.

"What the hell," I said. "Cooters feels about right. If I can get this applicator fixed and get Hayden to work, let's go."

Bobby pulled a U.S. Air ticket folder from his back pocket. "I had a hunch you'd say that, Coach. So Angela and I already got the tickets."

I couldn't help but think of the money that might cost. "Sure you don't want to drive?" I said.

Bobby shook his head. "Hey. We're professional golfers. We fly."

I could've said something about how the road was good enough for Snead and Hogan and Nelson, but I didn't. If Bobby wanted us to fly, it was his business.

A day later we were in the air, flying from Roanoke to Myrtle Beach via Charlotte. Bobby had insisted on the window seat, which I thought was ironic, then dropped off immediately to sleep. That was one of the ways he had of coping with nerves. He napped. I remember him napping throughout a ninety-minute rain delay one year at New Orleans when he was a stroke off the lead. By the time the storm passed he was groggy with sleep and it took him two holes—a bogey and a double-bogey—to wake up.

Angela was in the middle and I had the aisle. Even when the guy in the seat in front of me reclined and tried to drive my knees back into my hip sockets, it beat wrestling that truck six hundred miles.

I was thinking of being in competition again and how strange it would feel. We were going to be the only ones in the field playing by our own set of rules—the USGA rules for blind golfers. Basically, they're the same as for everyone else, except that the caddie for a blind golfer is allowed to stay behind the ball throughout the shot and he's allowed to place the golfer's club in the sand or a hazard so the player has a chance to size up the lie. But it was going to be different. I started to have more sympathy for Casey Martin.

Like him, we were going to draw some attention. The Cooters people weren't sponsoring their little tour because their hearts went out to struggling pro golfers. They were in it for publicity, and I was sure they figured Bobby would be good for some.

The beverage cart came down the aisle and I got Angela and me a couple of Cokes and the peanuts the airlines serve now in place of meals.

"I've been thinking about something you said," she told me, sipping on her Coke. "About being the piano player for Patsy Cline."

The notion that Angela Murphy had been thinking about anything I said was enough to deprive me of the power to do anything but nod stupidly.

"When did you learn to be a caddie, Mr. Mote?"

"Well," I said, "it's not exactly the same as, say, being a surgeon. You don't go to school for it."

"But who taught you? Did they used to have caddies at Eadon Branch?"

I laughed at the idea of miners employing caddies. "No," I said. "Just me."

She looked puzzled.

"My father taught me," I explained. "Clayton Mote."

She nodded and I felt like she wanted to know more.

"Clayton came home for a year or so just before he took off for good," I explained. "I was about twelve years old. He hadn't been playing good. Lost his card, I guess, though he didn't tell me about it. But he was not playing the Tour."

"And that's when you started caddying for him?"

I nodded. "He'd be playing in little tournaments around Virginia, you know, like the state Open or PGA, trying to win a little money and get his game back. And he said I was old enough to come along and be his caddie and save him a few bucks. "

"Did you like it?"

I thought about that. At first I'd liked it. I'd've liked it if Clayton Mote let me clean goose turds off his spikes. I thought it was great just to be doing something with him, even when he told me he wanted a caddie who kept his mouth shut and the clubs clean. Period.

But it wasn't long before his moods got to me. Sometimes he could be nasty. He'd yell at me for something like forgetting to rake a bunker so the grooves left by the rake pointed toward the hole. Mostly it was his silence. He'd go through weekend tournaments, two full rounds, where he'd never say a word to me. He developed hand signals to show what club he wanted, and they were a little confusing. Three fingers could mean a three-wood, a three-iron, or an eight-iron, depending on the situation. I had to figure it out and hand him the right club without saying anything to him. If I got it wrong, he wouldn't say anything, either. He'd just glower at me like he did the time I lost the shaft he gave me to learn the grip with. And he'd shove the wrong club back in the bag and grab the right one. That terrible, wrathful silence was worse than being yelled at.

I've since learned that practically all good golfers have their dark sides. If they don't get mad at themselves for making a bad swing now and then, it's a sign that they don't care enough to get good. But the best ones, including Bobby Jobe, can also see the beautiful part of the game. When he pured a seven-iron that covered the flag and then spun back toward the hole for a kick-in birdie, he enjoyed every second of it, enjoyed watching the ball fly, enjoyed saying "be the club," enjoyed watching that ball check up and draw back on the green, enjoyed swaggering down the fairway after it. And I enjoyed it, too.

Clayton Mote didn't know how to enjoy his good shots. To him, they were just preludes to what really engaged him, which was getting angry about his misses. And as time went by during that year, he missed more and more shots. I sometimes wanted to scream at him, tell him I knew he mishit some balls on purpose, because I actually thought he did. I thought he wanted to wallow in his anger. Of course, I never said anything to him.

But if the God's honest truth be told, when he disappeared the summer I was thirteen and I figured that it was just him going off somewhere to find some minor tour he could play on for a few months, I was relieved that I wouldn't have to caddie for him for a while.

"It was okay," I said to Angela. "He taught me the job."

That was partly true. He taught me where to stand and how to rake bunkers. But what I didn't know was what to say, how to keep a player like Bobby from taking his putter and using it to slit his guts open instead of put the ball in the hole. Clayton hadn't taught me that. He'd taught me to keep my mouth shut.

For half a second, I was tempted to tell Angela all about me and Clayton Mote, but I didn't. When your father disappears from your life, it's not something you like to talk about, especially if you were once actually relieved that he did go away and then, after he never came back, you started to think maybe it was partly your fault.

Angela looked at me for a moment as if she was expecting me to say something more. I just stuck my finger in my peanut bag and poked around for a little half-peanut that was still down there.

"Well," she said, "now the job's getting bigger. He needs you to think for him out there."

If she'd told me he needed me to walk out on the wing of the airplane and jump off, right then I might've done it.

"I normally have trouble just thinking for myself," I said. "But I'll do my best."

She smiled at me. "I know you will."

The plane banked out over the ocean and the strip of hotels along the shore just before it landed. You could see a dozen golf courses just between the water and the airport. Myrtle Beach has got almost as many golf holes as it's got mobile homes. During the spring and fall it fills up with guys on golf vacations; the airport is the only one I've ever been in with extrawide revolving doors so people don't get their golf bags caught as they leave. But it's too hot for normal people to play golf at Myrtle Beach in the summer and the course owners need some revenue. The Cooters Tour doesn't pay much to rent a course for the week, but it pays something.

This particular tournament was being held at a course called Egret Landing Plantation, which is ten miles inland. We were staying at a Holiday Inn across the highway. Eating being another thing Bobby does when he's nervous, Angela went with him to find some supper. They invited me to come along, but I figured I'd better take a look at the golf course and start making a game plan for the pro-am round the next morning. I walked across the highway.

Egret Landing Plantation had a few of the touches that developers think signal old money and charm in the South, like a brick gateway at the entrance and a clubhouse with white pillars. But it was set on low, swampy land covered with scrubby pines, and the water you could see from the entry drive looked stagnant and pestilential. If there were any egrets about, they were lying low.

"Welcome Cooters Tour Capitan Dick Grand Strand Classic Contestants" said a banner stretched between two pillars over the clubhouse door. They'd misspelled "Captain," but I guess they didn't want to spend the money for a new banner.

There was a tent pitched next to the clubhouse with a bunch of guys eating hot dogs and hamburgers. They were wearing shorts. They were amateurs. Out on the practice green, I could see a few guys in long pants. They were pros. Between them were about a dozen Cooters girls in their tight purple short shorts and little white halter tops that showed off a carefully measured dollop of cleavage. Oddly enough, they all wore pantyhose with this outfit, along with white socks and sneakers. "Tastefully tacky," it said on the backs of their halters. Well, that wasn't so far from right. Their outfits were so tacky they almost circled around and got to tasteful through the back door.

The sun was just sliding under the tops of the pines that framed some of the holes on the deserted golf course. No one noticed me as I stopped by the first tee and picked up a scorecard, then went to the eighteenth green to start seeing the course.

That's something I learned from Hale Irwin when he and Bobby played a Tuesday practice round together before the Honda Classic the first year they played it at Heron Bay. After he finished every hole, Hale would move to the back of the green, turn around, and look back toward the tee, making a few notes on his scorecard. I watched him do this a few times, then when we were waiting to hit on the tee of a three-par, I asked him what he was doing.

Hale said he always figured out his plan of attack by looking at a hole from back to front. First, he'd look at a green and figure out where the pin positions were going to be. Quite often at a Tour event, they'll paint little white dots in the grass that tell you. Or, if it was a course he'd played several times before, he'd check his old pin sheets and see if there was a pattern—some tournaments put the pins in the same spots year after year. If he didn't have anything else to go on, he'd just try to put himself in the position of tournament director and guess where the pins would be. Most greens only have a few difficult pin positions, and it was quite likely that they'd all be used.

Once he'd figured out where the pins were going to be, Hale would decide which pins he'd go for and which ones he'd stay away from. He liked to fade his approach shots, so he almost always attacked pins on the right sides of the greens. He stayed away from pins on the left, especially if there was water or a troublesome bunker on the left side. He'd plan the best angles to putt from; he told me he liked putts that were slightly downhill and broke a little left, so he tried to give himself those.

That done, he'd look down the fairway and decide where he wanted to be when he hit his approach shot into the green. The spot might vary, depending on where the pin was. Most players like to hit a smooth, full iron into a green, and most of them have a favorite yardage. With Bobby, for instance, it was 120 yards. With a wedge in his hands from that distance, Bobby could attack any pin. From ten yards closer in, though, he had a tendency to get tentative. I don't know what Hale's favorite yardage was. He always seemed to me like he was so good that it didn't matter, but I'm sure he had some distances that made him feel very comfortable. You plan your tee shot to try to give you that yardage for your approach. You can't always do it, but that's the goal. If, say, you have a short par four, maybe 360 yards, you might hit a three-wood or a two-iron off the tee just to leave yourself that favorite distance to the pin.

The eighteenth hole at Egret Landing Plantation was a long par four with a big green and a swamp that ran all the way down the right side and curled behind the green. There was a little vertical shelf halfway through the green and I could see three likely pin positions on the right side, the side toward the swamp. The only safe way for Bobby to go for any of them would be to hit a little cut with a short iron, no more than a seven-iron. He doesn't like to fade his longer irons and doesn't do it too well. That meant, in turn, that he'd have to hit his drive around three hundred yards down the left side of the fairway, a side protected by a long bunker. I decided I'd have to see how he was hitting the driver and what the wind was doing before I figured out where to aim him off the tee, whether it was worth it to flirt with that bunker. Otherwise, we'd be taking the conservative route, going for the left and middle parts of the green and figuring on making par. There usually aren't that many birdies on long par fours anyway. We wouldn't be giving much away to the field.

I walked the whole course that way in an hour and forty-five minutes. It was nearly dark by the time I finished. The cicadas and bullfrogs were making a fearsome racket in the pines and swamps. The last bits of light were glowing on the western horizon. The humps and mounds that lined the first fairway looked dark and flowing and halfway like nature, not a bulldozer, had put them there. I'd worked up a good sweat. It was nice to be back on a tournament golf course on the night before an event, even if this one didn't have the roped-off gallery areas and scoreboards that you see on the Tour.

I figured that it was a course on which you'd have to shoot eighteen or twenty under to win. Three of the four par fives were reachable if the wind didn't blow in your face. The greens seemed soft and receptive, and the rough was barely visible. The course was set up for tourists, not professional golfers. Yet it was tough enough that if you got too aggressive, tried to birdie every hole, it was going to cost you. For the first time, really, it struck me that I was going to be the only one of the two of us, me and Bobby, who would know this. As far as he would know, the course could be Augusta National or it could be Eadon Branch. I was going to have a lot more load to carry than the golf bag.

I walked back to the motel, ravenous. The car we'd rented was parked outside our rooms, so I knew Bobby and Angela had come back. I thought Bobby might want to sit down and talk about the course while I ate, hear what I'd learned. So when I got into my room, I dialed his number. The phone rang and rang, and it took me a few moments to understand that he wasn't going to answer it.

I figured he must be in Angela's room, broke off and hit the first three numbers of Angela's extension, which was 7224. I stopped before I hit 4, though. I didn't want to know that Bobby was in Angela's room. I sure as hell didn't want to have it ring and ring and then have an irritated, slightly breathless voice answer.

I left the room and walked out into the warm, fetid night, walked along the side of the highway, past a hot-tub dealer and a boat store, past a store that sold live hermit crabs as beach souvenirs. I felt like a damn hermit crab. I saw a fried chicken place and walked in.

It was not a good place to eat after dark. The fluorescent light made the chairs and tables look very cold, very plastic, and it made the racks of chicken pieces behind the counter look like so much dead flesh, the people serving it barely more alive.

But I ordered a three-piece meal, original recipe, with mashed potatoes and cole slaw and a Pepsi, wolfed it down with one of those plastic utensils the Colonel hands out which is half spoon and half fork, and tried not to look at the other single men in the place, eating similar meals. I walked back to the motel and slept.

I dreamed that I was arrested by a cop, for speeding I think, and when I got out of the car he started to poke me with his billy club, poking and poking until it got painful and I kicked out at him.

I woke up and saw Bobby Jobe. He was standing by the bed, poking me with the butt end of a putter, telling me it was time to get up.

"Show time, Coach!" he said. He was wearing cream-colored slacks and a cowboy belt and one of his old Callaway hats and shirts. Except for the Oakleys, he looked just as he had on days when he woke up leading a tournament—excited, pleased with himself. I looked at my watch. We had three hours before our pro-am tee time. Bobby usually liked to arrive at a course no more than an hour and a half ahead. If he was ready to go now, it could only be a reflection of how eager he was. I didn't like that. Bobby played best when he was nonchalant. But you can't order someone to get nonchalant.

"Complimentary continental breakfast downstairs," he said. "Angela's waiting for us."

He was alone. I could figure out how he'd found my room. There were metal numbers on the doors that you could feel with your fingers. But I expected he'd now wait around while I showered and dressed so I could help him downstairs.

He didn't. Once he was sure I was out of bed, he turned and walked out. He must've had that facial vision thing going for him, because he neatly got around the little table by the door. And I could see that, while he wasn't ever going to use a blind man's cane, he wasn't averse to employing a putter for some of the same purposes. He held it out in front of him a little bit as he went through the door, brushing it against the frame. And I could hear it scraping lightly against the wall outside as he turned and walked down the corridor.

I didn't know whether to feel proud of him for having the nerve to navigate by himself in a strange environment or horrified that I was about to go out and caddie in a professional golf tournament for a man who needed to drag a putter against the wall to figure out where he was going.

THE COOTERS TOUR PEOPLE HAD A TABLE SET UP IN A CORRIDOR BETWEEN the pro shop and the grill where players were supposed to register. The air-conditioning must've broken down, because it was hotter in the building than it was outside, and it was already a warm day. Sitting behind the table was a heavyset guy who jumped up with a big smile and extended a hand.

I remembered what Angela had said about having to do more than just carry the bag. So I introduced myself to the guy first and then let Bobby shake his hand. His name was Clifton Jackson and he was the executive director of the Cooters Tour.

Jackson pumped Bobby's hand and smiled and nodded like one of those punching bag toys with the weighted bottoms.

"I didn't think you all were really coming," he said. His accent was soft, like he came from Georgia or Mississippi. "I figured it might be a joke."

"No joke," Bobby said. "I'm here to play, pal."

Jackson looked like he'd just found a hundred dollars in a coat pocket. "Great," he said. "You all ready to play in the pro-am?"

"Countin' on it." Bobby smiled. "Need a practice round to learn the course, Cliff. Pro-am'll be fine for that, won't it?"

"Sure! We'll fix you up with some partners," Cliff said. "Sure 'nuff will."

I gave him the check for Bobby's entry fee and after Bobby changed shoes, we went to the range to hit some balls.

At a normal Tour event, they have bleachers set up behind the practice tee so that spectators can watch their favorites hit balls. Since the

Cooters Tour had few if any spectators, it had no bleachers. But after Bobby'd hit a few, I started to notice a crowd forming. First the players on the tee stopped their own practice and quietly watched. Then Clifton Jackson came over, and then a bunch of the amateurs who'd been warming up on the other end of the range. Then a few Cooters girls. Bobby started to hear a buzz of whispering voices every time he hit.

"How many watching us, Coach?" he asked.

I gave a quick glance around. "Maybe fifty," I said.

"Well, let's give 'em a show."

And he did. Bobby rose to the occasion. He hit about five crisp seven-irons right at the 175-yard marker, fading the fourth and drawing the fifth in. All I had to do was set him up and tell him what I wanted. Pretty soon we were working on something he used to take a little pride in on the practice tee, a precisely etched little patch of dirt that you make by setting each new practice ball just behind the divot from the one that preceded it. Amateurs leave a scattered collection of gouges in the ground when they practice, but not pros. We worked through the bag and the last few drivers he hit bounced off the fence at the end of the range. Bobby could hear it. Behind us, someone applauded. The applause spread.

I had a little sweat soaking through my shirt by this time, but I was feeling good. Bobby, I could tell from the way he was swaggering, was feeling better than good. We walked over to the putting green and started getting a feel for the speed. When Bobby curled a twenty-footer into the hole on his second try, a kind of collective gasp came out of the crowd, and I could see them starting to push in around the edges, straining to get a better look. Bobby could sense it, too. "Air's getting a little still around here, Coach," he said, pleased with himself.

Just as an experiment, I closed my eyes for a moment and tried to feel things the way Bobby was feeling them. He was right. The air did seem a little close. I could hear every whisper from the people around us.

Then there was a loud voice calling Bobby and I opened my eyes and saw Clifton Jackson coming over with a group of people trailing behind him. The first of them was a big, beefy man in a hat that looked like the one the Skipper wore on *Gilligan's Island*. He had a bushy gray beard and a blue shirt and khaki shorts that showed off thick, bowed legs. Jackson introduced him to us: Captain Dick Gootch, owner of Captain Dick's

Marina in Murrells Inlet and sponsor of the Captain Dick Classic.

He was one of those thick guys who seems intent on mashing your bones together when he shakes your hand. He introduced the men behind him—Paul Ledbetter, Jamie Forrest, and Paul Birkin, distributors for Bud, Coors, and Miller, respectively, in the Myrtle Beach area. They were our team for the pro-am. And then he introduced Amy.

Amy was a Cooters girl. She had a face that wouldn't normally have looked good to me. It led with her nose and her nose was beaky. But she had freckles and blue eyes and lightly frosted, short hair and a smile that seemed real, in distinction from those of her sisters in the Cooters sorority. And, of course, it was altogether evident that she was in superb physical condition.

"Amy's our drinks girl," Captain Dick explained. "When you sponsor the damn tournament, you get your own drink cart."

"Anything you want, you just ask," Amy said.

"Well, you might want to help Coach read my putts," Bobby said, and Amy giggled.

"Really admire what you're fixin' to do," Captain Dick said to Bobby. "Takes guts."

"Actually," Bobby said, "I'd say it takes more guts for you."

Captain Dick looked puzzled.

"But I think Coach here will keep me aimed away from you," Bobby explained. Captain Dick smiled, but he looked a little queasy.

"You do that, Coach," he said. I guess he thought that was my name.

I told the Captain I would do my best.

"You fish much?" he asked us. "Deep-sea fishin'?"

No, we hadn't.

"Be a good sport for you, since you can't see what's going on under the water anyway," Captain Dick said magnanimously. "Y'all wanna try it while you're down here, you come and be my guests, okay?"

"Sure," Bobby said. "If we have time." His tone was as cold as it gets.

A horn sounded and we took off—Captain Dick and the three beer guys and Amy in carts, Bobby and I on foot. We could have ridden, but we both wanted to do this the way it was done on the Tour. That meant walking.

It was a shotgun start, and we were on the tenth tee. Whatever annoyance Bobby was feeling about Captain Dick, it didn't interfere with his golf game. The tenth was a straightforward par four, 420 yards, and Bobby played it that way—a three-wood down the right side for openers, a seven-iron drawn into the pin, and a putt from twelve feet. Birdie. The couple of dozen people following us started to clap. Angela beamed. Amy jumped up and down. Bobby put his hand up, looking for me, and I gave him five. It felt good to make a birdie that counted.

"Way to start, Bobby," I said.

He didn't say anything. He was engrossed in a way that I had not seen before, not since he was blinded, not ever in the years we were on the Tour. He was even more focused than he was when he broke Clayton's record. I took it as a good sign.

I got that right. By the turn, he was four under. Nearly everyone in the place who wasn't actually playing had joined our gallery, and there was a camera crew from a Myrtle Beach station making videotape for the evening news. Clifton Jackson, I figured, had alerted the media.

That was when I started to get distracted.

Amy came up to me while we waited on the tee and put a tanned little hand on my forearm. With my eyes, I followed the line it started up past her tanned little elbow, tanned little shoulder, and tanned little neck.

"I just want you to know how much I admire what you're doing," she said.

I worked hard to keep my eyes fixed on her face and not on her breasts. "Thanks," I told her. "But Bobby's the one playing."

She just smiled as if we both knew that wasn't the whole story. "Are you sure there's nothing I can get you?" she asked me.

It was damn hot, one of those days in the low country when the air seems to rise right out of the swamps and your shirt quickly soaks through and sticks to your body like wet plaster and the bill of your cap drips like a bucket with a hole in the bottom. Amy's tanned body had a sheen of perspiration that made it look as if she had oiled it for a contest of some kind.

And then I saw Angela watching this little exchange between me and Amy. She didn't look happy. Her mouth was a thin, tight line. And even though it was generally my policy to stick to water on days like this, I told Amy I could use a Gatorade.

Amy had a little bounce in her step as she walked to her beverage cart, her tight little butt twitching in her shorts. She walked around behind it and leaned over to dig the Gatorade out. I watched a bead of sweat trickle down her chest and into the opening between her breasts. She had a small tattoo on the right one. I could just see the top of it.

"Ice, Coach?" she asked.

"That would be nice," I said. My voice was gravelly. She filled a cup with ice, poured the Gatorade in, and sashayed back to me. It went down fast.

Bobby had drifted away while this was going on, but he must've come back, because I heard his voice right over my shoulder. It was low, so just I could hear it. "Let's go, Coach," he said in a high-pitched voice like hers, teasing me a little. "Time to play. Is she cute?"

"Not bad," I told him. I thought about that last round at the PGA, about the time Bobby started paying more attention to that blonde, Lane or Blaine or whatever her name was, than to the tournament. "Let's play some golf," I said, half to Bobby and half to myself.

And we did. We parred the next two holes and Bobby put his tee shot into the heart of the fourth fairway, our thirteenth. As Captain Dick and the beer guys got ready to play off the white tees, someone from the Cooters Tour staff drove up in a cart and whispered in Clifton Jackson's ear. Jackson nodded, got out of his cart, and walked up to me.

"Don't know if you all want to hear this," he said quietly. "But four under is one off the individual lead at this point."

A pro-am tournament keeps two scores, the low individual score by a pro and the low best ball score by the team. No pro pays much attention to the best ball score. It depends too much on the way the amateurs play on the holes where they get a stroke because of their handicaps. But a pro likes to post a good individual score in a pro-am. It means he's got a little momentum and confidence going into the real tournament.

I looked over my shoulder. Bobby was talking to Angela and didn't seem to have overheard. I shook my head at Jackson. "We don't want to know," I said.

The way I saw it, if Bobby was actually going to play competitive golf again, he was going to have to take advantage of every small benefit that blindness afforded him. And one of those was going to be ignorance. He'd always been the kind of player who paid too much attention to scoreboards.

He always knew what the lead was, or what the cut was going to be. And two times out of three, that knowledge didn't seem to help him. It just distracted him, tempted him to shoot at sucker pins or try to hit over bunkers he should've laid up in front of, just like he did on No. 16 at the PGA. My theory was that he'd play better if he wasn't thinking of anything but the shot at hand. The way I figured it, his blindness could help him do that.

So I didn't tell him about the score, and it seemed to pay off. He hit a six-iron to fourteen feet on the fourth, leaving himself a putt up a gentle slope. I looked and looked at it, thinking there had to be a break of some kind, but I couldn't see one. So I lined him up to hit it straight at the hole. Bobby's stroke was like a metronome and the ball rolled exactly the way I'd foreseen. From the time it got six inches off the blade, I knew where it was going. That's one of the prettiest of the small sights in golf, watching a putt that you know has been hit exactly right as it rolls toward the cup for a birdie. It's almost like when you know you're going to kiss a girl for the first time and you know it's going to be spectacular and you move closer to her and take her in your arms and then your lips touch. The buildup, the anticipation—they're almost as good as the kiss itself.

We were tied for the lead.

Bobby hadn't had been able to see his putt go in the hole, of course, but he had sound to go by, the murmur of the gallery that started low right after the ball hit the club, then a few voices yelling "Get in the hole!" and then the little explosion of applause when the ball disappeared. It wasn't as loud as the big roar you hear for a birdie on a Sunday afternoon on the Tour. There weren't that many people. But it was still plenty loud. Bobby clenched his left hand when he heard and pumped it à la Tiger, and I could see that he was getting excited. He might not have known what the lead was, but he knew he was five under par.

I was getting into it, too. I kept trying to think that this wasn't really a tournament, just a pro-am, a glorified practice round. And I reminded myself that this wasn't a Tour course and that five under wasn't anything Bobby hadn't done before at Eadon Branch. But I couldn't help but start thinking that we actually might get back to the Tour. I could see us out there, could see the media crowding 'round, could hear the big galleries. I could taste the big money. It was all there in front of us. My chest got a little tight and my arms started to tingle.

I wasn't the only one. Amy, the Cooters girl, was jumping up and down and clapping in the gallery. Without being asked, she brought me another Gatorade on the next tee.

"You guys are making it exciting out here," she said.

I grinned back at her. "Yeah," I told her. "I'm gettin' a little pumped up myself."

She put that hand on my forearm and squeezed. "Keep it up, Coach," she said.

I just winked at her. She seemed to blush. Then she turned and walked back to her cart. I thought I saw a little extra twitch aimed in my direction.

I turned around and Bobby was facing in our direction, a little half grin on his face.

"What's she look like?" he asked in a low voice only I could hear.

"Normal," I said. "Two arms, two legs." I didn't like the look on his face or the interest he was showing. I wished we could hit the damn ball, but the group up ahead of us was taking its sweet time.

"Good lungs?"

"She's breathing," I said.

"Not airbags?"

"Shit, Bobby, how the hell should I know?" I hissed. "You think I've been squeezin' 'em?"

"It's important," he said. "You know I'm allergic to silicone."

"It's a good thing you're not allergic to horseshit, because it's coming out your ears," I said.

"Amy," he called out. "You think you could find me a Coke, please?"

She jumped out of the cart and came bouncing over with a cold can. "Cup of ice?" she asked.

"No thanks," Bobby said. He took a swig and handed the can back to her. "You just hang on to this for me while I'm playing, all right?"

"Sure," she said. "Glad to."

"You're sweet," Bobby said.

She smiled, lapping it up.

"You know the worst thing about being blind?"

Her eyes widened. She opened her mouth but no words came out. She hadn't ever been asked that question, I guess.

Bobby didn't wait. "It's knowing a woman is beautiful and not being able to see her," he said.

I almost gagged. But Amy bought it. Her eyes got shiny, and she reached up, put her hands on his shoulders, kissed him on the cheek. They hugged for a second and Bobby, facing in my direction, leered over her shoulder.

Bobby routined the next three holes. Amy kept bringing him his Coke and he kept taking short little sips on it, handing it back to her, asking her to carry it. She was focused on him now, not me. On the seventh tee, our sixteenth, she took a towel, reached up—she was a short girl—and mopped the sweat off his face. I could see her breasts brush against his ribcage. I tried to focus on the fairway ahead, planning our shot.

Then she did something I couldn't ignore. She twitched back to her beverage cart and sat down, one nylon-covered brown leg propped up against the dashboard. She had a soda in a can there, a Diet Pepsi with a straw in it. She stuck a fingertip on top of the straw and covered the opening. It was her index finger and she had long nails polished soft pink. She pulled the straw out. It was half full of pop, which hung in there because of air pressure or something. Then she stuck the bottom end of the straw in her mouth and sucked the Pepsi out of it. She did it two or three times.

It wasn't as if she was doing it for Bobby's benefit, 'cause he couldn't see her. And she sure as hell wasn't doing it to turn on me or Captain Dick or the beer guys. I doubt she even knew she was doing it. She was just in Bobbyland. I'd seen women there before. I looked back at Bobby. He was turned in her direction, and I could swear he was sniffing the air.

Captain Dick called over to us. "C'mon, Bobby," he said. "Let's bring this lead home!"

I winced. Captain Dick must've heard the score from Clifton Jackson and either didn't know or didn't care that I wasn't telling Bobby about it.

Well, I thought, it wasn't the end of the world.

"We're ahead, huh?" Bobby said, casually. "By how much?"

"I don't know," I told him. "Maybe a shot."

I looked down the fairway again and realized that the group ahead of us had already made it well out of range. They were almost on the green. It was past our turn to hit. The seventh was a dogleg right, fairly short, which called for a two-iron hit over the bunker at the corner. I pulled the club and told him the shot I wanted. We went into our shot-making routine. We had it down by this time. It took us no longer than a reasonably fussy sighted player to get lined up, get aimed, and get set. Bobby swung.

It was like so many other swings he'd made when he had pussy on his mind, or protecting a lead. He overdid it, reaching for that extra distance, wanting to hit a shot that would make Amy a little hotter. His timing went off and instead of flying the ball over the bunker on the right side of the fairway, he hooked it into the rough on the left. Instead of a seven-iron or so, we were going to be looking at a tough shot, a long iron from the rough.

"Not quite there," I told him after describing the ball's flight and the spot where it landed. I decided not to get mad at him. Not on pro-am day. I'd save mad for when it counted. "No trouble," I said, as soothing as I could.

We waited for Captain Dick and the beer guys to hit and then, as always, I shouldered the bag and poked the butt end out behind me, waiting for Bobby to put a hand on it so I could guide him down the fairway. This time, though, instead of keeping light contact with the end of the bag, he ran his hand up toward the end where the clubheads were jangling and walked considerably closer to me than he normally did. For a while he didn't say anything, and I could hear the sound of our footsteps on the short Bermuda of the fairway and the rhythmic sound of the irons jostling lightly against one another every time my butt shifted against the bottom of the bag. It's the second-best sound in golf, the best, in my opinion, being the sound a ball makes when it leaves the sweet spot of a driver. The sound lulled me for a minute.

"Definitely not airbags," Bobby said in a low voice only I could hear.

"Oh, Jesus," I replied. "Don't start this shit again."

"I do believe my sense of touch has gotten sharper," he went on, as if I hadn't said anything. "I could tell as soon as she brushed against me."

"Bobby, you're in the damn rough and we have to hit a good shot to make the green," I told him sharply.

"Course I'll know better when I get my hands on 'em," he said.

I stopped suddenly and shoved the bag back. As I'd intended, it hit him in the groin, just hard enough to get his attention.

"Shit," he yelped. "Why'd you do that?"

"I just remembered something and it brought me up short," I said mildly. "We're in a golf tournament."

"Don't get irritated, Greyhound," Bobby said. "It's not your most attractive quality."

I would've argued the point but I noticed Angela on the edge of the gallery. She was looking a little irritated herself. At me.

"Shut up and play golf," I said. "Being a lech isn't your most attractive quality."

He did shut up then. But he had a bad lie in the rough. The ball was down pretty deep. We tried to hit a five-iron out of there, but the grass turned the club over and he yanked it into the bunker on the left side of the green. Bogey.

I was furious as we walked to the eighth tee, our seventeenth. Partly it was the heat. It's hard to be patient when you've sweated out enough water to irrigate half the greens at Eadon Branch. Bobby didn't help me any. First he went through the little Coke ritual with Amy. Then he told me he didn't want to hit three-wood off the tee, he wanted to hit driver. That was going to bring fairway bunkers into play that he couldn't reach with his three-wood. It was the kind of risky play he liked when he was in the lead. But I was too steamed, too hot, and too tired to explain it to him in the calm, encouraging way a good coach would've done. I knew he wanted to hit driver because he figured Amy'd be impressed with the long ball, so I handed it to him, hoping he'd learn a lesson finally. I aimed him just to the left of it, and watched him cut it slightly, right into the sand.

We bogeyed that hole. We'd gone from five under to three under, from a stroke in the lead to a stroke behind.

"Damn, I hate cutting the ball off the tee," Bobby said as we walked to our final hole. "I think I came over the top a little bit."

"You're over the top all right," I snapped at him.

I caught Angela's eye. She was looking at us with a frown on her face. Even she'd figured out driver was a dumb club to hit on that last tee. I shook my head, hoping she'd also figure out that the driver hadn't been my idea. Then I thought she'd probably think I'd screwed up anyway, because it was my job to make sure Bobby was hitting the right club.

Walking down to the white tees, Bobby suddenly got friendly with Captain Dick.

"How we doing in the best ball?" he asked him.

"We're fourteen under, Bobby," Captain Dick said. "Might win something."

"Great," Bobby said as if he wasn't in the process of blowing a lead, even if it was just a lead in a pro-am on the Cooters Tour. "I think that calls for a celebration. Any of you guys know where we could get some beers after the round?"

The beer guys lit up with that question. They allowed as how it would be impossible for Bobby to pay for a beer in their company, anywhere in Myrtle Beach.

"Best lookin' women are at the Toy Chest on the bypass," one of them said.

Bobby leered a little. "One of the few good things about being blind is I don't care if they're ugly," he said. "Long as they're friendly."

The beer guys laughed. They and Bobby set a time—six o'clock at The Toy Chest. They looked thrilled that an actual big-name professional athlete was going to let them take him to a tittie bar.

"I want everybody to come," Bobby said. "You, Coach. Amy, you free?"

Why was I not surprised when he asked her?

"I'll need to make a couple of calls," she said. She almost blushed. "But I can be."

"Good." Bobby grinned. "I'm still partial to pretty, Amy."

She definitely blushed.

Bobby bogeyed that hole, too, and knocked himself back to three under, which was where he finished. What surprised me was how disappointed I was. Looking back on it, I should've been ecstatic. Here was a blind man, playing his first competitive round in more than a year. That was good enough. To post a 69 was damn near miraculous. But walking off the green, I was pissed off.

"I feel like I left sixty-six or sixty-seven out there," Bobby said to the two reporters who pounced on us, one from the local paper and the other from the TV station. "My swing's still a little rusty."

Cliff Jackson started pounding us on the back like we'd just won the Masters or something. "Great show, Bobby," he said.

Bobby just grunted. So I thanked him and asked about our tee time tomorrow.

"We're going to have you going out late—around twelve-thirty," Cliff said. "Reason is, I got to notify the media that you're here and playing so well. It's gonna be a big story. We gotta give 'em time to get here. Can you do a press conference around eleven?"

"Can't," I said. "Gotta be warming up. We'll do it after the round."

Cliff's round face sagged into a worried frown. "That might be too late for the evening news," he said.

"Sorry," I told him. One thing I'd learned watching Tiger Woods was that if the media really wanted you, they'd wait.

Amy picked that moment to bounce up and congratulate Bobby with a big hug and a kiss on the cheek. Then she kissed me on the cheek, only without the hug. She said she'd change clothes and meet us at The Toy Chest. She bounced away. The girl did not have a low gear. She made you wonder whether you were eating the right kind of breakfast cereal.

Angela, on the other hand, did not look happy. "The Toy Chest?" she said as soon as we were in the car and heading back to the Holiday Inn. She put the emphasis on the second word in the name. Her voice was hovering somewhere between angry and disgusted. "The night before the tournament?"

"You'll like it, Angela," Bobby said.

"The hell I will," Angela replied. "I'm not going."

"You gotta come," Bobby said. He was starting to get that jolly lech tone in his voice I remembered so well. "Coach might wander off with a dancer, then who'd take me home?"

"Let Miss Cooters do it," Angela groused.

"I don't want to go, either," I said.

I didn't. It's not that I had anything against topless joints, having been in a few. I just didn't feel like watching Bobby seduce someone or get drunk or make a fool of himself or all three at once, which seemed likely. I didn't feel like getting drunk, either, and I figured that was also pretty likely. Carrying a forty-pound golf bag in this heat was going to be tough enough without a hangover.

"What'sa matter, Coach?" Bobby grinned. "Amy's tits too small for your taste?"

"Will you two shut up?" Angela griped from the back seat.

"Why Angela?" Bobby said, getting down to his most obnoxious. "You don't think it's fair to call them small?"

"Not when your brains are around for comparison," Angela grumped.

"Whoo-ee," Bobby said. "What's got into you?"

"Nothing," Angela said. In the rearview mirror I could see her staring intently out the window. She had her arms folded in front of her.

"Something's ticked you off," Bobby persisted.

"Nothing, damn it," Angela said.

Of course, Bobby knew damn well that what ticked Angela off was the way he flirted with Amy. I started to wonder then just what kind of relationship Bobby and Angela had. Even when he was breaking up with Paula, Bobby'd never gone and picked someone up right in front of her.

I kept my mouth shut. Bobby didn't.

"We need you in a good mood, Angela. We need you happy."

Angela just stared out the window for a while. Then she spoke. "Henry, you have to go," she said. "Keep him out of trouble."

So I went.

THE TOY CHEST HAD PINK NEON TUBING RUNNING ALL AROUND THE BUILD-ing and a silhouette of a showgirl, also in pink neon, over the front door, which I guess was to make sure no one wandered in looking to buy Pokemon cards or something. There was a GoKart track, the Myrtle Beach Grand Prix, across the highway. As soon as Bobby got out of the car, the sound of the engines, high and flighty like hornets swarming, attracted his attention. He stood and listened to it. He sniffed the air.

"We used to have one of those in Dalton," he said. "Coach, you know I won my first trophy for racing GoKarts, not for golf?"

"No," I said. "But I'm sure NASCAR lost a great driver when you decided to play golf."

We went inside. It took a minute for my eyes to open up and adjust to the dimness. Then I could see that Captain Dick, Amy, and the beer guys were already there, at a table up near the stage. A redhead was dancing to something by Aerosmith. Actually, she was past dancing. She was hanging on with her hands and feet both to the brass pole that ran from the stage to the ceiling, swiveling around on it till her butt was about six inches from Captain Dick's nose.

A guy in a white suit—the likes of which I hadn't seen since Colonel

Sanders died—greeted us just inside the door, next to a velvet rope. "You Bobby Jobe?" he asked me.

"He is," I said, jerking a thumb in his direction.

Bobby was somehow trying to take it all in, standing there, bobbing his head up and down, inhaling.

"Welcome to the Toy Chest," the guy in the white suit said. "Mr. Gootch has taken care of your membership and cover charges. Have a great time." He parted the rope for us. I gave Bobby my elbow and steered him over to the table.

They cleared space between Amy and Captain Dick, and we sat down. Five minutes later, Bobby was working on his second Scotch and Jamie, the Coors guy, was on his third lap dance.

Bobby didn't indulge in that. I could see that Bobby was already going to work on Amy, telling her how impressed he'd been with her work on the golf course. "You had real panache," Bobby told her.

Amy beamed. It's amazing what women will buy from the right salesman.

"All these years we've been working together and I didn't know you spoke French," I said to Bobby. He pretended not to hear.

One of the dancers came up to Bobby. She was a blonde, I guess; the light in the place was red fluorescent and it made her hair and skin and even the bangly little bikini she wore look faintly glowing pink. She was one of those women who look so hard you think there's steel in their rouge, and her eyes were not there. But I'll say this for her. She worked out. She had abs you could've bounced quarters off of. She snaked an arm around Bobby, winked at Amy, and stuck a tongue in his ear.

"Like a dance, Pro?" she asked him.

Bobby smiled at her, reached out and patted her on the hip, then pulled out his wallet and told Amy to take a hundred-dollar bill out for him. She did. He handed the money to the dancer.

"I'm busy," he said. "But my coach here needs to get happy." He gestured to me.

It pissed me off. For one thing, he didn't have hundred-dollar bills enough to be throwing them around like that. And it was bad enough he'd never noticed the Cooters girl till she started to flirt with me, then he'd moved in on her. Now he was using me to make himself look good, to help him score with her. And on top of all that there was Angela, but I couldn't have told you where she fit into my irritaton.

The dancer's empty eyes never reacted to the size of the bill. She just reached out, snagged it, and stuffed it under her garter. It reminded me of the way a frog sits still and blank-faced till it sees a bug and then—zap— the tongue goes out and nails it.

"Can't do it, Bobby," I said in a voice low enough so that only he could hear it. "I'm in training. I'm involved in a golf tournament."

I shook my head at the girl and she shrugged and moved away, managing rather easily to hide her disappointment over not being invited to wave her tits in my face and show me those abs close up.

Bobby didn't respond to what I said. He turned away like I wasn't there. And as far as he was concerned, I wasn't. He had only one thing on his mind, and that was Amy, or rather, screwing Amy. If he'd worked at his golf game with half the concentration he devoted to Amy, he'd've retired the trophy at the Masters. He was that into it.

A black dancer came out on the little stage in front of our tables and the deejay, of course, played "Brown Sugar." He had as much imagination as my old high school football coach, who never called a pass till it was third and forever. The girl gave it an equally imaginative performance, right down to the obligatory crotch flash whenever the Stones went "whooh!"

I couldn't hear all of what was passing between Bobby and Amy. For a while, he was apparently agog to hear about the time she finished second runner-up in the Miss Dillon County pageant. Then he was telling her how much more sensitive he'd gotten since his blindness, how he could hear and smell things much better, like the perfume she was wearing. About that time, "Brown Sugar" ended and there was a lull in the music, which made all the voices in the room seem suddenly louder.

"Isn't anything I can't compensate for," Bobby was saying. "I bet I could even drive one of those GoKarts across the road."

"Now how could you do that?" she asked, like she knew it was true but just couldn't figure out how.

"Well, I'd have to learn the track somehow," Bobby said. "Memorize the curves. Wouldn't be hard."

"I'd pay to see that!" Captain Dick butted in. He'd been listening, too.

"Me, too," Paul the beer man said. "Matter of fact, I got five hundred dollars says you can't do it."

I thought they were joking. But when I looked in their faces, I could see they weren't. And I could guess why. I wasn't the only one irritated by being a spectator while Bobby got Amy's pants off. It must've seemed to Captain Dick and Paul that he was peeing in their territory. They were drunk enough to do something about it, to offer a bet that Bobby would have to back away from, to show him up.

"You're on," Bobby said.

"Wait a minute," I objected. "This is the stupidest thing I ever heard of. You're not going to drive some damn GoKart. We're here to play golf."

"Greyhound," he said, "you ever see me lose a bar bet? I know how to do this."

"This isn't juggling shot glasses," I started in, but Bobby just patted me on the back and stood up.

"Let's go," he said to me. "I can't walk out of here myself."

I shook my head for a second before I remembered he couldn't see that. "No way," I said. "I like it here."

He didn't hesitate. He turned to Amy. "Sweetheart," he said, "let's you and me take a stroll."

She looked around at the table for some idea of what to do. The beer guys and Captain Dick were getting up and grinning. So she got up, too. Bobby didn't put his hand on her shoulder. He took her hand in his. They started making their way to the door.

I sat there for a moment, wondering what I should do. I thought about calling Angela, seeing if she could talk some sense into him. But by the time she could get to the Toy Chest, it would be too late. I thought about sitting there and waiting till he came to his senses. I decided against that, on the grounds that he probably wouldn't.

So I got up and went after him. When I got outside to the parking lot, it had gotten completely dark. The air was heavy and foul, full of swamp vapors and pine tar smells and diesel fumes. Clouds of insects swarmed around the streetlights on the perimeter of the parking lot. The hornet-swarming sound of the GoKarts across the highway rose above the deeper rumbles from the cars and trucks on the bypass. You couldn't have told it was a beach town and there was an ocean nearby. Not by smell, anyway.

I could see that Bobby's little group was already across the highway. They'd picked up a few spectators as they exited the Toy Chest, so there were a half-dozen of them. I had to wait a minute more before the traffic cleared on the highway enough for me to jog across.

By that time, Captain Dick had already pulled out his wallet and he was negotiating with the owner for a half hour of track time, alone. Bobby had somewhere picked up a golf club, probably from the trunk of Captain Dick's car. It was an iron, maybe a three-iron. He was still holding Amy's hand. She was holding his Scotch in her other hand. A big wad of cash went from Captain Dick to the track manager.

I started to run, then I stopped, hung back and just watched. What would I have done if I'd caught up to them? Talked some sense into his head? I'd've had better luck persuading a turnip it was an apple. Coldcocked him? Might've hurt him.

Besides, if the truth be told, I wanted to see how he'd try to do it and whether he could.

It took about fives minutes for the manager to call all the karts off the track and announce a special exhibition. The kid drivers came off grumpy and sullen.

Bobby stood seemingly idle during all this, holding onto Amy with a long, snaky arm around her bare shoulder and rubbing the butt end of the three-iron along a wall. Finally, the track grew quiet enough that you could hear the mosquitoes being incinerated by the electric traps mounted over the hot dog stand. All the karts were off. Then an engine started up, whining like a chain saw, and a mechanic drove it to the middle of the track, where Bobby and Captain Dick were standing.

I decided I had to make one final effort to talk him out of it. I got there just as the two of them were going over the terms.

"One full lap," Captain Dick said. "No stopping. Gotta stay on the track."

"No stopping," Bobby agreed.

The mechanic handed Bobby a helmet.

"Bobby," I called to him. He turned in my direction. I walked up to where I could speak to him in a normal tone.

"Angela and you and me haven't worked so hard to toss it all away on a stunt," I said. "Think of all that sweat."

"I am thinking about it, Coach," Bobby said. He grinned. He jammed the helmet on.

He took Amy in his arms and gave her a kiss that lasted about as long as one of his best tee shots took to come down. She ground that little body of hers into him. Captain Dick half smiled, but he looked like he was smiling in anticipation of seeing Bobby run the car into a wall and lose the $500.

"Bobby . . ." I started. He waved me off.

"Don't worry, I'll tell Angela you tried to talk me out of it," he said.

He started for the GoKart.

There was only one option left—coldcocking him. But by this time, I was halfway with Captain Dick. I wanted to see him run the damn thing off the track and knock the cocky grin off his horny face. Besides, if I'd coldcocked him and he played lousy the next day, I'd've got the blame.

Bobby got in the kart and told the mechanic to roll him over to the inside lane. He still had the three-iron with him, and suddenly I understood what he was going to do. He squeezed himself into the kart, with his big heavy legs bent up near his ears. He told the mechanic to set the kart up within a foot or two of the inside curb. He grabbed the steering wheel in his right hand and got the butt of the club down on the curb, holding it in his left hand.

He let the clutch out real gradual, so the kart was barely moving. And he dragged the butt of the club along the curb as he moved, so he could feel the curves as they came.

He drove that way through the first couple of curves and under the pedestrian overpass that got kids into the pit area. It was like watching a turtle cross a road. Sometimes the kart slowed down so much I thought he'd stalled it, but the engine never quit and it was always in motion.

"Yes, Bobby!" Amy shouted. "Whoo!"

"Shit," Paul the beer man said. "Is that legal?"

"Dunno," Captain Dick said. "Whyn't you look up the rules for blind race-car drivers?"

Some of the kids got into it as they realized what was going on. "S-curve ahead, man!" one of them yelled.

Bobby got through the S-curve, through the backstretch. The track was only maybe two hundred yards long, laid out like a rubber band sitting on a table with some kinks in it.

"Whoo! Whoo! Whoo!" Amy was starting to sound like a choo-choo train, 'cept she was hopping up and down. The kids had pressed over the barrier and onto the track and they were whooping it up big as Bobby rounded the final curve and headed for the finish line.

"Twenty yards!" I yelled out. I was rooting for him, too, by this time.

Ten yards from the finish, he started to accelerate. He didn't stop as he crossed the line and heard that he'd done it, just nodded his head, a big grin on his face. He got it up to where the kart was moving a little quicker, maybe five miles an hour, still with the three-iron rubbing against the inside curb.

"Okay, Bobby, you did it! Stop!" I yelled out. But I could see he didn't care. He wasn't satisfied.

He punched it up to ten or fifteen miles an hour. The engine's pitch got higher, faster. The whooping died down and Amy stuck a polished pink fingernail in her mouth and nibbled on it.

He got through that lap, and he started a third, this time around twenty miles an hour. The kids started to whoop again, egging him on. Captain Dick turned to me. "Why doesn't he stop? He's won the damn bet."

"If he had sense enough to stop, he wouldn't've made the bet," I said.

Coming around the third time, he slowed down, and I thought he might've had enough. Instead, he got to the finish line, slowed to a crawl, and waved the three-iron in the air. I could see the track lights gleaming in his Oakleys and off his teeth. His grin was huge, like a kid's, and it was clear he was jazzed.

"Watch this," he yelled.

He threw the three-iron away. It clattered to the asphalt in the pit area. Slowly, Bobby started driving a fourth lap.

"Oh, Jesus," I said.

He must've had a pretty good memory for the turns, because he moved left at about the right time going into the first one. But he went wide, and I could see what was going to happen a second or two before it did. He didn't know that the pedestrian overpass was there. He was probably figuring if he hit the little curb on the outside of the track, he'd have room to stop before he hit anything. Anywhere else on the track, he would have.

"Look out!" I yelled, which may not be the absolute stupidest thing you can yell to a blind man, but is probably in the top ten.

He hit the overpass abutment almost head-on. It was an odd-sounding collision. Usually, when a car hits something, you hear the squeal of tires as the driver tries to stop. Then you hear the crunch. This was just crunch.

The front end of the GoKart bent in half and a little wheel came bouncing back, rolling in half circles on the track. Bobby sat, motionless, behind the wheel. I started running toward him. Everyone else was a step behind me.

As I ran, I could see him move, try to get up. When I got there, he was half out of the seat, hanging on to the steering wheel. He was like a fighter who's grabbed the ring rope, trying to get back on his feet. But he was sagging, about to go down. I grabbed him under the arms and pulled him up.

"Ouch. Shit," he said. He shook his head to clear it, got a little steadier on his feet and pulled away from me, standing straight up.

"You okay?" I asked him.

"Henry?"

"Yeah."

"I'm fine," he said, curtly, like it wasn't worth discussing and he didn't want to hear any more about it.

But then he tried to pull his shoulders back and throw his chest forward. I saw him wince. I could see he'd banged himself pretty good on the steering wheel.

"Too bad you hit your chest and not your head," I said. "If it'd been the head, you wouldn't've hurt anything important."

7

▼

So, HOW'D IT GO LAST NIGHT?" ANGELA ASKED.

We were having the continental breakfast in the lobby of the motel. Or, at least, she was. She was eating a muffin and drinking orange juice. Bobby was drinking coffee. I didn't have any stomach for food, either.

"Umgh," Bobby grunted. He was wearing his full Callaway outfit, all the patches and logos and stickers in the right places. He'd even somehow managed to get a crease pressed into his pants. He looked ready to play tournament golf.

I knew he wasn't. He hadn't said anything to me, but I could see by the way he was carrying himself that his chest hurt him. He was hunched over his coffee like it was too painful to sit up straight. When he moved the cup to his mouth, he did it gingerly.

Angela waited for a second, like she was wondering if she'd get more from Bobby in the way of an answer. Then she turned to me.

"I assume you had a marvelous time, too, Henry," she said. She wasn't usually sarcastic, so I could tell she was still chapped about the fact Bobby'd gone out and I hadn't somehow stopped him. She'd've really been ticked if she'd known what'd happened.

I almost told her. I wanted her to light into Bobby, hurt him, make him feel bad. But I didn't. Last vestige of the caddie code, I guess.

"Smashing," I said, trying to sound like Colin Montgomerie.

Angela sniffed. Bobby didn't look up from his coffee.

"I'll assume," she said, "that when you guys are so talkative it means you're getting focused on your round. That's good."

In fact, I was trying to talk myself into going out for the round. I was close to quitting. Not as close as I had been when Bobby and I had finally got back to the motel the night before. But close.

"Yeah," I said. "Focused."

Bobby, sounding a little guilty and nervous, changed the subject. "I got a call from the Tour just before I came down for breakfast."

"The Tour?"

Bobby nodded. "One of Finchem's flunkies. Said they wanted me to know how pleased they were I was trying to come back. Said they'd have someone watching us today."

Damn, I thought. Just what we needed. A distraction. But the news that the Tour would have an observer settled the question of quitting, at least for the moment. It reminded me that whatever I did wouldn't just be between me and Bobby. Lots of people would be watching, judging. If I ever wanted to work on the Tour again, I couldn't quit on him.

"Why?" Angela asked.

"They didn't say," Bobby replied. "But I think it might have something to do with the medical exemption."

"What medical exemption?" she asked.

"Say if a guy hurts his back or something in April and misses the rest of the season and doesn't make enough money to keep his card. He can petition for a medical exemption," Bobby explained. "Then the Tour can let him play in the same number of tournaments that were left in the season when he got hurt. If he makes enough money to qualify, he gets to keep his card and stay on the Tour."

"They can give him an exemption or they must?" she asked.

"Can," Bobby said.

"Let's not think about that," I said. "We got enough to think about."

Of course, that was like not thinking about presents on Christmas Eve.

WE PARKED NEAR THE BACK OF THE LOT, NEXT TO A DENTED WINNEBAGO that one of the Cooters Tour players used to save money on motels. I pulled the clubs from the trunk and Angela spoke softly to Bobby, helping him get oriented for the walk to the locker room.

We had no more chance of getting there easily than I would have carrying the ball through the Packers' defensive line. A squad of reporters and technicians spotted us and started moving at a sloppy double time toward us. With their grungy clothes and their bristling array of boom mikes and cameras, they looked like a bunch of homeless men making a getaway after looting an electronics store. The questions started flying at us as soon as the microphones were close enough to stick in Bobby's face.

"Bobby, is it true you're trying to get back on the Tour?"

"What's the secret to playing golf blind?"

"Do you hit the shots or does your caddie?"

I told Bobby to grab hold of the bag, started yelling that there'd be a press conference later, and lowered my shoulder. I pushed ahead, just like I was back playing left guard for Allegheny Gap High School and Junior Edmisten had called his favorite play, the quarterback sneak. Bobby and Angela trailed in my wake, but Angela lost her hat when some clod knocked it off with a boom mike and another one stepped on it.

On the Tour, the locker room would've been a sanctuary; the Tour has guards to keep out anyone the players don't invite in. But the Cooters Tour, not being regularly besieged by the media, didn't. So the cameras and mikes just followed us in. They filmed as Bobby changed his shoes, and I could hear a little murmur go up as he knotted the laces.

"He can do it himself," someone whispered.

"Y'all want to come watch us take a leak?" I asked. "He can do that himself, too."

Clift Jackson came in at that moment. I guess he'd never had to deal with a crowd of reporters before, but his instincts were good. "Please, step back, fellas," he said. "Bobby'll be having a press conference later."

A few of the media people stepped back, but the crush remained, and it followed us, like a swarm of angry bees, out to the practice range. Clifton helped me run interference. "Sorry about the mob," he said.

"Doesn't bother me," Bobby said. "I can't see 'em."

"It'll bother you if one of 'em gets a little closer and you put a driver up his nose on your backswing," I said.

"Didn't expect quite this many to show up," Jackson said. "You're a big story."

He lowered his voice. "Um, I shouldn't say this, 'cause I can't have favorites. But I'll be rooting for you out there. I like what you're trying to do."

I looked at him. He looked sincere. Bobby didn't say anything to him, but I thanked him.

Fortunately, there was at least a rope to hold folks back at the practice range, and I was happy to slip under it. Tiger Woods used to say that the place he felt the least nervous and the most comfortable was between the ropes at a tournament, because that was the one place no one could ask him a question, or try to get his autograph, or offer him a business deal he couldn't refuse. I was beginning to appreciate what he meant.

The media crowd only got bigger, though. And it was supplemented by actual spectators, lured by the stories on the evening news and the fact that the Cooter's Tour didn't charge admission. That was because they didn't usually have enough spectators to justify paying someone to take tickets.

There must've been five hundred people stretched out behind the ropes by the time Bobby started doing his warm-up stretching. Every time he moved, there was a rustling like cicadas in the evening, the sound of electric motor drives in the still photographers' cameras. Take a club out of the bag. Whirr, click click. Put it behind your back and loosen your chest. Whirr-whirr, click-click-click. At the rate they were going, Kodak was going to run out of film before we finished our round.

I smelled cigar smoke and took a quick look around. Off to one side, I spotted two familiar faces. One of them was Ken Alyda, the AP golf reporter. He was puffing on one of those Dutch Masters of his. And next to him, wearing sunglasses and a big hat, was Cade Benton, a leathery-faced public relations official from the Tour. They both caught my eye and they both nodded.

Angela had edged her way to the front of the group, right behind us, and she saw what I was doing. "You know them?" she asked me.

She was shading her eyes with her hand, and the sun was starting to beat down. So after I told her who they were, I unzipped the bottom pocket of the bag and fished out an old Callaway visor of Bobby's for her to put on. She was, I couldn't help noticing, trending toward the cover-girl end of her appearance spectrum and away from the Raggedy Ann end. When she ran her fingers through her hair to put it under the visor, I couldn't stop watching. I told myself to get focused on golf.

The whirring of the cameras intensified as Bobby started hitting lob wedges. Normally, I liked him to hit a lot of wedges a lot of different distances when we warmed up, because Bobby's game depended on being able to respond with the right stroke when I told him eighty yards, or sixty yards. He needed to tune up his touch every day.

He hit a few wedges and his swing was fine. Of course, wedges don't take a full swing. He told me to give him the two-iron.

"You don't want to hit more wedges?" I asked. "Loosen up a little more?"

"Nope," he said. "Two-iron."

I gave it to him and lined him up. He took the club back normally, but he didn't quite finish the swing. I was watching the ball, and not him, so I couldn't see if he grimaced or not. But the ball flight told me he was flinching instead of following through, leaving the clubface a little open. Obviously, he was having trouble with the bigger arc of the two-iron.

"Hurt?" I asked quietly.

"No," he snapped.

He took a half-swing and stopped at the top, looking back over his right shoulder to check the position of his hands.

As if he could see them. As if that was the problem. I didn't know whether he really thought he had a hitch in his swing or whether he was just trying to show the spectators that he did, trying to give himself an excuse for the way he was going to play.

"If you're not feeling right, let's W.D. now," I said.

"I feel fine." He smiled. Suddenly, he was trying to charm me. "You know I always play best when my brain's feeling a little loose in my skull."

The smell of cigar smoke got stronger and I turned around. Alyda and Benton had moved right behind us, and Benton took the opportunity to stick his hand out and say, "Hello, Greyhound. Cade Benton from the PGA Tour office. Nice to see you."

I shook hands. That, of course, got Bobby's attention, which was no doubt what Benton had intended. I'd been thinking I wasn't going to point him out to Bobby, hoping that he'd stop thinking about the presence of a Tour representative as he played. But Benton wasn't going to allow that.

Bobby stepped toward us, sticking his hand out in the direction of Benton's voice. Benton found it and shook it.

"Bobby, Tim Finchem asked me to tell you we all admire the hell out of what you're doing and how far you've come and we're rooting for you," Benton said. He was nice about it, but I still wished he'd just kept quiet.

"Well, tell Tim I expect to be back out there soon," Bobby said. "I'll expect more support than I've been getting."

Bobby felt, rightly or wrongly, that the Tour had abandoned him after the accident. It hadn't surprised me. Golf is a tough business, and lots of people fall by the wayside every year. The Tour doesn't waste any energy thinking about them. If Bobby thought an ex-player was forgotten, he should've tried being an ex-caddie.

Benton flinched a little at what Bobby said, and it struck me that Finchem and the people at the Tour must've been seeing Bobby as a potential problem. They'd been burned by the Casey Martin case, and I don't think they wanted to be burned again.

"We hope you are back, Bobby" was all Benton said.

Alyda was quiet through all this. I caught his eye and he nodded again. I had the feeling he was watching me, rather than Bobby.

I looked at my watch. We had only a few minutes left. So I prodded Bobby back to the tee and he managed to hit a few drivers and a few putts before we had to go to the first hole. I hoped his chest was loosening up.

I was sweating piggishly by the time we got to the tee. So was Bobby. He looked like the kind of horse you don't bet on because he's too lathered up in the paddock.

Our playing partner was already there—a big, broad-shouldered kid named DeWayne Elston, out of the University of Texas. He looked like Ernie Els with dark hair, but he didn't have Ernie's laid-back friendliness. He shook hands kind of stiffly. So did his caddie, who also happened to be his wife, Christie. On the Cooters Tour, there weren't a lot of professional caddies. Players couldn't afford them. They carried their own bags, or had old roommates and little brothers do it, or girlfriends.

I looked at the pin sheet. As I'd expected, the first pin was set toward the right edge of the green, behind a big, deep sand bunker. That meant that if you wanted to go for the pin, you'd have to either flirt with that bunker or approach from the left edge of the fairway. Marsh ran down the left side of the hole nearly all the way to the green. We were going to play down the right side, stay away from the bunker and the pin on our approach, and make par, bogey at the worst. No point in risking a bad start.

Elston won the toss for the honor and he wasn't playing safe. He had an upright swing with a big turn and a little hitch in it that he'd probably have to straighten out if he wanted to get consistent enough to make the Tour. But he got all the parts working together on this swing, and he drove the ball about three hundred yards, left center. It was Bobby's turn.

Quietly, I set up the situation for him. "Okay, Bobby. Nice, easy starting hole. Four-eighteen. Flat. Straight. Plain-vanilla. It's cut out of the trees, but there's a lot of room. No wind. It's a pretty hole and a pretty day. We're going to drive the ball down the right side. No trouble to worry about. Just swing nice and easy."

Then Bobby broke out of his routine. Instead of waiting till I put the driver in his hands and got him lined up, he put his hands together and took an imaginary backswing, cocking his head back the way he'd done on the practice tee—like he could see his hands.

"You're gonna make a great swing, Bobby," I told him. "Trust."

He nodded and got back into the routine. I lined him up and set the clubface behind the ball. As I stepped back, I saw his lips move. "Let it happen," he whispered to himself.

But he swung as stiffly and awkwardly as an old man getting out of his car after a long trip. It was his choke swing, paying a visit at the worst possible moment. Could've been nerves. Could've been bruises. I don't know. The ball took off down the left side instead of the right side, and then it started to veer more left. A gust of wind capriciously blew it further. It touched down on what must have been the hardest piece of ground on the golf course because it kicked even farther left, sickeningly left, and disappeared in the direction of the marsh. The crowd moaned a little, the way they do after a bad shot.

Bobby was off balance as he finished, and he knew that it was a bad shot. "Shit!" he cursed. "Left. Left of left."

"Yeah," I said. I guess I didn't muster the required tone of stolid confidence in the face of adversity.

"What happened?" he demanded. "Where'd we wind up?"

"In a hazard," I told him.

"Hazard? You mean a bunker?"

"No, a swamp."

"Swamp?"

I felt sorry then. I hadn't told him there was a swamp because I didn't figure he needed to think about it, even though it was generally my policy to give him a full description of the shots he faced. But I guess it reminded him of how dependent he was, and he reacted like I'd deliberately let him walk into a streetlamp.

"There's a swamp on the left?" he hissed.

"Maybe 'marsh' is a better word," I said. "Sorry. Didn't think it was really in play."

He face got red and twisted. "Didn't think it was in play? Didn't think it was in play? How many years've I been goddam drawing the ball?"

"Sorry," I repeated. I was starting to feel like we were back on the sixteenth hole in the last round of the PGA.

Bobby took a deep breath and visibly tried to compose himself. He couldn't.

"Biggest round of my life and he doesn't tell me about the swamp," he muttered to himself.

I started to say something about how if I'd been about to play the biggest damn round of my poor life, I'd've been in bed last night instead of trying that fool stunt in the GoKart. But I didn't. I made up my mind then and there that whatever Bobby did or said, he wasn't going to get to me. Not on the course, anyway. Cade Benton and Ken Alyda were going to see and report on a model caddie.

"I'm not sure it went in all the way," I said as mildly as I could. "Might be playable."

"Let's go," he said. He listened for the sound of clubs rattling as I shouldered the bag and backed the butt end up toward his hand. He latched on. "From now on," he said, "Don't leave anything out when you tell me what we're looking at."

"You got it," I said.

It was a long walk up the first fairway. Angela walked along with a slightly sick expression. Ken Alyda and Cade Benton looked grim, like they were walking into church for a funeral.

A bad tee shot on the first hole can give you that feeling. It's like you've taken a fresh white shirt and spilled bacon grease on it at breakfast except you can't go to your room and change into another shirt, much as you'd like to. You'd like to yell "do-over" and hit again before the other kids can object. But in real golf, like the sign said at Eadon Branch, there are no mulligans. I guess that was why the sign painter had written "mullicant."

The fairways at Egret Landing turned to light rough and then sloped down and faded gradually into the marshes. The builders had spent money on railroad ties and bulkheads only around the greens, so it was quite possible for a ball, watched from the tee, to disappear into a hazard without reaching the water. It turned out that Bobby's Titleist had done just that. It was sitting in a little three-foot-wide strip of gray-brown mud between the edge of the rough and the dank, murky water. If there'd been more rain in the weeks before the tournament, it would probably have been in the water. But you could see it.

That didn't mean you should play it.

I told Bobby the situation, and this time he demanded all the details. I gave them to him. That wasn't enough. He wanted to feel the situation with his hands and feet. So, gingerly, I walked down the grassy slope with him leaning on my shoulder. We got to the mud strip, and our shoes sank several inches deep. But Bobby wanted to take a stance by the ball and see how it felt. He could barely do it. The water was lapping gently at his heels and pond scum was squishing up around his shoes. He bent over and I helped him brush a finger over the mud behind the ball. It just was not a good place to be trying to hit a golf ball.

"I think we should take a drop," I said. "It's a lateral hazard, just a stroke penalty. You can hit onto the green and the worst that'll happen is a bogey. We go on."

But Bobby was not having it. "How far are we from the green?" he asked.

"About one-sixty," I estimated.

"And the bank we just came down is about three feet high?"

I looked at it, and at the two lines of spectators peering down at us, murmuring like conferring judges.

"About four feet," I said.

"And what's between here and the green?"

"Nothing," I said. "There's a bunker on the right side, but it's not in the way from this angle."

He wiggled his feet in the muck and sank in a couple of more inches. "I think I can get a seven-iron onto the green," he said.

I wasn't going to argue with him. He knew what I thought. Mosquitoes were buzzing in my ear, the marsh stank, and I just wanted to get out of there.

"Make it smooth," I said.

There was no way for me to get behind him except to squat in the marsh, so I did, ankle deep in the water. I could feel my sneakers getting sucked into the ooze and I worried for a moment that when I tried to step out, they'd be sucked right off my feet. I gave him the club and lined him up. I put the clubhead down behind the ball.

"But he's in the hazard!" someone in the gallery said, just after everyone else had hushed.

I looked up. Bobby had heard it. So had everyone else.

Of course, a sighted player couldn't put his club on the ground behind the ball if the ball lay in a hazard, as Bobby's did. The rules for the blind gave Bobby an exemption, but not many people knew that. Neither, I guessed, did DeWayne Elston and his wife, because I could see them looking shocked. She was pointing and he was shaking his head.

"Don't worry about them," I said to Bobby. It wasn't the time to educate people about the blind rules. "Trust it."

I stepped back farther into the marsh to get away from his backswing, only the bottom beneath me dropped off quicker than I thought it would. My left foot found nothing. My right foot slipped in the ooze. I fell back into the water, making a sound like an old refrigerator makes when someone tosses one off the highway bridge into the Gaulor River. The water felt slimy as my head went under, and my mouth must've been open, because I got a bellyful of it.

I came up sputtering and coughing and when I opened my eyes, I saw that people in the gallery were laughing. Bobby was stopped in midback-swing, his head swiveled back toward me, trying to figure out what the hell was happening.

"Sorry," I said. "Slipped."

I sloshed to my feet, dripping and looking, I'm sure, just as stupid as Hardy looked when Laurel innocently bumped him into a pond. My hat was off, no doubt floating somewhere behind me. I didn't bother to look for it.

"Needed to cool off anyway," I said, trying to make light of it. But it didn't work, at least not with Bobby. I saw his jaw jut. Then he shocked me. Rather than wait for me to come back, squat down again, and reset him, he turned his head back in the direction of the ball and swung.

He missed. Missed the ball, that is. He dug that club into the mud like a steamshovel ripping open a coal seam, sending a big, brown splash of water and muck up the slope of the bank. The ball moved a little bit in the general explosion. It ascended like a bad bottle rocket, weakly, about two feet in the air. It hit the bank, seemed like it might die in the grass there, then slowly rolled back and curled to a stop right against Bobby's left foot.

For some reason, I yelled, "Don't!" as in "Don't swing!"

Of course, he'd already done it. We were now lying three in the hazard—one for the original tee shot, two for the misbegotten swing he'd made after I fell into the water, and three for the penalty when he let the ball hit him.

I thrashed toward him to try to get him away from the ball before he stepped on it, and my right sneaker came off. I left it behind.

I grabbed him like you'd grab a child who'd stepped off the curb into traffic, pushing him toward the bank.

"Did the ball hit my foot?" he asked me.

"Yeah," I said. "'Fraid so."

He didn't get mad. He seemed more shocked than anything else—maybe even a little scared. "When I heard you fall in, I got flustered," he said.

"It's all right," I said. "My fault."

I glanced over his shoulder and caught a glimpse of Alyda and Benton standing in the grass above us. They looked like they had just watched us unexpectedly pull long swords from Bobby's bag and disembowel ourselves—like what they had seen was both too ugly to watch and too fascinating to turn away from.

I felt ashamed and I cast my eyes to the ground. When I looked down, I noticed again that I was dripping, muddy, and minus one sneaker. I looked a complete fool, and it occurred to me that everything I had been doing since Angela Murphy showed up at Eadon Branch was utter foolery.

The strange thing was, though, that at the same time, I was thinking that, all right, we've given away a few, but we can get 'em back, we can still shoot 69 or 70, we can still be in this thing. Golf is like that. No matter how it humbles you, it never leaves you quite hopeless.

Almost never, anyway.

It was clear to me that someone had to take charge, and Bobby still seemed shocked. He hadn't said anything.

"I think we better . . ." I began.

"Oh, Jesus," he whispered. "Oh, sweet Jesus."

He sounded like one of those kids in those Freddy Krueger movies when they finally realize that havoc and hell are breaking out in their high school and will not be contained. He sounded shaky.

I tried to make a joke.

"The good news," I said, "is that you don't look as stupid as I do."

Bobby did not laugh.

"I think we better take our drop up on the grass and get the hell out of here," I said.

He nodded, and I pushed him up the slope until someone in the gallery took him by the hand and helped him up the rest of the way. I picked up the bag and looked out to where I'd fallen down, thinking of my lost sneaker. I could see a faintly lighter spot in the muddy water where the bottom of the marsh had been churned into a cloud of muck. It reminded me, for some reason, of the oil slick they always talk about on the TV news when an airliner goes down in the ocean and no one survives. I decided I'd be better off without the sneaker.

So I scrambled up the embankment as best I could, leaving the damn golf ball behind. It was Alyda who reached out and gave me a hand getting up the last few feet. For a reporter, he had a surprisingly strong grip.

Bobby was standing there, listening to the sound of the clubs rattling as I rose. They were a little noisier than usual because of my lost sneaker. It made me limp a little and that made my butt twitch more, so the clubs sounded like they were falling down stairs. Of course, the sound was magnified by the funereal silence that had descended upon our gallery.

Bobby clamped a hand down on my shoulder as if he'd been able to see it. He leaned close to my head so only I could hear what he was saying. "Well, Coach," he said, "worst thing can happen to me is I look like a guy trying to play golf with his eyes closed."

It wasn't quite as ugly as the way he used to react to screw-ups on the course, but it wasn't what I wanted to hear.

"We can afford to spot these guys a few," I said. "Golf tournament starts now."

He grinned and shrugged and held out his hand for a new ball.

I gave it to him and helped him get oriented two club lengths from the red line that marked the edge of the hazard. He dropped it.

We went through the whole routine, and Bobby did a good imitation of someone trying his best to knock an eight-iron onto the green. But I could tell he didn't believe in the shot, didn't have any real expectation he could hit it. Instead of snapping a hook, this time he blocked the ball weakly right of his target line. It headed straight for that big, deep bunker like a sand crab going home. It dove in.

When I told him that had happened, he didn't say anything. He just swallowed, nodded, and put his hand on the butt end of the golf bag. We moved on.

We moved gingerly, because my right foot had only a filthy, wet sock that was dropping down over my ankles and seemed likely to fall off entirely before too long. My wet clothes chafed and weighed me down. The sun was beating down on my head and there was a mosquito checking out real estate around my left ear. I looked toward the sky, half expecting to see vultures circling, but there was nothing. No clouds, no birds. Just the small, noontime disk of the sun, white-hot and burning.

The score got worse from there. Bobby took two to get out of the bunker. And after he did put the ball on the green, DeWayne Elston—prodded, it seemed by Christie—sidled over to me.

"You do know," he said, "that it's against the rules to ground your club in a hazard?"

Bobby heard him. He ignored him.

"Not the blind rules, kid," I said. "But thanks for your concern. We spent four years on the Tour, and we never knew that."

I was a little steamed.

Elston's face got rigid, and he stalked away.

I looked at the putt, looked at it again, and for some reason decided it would break left. It broke right. Add three putts to the score and we were already in double figures.

The scores didn't get much better after that. We bogeyed two and doubled three. Bobby's face was looking numb, like he'd been in the dentist's chair and gotten a shot to kill the pain. He followed our routine on every shot, and I suppose he tried his best. But he just couldn't put the disaster of that opening hole out of his mind. By the end of two holes, I'd put a club in Bobby's hands and he'd hold it tentatively, as if he was thinking, What is this strange tool and how am I supposed to use it?

The only good thing that happened was on the third tee. Angela came up to me carrying a hat, fresh socks, and some new shoes she'd just bought in the pro shop. She smiled bravely.

"Thanks," I said. I meant thanks for the clothes, thanks for being nice to me, thanks for talking to me, thanks for smiling.

"I hope they fit," she said.

They were close. Grandly, I tossed my old sneaker into the little trash basket under the ball washer. I put the hat on.

The thought of Angela doing me a favor made me feel better. So did having clean socks and two shoes.

But the golf didn't make me feel better. Bobby couldn't have been more lost if you'd dropped him on the stage of the Grand Ole Opry, handed him a fiddle, and told him he had to play "Rocky Top." He had no swing. Either it hurt him to swing right or he'd forgotten how. He kept playing, wanly.

"Sorry about that, Coach," he'd say after he hit another bunker or blew a three-footer. And that was all. I started to wish he'd blame me, or break a club, or shake another two-iron at God. Something.

We made the turn in forty-six strokes. Half the gallery, including Ken Alyda, dropped away. But Cade Benton stayed, taking everything in for his report to the PGA. So did Angela. I didn't care about the rest.

By the time he three-putted the tenth, Bobby was starting to throw a pity party for himself. "I never could putt worth a shit," he muttered. "What made me think I could do it blind?"

I didn't say anything.

"How many holes do we have to go?" he asked me.

"Last time I checked, eighteen minus ten was eight," I growled at him.

"Think maybe they'd let us phone in the last few?" he asked.

A few minutes later he started whining. "Wonder if they'll put that on

Sports Center?" he asked when his tee shot on the eleventh found a bunker. "No, I guess they'll stick with getting hit by my own ball on the first."

I was beyond trying to talk him into trying. I just wanted to get the round over with.

The back nine was like walking through a coal mine barefoot. It was a tough slog. I even tried telling Bobby a joke or two to loosen him up. They were horrible jokes. I won't repeat any of them here, but the best of them involved a Great Dane, a pretty aerobics instructor, and a visit to the veterinarian to have his forepaws clipped.

It didn't matter. Bobby kept whining.

We got to the eighteenth tee hot, sweating, heads hanging. Nearly all the spectators had gone. It was as if someone had told them they'd be able to watch a bullfrog fly out at Egret Landing that day. When the bullfrog didn't fly, they walked away, feeling like someone had taken advantage of their naïveté, even if they hadn't had to pay to watch.

I slurped down some water and handed some to Bobby. He drank it, groped down the bag till he found one of the towels hanging off it, then mopped the sweat off his face.

"Where do we stand?" he asked me. I knew exactly what our score was—87 to this point.

"I don't think we're going to be the overnight leaders," I said. "But since there's no scoreboards out here, it's hard to tell."

Bobby grimaced. "We going to break a hundred?"

I wouldn't tell him.

"Just pretend you're a professional golfer, okay?" I said. "Hit the fucking drive where I tell you."

He flinched a little. My tone must've been pretty nasty. By that time, I didn't care. I just wanted to go somewhere and drink a lot of cold beer.

Elston was up first, of course. He'd had the honor all day. He was working on a 68 or 69 that could've been a few strokes lower except he had heavy hands around the green. He banged the ball down the middle, but not his usual three hundred or so. "Didn't catch it," he said to his wife.

I aimed Bobby down the left side, figuring that the bunker down that side was a better alternative than the marsh down the right. At that point, if St. Peter'd told me my condo in heaven had a view of a marsh, I'd have told him I prefer a warmer climate, thank you very much.

He hit it down the left side, and he hit it pretty hard. It was almost a good shot. But he hooked it again, and he wound up in that bunker, maybe 180 from the pin. It was the first time all day we'd been past Elston off the tee.

Elston hit first, and he tried to cut a four-iron into the pin; as I'd expected, they'd put the hole on the right side, close to where the marsh curled around the green. Elston overcooked it. The ball faded too much. It came down smack in the water. For some reason, Christie Elston looked over at us and glared, like we'd been responsible. And maybe she thought we were. When you hit a bad shot, you're tempted to pin the blame anywhere you can. If you've got a playing partner who's blind and not breaking 90, that's a handy target.

Bobby, of course, didn't see this. He was busy tromping around in the back of the bunker, trying to get a feel for it. I had a sudden desire to finish with some style. I think Bobby did, too. "Okay," I said. "Elston's in the water. Our turn."

I looked at the lip of the bunker, maybe eight yards in front of our ball. The lie was pretty good. I figured it would take a five-iron to get to the green if he could pick it relatively clean.

If we'd been protecting a two-shot lead, I'd've probably given him a wedge and made sure he got the ball out of the sand and didn't do worse than five for the hole. But we sure as hell weren't protecting anything, so the five-iron seemed like the play.

"Let's do this one right," Bobby said as I set him up.

"Okay," I said. "Wind's in our face, but no problem. Bunker's got a two-foot lip, but you got room to clear it. We got Jerry Kramer to the front edge, Jerry Rice to the hole, and Dennis Rodman to the back. There's water on the right side of the green—"

"What number was Jerry Kramer?" he interrupted me. "I forget."

"Sorry," I said. "Sixty-four. One-sixty-four to the front, one-eighty to the hole, one-ninety-one back."

I don't know what made me say "Jerry Kramer." He was definitely before Bobby's time. I think it was that I could remember one Christmas I got Clayton Mote, who liked the Packers, a copy of Jerry Kramer's book as a present. Clayton Mote was a big Vince Lombardi fan.

"I wonder if that butthead's gonna have anything to say about grounding the club in a hazard," Bobby said. "I'm sure tired of hearing that."

"We've sure given him a lot of chances to say it, though," I said.

Bobby sighed. "I know," he said. He looked whipped.

"Ready?" I snapped.

He got serious again, flexed his hands on the club, and nodded.

"See the shot," I said. "Trust it."

I stepped back and he swung.

It wasn't the greatest swing he ever made, but he put a lot into it, which may have compensated for the fact that he caught the ball just a hair heavy. He sent a spray of sand out of the bunker and I thought I heard a little flicking sound as the ball clipped a bit of high grass atop the lip. But then I saw the ball take off, covering the flag. I stepped outside the bunker to get a better look.

The ball hit on the front edge of the green and started to roll. It took some break as it slid over the little ridge in the green. It was headed toward the flag, but too fast. I could see that it was going to roll right off the green and into the marsh. Then, with a muted clank, it hit the flagstick, caromed about six inches into the air, and dove into the hole.

"Goddamn," I said.

"What happened?" Bobby asked me. "I know I caught it heavy. I know it brushed the lip. Where is it?"

I guess one of the worst parts of being a blind golfer is not being able to see your occasional miracle.

"You sure did hit it heavy," I said. "And you did catch the lip."

I was going to prolong the suspense a little more for him, but out in the fairway, Angela recovered from her own surprise and started whooping and clapping.

"But it hit the pin, didn't it?" Bobby said. He started to grin.

"And went in," I told him.

He dropped his head and shook it. His grin was a little embarrassed.

"Funny game, isn't it?" he said. "At least I didn't shoot in the nineties."

He'd known all along what the score was.

•   •   •

As we walked down the last fairway to the green, I was thinking hard. You might think that an eagle would make me eager for another chance the next day. You'd be wrong. It just meant that the round was over and I didn't have to think about the next shot. That last shot was just a teaser, a final way of the golf gods smirking and saying, "See, look what talent we put at the disposal of a ten-cent head."

"Sorry I made you go through this, Greyhound," Bobby said after I plucked the ball from the cup and handed it to him. "It'll go better tomorrow."

I didn't snap at him or anything. I just shook my head before I remembered that he couldn't see that.

"No, Bobby," I said. "it won't."

"Hey." He smiled. "I'll know where the marsh is."

"Yeah," I said. "You will."

We waited until Elston putted out and started walking toward the clubhouse. Cade Benton stepped into our path. He looked like an old, wattle-necked judge, assuming a judge would sit in khaki pants and a white polo shirt with a PGA Tour logo on the breast. His voice sounded throaty and harsh.

"Bobby," he said. "That shot on eighteen was the damnedest thing I've ever seen. Thanks for the chance to watch. Sorry it didn't go so well out there before that, though. Looks like you've got a ways back yet." He stuck out his hand and Bobby groped for it, found it, shook it.

"I hope you stick with it," Benton concluded.

"I will," Bobby said. "Stay around for tomorrow."

"Got to be in Ponte Vedra," Benton said. "But good luck."

He was being polite, but he was clearly saying there would be no medical exemption for someone who had to hole out a bunker shot on the eighteenth just to break 90.

Benton was halfway to the parking lot before Bobby said anything. "He should stay for tomorrow. I'll play better tomorrow," he said.

The television guys were on their way, moving out of the clubhouse. Someone from ESPN was in the lead. They'd gotten their action film on the first hole. Now they needed a few quotes to wrap up their stories.

I had about a minute to talk to Bobby. "You're not going to play better tomorrow," I said. "You're gonna withdraw."

"Withdraw?" he asked, like he didn't know what the word meant.

"We're not ready for tournament golf," I said, putting it as tactfully as I could.

He shook his head. "I don't wanna withdraw," he said.

"You don't have a choice," I said. "You can't play without me, and I'm not doing it."

He clapped me on the back. "Hey, you're just pissed off about going in the swamp," he said. He tried to sound cool about it, but his voice quavered. "I understand. We'll get a few beers and cool off . . ."

"No," I said.

And in fact I wasn't mad anymore at that point. I was past that. I just knew that there was no point in continuing. At some point, Bobby wasn't going to be able to do it.

"What're you saying?" he asked, suspiciously.

"I'm saying I quit. I've had it. I'm finished. I'm going back to Allegheny Gap."

His mouth dropped open and stayed that way till I was afraid some mosquitoes might nest in there. Then his face got a little redder.

"You think *this* was my game?" he yelped.

"Yeah," I said. "Looked very much like you playing out there."

"But I holed out that shot . . ." he started. His voice slowed. "I can hit the shots," he finished weakly.

"That's not enough," I said.

He whined a little. "But tomorrow my ribs'll be better. I just need another chance," he said.

"You've run out," I replied.

God help me, but there was a part of me that enjoyed saying that. It was payback for a lot of things.

He scowled. "It's 'cause I'm blind," he accused. There was an undertone of anger and bitterness in the words. "You think—"

I cut him off. "Don't tell me what I think," I said. "It has nothing to do with your being blind. It has to do with you."

He stiffened, but before he could say anything, the reporters were on us. They lined up in a row, pointing their cameras at Bobby. A couple of the Cooters girls, no doubt prompted by Clifton Jackson, moved in behind us so they'd be on camera in the background. We were surrounded.

"How do you feel?" the ESPN guy asked.

Bobby grimaced. "Hot as hell. Thirsty. Humiliated," he answered.

"Do you still think it's possible for a blind man to play tournament golf?" the guy asked.

Bobby paused for a long time before he answered. "Yes," he said. "I do. But I'm not sure if I'm the blind guy to do it. I mean, I guess I'm not. I'm withdrawing from the tournament."

I caught a glimpse of Angela out of the corner of my eye. She was starting to cry. From out of the shadow cast by the brim of her hat, a tear rolled down her cheek, glistening in the harsh sunlight on her face, mingling with the perspiration there. She was a hair away from jumping between Bobby and the cameras and telling them to leave him alone. So was I.

But there was no stopping this interview.

"What are you going to do now?"

Bobby smiled that old rueful, aw-shucks smile I could remember seeing when he shot 73 or something and blew a tournament. "I'm going to start thinking about some other way to make a living," he said. "Maybe I'll tune pianos."

Now Angela was crying freely. She wasn't sobbing, and her head was up. Tears just rolled down her cheeks. The bag felt heavy on my shoulder, and I dropped it to the ground and started wiping off the clubs, giving me an excuse to hide my eyes and my burning cheeks. I felt ashamed of myself. I felt like Bobby was doing the right thing, but I still felt ashamed of the way I'd bullied him into it, ashamed of the way it hurt Angela.

"It took courage to come out here," the ESPN guy said. "You've won a lot of fans."

Bobby shook his head. "I just hope I haven't discouraged any blind people," he said.

I figured that was about enough. I picked up the bag and stepped in between Bobby and the cameras. "Gotta get to the locker room and cool off," I said. I shoved the butt end of the bag into Bobby's belly button and waited till I felt him latch on, then I plowed straight ahead, forcing the reporters to make way.

Bobby sat down on a bench in front of his locker, sagging like a three-day-old balloon. The little bit of charm he'd managed to muster for the TV people was gone, and when he turned his face toward me, I could see that he hated me for making him quit, hated being in a situation so dependent.

"Do me a favor," he said. "Get outta here."

I got.

I left the locker room and went looking for the bar. It wasn't hard to find. The bar was one of those new places that tries to look old, with forest-green wallpaper and prints of Scottish guys in long coats hitting golf balls at St. Andrews or Prestwick or someplace, their urchin caddies at their sides. I was feeling pretty urchinly myself.

I ordered two Coors because they're the thinnest beer I know and they go down the easiest when you're really thirsty. I finished the first in about four seconds. I was starting on the second when Angela walked in.

Her eyes were red, but not as red as her nose. Her sunblock must've failed her again out there. She was composed, but barely, dry-eyed, but barely. Beautiful, but barely. And I realized then that if Bobby quit, she'd never be in Allegheny Gap again.

She sat down next to me, her shoulders slumped forward a little, her shirtsleeves still damp and sticking to her arms. She took off her hat and pushed that thick red hair off her temples. I just watched her fingers run through it, unable to say anything.

"Buy me a beer?" she asked.

I gestured to the bartender.

"You sure you can handle it?" I asked her, trying to tease her a little, make her smile. It didn't work.

"I don't care," she said.

I nodded. There were a lot of things I wanted to say to her, like how much I admired the work she'd done with Bobby and how much I'd liked having her around Eadon Branch, but I'd long since gotten used to the fact that I never could tell a woman the things I wanted to say.

She took a long pull on her Coors. I matched her.

She turned to me. "How can he quit," she asked, "after that last shot?"

"That last shot was just a chain yanker," I said.

"Okay. Tell me what a chain yanker is."

"Well, golf is a game that likes to yank your chain. Just when you think you've got it, you hit one sideways. And just when you think you'll never get it, you hole one out of a fairway bunker like Bobby did. It's like a joke. It's one of the reasons that when you throw your clubs into a pond, you usually wind up wading in after them."

Her eyes widened. "But it shows what he's capable of!"

"Sure," I said. I finished my second beer. "But not what he can do when he has to."

"Can't you talk him out of it?" she asked me. "Everybody who's blind has this kind of problem. They have to get past it."

"I don't want to," I said. "I don't want to do this anymore."

She looked sad. "Why not?"

I thought about telling her about what Bobby had done the previous evening. I thought about telling her that I was tired of working in a boy's role for a person who wasn't yet a man himself.

"Bag gets heavy," I said.

She looked like she wanted to argue with me, then decided against it. She just took a long swallow on her beer. She was learning to drink the stuff. Another thing for me to feel good about. I asked what she'd do next.

"Well, I've committed to work for Bobby for the rest of the year," she said. "But I don't know if I can do him any good if he doesn't want to see this through. Maybe I'll go back to the hospital staff. What about you?"

It felt like we were in a band that breaks up in Paducah or someplace and the musicians have to figure out what they're going to do now that they won't be on the Grand Ole Opry.

"I don't know," I said. "Hadn't thought about it."

"You've got Eadon Branch," she said.

I guessed Bobby hadn't told her about our money problems. I wasn't about to.

"Yeah," I said. "There's that."

"Will you go back there? Or try to get back on the Tour?"

"Maybe I'll teach line dancing," I told her, trying again to be funny.

For a short moment, I thought I saw her eyes soften a little, remembering that time we danced.

"I never got to take another lesson," she said.

And then I should've said something about how we could still do something about that. I should've gone over to the jukebox and put a quarter in the machine and punched the button for "Crazy" by Patsy Cline and taken her in my arms and danced her around the room till she fell in love with me. But there wasn't a jukebox or a dance floor—just some Muzak and a bunch of guys drinking Jack Daniel's and hassling each other over two-dollar Nassaus and a few guys from the Cooters Tour who hadn't learned yet that if you started drinking beer after every bad round you could soon be a lush. And I probably wouldn't have had the nerve to dance with her even if there had been a jukebox.

So I sat there a moment, feeling awkward, and probably would've said something really inspired, like, "Well, take care of yourself," if Ken Alyda hadn't walked in.

He had another cigar going and he was scanning the room. He headed my way and I realized I was the one he was looking for.

He sat down on my left and I introduced him to Angela.

"Tough day out there, Greyhound," he said.

He exhaled some cigar smoke, trying to turn it away from me, but the vent for the air conditioner blew it toward me anyway. His cigars were the kind a caddie might smoke. I think that instead of tobacco, they were filled with dried reeds from that marsh I fell into.

"Tell me about it," I said.

"Amazing he made that eagle on the last," he said.

"Yeah," I agreed. "Too bad it wasn't on the first."

Alyda nodded sympathetically and shifted on his stool a little bit, like he was sitting on something uncomfortable. "Uh, Greyhound, I'm glad I ran into you, because I've been meaning to try to call you. Didn't have your number."

"Oh?" I couldn't imagine why.

"Yeah," Alyda said. "It's about something kind of personal."

"I'll excuse myself," Angela offered.

She hadn't finished her beer, and I didn't want her to go.

"No, stay," I told her. I put a hand on her forearm. It was warm and bony.

"She's a good friend," I told Alyda. I sipped on the beer.

He nodded. "Well, it's about your father."

I didn't gag on the beer or anything else you might expect. Once he said that, I just got real cool, real detached. I nodded. I sipped again.

"I know where he is," Alyda said, like he was challenging me to deny I knew where he was.

"Well, you're ahead of me then," I said. "Like I told you, I haven't seen him since I was thirteen."

"Maybe I shouldn't have looked into it," Alyda said. "But I kind of liked your father. He was civil with me. Not like Hogan or some people. When I asked him a question, he answered it. He was grouchy, and a little spacy, but so am I."

I nodded. "So where is he?" I asked him.

"You really don't know," he said.

"No," I told him.

Alyda looked sad, like he was telling me about a death.

"He's at the V.A. Hospital in Staunton, Virginia," Alyda said. "Has been for fifteen years."

"A hospital?"

I couldn't quite figure this out.

Alyda nodded.

"Is he sick?"

Alyda put the cigar down and looked me straight in the eyes. He was being kindly, I could see, and truthful. He was too old to jerk people around.

"It's a psychiatric hospital, Greyhound," he said.

8

▼

$\mathbf{A}$ GOLF COURSE IS MAYBE THE MOST FRAGILE THING I KNOW OF OUTSIDE of a woman's feelings. If you don't tend to it every day, you start to lose it. In a couple of days the greens get shaggy. Within a week, the fairways are overgrown and weeds are setting in. Let it go for six months and you might as well buy some cows, because all you're going to have is pasture.

When I got back to Eadon Branch, late on a Friday afternoon, I could see the beginning signs of neglect, even though I'd only been gone a few days. The ninth and fourth greens had burned away at a couple of high spots that always gave us trouble, and there was goosegrass growing in the fairways.

I walked into the clubhouse. There were no customers around, though I'd seen and heard a few out on the course. Eudora had the television and her apron both on. She was watching Oprah while cleaning up the grill. I didn't know whether to hug her or yell at her, so I did neither. I just said hello, and she said hello back. Eudora wasn't the hugging sort of mother most of the time.

"How'd it go in Myrtle Beach?" she asked. "Miss the cut?"

The question seemed a little wary and it occurred to me then that I was not the first person to walk through this door late on Friday with a sour expression on his face and no paycheck in his pocket. It must've happened dozens of times with Clayton Mote.

"We shot a bunch over and withdrew," I said.

Eudora wiped her hands on her apron and said she was sorry.

"Where'd Bobby and Angela go, back to Nashville?"

Yes, I said. They'd dropped me off and headed down the road to the interstate.

"They coming back?"

I didn't think so. If Eudora wondered why, she didn't press me about it. She must've sensed the mood I was in.

I asked her about the burnt patches on the greens. "Didn't Hayden remember I told him to syringe those greens if it got up to ninety?"

"Hayden's gone," she said.

"Gone?"

"Quit to go work on the grounds crew at the Homestead."

"Why'd he do that? They won't put up with him long."

"Word's out," Eudora said.

"What word?"

"Word's out the bank's foreclosing."

She said this in a flat, stoic tone, as you might say that one of the mines was closing, or that a shoe store downtown had given up competing with the Wal-Mart and gone out of business. She kept her head down and took a rag and wiped off the three little tables in the lunch area. I started stacking the chairs.

"Well, what's the Powerball up to now?" I asked her.

She didn't smile. "Twenty-four million," she said.

"That oughtta be enough," I said.

She just nodded and wiped another table down.

I got the broom out of the closet and started sweeping up. The dust and bits of turf off players' shoes slid across the linoleum into the bright light coming in from the setting sun.

"Had an interesting talk with a sportswriter down in Myrtle Beach," I finally said. "Fellow that knows where Clayton Mote is."

She stopped wiping and I could see from the rigid expression on her face that she knew.

"Why didn't you tell me?" I asked her.

I half expected her to stop what she was doing, pull a couple of chairs down, and maybe pour us a couple of shots of the Jack Daniel's she kept in the refrigerator behind the gallon jar of mustard, then sit down for a long talk. She didn't. She turned her face back to the table and kept wiping.

"What'd he tell you, this writer?"

"That he's in a V.A. hospital up in Staunton. Has been for fifteen years."

She nodded, tight-lipped. "That's right."

"Why didn't you tell me?" I asked her again, more insistent this time.

Now she stopped wiping, put down the rag, and faced me.

"I thought about it. I kept thinking I would," she said. "But I didn't want you to think—well, Henry, to be honest, I didn't want people around here to think that we had insanity in the family. Men run off here. People talk about it for a while, then it's accepted. But insanity is like a stain that stays on your family name for generations. If we were in Roanoke or someplace like that, people might see it differently. But this is a small town."

I could see how she'd thought about the town. I didn't necessarily agree with it, but I could see it. I still couldn't see why she'd never told me.

"But you lied to me, Eudora," I said.

She sighed. "When you were little, you were used to your father being gone for weeks at a time," she said. "It was easier at first just to let you think he was off playing tournaments again. After a while, it seemed to me you'd accepted that and it would just be harder on you if I told you the truth. Since you've been back, I've been meaning to tell you, but the right moment just never seemed to come up."

I almost told her what it'd felt like to hear it from a stranger, hear it in front of Angela, ask her if she thought *that* was the right moment. But I checked myself, partly.

"You should've told me," was all I said.

She didn't argue with me. She just kept wiping tables down, and I wouldn't've even had a clue of how upset she was if I hadn't noticed that she was wiping the same table for the third time. Eudora was not the type of woman to spend an extra second cleaning.

I didn't expect her to apologize. In the Mote family, there's an unwritten code that takes effect when you hurt the people around you. They don't complain and you don't apologize. After a while, everyone forgets about it and life goes on. Or, at least, I used to think so.

"Do you ever go see him?" I asked her.

"I used to," she said. "I haven't been in three years."

"When you got that divorce."

She nodded. I thought that might be the end of it, but after a second, she raised her head and decided she needed to say something in her own defense.

"You don't know what it's like," she said. "The first few times, you go up there and you listen to the doctors and you think, He really must be sick. And you try to help him get better."

"What do they say is wrong with him?"

She shook her head. "He's schizophrenic, or so they say. Violent and delusional."

The Clayton Mote I remembered was grumpy and weird, but he knew which hole his food went in and where it came out. He wasn't delusional. About violence, I wasn't so sure. I'd seen him walk into the woods along the side of a hole at the Virginia State Open and wrap his putter around a pine tree, snapping the head clean off. Putted the rest of the round with his two-iron. But there are plenty of players with tempers and they aren't locked up for fifteen years.

"Violent?" I asked her.

She spoke very quietly, as if afraid that someone out on the road might hear her. "He attacked Sam Snead in the locker room at Greensboro fifteen years ago. Supposedly tried to kill him. The Tour kept it quiet, but if your father hadn't been hospitalized, he was going to be arrested and tried for assault with a deadly weapon."

"A deadly weapon?"

She grimaced. "I think it was a four-iron. That's how the police are."

I tried to imagine Clayton Mote attacking Sam Snead with a four-iron. The idea was painful and screwy and I wouldn't have believed it possible except that Eudora had no reason to be making it up.

"Maybe he didn't have enough club," I cracked. "Maybe he should've used a driver."

Eudora didn't appreciate my sense of humor. She scowled. "That's a bad habit you have, Henry," she said. "Making jokes when you should be serious."

"Sorry," I said.

"That's not why I gave up and divorced him," she said.

My head was starting to hurt and I had an urge to go outside and pull weeds or something. But Eudora seemed like she wanted to get this off her chest, to explain herself to someone.

"Why did you?"

"They have drugs now. They can control it, the schizophrenia. But when I wanted him to leave the hospital and come home, he wouldn't do it."

"Wouldn't? Why?"

She looked exasperated.

"I don't know, Henry," she said. "It depends on who you believe. The doctors up there say he's still delusional. They say he thinks I'm involved with someone named Joe Dey and with Sam Snead in a plot of some kind to drive him off the Tour. I think they're the crazy ones. I think he's just decided he'd rather stay there and eat free food and work on his damn golf swing."

"In a nuthouse?"

She nodded angrily. She'd about worn her wipe rag down to threads. She was worked up.

"I don't even know who Joe Dey is," she said, nearly spitting, she was so mad.

I had vaguely heard of Joe Dey. He'd been the Tour commissioner back before Deane Beman. And of course I knew who Snead was. But Snead, by the time Clayton Mote played the Tour, was no better than a ceremonial golfer.

"You think Clayton wants to work on his golf swing?"

"That's all he'll do. I drive two hours up there and he's out in a field somewhere hitting balls and he says, 'Hello, Eudora,' but he won't come inside to visit. He just stays out there hitting golf balls. If you try to make him go inside to talk, he throws a fit."

I didn't know what to say.

Eudora's body started to quiver and then she started to cry. I hadn't seen tears on her face in so long, I thought for a second she might be sweating. I realized then how hard this must've been for her—not just me finding out, but the whole fifteen years of secrecy and shame and the unfairness of it and blaming herself for it.

So I walked over to her and put a hand on her shoulder and she spun into my arms, put her head on my shoulder, and just wept. She cried until I could feel my shirt getting wet and I had misty eyes myself. It was the second time I could remember our roles being reversed, with me being the one to comfort her.

"I'm sorry, Eudora," I said. "I'm sorry."

"No," she sobbed. "I'm sorry."

"No one's to blame, no one needs to be sorry," I said, not sure if it was true.

I patted her head like you'd pat a child's head, even though I'm not much taller than she is, caressing it a little, trying to establish a soothing rhythm. After a minute or so, she snuffled once and stopped.

"He blames me, Henry," she said. "He blames me."

"Well," I said, "He also blames Sam Snead. He'd probably blame me if he saw me."

I was just jawing, trying to say something to make her feel better, but I had to stop there, because it struck me that maybe he would blame me and maybe I was to blame. I certainly hadn't been the perfect child. I'd even lost the shaft he gave me to teach me the grip.

And then I stopped myself. That was crazy. I hadn't done anything wrong, at least not to Clayton Mote. But I could see how Eudora had reached the point where she just couldn't stand carrying around that blame any longer and she'd decided to stop going to see him.

So I started laying it on thick, telling Eudora that she was blameless, and he'd probably have gotten sicker sooner and a lot worse if it hadn't been for her.

But it did seem like a long time for someone to be sick.

"Don't they have drugs?" I asked her. "Prozac or something?"

I was already developing this idea that somehow the doctors needed to be bullied into trying to cure him and maybe they hadn't paid atten-tion to Eudora, but they might pay attention to me. I'd be Clayton Mote's rescuer, the boy who rode into the hospital on a white stallion and put his family back together again.

"They've tried 'em all," Eudora said. "He won't keep taking 'em."

"Can't they put him on a couch and talk to him till he's better?"

She shook her head. "Henry, he's got to want to get better. They've tried everything."

I still had this white-horse idea. "Well, I think I should go see him and talk to him, talk to the doctors."

Now she patted me on the back. "You can if you want, Henry. But you might be sorry you did. You might be happier if you just keep thinking that he ran off 'cause he couldn't stand me."

"I never thought that, Eudora," I said.

Her eyes teared up again. "I wish you had," she said.

I hung around the clubhouse for a while after Eudora left, till it was almost dark. Just as the sun was going down, I stepped outside and heard the sound of a small plane coming into the airstrip. I searched the sky and caught sight of it. It looked like a two-engine Beechcraft with a green stripe. I'd never seen it before. The sun shining off the fuselage made it look almost golden.

There was no one else around. I yanked my TaylorMade out of the golf bag I kept in the corner of the shop and opened up a new sleeve of Titleists from the ball rack Eudora had by the register. I hustled outside.

The plane was nosing down toward the airstrip, coming into range. It looked big and slow. I teed the ball up, looked at the plane, then looked at the place in the sky where I expected it to be in about three seconds. Then I swung.

I cut it some and missed by at least sixty yards.

I SPENT THE NEXT COUPLE OF DAYS THINKING ABOUT WHEN AND HOW I might go to see Clayton Mote, all the while trying to do something to save the greens that were burning up and get rid of the goosegrass without spending a lot of money on chemicals. Basically, there wasn't much I could do except get down on my hands and knees and pull the stuff out by the roots, which was ridiculous, since there wasn't likely to be a golf course on this ground much longer. It was like doing paint-and-chrome work on an old truck just before entering it in a demolition derby.

And then a very odd thing happened. A storm called Hurricane Gabe came out of the Caribbean, up through the Florida panhandle and Georgia. And it kept going. Normally, hurricanes petered out before they got to Allegheny Gap, but not this time. Gabe swept up through Georgia and into Tennessee and Kentucky and just sat there for three days.

By the second day, Eadon Branch was two feet over its banks and the ninth, third, and fifth fairways were partly under water. The ground that wasn't underwater could suck your feet in up to the ankles if you didn't watch where you stepped. I spent a lot of my time down by the fourth green, making sure that nothing blocked the flow of water over the dam Clayton Mote had built to enlarge the old farm pond. If that little spillway got clogged, the water would back up over the fourth green and wash it away.

But it was a tough little dam and it kept doing the job as long as I kept clearing the limbs and leaves and assorted junk that flowed down off Eadon Mountain. The fourth green wouldn't go under unless the whole golf course did, a possibility that began to seem a lot less remote around evening of the storm's second day. It stopped raining and cleared up for a while, and the sun actually shone briefly. But then more clouds rolled in, and as darkness fell, so did more rain.

I went up to the pro shop, which was deserted, pulling my muddy boots off as soon as I'd walked inside. My clothes were soaked through, though, and they dripped little streams of water onto the floor. I didn't care. We also had a couple of leaks in the roof, and Eudora had placed a bucket under each of them and moved the clubs and shirts and hats out of harm's way. I found Eudora's remote, turned on the TV, and flipped around till I found the Weather Channel.

I watched some guy in a suit the color of the bunkers at Oakmont point to swirling masses of blue and green and a yellowish color that were superimposed on the map of the eastern United States. It looked like a whirlpool of poison chemicals. That was Hurricane Gabe. And then the scene cut to a picture of a golf course. I recognized it. It was Horsehoe Bend Golf Club, outside Cincinnati, where that summer's PGA Championship was scheduled. The tape showed half the twelfth green washing away into a swollen, brown creek. It looked like an earthquake had struck. The green just cracked in half, showing a dark, gaping black fissure. The lower part fell away, dissolving into the flood.

"The PGA Championship has been postponed," the weatherman said. He switched to a view of people in Cincinnati piling sandbags outside of Cinergy Field.

"And it may be a while before the Reds can play again at Cinergy," he said. "The storm is probably going to stay just about where it is until Thursday, when it will gradually move north and break up."

If he was right, that meant another full day of rain.

The phone in the pro shop rang.

"Eadon Branch Golf Course and Swim Club," I said.

"Oh, may I speak to the cabana boy, Mr. Mote?"

It was Angela.

I should've said something witty about waterskiing in the bunkers or something, but I just said, "Angela, is that you?"

"Anyone else call you Mr. Mote except a state trooper?"

"No," I said.

"Then it must be me, huh? So, how's your father? I've been wondering about him. And you."

"Well, I don't know," I said.

"You haven't seen him?"

She sounded genuinely surprised that I hadn't gone. That was Angela's way. She saw the right thing to do as clear as Deion Sanders sees the end zone when he's returning a punt. And she set out to do it with all the confidence Deion has when he tucks the ball under his arm. So it hadn't occurred to her that I'd been dithering about seeing my father, that I'd been thinking about all the things Eudora had said and telling myself that maybe I was better off not disturbing him.

Instead, I started to see myself on that white horse again.

"Haven't had a chance to, yet," I said. "I'm going as soon as this rain lets up and Eadon Branch goes down. We're damn near losing the fourth green."

"You saw what happened at Horseshoe Bend," she said.

I told her I had.

"I heard they're not going to be able to find a new course for the PGA for at least a month," she told me. "You know what that means?"

I knew what she meant, but I didn't want to encourage her.

"It means they'll have it no earlier than September," I said. Witty.

"It means Bobby can still play."

So that was what this was about.

"I guess he could," I said as coldly as I was able. "He finished in the top fifteen last year. He's exempt."

"He'd need you," she said.

"No," I told her. "He can get someone else."

Her sigh sounded raspy over the phone line, like she'd blown into the mouthpiece.

"You haven't changed your mind, Mr. Mote?"

I wished she'd start calling me Henry again.

"Why are you so sure he has to do it?"

"He has to do it because he knows he can do it, Henry," she said. "If he doesn't do it, he'll start settling in everything. He'll give up."

I wanted to tell her to wake up and notice that 99.9 percent of humanity did that every day and that half the ones who didn't were insufferable asses. I wanted to point out that as man and golfer, Bobby Jobe had been getting along fine on less than his best for all his life.

"Not much chance of that happening while you're around," I said.

She laughed a little, as if she were pleased.

"We miss you, Henry," she said. "Say hello to your father for me, okay?"

I promised her I would. Then I dithered around some more.

TWO DAYS LATER, SHE SHOWED UP.

It was midmorning, a Thursday. No one was playing, though the course had dried out enough to mow the fairways again. When I saw her, I got out from under the tractor I was trying to start and wiped my hands on my T-shirt, making big grease marks.

"I figured that with the rain stopped and the branch going down, you'd be ready to go visit your father," she said. "I'd like to go with you."

Of course, I didn't say "Great!" or anything like that which might have let on that I was glad to see her.

"Why?" I said, like she'd asked to look at my tax return.

"I don't know," she replied. "I just do."

I still couldn't get it through my head that she wanted to spend at least six hours alone with me—three hours up the road to Staunton and three hours back. I still managed to sound like I didn't want her company.

"What about Bobby?" I asked.

"He's taking a few days off," she said. "Licking his wounds."

I wanted Angela to think that there'd never been any doubt in my mind about going to see Clayton Mote. So I told her I was ready to go as soon as I could change my shirt.

She smiled so sweetly I almost thought I'd fooled her.

We took the old blue Ford truck. I'm not sure why, since her car would've been more comfortable. But the Ford was running all right, and I guess I had this notion that maybe we'd take Clayton for a ride and maybe he'd be glad to see his old truck. The sky was fresh and clean and blue after all that rain and the air had a trace of crispness in it, the kind that makes you think of apple harvests in Virginia. We had the window down since the crank on the window on my side was broken, and I thought I could smell her a little in the air that rushed around her.

We listened to a Patsy Cline tape while we rolled up the highway toward the interstate, but it ended and the silence got to be a little noticeable. I tried the radio, but there were only country stations and preachers, and I was thinking that Angela was, after all, from New York and a Catholic by birth and she might not like that stuff too much. So I turned it off and tried to think of something to say.

"How about an audio book?" Angela asked me.

"Sure," I said.

"I got started listening to these with my students," she said. "They have to learn to retain what they hear, so I'd play a tape and then ask them questions about it. But I got to like listening to them when I drive."

She pulled one out of the bag she was carrying. "I've got *Heart of Darkness,*" she said. "Conrad."

"Not the Conrad who plays at Eadon Branch," I said.

She laughed, and I felt a little better about myself.

Conrad was all right with me, so we put it in and listened as I swung onto I-81 and headed north through the Shenandoah Valley. The story was about a guy named Marlow, who's a river ship pilot. He gets hired by a company to go up the Congo in search of a mysterious guy named Kurtz, who's an ace rubber trader. It's a pretty gruesome story, and I was half into it and half repulsed by it when we stopped for gas outside of Lexington. It was one of those Sheetz places, with a red plastic roof and a beer section longer than your average cement truck. I told Angela she should watch out for dying natives as she walked inside to get some food. She smiled.

I pumped the gas and went inside to pay. She was wandering in the middle aisle and when I approached her, she looked up and said, "There's nothing to eat here."

"This place is full of things to eat," I said, and I picked up a jumbo bag of nacho-flavored Doritos and a tube of Pringles. I added a six-pack of Miller.

"Gourmet dinner in caddie class," I said. "And you're traveling caddie class now."

She looked dubious.

"Well, if you want carrots and lettuce and stuff, it's gonna take a while," I said. "'Cause first they'll have to plant 'em."

She shrugged and said okay. That was one of the things I liked about Angela. I don't have any doubt that back in Nashville, she had an apartment unsullied by Miller beer or Doritos. But once she got into a situation where Miller and Doritos were inevitable, she found a way to enjoy them.

Back in the truck, she cracked a couple of cans and ripped open the bag, and we sipped and munched for a while as Marlow got the boat repaired and set off up the river to find Kurtz, if he was alive. And it suddenly seemed to me that the story was uncomfortably close to what I was doing, and I reached out and turned it off.

She understood immediately. "It was getting a little too eerie," she said.

I finished a beer and stuck the can in the bag under her feet. She looked at the can. "I thought good old boys tossed the empty cans at signs."

"That's not precisely true," I said.

"Oh?"

"We only toss empty bottles at signs. Cans don't have the right heft. Bad aerodynamics."

She nodded, lips pursed.

"You disappointed? We can go back to Sheetz and buy a few bottles."

A look that I hadn't seen before crossed her face. It was like she'd walked up to a pond and found that her ball hadn't rolled in, that it got caught up in a clump of wire grass just short of disaster. It was a pleasant-discovery look.

"Henry," she said, "you don't throw bottles—or cans. I've seen you walk halfway across a fairway with that bag on your back to pick up a gum wrapper."

"Well," I said, "Clayton Mote taught me that. Back when the course was just open. That was my first job in golf. 'Policing the property,' he called it. Had to be perfect, or he'd make me go out and do it all over again."

"But I'm right, aren't I? You don't throw bottles at signs."

"Not since I was sixteen or so," I acknowledged.

"So why do you encourage people to think of you as some kind of ornery, bottle-throwing redneck?"

I shrugged. "I've always been doing it, I guess. If you're a caddie from Allegheny Gap, people expect it."

She sipped some beer. "I don't expect it," she said.

I smiled at her across the seat of the truck. A tendril of curly red hair had escaped from the tight bunch she'd created to stuff it all under her baseball hat, and fluttered over her left eye.

"All right," I said. "With you I'll be my intelligent, environmentally sensitive, true self. But you have to promise not to tell anyone about it."

She laughed again, quietly, tilted her beer can back and finished it off. But she couldn't handle that much beer, and she started coughing and gasping till her eyes were red.

I waited till she'd recovered. "Now that we've discovered my secret, sensitive side," I said. "Can I ask you a personal question?"

She looked a little startled, but she nodded.

"How come you can't drink beer?"

She flushed. "Where do you think I was supposed to learn?" she demanded.

"In college?"

She seemed indignant. "What do you think I did in college?"

"I don't know," I said. "Never went. But I know they drink beer there. I think Bobby majored in it."

She pulled her legs up until her knees were under her chin, folded her arms over her shins, cocked her head, and looked straight out at the road.

"Well, that wasn't offered at my school."

"Where'd you go?"

"I went to a little Catholic girls' school called the College of the Annunciation."

I wanted to ask her why, but I didn't.

"They gave me a scholarship," she said, still looking out at the road, like she knew what I wanted to ask without me opening my mouth.

"Not a big party school, I imagine?"

"No. And I was a commuter."

Being sensitive and all that, I cracked another beer. I offered her one, but she declined. A sign said, "Staunton, 27 miles," and I felt even more like that guy Marlow, getting deep up the river, up where the banks squeezed the stream and the jungle was close and thick and you sensed that the heart of darkness might be just around the next bend. Except that in our case, what was actually around the bend was a crossroads called Stuart's Draft.

"It wasn't a convent," she said. "Some people think it was and I was almost a nun."

I figured she might be talking about her ex, but I didn't ask.

"I didn't think it was a convent. I didn't think you were almost a nun."

"You danced with me like I was almost a nun," she said.

That brought me up short.

"Sorry," I said. "I was just trying not to step on your toes."

"It's all right," she said, still looking straight out at the highway, still with her knees drawn up under her chin. "I'm kind of socially retarded," she went on. "If you want to know the truth."

An eighteen-wheeler nearly blew my door off in the left lane, going up a little grade. I looked at the speedometer. I'd gotten so engrossed in what she was saying that I'd slowed down to about fifty.

"I wouldn't say that," I said.

She let her legs down and turned my way.

"Oh, I would. After my father died, my mother was worried I'd be wild, so she made sure I went to Catholic girls' schools all the way. Then I went into the Peace Corps in west Africa, working with people who had river blindness. You didn't want to mess around over there. Every third male has AIDS. And then I went to graduate school at Vanderbilt in blind education, which isn't exactly a party scene, either. I married the first guy I ever dated much."

"What happened?"

She flicked her eyebrows toward the roof of the truck. "He was a software salesman. On the road all the time."

"That was it?"

She frowned. "Well, let's just say he would've wondered why you and Bobby waited so long to hit on that Cooters girl."

"Oh."

"I definitely have a talent for picking inappropriate men," she said.

I didn't know what to say to that, and I was relieved to see a sign along the road saying the V.A. Hospital was the next exit. We got off onto a two-lane state road that carried us through a couple of miles of apple orchards and dairy farms, sweet green land, a little brown at the edges in high summer, looking placid and fertile.

"I sort of thought we'd be going through a forest of thornbushes by now," I said, trying to start a conversation again. She didn't answer.

Then there was a fence—an ordinary, chain-link fence, that seemed to enclose a large piece of property, and a gate with a little guardhouse that said "Staunton Hospital, U.S. Veterans Administration," with several flags flapping lazily on poles right behind it.

We parked in the visitors' lot. There was hardly anyone there. I'd expected a place with grim brick walls and bars on the windows, but it just looked like a hospital, plain and antiseptic.

We walked into the lobby. The place was almost clean, but it was worn. The furniture was spare and institutional, but it had a sixties look, with odd plaids on some of the cushions and curtains, a lot of orange. It struck me that this was a hospital built for the post-Vietnam era, stuck forever sometime around 1971. There was an information desk in the lobby, and beyond that we could see a corridor where two guys in hospital gowns, both heavy, pot-bellied men with long beards, were slowly shuffling along behind walkers. Their butts were visible through the opening in the back of the gowns, big and hairy.

Someone directed us out of the main building to the psychiatric division, which you could see through a grove of trees, sycamores and elms mostly. It was white, about five stories high, and it looked odd. Then I figured out why. Its windows were like slits, as if it were a modern-day fortress but with archers defending it and they only wanted enough of an opening to sight an attacker and fire an arrow through. Of course, it wasn't that at all. These windows weren't designed to keep people out. They were designed to keep people in. If you wanted to kill yourself at Staunton Hospital, you'd have to be a little more creative than just opening a window and jumping.

This time, there was no big lobby, just a little entry cubicle with a thick, locked door behind it. This door had a window about the size of a book in it, but if you looked through it, the view was dim and blurred. The glass was thick.

The receptionist was a guy named Martinez in a white orderly's uniform. He was about five feet tall and six feet wide, built a lot like the desk he was sitting behind. When we told him why we were there, he replied immediately, "You're not on the visitor list for today."

He hadn't pulled out a list to check, so I assumed the list was short enough that he'd memorized it.

"I know," I said. "But he's my father and we've come a long way."

If Martinez sympathized, he was a guy I wouldn't want to play poker with. His expression didn't change.

"You'll have to see Dr. Mehta," he said.

He picked up the phone, punched a couple of numbers, and spoke briefly into it.

"Okay," he said. "Through that door, third office on the right." He reached out, pressed some kind of button, I guess, and we heard a buzzer. I tried the door, and it opened.

By that time, I expected to see someone in a straitjacket or lost souls sitting around drooling on themselves. But I didn't. It was just a corridor with green walls, linoleum floors, and doors on either side. It could've been a school.

There was a guy mopping the hall, a patient, I guessed, or an inmate. He didn't make eye contact with us and I didn't try to make eye contact with him.

He'd left a wet patch on the floor and Angela slipped on it.

"Whoa," she said, and she fell backward. Her feet almost went out from under her, and she grabbed my shoulder for support. She was light, no load at all, I noticed. I inhaled the smell of her hair while she got her balance. Then she let me go and I exhaled.

"Sorry," she said. "You're right. I'd give klutzes a bad name."

The sign on the third door said "Dr. Mehta." I knocked. After a second, a voice said, "Come in."

Dr. Mehta didn't look like I'd expected, either. He wasn't wearing a white coat and he wasn't cold. He was a dark-skinned Indian from India, with a big head on a skinny neck and glasses that made him look goggle-eyed. He reminded me of the finches that eat at a feeder Eudora's got and sometimes come up to the window and peer inside, their heads a little wobbly, like they're too heavy for the rest of their bodies. Mehta looked like he had no muscles in his body at all, just bone. And his posture suggested he'd spent a lot of years with a pack full of books on his back. But he was a cheerful guy. He smiled at us, asking us to sit down, telling us this was an unexpected pleasure. He had one of those Indian accents, the kind that pronounced every letter when he said "unexpected," right down to the last c, t, e, and d. I imagined that in Staunton, like it would in my part of Virginia, that just made him seem like more of an alien.

He had a thick file folder on the desk in front of him, and I could see from the name on the tab that it was Clayton Mote's.

"So you're the pro's son," he said, leaning back and looking at me. "I think you must favor your mother, but I can see a little of your father in your face as well."

"Yeah," I said. "See, I only recently learned my father was here. My mother didn't tell me. That's why I've never been to visit him."

I don't know why I felt like I had to justify myself to this guy. He didn't look like he was blaming me for anything. I glanced at Angela, who was seated in the chair beside me. She looked quiet and composed.

Mehta waved his hand, dismissing my explanation as unimportant. I got the sense he wasn't too concerned about why I'd never been there. Or surprised.

"You call him the pro?" I asked.

Mehta smiled. "Yes, well, that was the name everyone used when I got here two years ago," he said. "Your father seems to like it."

"You're his doctor," I said.

Mehta nodded. "That's right. His psychiatrist. At first, your father was a patient of Dr. Lincoln. But he retired several years ago. Your father has been here a long time." He tapped the file with his open palm, emphasizing its thickness.

"Yeah. Why is that?"

Mehta didn't answer for a moment.

"Perhaps I should tell you something about schizophrenia," he said. "Do you know what it is?"

"Like a split personality?" I said.

Mehta smiled a little. "I see you watch American Movie Classics," he said.

He was right about that, and I blushed. I'd got my fill of Tyrone Power and Ronald Colman movies, sitting alone in the clubhouse or a motel room at night. But I didn't want to admit it in front of Angela, so I just grunted.

"That is the way Hollywood used to describe it," Mehta said. "But schizophrenia is a disease—probably a collection of related diseases—of the brain. Probably genetically based, but it does seem as if psychological trauma can trigger it in some cases. It generally develops in late adolescence but in rare cases, like your father's, it can come on in adulthood. The symptoms usually include delusions, perhaps paranoia, hallucinations, thinking disorders."

"Like my father thinks Sam Snead and my mother are out to get him," I said.

Mehta nodded. "Your mother briefed you, I take it."

I nodded.

"We know it's a physical disease," Mehta went on, "because in some rare cases, it can be cured immediately by measures like dialysis of the blood. Apparently, dialysis filters out chemicals that in some kinds of schizophrenia interfere with normal functioning of the brain."

"Did you try that with Clayton"—I stopped, thinking that Mehta might wonder why I called my father by his name—"with my father?"

Mehta looked at the file, squeezing a pair of half-lens reading glasses onto his fleshy face. "Yes. That was tried in"—he ran his fingers down a page in the file—"1991 and 1993. Unsuccessfully."

"What else have you done for him?" I said, trying to sound challenging, even though I was beginning to feel that if there was something easy that they could've done to cure Clayton Mote, it would have been done. Mehta just struck me as that competent and that caring.

"The usual treatment is drugs. Chlorpromazine. Haloperidol. Fluphenazine. Trifluperazone."

"And you tried them?"

Again, Mehta referred to the file, riffling the pages. But I could tell he wasn't really looking at them. He was just letting me know that if I wanted to read till my eyes glazed over, I could.

"We've tried them all," he said. "In varying combinations, varying doses."

"Nothing worked?"

Mehta shook his head. "I wouldn't say that. They all had some effect, generally for the better. The main problem was that he refused to take them once he was on his own. We made several attempts to move your father to a halfway house we have in Staunton to see if he could get along with less intense supervision. But the first thing he always did was stop taking the medication."

"Why?"

"Well, one of the side effects of the drug is stiffness of the muscles. Your father claimed that it interfered with his golf. So he stopped taking it."

That matched what Eudora had told me.

"He still cares about his golf, still thinks he can play?"

Mehta chuckled out loud. His Adam's apple jiggled in his neck. "Oh, my, yes," he said. "I should say so."

Angela looked a little impatient for the first time. She leaned forward in her chair, breaking into whatever was making Mehta laugh. "Can we see him?" she asked. It was not a demand, but just short of that. She was insistent.

Mehta responded by growing serious again. "Yes, of course," he said. "But, Mr. Mote, I should warn you about something."

Now I had two people calling me "Mr. Mote."

"What?" I asked.

Mehta's eyes seemed to droop down toward the loose flesh of his cheeks. "He may respond well to you. He may not. You must not take anything he says personally."

I started to see why Eudora thought the doctors were as crazy as the patients here. How the hell else besides personally was I supposed to take the first things my father said to me in fifteen years?

"Okay," I said. I didn't want to give the doctor some reason to postpone the visit.

"It's more than that," Mehta said. "He may simply be unable to recognize you. The disease won't let him."

"All right," I said. "I'll introduce myself."

"I am not sure I would do that, either," Mehta said. "It might be best not to tell him who you are right away."

I wasn't expecting a teary reunion like they'd have on the Oprah show or anything, but I had figured I'd say, "Hi, Dad," or something.

"What should I do?"

"Just tell him you have come to talk about golf," Mehta suggested. "Don't tell him your name. Or use another one. Do you have a nickname he does not know about?"

I was starting to feel like maybe I'd made a mistake coming.

"Greyhound," Angela said. "Some people call him Greyhound."

I couldn't figure out was why she was pushing so hard for this meeting.

"Yeah," I said. "Some people."

"That will do," the doctor said.

"Let's go then," I said. I actually didn't much feel like going through with it at that moment. It wasn't just what Mehta had said. It was the whole idea of stirring things up. I'd gotten along without Clayton for fifteen years and I'm a believer in not fixing things that aren't broken, starting with golf swings and extending to most stuff. If Angela hadn't been there, I might've told Mehta to forget it.

But she was there.

Mehta nodded. But instead of taking us into the bowels of the psychiatric building, which I expected, he led us outside. When we stepped into the sun I blinked. I could feel it warming my skin. It felt good. It was one of those hot, muggy days when by late afternoon the air is getting old and used. But it still smelled great after the air of the hospital. You work in golf, you tend not to notice how much you like fresh air until you can't have it.

"Your father will be over by our golf area," Mehta said. He said it with a certainty, and he hadn't checked with anyone, so I got the impression that Clayton Mote was at this golf area, whatever it was, every day. Mehta led us down an asphalt path, kept neatly swept and lined with whitewashed rocks the way the military does.

"You have a golf course?" I asked.

"Well, we have some grass and a couple of flags in the ground," Mehta said. "But some of the patients like it."

He was describing it accurately, I could see as we walked on. The hospital had a big sports field with a couple of softball diamonds. Back in the outfield area, against a backdrop grove of pine trees, I could see a couple of droopy flags, white gone to gray with red numerals on them. They weren't real golf holes, just flags and grass and maybe the mower guy cut a little closer around the holes.

There were two guys playing, about to tee off, and for a moment I thought one of them might be Clayton Mote. But as we got closer, I could see that one was in a wheelchair and the other had an artificial leg in an unreal shade of flesh. It glinted in the sun. They were both younger-looking guys, wearing shorts and T-shirts, and I wondered what war they'd fought in. They didn't seem old enough for Vietnam. The guy in the wheelchair was hitting. He had one of those devices that extend the seat up and out a little so he could let his legs dangle and swing a club. There's a trick-shot artist in a wheelchair who goes around the country giving exhibitions and he can actually hit it pretty good that way. This guy couldn't. He dribbled the ball about forty yards off the tee. The guy with the artificial leg couldn't turn and he had no balance, but he managed to hit it a hundred, then jabbed the club into the ground to keep from falling over. I started to feel sorry for them both, but they were grinning and chattering like nursery school kids as they set off after their golf balls, the one hobbling with a club for a cane and the other bumping along in his wheelchair over the humps in the grass. They were having fun.

I could see no sign of Clayton Mote. Then I heard one. It seemed to come from the pine grove. It was the sound of a club shaft hissing through the air, followed by the thwack of a golf ball being crisply struck. It was the sound of a good player. Milliseconds later I heard a dull bonking sound, like a ball striking a tree. I'd heard that one before, too. And from good players.

"He's over there," Dr. Mehta said, pointing into the pine grove. "At his practice ground."

I looked in that direction and the sun bounced off a steel club shaft into my eye and I could see him. Or part of him. He was half hidden behind three or four files of trees, the kind of trees they have at a place like Pinehurst, longleaf pines with straight, tall trunks and little clusters of green needles at the top, like a flower, trees that cast long shadows late in the afternoon. The trees and their shadows made it a little like watching someone in one of those nightclubs where they use a strobe. My eye got quick little pieces of him and he looked like he was moving jerkily, speeded up.

We walked through the pines toward him, our footfalls quiet on the brown straw underneath us. I hesitated. I wanted this meeting, but I was afraid of it, too, still afraid of my father. Then I felt Angela's presence beside me. So I lengthened my stride until I was again half a pace ahead of her. We stepped into the clearing.

He was smaller than I remembered. But it wasn't just the change of perception you'd expect, like when you go back to your old elementary school as an adult and realize it only seemed enormous because you were six years old when you started going there. Clayton Mote actually was smaller. It started with his hair. He'd had a thick head of wiry black hair that he'd been forever unable to stuff neatly underneath a golf cap. He'd had thick, dark eyebrows. They'd made him look bearish when he got angry with me. But the hair was almost gone. The hospital barbers had shaved his head like a boot camp recruit's, and the stubble had more gray in it than black. His eyebrows were still bushy, but they, too, had gone gray.

But it wasn't just that. He was thinner than I remembered, dried up and wrinkled like an old, bleached raisin. He was not quite an old man, but he was getting there.

His clothes suggested how much he'd changed. He'd always taken clothing seriously. I could remember one time, when I'd caddied for him at the Virginia PGA and we'd stayed in a cheap motel outside of Richmond and he called the front desk and harangued them for ten minutes for not having an ironing board and an iron so he could press his pants before we went to the course. But he wasn't dressing well anymore. He had a plain white T-shirt on, soaked with sweat under his arms. And he had on some kind of floppy khaki shorts, black socks, and white sneakers that were old and scuffed.

One thing that hadn't seemed to change were his hands. They looked the same, thick and powerful and oddly, delicately clean, with long, precisely clipped nails. And he still had a slightly weak grip, a one-knuckle grip that kept him from hooking the ball.

The other constant was his equipment. He was swinging the same Hogan driver I remembered, a deep, sorrel-colored persimmon head with a steel shaft, the kind of driver that you don't see anymore. The finish on that driver still gleamed. So did the shine on the shaft. And so did the other clubs arranged precisely in the red-white-and-blue Hogan Company bag with "Clayton Mote" embroidered in white block letters. I saw that he still arranged the clubs in precise order, with the putter and the two wedges in the bottom compartment, the irons in the middle compartment in numerical order, and the woods in the top compartment.

Maybe it was the sight of the golf bag that triggered it, but I suddenly wished I was dressed differently. I had on jeans and an old golf shirt. They were clean; I'd changed into them before Angela and I had left. But Clayton had always insisted that jeans were not allowed at Eadon Branch, that they weren't acceptable golf attire. I felt like I wanted to have on better clothes. Clayton Mote himself looked far from dapper, but I guess it just shows that no matter what the circumstances, you don't stop wanting to impress your father.

It didn't matter. I could've been naked for all the attention he paid.

He had a ball, an old, scuffed ball, teed up in front of him. He was standing with his head cocked a little to the right, as if he was listening for something, focusing all his attention on it. He seemed to nod. Then he addressed the ball, his head still cocked. He waggled three times, just like he always had. He swung.

His swing had changed, I thought. His rhythm was slower, more deliberate. The swing had been pared of a couple of small but unnecessary loops and hitches at the top. It was simpler, more compact. It was, to my surprise, better.

He swung powerfully and the contact with the ball produced a loud crack, the kind of sound a well-struck wood club makes, different than the sound a metal clubhead produces. The sound echoed off the pine tees, amplified. From my angle, it looked like he was hitting straight into the woods, and I waited for the sound of the ball bouncing off a tree, the sound I'd heard a minute earlier. But I heard nothing but the faint reverberations of that clean, solid impact.

He finished on balance, looking oddly graceful, considering what he was wearing and where he was. We walked carefully closer to him, the way you might approach a skittish foal.

I could see then that he hadn't hit it into the woods but rather down a narrow little alley in the woods, the kind of alley that maybe a power company might make if they were stringing electrical lines through a forest, a cut maybe fifteen feet wide and at least 250 yards long. If Clayton Mote practiced by hitting balls down that tight little chute, then it was no wonder his swing had got better. You had to pipe it just to stay out of the trees. If you gave me a driver and a full bucket, I doubt I'd hit two balls out of fifty down that chute without touching wood.

He'd been practicing there a long time, I could tell. The ground around him was bare, packed earth. Whatever had grown there he'd worn away with those sneaker-shod feet.

He still said and did nothing to acknowledge our presence. He came out of his follow-through stance and reached down behind him to a small pile of old golf balls. He teed one of them. Then he straightened up and appeared to be listening to something again.

"Hello, Pro," Mehta said. "How are you?"

My father didn't answer. Instead, he went through the same preshot ritual, made the same smooth, economical swing, and produced nearly the same shot—a drive that took off low and straight and stayed that way, climbing until it was two-thirds the height of the trees that surrounded its flight, fading ever so slightly as it came down, and dropping to earth beyond my sight.

"Two," Clayton Mote said, but not, it seemed, to us. "That's two."

His voice sounded odd, raspy, and higher than I remembered. But maybe that was just perception, since the father's voice in my memory was like Darth Vader's, only deeper.

He teed another ball up and swung again. But this time he got a little quick and pulled it just a bit. It was still a good shot, a useful drive on any golf course I've ever seen. But about two hundred yards out, it hit a pine with a tight, faint little thwock.

Clayton Mote's expression did not change. "Zero," he said. "Back to zero."

I didn't know what to do. I wanted him to recognize me, to say, "Hello, son. You're looking good." I was smart enough, barely, to see that wasn't going to happen. I thought that maybe I should just step forward and hug him, but I couldn't do that, either.

Mehta intervened. "Pro, you have some guests," he said. He walked up to Clayton and gently put a hand on the golf club, preventing him from getting set to hit another ball.

My father looked up in what seemed to be mild surprise. He didn't look at Mehta and he didn't look at me or Angela. He seemed to be focusing on the sky over our shoulders somewhere.

"Gotta hit a hundred," he said, sounding a little annoyed. "Hogan says, gotta hit a hundred."

I couldn't just stand there anymore, so I stood right in front of him and reached out. His hand was lying loosely on top of the shaft. I took it. The fingers were limp and unresponsive, dead. Even from that, though, I could feel the calluses he'd built up over fifteen years of hitting golf balls in this far corner of a madhouse.

"Hi," I said. "I'm Greyhound. This is Angela."

I looked back. Angela smiled and nodded at him.

Clayton Mote looked at me. "Hey, Henry," he said, like I'd been coming to see him every day for the past fifteen years. No my-you've-grown. No apologies. No glad-to-see-you. No what've-you-been-up-to. Just "Hey, Henry."

I had an urge to hug him, and I started to do it. But he shied away like my hands had shocked him. Mehta laid a hand on my elbow, telling me to go easy. So I stepped back.

"Been a long time," I said to Clayton.

He just looked at me and blinked. For some reason I remembered something I'd long forgotten. I was three, I think, maybe even a little younger. It was Christmas time, I know, because there was a tree in the living room with colored lights. And Clayton Mote was lying on the floor. Playing dead, he closed his eyes, lay very still. At first, in my little brain, I'd known he was playing, and I'd just kind of crawled on top of him, waiting for him to wake up and play a new game. But he didn't. And I'd panicked and started thinking maybe he really wasn't going to wake up and clawing at his eyes and crying until finally he gave up on the game and laughed and picked me up and threw me in the air. And that's what I felt like doing again, like panicking and clawing at his eyes and making him wake up and be himself.

But, of course, I didn't.

Instead, I did what Dr. Mehta wanted me to do and stepped back a little, gave my father some room. And he went right back to what he'd been doing. He picked up another ball—he had maybe two dozen of them in an old black shag bag—teed it, and hit it straight down the chute.

"That's one," he said. "Gotta hit a hundred. Hogan says gotta hit a hundred. Get out of here."

"Nice swing," I said.

He perked up. "Not flat? Didn't lay it off?"

I shook my head. "On plane," I told him.

For the first time, he smiled. "Good," he said. "I got a tendency to get a little flat."

I looked at Angela. She was standing there, impassive, taking everything in but not showing what she thought about a father and a son separated for fifteen years whose first conversation is about swing plane.

"Your swing's fine," I said. "Hey, I'm sorry I haven't been here to see you. I only found out where you were a couple of days ago."

I thought he might've picked up on this, asked me why I didn't know, or explained why he never wrote, or just tried to catch up. I could've told him about caddying on the Tour, about Bobby, about Bobby setting the course record at Eadon Branch.

He shrugged. "'S okay," he said. Like he hadn't minded not seeing me.

"Eudora's fine. Eadon Branch is . . . still there," I said.

He nodded, but he was looking at his grip, flexing his fingers, getting ready to hit another shot. He wasn't paying attention. If his wife and his golf course still meant anything to him, he wasn't letting on.

"Stand behind me," he said.

We all moved. We watched him hit another ball, another pipe job. "Two," he said. "On plane?"

I just nodded. I didn't want to talk about his swing anymore.

Clayton grunted. "Good. Plane was Hogan's big problem," he said.

Mehta took my elbow and prodded me back a little farther. "Do you know," he asked me in whisper, "if your father knows anyone, or knew anyone, named Hogan?"

I thought everyone knew Hogan, but I guess I hadn't counted on Indian psychiatrists. "Sure," I said. "I don't know as he knew him personally, but Hogan would be Ben Hogan."

Mehta blinked, a cautious, pleasant, completely befuddled look on his face.

"A great golfer," I said. "Maybe the greatest. He died a few years ago."

"I see," Mehta said.

"He talks about him a lot?" I was whispering, too.

"Yes." Mehta nodded. "He thinks he hears voices, particularly this Hogan."

"Maybe Hogan's telling him how to swing the club," I suggested. "His swing looks more like Hogan's than I remember it." Then I realized what I'd said. "I mean, he thinks Hogan's telling him how to swing."

The doctor nodded. "And is—was—this Hogan known for having a secret?"

This was starting to sound goofier and goofier. "Yeah," I said. "Hogan liked to say he had a secret. Something about the way he cocked his hands at the top of his swing. Least, that's what people think it was. He was a great ball striker. People think he must've known something no one else did."

Mehta nodded like he even knew what the top of the swing was.

"Why?" I asked. "Does he talk about Hogan's secret?"

The doctor's eyes widened, like I was asking if they got people in New York City.

"Quite," he said.

Clayton swung and hit yet another pure tee shot that stayed between the trees.

"Three," he said. "Gotta hit a hundred."

"What's this 'gotta hit a hundred?'" I asked Mehta.

"It's a part of an obsessive behavior that your father's been exhibiting for many years," he said. "Dr. Lincoln's notes indicate that your father believes that if he can hit a hundred golf balls down the alley in the trees without hitting a single tree, he'll be cured and he can leave the hospital. But your father has not confided this to me."

Angela had sidled over toward us and was listening to what we said as she watched Clayton Mote prepare to hit another tee shot.

"Is that possible?" she asked me.

"What? Hit a hundred drives down that chute?"

She nodded.

No, I thought, it wasn't possible. Hogan in his best year, in 1953 when he won three legs of the Grand Slam, couldn't do that. Byron Nelson in 1945, when he won eleven tournaments in a row, couldn't do that. Hell, I doubted that Iron Byron, the ball- and club-testing machine the USGA named after Nelson, could do that. Golf balls and golf clubs weren't that perfect.

And yet I'd seen guys on the Tour do things I'd thought were obsessive and impossible. I'd seen Tom Kite one time insist that he wouldn't leave the practice green until he'd rolled in ten in a row from fifteen feet. And he'd done it—after a couple of hours, when it was damn near dark. I lost twenty bucks to his caddie, Mike Carrick, on that one. The best players may say they're not seeking perfection, may acknowledge that they can't ever own perfection. But a lot of them think they can at least touch it once in a while, hold it in their hands, like water, before it gets away from them.

So I didn't know how to answer Angela.

"It's not very likely," I finally said.

Clayton Mote, seemingly oblivious, swung again and piped another one. "Four," he said to the air and the trees.

And then he started to sing a little as he rooted around in his shag bag for another ball. It was quiet, and you had to strain just to make out the words. "Go Greyhound," he sang. "And leave the driving to us, Greyhound bus, Greyhound bus."

That got my attention like a swift kick in the groin. As far as I knew, only Bobby Jobe and I knew the connection between my nickname and the bus company. Eudora didn't know. And here was Clayton Mote, out of my life for fifteen years, singing about it. For a moment, I thought he did know, that this whole schizophrenia thing was just an act. I couldn't help myself. I walked in front of him and put a hand on the club just like Dr. Mehta had done. He stopped, frozen, in midwaggle. His head was still cocked, in that odd way, now looking somewhere down around my feet, where the ball was. I leaned over until his eyes were at least pointed in the direction of my face. What he was seeing I can't say.

"What do you know, old man?" I whispered to him. "You sandbagging us?"

He didn't say anything, just blinked, caught with his body tilted at an odd angle. I could see blackheads in the pores of his nose, see the wild hairs growing sideways from his eyebrows, smell the chili he'd eaten for lunch, see the tufts of stubble where whoever shaved him had gotten careless that morning. I just couldn't see my father behind that face. I had the feeling that if I could have stayed there like that forever, he wouldn't have moved, couldn't have moved. And I realized that I was being foolish, that in some fashion, I was frightening him, challenging him to respond in ways that his sick brain wouldn't let him do.

And I realized something else, realized that I was as big as, if not bigger than, he was now, even if he was technically still a couple of inches taller than I was. I realized that I no longer had to be afraid of this man and that however angry I got with him, it wouldn't do any good. Whatever he'd done to me he'd probably done because he was sick, but we just didn't know it at the time.

I let him go.

When I'd stepped back beside Angela and Dr. Mehta, he slowly unfroze himself, started waggling right where he'd left off, and hit another drive that split the chute.

"Five," he said.

The sun was sliding toward the top of the pines and a black man, an orderly in white pants and a white T-shirt, appeared, walking across the athletic field toward us. Dr. Mehta looked at his watch. "Almost time for dinner," he said.

It was about five o'clock. They eat early in hospitals.

Clayton Mote looked up, saw the orderly coming, and started mumbling. "Gotta hit a hundred," he said. "Gotta hit a hundred."

Dr. Mehta put a hand on his shoulder. "Sorry, Pro. Recreation is over. Time to eat."

I thought he'd protest, but I guess the years in the hospital had conditioned him to a routine. He just nodded. He picked up the shag bag and counted the balls inside. Then he walked down toward his landing area. I guessed that the count let him know whether he'd collected all the balls he'd hit.

The next time I saw him, I decided, I knew what I'd bring as a present.

"I'm going to help him," I said to Angela, and I started out after him.

She followed me, and then it was the three of us walking side by side down that alley in the trees. When we reached the first ball, I stepped ahead, reached down, and flipped it toward my father. Wordlessly, he caught it and slipped it in the bag. Angela saw one and she did the same thing. Of course, being so unathletic, she threw it behind him and he couldn't catch it. He didn't mind, though. Just turned around and picked it up. And for half a second, I almost forgot where we were and why, and it was just me and my father and Angela at the end of a practice session, picking the range. We kept flipping him balls and he kept catching them and I could imagine that he was glad we were there and we were connected somehow, even if it was a connection forged around a crazy obsession. We picked up maybe two dozen golf balls, finding a few in the pine straw to the left and right of the alley of his cleft in the trees, but most of them in the cropped, bumpy grass. The air was cooler than it had been earlier in the afternoon and there was a smell of cut grass in the air and it was almost pleasant.

But the connection I felt proved bogus. Once the balls were in the bag, Clayton Mote neither thanked us nor acknowledged our help. He zipped it closed and walked back the way he came, seeking the orderly. Without a word to anyone, he took a position half a step behind the man, to his right. And they walked off toward the main building.

"Can we eat with him?" I asked the doctor as we walked behind them. "Or maybe take him out to McDonald's or something?"

He shook his head. "Not tonight," he said. "The cafeteria is off limits to visitors and normal visiting hours end at five."

"No exceptions?" I asked.

"Not without prior arrangement," Mehta said. He seemed genuinely sorry. "Perhaps the next time you come."

"You think it does him any good to see me?" I asked him.

"Oh, yes," he said, and again, he seemed genuine.

"How?"

"Well, I don't know. I'll be observing him to find out. But anything that reminds him of the world that exists outside of his delusions is helpful. And I'm encouraged by the way he allowed you to interact with him."

I could only imagine what Mehta would find discouraging if he thought what had just happened was hopeful.

"What's going to happen with him?" I asked. "Is there any chance he'll get better?"

"With a patient like your father, you never know," Mehta replied. He seemed to be choosing his words carefully. "It's not uncommon to find that schizophrenic symptoms ease as a patient ages. But as I said, it's a disease with many variants. We don't know which one, exactly, your father has. We review his medication history every few months and try something different with him—a changed dosage, a new combination. And there are new drugs coming onto the market all the time. Perhaps something will have a more positive impact."

"But if nothing does?"

"Well, your father is fortunate, in a way," Dr. Mehta said. "If he were a normal patient he would be treated until his insurance ran out. Or until the state's hospitalization limits were reached. And then the hospital would be required to prescribe the best combination of medications it could and release him."

"He couldn't survive," Angela said.

"No, he would probably wind up living under a bridge somewhere," Dr. Mehta agreed. "But because he's a combat veteran, we can keep him here as long as we think it is the best place for him. And hope that time, or some new medication, eventually makes a difference."

I looked ahead at the docile figure of my father, following the orderly to his dinner. "What if he hits a hundred in a row down the chute?" I asked. "Could that cure him?"

Dr. Mehta laughed softly, indulgently. "I hardly see how," he said.

I was embarrassing myself, but I blathered on. "Well, I just thought, you know, that if he *thought* he was cured, it might have an effect, you know?"

The psychiatrist seemed miffed with me now for the first time, like a teacher with a kid who doesn't get it because he hasn't been paying attention. "And if a paralyzed man awoke one morning thinking he could walk, could he walk?"

"Sorry," I said.

The doctor softened. "Stranger things have happened, Mr. Mote. I don't pretend to know why your father is ill or what can cure him. I do not want you to give up hope."

"Thanks," I said.

We passed the ragged gray flag that marked the second hole on the hospital's two-hole course. I heard the murmur of the cicadas and the other night bugs, growing louder as the afternoon edged toward evening.

Something else occurred to me. "You said he was a combat veteran. I didn't know that. I knew he'd been there, in Vietnam, but he never talked about it. Could something in combat have brought this on?"

The doctor shrugged. "I don't know. Many things can contribute to triggering the disease in someone with the genetic predisposition to have it."

"It's genetic?"

"Yes. If one parent has the disease, a child has a ten percent chance of having it. If both parents have it, the child's risk is forty percent," the doctor said.

"Hang in there, Eudora," I said, trying to sound as if I wasn't really worried about it.

Fifteen yards up ahead of us, Clayton Mote and the orderly escorting him turned toward the psychiatric building where Dr. Mehta's office was. It struck me that I wasn't even going to get to say good-bye to him, not that it would have mattered. And for some reason, at that moment, I saw him in a detached sort of way. He was just a rapidly aging hillbilly from the mountains of Virginia who'd had a few years on the Tour, never won anything. Like uncounted rural southerners, he'd borne the brunt of things in Vietnam. And somewhere along the way, his brains got scrambled. Maybe the only thing of permanence he'd left behind was a half-finished golf course, and I was about to lose that for him.

It was Angela who broke the silence. "Pro, wait," she called. And she jogged ahead and got in front of Clayton Mote and the orderly just before they went through the steel door into the psychiatric unit. She got right in his face and smiled at him.

"Pro, do you give lessons?"

Clayton Mote smiled back at her like she'd just asked him to run off to New York City with her for the weekend. He seemed to connect with her in a way that was close to flirtatious, uncomfortably close. "Yeah," he said in that odd, raspy voice. "I give lessons."

9

▼

Halfway between Staunton and Lexington, the sun went down over the Blue Ridge. We'd gassed up and Doritoed up and took on a fresh six-pack of Miller just as we hit the interstate. The truck, as far as I could tell by the sound of the engine, was unlikely to throw any rods for a while. It was humid, a good evening for riding with the windows down. That was fortunate in a truck that offered no other option.

I wasn't saying much. I was thinking about Clayton Mote. Even though I was ready for it, even though I knew he was sick, I guess it'd shocked me that he didn't seem to care about his own son. Hurt me, to be honest about it. I'd had those white-knight fantasies.

The odd thing was what happened inside my head when I thought about him. It used to be that the Clayton inside my head was the Clayton I'd caddied for when I was thirteen, the one with the hand signals and silent glower. That Clayton was gone. I couldn't conjure him up anymore. All I had was this smaller Clayton, hitting drives down an alley in the trees, listening to instructions from Ben Hogan that only he could hear, trying to stripe a hundred in a row.

Angela seemed content to let me be quiet. She didn't quiz me about my feelings or any of that crap. She just let me stew. Finally, I opened the glove box and rooted around. I found a Patsy Cline tape. I put it in the player and Patsy started singing "Three Cigarettes in an Ashtray." It was slow and sad. Matched my mood.

I took my eyes off the road and peeked at her. She was sitting with her right elbow propped in the open window, bobbing her head a little in time with the music and humming some. The breeze was ruffling her hair just a little, and the sky outside was feathery bands of orange and pink and purple, the way it gets at twilight sometimes.

I pulled a couple of beers from the bag at my feet and offered her one. She said yes. I cracked it and she took it. I felt her fingers slide briefly over mine when she did.

"How you feeling, Henry?" she asked me.

"Okay," I said.

"I think your father's going to get better," she said.

"What makes you think so?"

She shrugged. "I just do. I liked Dr. Mehta. I think he'll help him."

"Hasn't yet," I said.

I wished then that I could look at things the way she did, optimistic. I couldn't, though. It wasn't my nature.

"I kind of liked Clayton Mote," Angela said.

"Huh," I replied. "I think he liked you. 'Course, all that sweetness could've been a facade."

"Don't be harsh on him, Henry," she said. "And don't give up on him."

"I won't."

It was true. I didn't feel like giving up.

"Or on Eudora," she added.

I just nodded. There were a lot of good reasons to be mad at both of them, I wanted to tell her. But I didn't. She had that kind of effect on me. She made me want to do better.

Maybe it was the idea of giving up on people that caused it, but I asked her how Bobby was.

Her voice got a little edge in it. "He's been pretty down," she said. "But I think he's feeling better."

"Good," I said.

"Paula called him and took him to dinner."

"That made him feel better?"

She swallowed some more beer, finished off the can. She nodded. "I think so," she said. Patsy started doing "Cry Not for Me."

"You got another beer?"

I cracked a couple more.

"I like Paula," I said. "I'd be happy if they got together, but I don't think Bobby can manage it."

She slugged down half a can, it looked like. "I'm not happy," she said.

I think she expected me to be angry or surprised or something, but I wasn't. I just kind of nodded and kept my eyes on the road. We were drafting a couple of semis from that J. B. Hunt outfit down in North Carolina.

"I mean, I know I should be happy," she said. "How can you not be glad if a couple has a chance to get back together?"

It was painful to hear her say this.

"But I'm not," she said. She considered her beer for a minute and I could tell she was getting ready to heave up another truth that she figured I didn't know.

"I kind of have a thing for him," she said.

I looked out at the road. Runaway trucks, I realized, are like I've heard cabs are in New York City. Whenever you really need one, you can't find one. I would've liked seeing one hop the median and squish us like a bug when I heard her say that. But none did.

"I know," I said.

She looked at me like I'd just described a birthmark that only she and her mother knew about.

"You knew?"

"Sure," I said. I know it was evil of me, but I wanted to make her suffer a little. "It was obvious."

"Obvious?"

"Well, I don't think Hayden Pritchett knew. But he's not too swift, you know."

"But everyone else at Eadon Branch knew?"

"Pretty much," I said.

For all I knew, it was true. If you wanted to mess around secretly, Allegheny Gap wasn't the place. You might as well do it on the football field at halftime of a Hilltoppers game as do it at the Econo Lodge.

"I never slept with him, you know," she said.

I damn near spit up some beer when she said that.

"Oh?" I said.

She couldn't face me to talk about this, looked out to the west, where the Blue Ridge was turning black and stars were coming out in the sky.

"It never happened," she said softly.

Now I was surprised. "Excuse me," I said. "Are we talking about Bobby Jobe here? Or is there some other Bobby in your life I don't know about?"

"Well," she said, still with a trace of that anger in her voice. "He made a couple of passes at me early on. He was drinking and it was professionally inappropriate, so I made him stop."

"How'd you do that?"

"I slapped him," she said.

"That'd work," I told her.

She smiled, not happily. "Then, after a while, I started to feel differently. Bobby grew on me, especially after we came to Allegheny Gap. But he didn't do anything and I'm, um, not too good at figuring out how to get that sort of thing started, you know?"

You could with me, I thought. But I just nodded.

She looked at me. "You don't believe me, do you?"

"Sure I do," I said.

"Well, it's true. I hold the single-season record for scoreless nights in an Econo Lodge."

"Only because I prefer Motel 6," I said.

Thank God she smiled at that.

"Let's have another beer," she said. It sounded like a good idea, so I cracked the last two in our six-pack. They were getting a little warm.

She held her can up toward the middle of the cab. "A toast," she said. "To record holders."

"To record holders," I agreed, and we clinked cans together.

She started to sip hers. A high rig passed us on the northbound side and in the glow from its headlights, I thought I could see her eyes glistening.

"He doesn't want me."

"Give yourself a break," I said. "After all, he *is* blind."

She laughed and leaned my way and the wind blew in her window and I could smell her. Then she straightened up. "No," she said. "I think he wants Paula back. He just can't figure out how to do it."

"She'd be good for him," I said.

She nodded, but she looked hurt. It took me a second to figure out why.

"Not that you wouldn't be," I added.

She shook her head. "Sometimes I think I'm the one who's blind," she said.

"Whattaya mean?"

"I mean with men. When a man comes along who'd be good for me, I can't see myself with him. So I wind up either with losers who treat me badly, like my ex-husband. Or I wind up alone, waiting for unavailable men like Bobby. Doesn't that sound stupid?"

See me, I thought.

"No," I said. "Sounds too damn familiar for me to call it stupid."

She laughed. "Henry, I'm glad we're finally friends," she said.

Great, I thought. Friends.

I wanted to ask her why it was that since the eighth grade, the girls I've really wanted have been falling in love with guys like Bobby Jobe and telling me they were glad I was their friend?

But I didn't. I just turned the music up a notch and we covered the last seventy miles to Allegheny Gap in companionable silence, broken up by a quick pit stop for more gourmet caddie food—Cheez Doodles this time, washed down by Budweiser.

THE NEXT FEW DAYS AFTER ANGELA LEFT I WORKED ON THE LATEST PROBLEM we were having with the turf, a bout of gray leaf disease that was killing the ryegrass. Just for the hell of it, I called the agronomy service at the United States Golf Association in New Jersey.

"We're recommending that courses in your region go completely to a new type of creeping bent grass. The rye's going to be too tough to keep with this disease," the agronomist told me. Bent grass was the type we had in our putting greens. It was susceptible to at least six different diseases and fungi and it burned out when the weather got hot. Keeping the greens cost us as much each year as the rest of the golf course.

"The Homestead's making the change this winter," he said, all helpful.

"Thanks for the advice," I said. "We'll give it some thought. We could be making changes this winter, too."

I didn't tell him the changes included tearing the place up for a coal mine.

So I was thinking about money when Eudora came out of the shop and called me to the phone, saying Bobby Jobe was on the line.

"Coach, I need a ride," he said. No preliminaries, no how-are-yous. It irritated me.

"They got taxis in Nashville?" I said, a little nastier than I meant to be.

"I'm not in Nashville," he said.

"Where are you?"

"Well, if they're telling me the truth, I'm at the bus stop in Allegheny Gap."

That didn't register right away.

"Where?"

He repeated it.

"How the hell did you get there?"

"How do you think I got to a bus stop—by airplane? I took the bus."

I looked around the shop. Eudora was the only one in there. If I'd seen anyone in the corner or at the counter, listening and grinning, I'd've known it was some kind of joke. But Eudora just looked curious, the way she usually did when I took a call. Maybe a little more so.

"You took the bus?"

"Yeah. Why d'you sound so surprised?"

"Well . . . ," I said.

I could barely imagine a very determined blind person riding a bus, asking directions, listening to the drivers call out the stops, relying on people to steer him to the platforms and ticket windows and the waiting areas. It was hard, but it was possible. But it was impossible to imagine Bobby Jobe doing that. He thought it was beneath *his caddie* to ride the bus. Besides, I didn't think he had the nerve.

"Don't underestimate me, Coach," he said. "So, you gonna come and get me or do I have to hitchhike out to Eadon Branch?"

I took the Ford down to get him.

Allegheny Gap didn't have much of a bus stop. It was just a brick shed down by the railroad yard in the most tired part of town. When I got there, Bobby was sitting on the bench outside, facing in the opposite direction from Eadon Branch. At his feet he had a valise and his golf bag, inside its travel shell. There was no one around.

I parked the truck fifty yards away for a second and looked at him. He looked a little lost, but also a little jaunty, like he was proud of himself for making it. And I guess he should've been. It would scare the hell out of me to do what he'd just done.

Once I saw the golf clubs, of course, I thought I had a pretty good idea what he came for. And I still wasn't buying it. But I shook his hand and got his stuff in the back and him in the passenger seat, and headed back to Eadon Branch. We passed McDonald's and Jimmy Edmisten's place and settled in behind a slow-moving, muddy old rig hauling a bulldozer big enough to slice off a mountaintop in an afternoon. Bobby chattered about little things: Robby's recent birthday, the flooding out in Tennessee from Hurricane Gabe—everything but the bag full of golf clubs in the back and why he'd brung them.

"Bobby, you're welcome to visit," I warned him. "But if you want to try to play golf again, you're wasting your time here. You gotta find yourself another caddie."

"Don't want to play golf exactly," he said. "Want to take a lesson."

"And I'm not going to give you a lesson," I said firmly.

"Don't want a lesson from you," he said. "Angela says I should take a lesson from Clayton Mote."

If the rig with the bulldozer had slowed down at that moment, we'd've been splattered on its treads.

"Clayton Mote?"

"Clayton Mote. I figure you must know him. You're the only Mote I know."

"Did Angela tell you why she wanted you to take a lesson from Clayton Mote?"

"Nope. I wanted to ask her, but she just said, "You should take a lesson from Clayton Mote' and hung up. And since then, she's had her machine answer the phone and she won't call me back."

"So you just got on a bus and came here."

"I figured if I called and asked, you'd tell me to stuff it, but if I showed up, you'd help me."

I shook my head. You can't exactly turn away a blind man after he says something like that. He was right.

"So who is Clayton Mote?"

I told him then about my father and how he'd gone off years ago and what Ken Alyda had told me down in Myrtle Beach. I told him how

Angela had prodded me to visit him. I told him about the mental hospital and the practice range in the trees. And I said that I thought Clayton was too squirrelly to give a useful lesson. "He thinks he hears things from Hogan," I concluded.

Bobby was undeterred. "Well, Hogan had a good swing," he said. "Better he listens to Hogan than someone who doesn't know his ass from a hole in the wall."

"Jesus," I said. "You're as crazy as he is."

We pulled into the parking lot and parked by the shop. Bobby got out of the truck and stood for a second with his nose in the air, sniffing.

"Eadon Branch," he said. That was how he recognized the place now, I realized. By the smell. He sounded happy to be there.

"So," he said. "You going to take me to see your father for that lesson?"

I had to respect the fact that he'd gotten into a bus and gotten himself to Allegheny Gap.

"I'll call the doctor and see if we can go tomorrow," I said.

THE NEXT MORNING, I FINISHED A FEW CHORES AND WENT INTO THE SHOP to get Bobby and get started. Eudora was putting the finishing touches on some pimento cheese sandwiches she intended for us to take on the trip. She hadn't asked any questions about my first trip to see Clayton and I hadn't volunteered anything beyond the fact that I'd seen him and watched him hit golf balls.

"You like a little ham on your sandwich, Henry?" she asked me.

Eudora didn't often customize her sandwiches. Hell, she didn't make 'em that often unless she knew someone was going to buy them. So I figured this was a pretty symbolic batch of pimento cheese.

"Yes ma'am," I said. "That would be nice."

She looked at me.

"Please," I added.

She didn't smile or anything, of course. She just cut a little slice of ham and laid it on the sandwich, then wrapped it up in cellophane, put it in a bag, and handed the bag to me. I grabbed a couple of dozen new Titleists from behind the register and stuffed them in the bag with the sandwiches.

"Drive carefully," she said. "Say hello to him for me."

Bobby was moved by the occasion. "You got any beer back there, Mrs. Mote?" he asked.

"Beer?" she asked.

"It's okay. I'm not going to be driving," Bobby said.

Eudora gave Bobby a big smile, opened the fridge, and handed him two six-packs of Bud. This was a woman who counted every damn one of the beers I took from that fridge. But for Bobby she had two six-packs and a big smile.

"Someday," I said to him, "you're going to have to tell me the secret of your charm with women."

"The first thing," Bobby said, "is never use it on women who are less than beautiful."

Damned if Eudora didn't blush.

In the truck, we put on some Willie Nelson and we were listening to him singing "On the Road Again," when we hit I-81 and headed north. The song reminded me of a couple of times when Bobby and I had driven from one tournament to the next, like the little trip from Palm Springs to San Diego or the jump from Tucson to Phoenix. We did it then the way we were doing it now, with me behind the wheel, Bobby in the front seat, orchestrating the music and sucking on beers.

"Remember the time that cop stopped us in Arizona?" I asked Bobby.

He smiled. "Yeah. I thought we'd be sleeping in jail for sure that night. What were you doin', a hundred?"

"Only ninety," I said. "It was all those empty beer cans you'd dropped on the floor that really got him ticked off."

"Gave him a little swing lesson there by the side of the road. Used the headlights."

"Was that a Riviera we were driving then?"

"Don't think so," Bobby said. "It was a Park Avenue they gave us."

I didn't say anything, struck for a moment by the lavishness of life on the Tour. Want to drive to Phoenix so you can play in our golf tournament? No problem, sir. Just sign for the keys to this new car. Even caddies got a taste of the honey. There was so much that it sometimes slopped over the edge of the bucket.

Bobby shifted around on the seat a little, like he was sitting on nails.

"Be nice to have a courtesy car again," he said. "One of them big Lincolns, maybe."

"Don't start," I told him.

DR. MEHTA WAS EXPECTING US THIS TIME; I'D CALLED AHEAD. HE WAS wearing a wide flowered tie that looked like it could have been made from gift wrapping. It was bright and warm—like him. I introduced him to Bobby. His head bobbed on that pencil neck of his as he shook hands.

"How's the pro?" I asked him as we walked out of the hospital building toward the playing fields.

"It's been interesting to observe," the doctor replied. "He has not said anything, but I sense that he has been agitated by your visit. The orderlies tell me he hasn't been sleeping much. When I speak to him, he seems completely preoccupied with his Hogan delusion. And he practices his golf more obsessively than I can recall."

"That doesn't sound good," Bobby said.

It didn't sound good to me, either, but Mehta didn't see it that way.

"On the contrary," he said. "Change is almost always positive in a patient with Mr. Mote's history. If change is possible, progress is possible. So when I see him reacting in any way to things that happen to him or even around him, I take it as a positive sign. "

"How do you think he's going to react to a blind golfer?" Bobby wanted to know.

"There's no way of predicting," Dr. Mehta answered. "I imagine he's never seen one. I hope he'll be curious. I know I am."

I started to sweat before we got halfway to Clayton Mote's little practice area. The bag strap felt sharp on my shoulder. I shifted the load around, trying to find a comfortable spot. I couldn't.

A hundred yards away we heard the first sound of ball striking club.

"What's he got there? Wooden clubs?" Bobby asked.

"Hogan persimmons," I said. "Classics."

We walked closer and heard the sound of another shot. "Damned if he *isn't* practicing in the trees," Bobby said. "I can hear the echoes."

Clayton Mote's voice became audible to us. "Two," he said. "That's two."

I could see him about then and what struck me was how absolutely identical everything was to the way it had been a few days before. Same clubs, same balls, same sweaty T-shirt and black socks, same wide, unseeing look in his eyes. Same stubbly head of gray hair. I thought about how similar his days must be, laid end to end for all those years, with nothing ever changing except maybe the advice he thought he was hearing from Ben Hogan, the occasional haircut, and the slow deterioration of his body.

He looked at us, then looked back down at the golf ball teed at his feet. Looked at us, looked back down. It was like his head was being jerked up and down and he had no control over what he looked at. He swung, and it was the worst swing I'd seen him make, hurried and flat and wristy. He hit a duck hook that got barely fifty yards from the tee before it disappeared into the trees on the left.

Bobby heard the clunk as ball met pine bark. "That didn't sound too good," he said.

Clayton Mote stared at him for a moment and I thought he was actually going to say something to us. But after a moment, his attention snapped back to the golf balls at his feet and he teed another one up. He was nodding at something the voice in his head was saying, and he slowly and deliberately regripped the club as he did. So I guess Hogan was telling him how many knuckles should be showing on his left hand or something like that.

Before he could swing again, I walked up to him, remembering how Dr. Mehta had done it. Friendly and slow. I put a restraining hand on the shaft of his driver.

"Hi. We're here for that lesson we talked about the last time. Remember?"

With my hand immobilizing his club, Clayton Mote seemed better able to focus on us.

"Lesson?" he asked. Then, "Where's the girl?"

I winced, I guess because it seemed clear that he cared more about Angela's absence than he did my presence. He was sick, I reminded myself.

"She couldn't make it this time," I said.

"You want a lesson?" Clayton Mote asked. And he smiled. His teeth were small and yellow. It was the first time I'd seen him smile at me in so many years that I couldn't remember the last time.

"No, Pro," I said. "I've got a player here named Bobby Jobe wants a lesson."

"Not you that wants the lesson?" he asked.

"Some other time, I want you to teach me, Pro," I told him. "Right now, Bobby needs a lesson."

Clayton nodded. "I charge seven-fifty for half an hour," he said.

"Seven-fifty!" Bobby snorted. "Leadbetter only charges five hundred."

"I think he meant seven dollars and fifty cents," I whispered to Bobby.

"Who's Leadbetter?" Clayton Mote wanted to know.

"He's a teacher," I said. "But it doesn't matter. Seven-fifty is fine."

Clayton looked at me for a long second. His eyes focused on mine and I thought there was some contact there, some glimpse of the man he used to be. But he didn't say anything to me and when I blinked his eyes were wide and blank. I had the sense that maybe his brain was like a camera that's got out of focus and he was seeing everything blurred and distorted.

"Let's not hit here," I said. "I want Bobby to have some room. Let's go over to your first hole there."

So we did. Bobby and I assumed our usual posture, his right hand lightly draped over the butt end of the golf bag, and I walked over to the little tee box. It was just a patch in the grass mowed about half an inch lower than the rest of the field, with two pieces of wood, cut from an old two-by-four and painted blue, as tee markers. The grass was clumpy and weedy and there was a bare spot of dirt and brown grass where most of the players stood when they teed off. I thought for a moment about Augusta and the impeccable, closely mowed turf of its tee boxes. I remembered the last time Bobby and I had stepped onto that first tee for a Tuesday practice round, when the grass was virgin new.

"Whyn't you warm up and I'll watch you swing," Clayton suggested.

He sounded so damn normal suddenly. I was starting to understand a little more about Clayton's disease—well, not understand it, but at least be familiar with it. His mind seemed like a tractor that's got only one gear and one attachment. It can go straight ahead and pull a plow. It can't reverse, it can't disk or furrow or any of the other things a tractor normally does. Clayton could engage with someone about golf. Other than that, the disease had control of his mind. He might recognize me in some way, even know my name. But he couldn't really talk to me about anything but whether I thought his swing was laid off.

So Bobby stretched for a minute, then hit a few wedges, then some seven-irons. He was making precise contact and his balls had a tight, low trajectory with a little fade at the end. They were damn near perfect.

Clayton Mote made a clicking sound with his tongue as the sixth or seventh shot took off and spoke for the first time.

"You know, your caddie's not allowed to stay behind you when you swing like that," he said to Bobby.

Bobby and I stopped in the midst of preparing a shot.

"Pro, he has to," Bobby said. "The rules make an exception for the blind."

Clayton looked at him like he'd stuck a third arm out of an extra hole in his shirt. "You're blind?"

"Uh, yeah," Bobby said.

"Can't see?"

"Nope."

"Horseshit," Clayton said. "No blind man can hit it like that. This some kind of a joke?"

"It's no joke," I said. "He's blind."

Clayton took a step toward Bobby and threw a left jab at his face, a punch that stopped a few inches shy of his nose. Bobby, of course, didn't flinch.

"Well I'll be damned," Clayton said. "Hit some more."

Bobby worked his way down to a driver and crushed a few toward the distant flag, which I figured was about 350 yards away.

"Let's see your position at the top," Clayton said.

Bobby drew the club back till its shaft was parallel to the ground.

"You got a tendency sometimes to close the face and snap it, don't you?" Clayton said.

Bobby reddened. "Sometimes," he acknowledged.

I thought about that first tee shot down in Myrtle Beach.

"Once in a while," I confirmed.

Clayton had figured out in a few minutes what some of the Tour's swing doctors took half an hour to see. That was in fact Bobby's most persistent swing flaw.

"Let me show you what to do," Clayton said. And he took Bobby's hands and placed them in the proper position at the top. He tapped Bobby's left shoulder. "Feel that stretching?" he asked.

"Yeah," Bobby said.

"Go for that feeling," Clayton said. "Try to feel like you're going to tear the sleeve of your shirt, you're stretching so much in that shoulder."

Bobby nodded. I could tell he was as impressed as I was.

"Other than that, your swing's perfect," Clayton said. "Don't change anything."

Dr. Mehta was beaming, so I guess he was impressed by the way Clayton was handling himself. I could imagine him starting a golf therapy program for the patients, with Clayton teaching.

But then Clayton slipped away from us, from reality. "Learned that from Hogan," he said vaguely as if he was talking not to us, but to gnats in the air. "Hogan knows. Hogan hates Snead. Snead screwed me."

I felt mortified, somehow, even though I'd warned Bobby my father was not normal. You can't help but he embarrassed when your father starts raving.

Bobby didn't object to what Clayton was saying, though. He seemed to accept it. In fact, he seemed intrigued by it.

"You saw Hogan play?" he asked.

Clayton nodded. "I saw Hogan. Hogan knows the secret," he said.

Bobby turned toward me as if asking me to verify that Clayton Mote had indeed seen Hogan play. I didn't know. I couldn't remember when Hogan had retired, exactly. The years didn't seem to match. But it was possible. I didn't say anything, and Bobby turned back toward Clayton.

"Is that Hogan's secret?" he asked. "Stretching like that in the shoulder? I thought Hogan's secret was cupping the left wrist at the top. I try to do that, you know."

Clayton didn't respond, directly. He was disengaged. "Hogan knows the secret," he murmured.

"Yeah, but what is the secret?" Bobby asked again.

Clayton's eyes flashed. "Hogan hates Snead!" he said, emphatically. "Hogan knows. Snead screwed me."

I didn't like the way the conversation was going. I didn't think Angela had sent Bobby up here to grill Clayton about Hogan's secret. I had an idea, and I figured the doctor would let me try it.

"We've still got twenty minutes left," I said. "How about a little playing lesson? These two holes."

"Playing lesson?"

Clayton Mote looked worried by the idea. The bushy gray eyebrows knit together and the brow furrows deepened and he started to shift from one foot to the other like he was getting ready to run off.

"Yeah, you know," I said. "Play a few minutes. Watch Bobby play. Show him how it's done. Pick up on little mistakes he might be making. Playing lesson. Give us the benefit of your Tour experience."

I tried to be as casual as I could about it, like it was nothing he hadn't done twice a week for the past fifteen years.

"Snead screwed me," Clayton replied, like a parrot. "Gotta hit it straight down the middle."

He was wavering, again, between being with us and being with the voices in his head. The teacher part of him was with us. The golfer was somewhere else.

"I'll hit first," Bobby volunteered.

Casually as I could, I picked up Clayton's bag and placed it over my other shoulder, so I was carrying both. The weight of both bags damn near tore my kneecaps off when I squatted down to line Bobby's driver up. Ahead of us, I could see the flag, just a little bit past Bobby's range. A shaft of bright sunlight broke through the clouds and haze, lighting up the hole. The distant flag glinted a little as it flapped in the slight breeze. The grass looked a little less tired, a little fresher. The tallest pines from the wooded area threw sharp black shadows along the fairway.

When Bobby was lined up, I stepped back. "Let it go," I said.

And he did. It was a titanic drive, a shot that looked at first like he'd popped it up except that you could tell by the sound that he'd caught it dead flush. It set off a little to the left of the flag and then faded in just a touch. I couldn't see well enough to tell if it was on the green or not, but if it wasn't, it was close. Of course, on the green was a concept that didn't matter too much on this course.

"Not bad," I told Bobby.

Clayton hung back on the edge of the tee box. I walked up next to him and let the bag drop off my shoulder. I propped it in front of him, the way he'd trained me to do. He blinked, looking down at the clubs, polished and gleaming, reflecting that sudden shaft of sunlight that had broken through the clouds.

For a long time, he just stood there. His lower lip trembled slightly, so slightly you could barely notice it. That was his only movement.

Then he turned slowly toward the target in the distance. And as if someone else were controlling his arm, he reached toward the bag and extended his right index finger. I understood the signal. He wanted the one-wood, the driver.

Wordlessly, I gave it to him. He wrapped his hands around the grip, hefted it. I thought he had to be remembering the summer I caddied for him, but if he was, he said nothing about it. His eyes were fixed on the flag in the distance.

Bobby had left a ball on the ground, a fresh Titleist. Clayton bent over and teed it up. I pulled the bag back and gave him room.

Clayton appeared to be listening to his Hogan voice again. He had an ear cocked toward the sky and he was nodding. He stood over the ball long enough to make me think he wouldn't be able to swing, that his brain had frozen. But then he turned toward the ball and, to my relief, he hit it.

And he hit a fine shot, left center of the fairway, not as long as Bobby's but not bad for a fifty-year-old guy who's spent the last fifteen years in an institution.

"Nice drive, Pro," I said.

I humped the bags up onto my shoulders and took a couple of steps toward the distant green. I reached for his driver, figuring I'd stick it back in the bag. But he held on. He didn't move.

"Wait," he said. "Mullicant."

It stopped me like he'd driven the clubhead into my gut. I remembered then who'd posted the "No Mullicants" sign at Eadon Branch. It was Clayton Mote, of course. I remembered how he'd scorned the miners who'd hit their tee shots out of bounds on No. 1 and award themselves mulligans. There were no mulligans, he'd taught me, no do-overs. That's why he called them mullicants.

"Gotta have a Mullicant," he said. He was talking not to us, but to himself. "Gotta be down the middle. Gotta be straight."

His grip on the club was fierce, determined. He was not going to let go. So I let him have it.

Dr. Mehta looked puzzled. He whispered something to Bobby, and Bobby whispered back. But I suspected that Bobby was as puzzled by what he was hearing as Mehta was. To him, Clayton's shot must've sounded pretty good. He'd heard me tell him it was good.

I opened the pocket on Bobby's golf bag and handed Clayton another fresh ball. He went through his listening ritual again. He swung again. And he hit another good shot. This one was a power fade that lit about 230 down the fairway and skipped a couple of times, stopping right of center about 260 yards out.

This time I assumed nothing. And sure enough, he turned to me with his palm open. "Mullicant," he said again in that voice that was both high and harsh.

I opened one of the gift boxes of Titleists I'd brought and handed him another ball. He hit a third drive and this one, to me, was perfect. If there'd been a sprinkler line on this hole, it would have been right on it.

The sweat shone on his forehead. He scowled. "Mullicant," he said.

"But why, Pro?" I asked him. "You've hit three good drives. The last one was pured."

His face twisted a little and he looked like he was suffering. He looked as if he thought he'd landed in England and he was speaking English but the Englishmen couldn't understand him. He looked frustrated. He bit his lip as if he wanted to hit me. "Ball," he said.

I did, and he hit a fourth fine drive. "Okay, let's go pick one and play," I said. I reached for the club again.

He yanked it away from me and held it over his head. "Gotta be down the middle!" he said, raising his voice till he was almost yelling. "Down the middle!"

I backed off, afraid he was going to swing at me.

Bobby ambled toward the sound of Clayton's voice. Dr. Mehta, looking concerned, put a guiding hand on his elbow.

"Look, Pro," Bobby said. "I know you want to hit it perfect. So do I. But you can't. That's not golf. In golf, you gotta take your best shot and live with what happens. Let it all hang out. Sometimes you hit it great. Sometimes you don't. Doesn't matter, y' know? That's golf."

"Down the middle!" Clayton insisted, as if he was about to boil over. He was jerking like a steam pressure cooker, damn near levitating himself. "Down the middle!"

"But that's not golf, Pro," Bobby said softly, more sympathetic than he'd ever been with me.

I figured this was maybe what Angela'd wanted Bobby to learn from Clayton. 'Course, with Bobby, sometimes you had to beat him over the head with it a few times.

But this time Bobby looked like he'd figured it out. "Guess we don't need to finish this hole, Pro," he said. "It's been a good lesson."

"Down the middle," Clayton said, his own voice softer and lower now. It was like he hadn't been listening to us, or even aware we were saying anything. "Gotta be straight down the middle. Snead . . ."

He looked like he might start crying, which is something I'd never known my father could do. I handed him the rest of the Titleists I'd brought. I'd had this fantasy that he'd be pierced by the gesture of giving him fresh balls to practice with, that he'd bubble over with gratitude, embrace me.

He didn't. He stripped the wrapping off them and dropped them into his shag bag without a word. He never even looked at me.

10

▼

"YOU HEARD THE ONE ABOUT JACK NICKLAUS AND STEVIE WONDER?"
Bobby asked.

He sipped at his beer, a Coors. Bobby had been a Scotch man on the Tour, but he was always a flexible drinker. In his current circumstances, he was adapting well to caddie tastes. We were sitting in Gully's and the place was as quiet as it ever gets. It was Thursday, close to midnight, and there were a couple of guys hanging around by the pool table. The dance lessons were long over and the jukebox was quiet. Down at the end of the bar, a guy I didn't know, trucker probably, was stubbornly trying to hustle Rebecca Pollard, an Allegheny Gap woman who liked her beers and didn't like being hit on and had been known to belt guys who didn't get the message the first time she delivered it. Rebecca had a pretty good right hand, which is why I figured the guy was just passing through.

"Haven't heard that one," I said, "but it sounds like category four."

A voice came from behind us. "Category four?"

It was Angela. She was wearing jeans and her Eadon Branch shirt. She was tipping heavily toward the freckled end of the Angie Everhart–Raggedy Ann spectrum. But I was still glad to see her.

Bobby recognized the voice and turned on his stool. I suddenly remembered manners Eudora had taught me years ago and stood up. To my surprise, she hugged me, smiling. Not a long, passionate hug, but a very convincing glad-to-see-you hug. Then she kissed Bobby on the cheek.

"When'd you get here?" he asked her.

"Just drove in," Angela said. "Thought I'd find you here."

I must've looked a little more stupid and puzzled than I usually do when I'm on my fourth beer.

"I called Eudora. Today. She told me you'd gone up to see your father. I figured I'd come on up and find out how it went."

"Went fine," Bobby said. I just grinned, stupidly.

"So what's category four?" she repeated.

I signaled for another round of beers and Angela took the barstool next to mine.

"Category four," I said, sounding authoritative, "is blind golfer jokes. They all end with something about playing at night."

"I didn't know they were common enough to have a category," Bobby said.

Angela smiled like she was bemused. "What do you mean, category?"

"It's caddie-tent talk," Bobby said to her. "What simple minds do when they have too much time on their hands."

"As opposed to the intellectual stuff golfers talk about," I said. "Shaft flexes and which hotels have the best free breakfast."

"What do you mean, category four?" Angela persisted.

"There are only a handful of basic golf jokes," I explained. "They go round and round in variations that only seem new if you haven't been listening to 'em for years. Once you know all the basic jokes, you can tell within the first line or two what category a new variation falls into."

"Like what?"

"Well, category one is your basic God-Jesus-and-Moses-play-golf joke. Category two is the golf-not-interrupted-by-death joke. Category three is your antiwife joke. Category four is blind golfers. Category five is sex-on-the-golf-course jokes."

I was putting her on, of course. Although caddies had heard all the jokes and they did classify them, and they did delight in heaping scorn on someone, usually a player, who tried to pass off an old joke as new, they were in no way organized enough to have agreed on a list of categories like I'd just spouted.

"I didn't think blind golfer jokes were that common," Bobby said, sadly. He sucked down the last of his beer, smacked the bottle on the bar, and ordered another.

"What's your least favorite religion?" I asked him.

"Holy Rollers," he said.

I could hardly imagine what prompted him to say that, but I didn't stop to ask.

"Okay. A priest, a rabbi, and a Holy Roller preacher were playing golf one day. The group ahead of them was terribly slow. It took six hours to play. They finally finished the round and went to the pro to complain. And the pro said, 'Didn't you know? Those players ahead of you were blind.'

"'God forgive us our impatience,' the rabbi said.

"'I'll say a rosary of repentance,' the priest said.

"The Holy Roller preacher thought for a minute. Then he says, 'Couldn't they play at night?'"

Angela smiled.

Bobby's face sagged a little behind his Oakleys. "Mine ended with Stevie telling Jack he could play him any night that week."

"It's a category," I said, shrugging in my most worldly way.

He shook his head. "I didn't know that. I figured, you know, I'd use blind jokes in my motivational speech. Put people at ease about me?"

"Try something else," I suggested. I sipped a little of my own beer and looked across the room at the jukebox. I was thinking that maybe if I put the right song on, I might get Angela to dance and not treat her like a nun.

The new beer came and Bobby took a small swallow.

"Shit, I'd be a lousy motivational speaker anyway. What do I know about motivation? All I know about is trying to have a good time."

He swallowed again and started looking philosophical, or as philosophical as a former golden boy golfer with a bent nose and dark glasses in a dim bar can look halfway through his sixth beer.

"But you know, I'd forgot that golf was supposed to be a good time. I realized that with your daddy this afternoon."

I nodded. "I don't think he ever got that part."

Bobby shook his head. "I bet he did once. Otherwise he wouldn't be such a good player. But he forgot. The thing about golf is that you know all the stuff you need to know. You just are always forgetting it. Like that it's fun."

"When I first played golf, I probably shot a hundred and ten, but I had a great time," I agreed.

"Well, I shot eighty-seven, but I had a great time, too," Bobby said. He still had that touch of arrogance, and he knew that he was pointing out the difference between his talent and mine. Untutored, he's broken ninety the first time out. It took me three years to do that. Of course, I was only eleven.

"The difference between me and you is that my scores have gotten better since then," I pointed out.

"Careful, Henry," Angela said. "We want Bobby to forget that round."

"What round?" Bobby answered. I was looking straight ahead at the mirror behind the bar. In it, I could see he was grinning.

We were all feeling pretty good, for reasons that seemed as divorced from reality as the swing tips Clayton Mote heard from Ben Hogan. Bobby was still blind, functionally broke, and a very short distance away from selling pencils. I was still lonely, quietly carrying a heavy jones for Angela, and about to lose Eadon Branch. Angela was still pining for Bobby, I guess, but telling herself to be glad he was thinking about Paula. Maybe we felt good because the thunderstorm we'd driven through just north of town had cleansed the air, made things a little cooler. Maybe it was the way Dr. Mehta had thanked us for coming and encouraged us to come again. Clayton hadn't made any progress that I could notice, but Mehta seemed to think good things were happening.

On the TV set, the first Thursday night college football game of the season on ESPN ended and they switched to *SportsCenter*. A guy named Duke was doing the news by himself for some reason. They usually have two anchors. Duke gave the baseball scores, and a little about the NFL injury list for Sunday's opening games.

"And in golf," Duke said, "the PGA Championship has a new home. You remember that the tournament was washed out by Hurricane Gabe last month. Horseshoe Bend Golf Club couldn't repair its greens in time to hold the event this season. So tycoon F. Rockwell Peddy stepped up with an offer the PGA couldn't refuse. Peddy's putting up three million dollars and the PGA is putting on its championship two weeks from now at the legendary Sand Valley Golf Club, in the New Jersey hinterlands between Philadelphia and Atlantic City, where Peddy owns several casinos. Sand Valley is perennially ranked as the best, toughest, and most intimidating course in the world, but it has never hosted a professional championship. The exclusive club felt it didn't have the facilities to accommodate the spectators and the media that accompany a major event. But Sand Valley recently added some new, longer tees to bring the course up to modern length. With the PGA in a bind, the club decided to make a onetime exception. Small gate receipts won't be a problem with Peddy putting up most of the purse. And he'll house the players and the press at his Atlantic City hotels. The golf world will finally get to see the best players testing themselves on the game's best course."

The television cut to a beer commercial. I grabbed the remote from the bar and turned it off. No one said anything for a moment.

"You get the feeling someone's trying to tell us something?" I asked.

"Sand Valley," Bobby said. "Wow."

I knew what he was thinking. He'd finished tenth in the last PGA. That meant he was exempt from having to qualify for this year's tournament. But the way I saw it, if he couldn't handle a Myrtle Beach course in a Cooters Tour event, how could he even think about playing Sand Valley in a major championship?

"You could play, Bobby," Angela said, ever the cheerleader.

Bobby made like he really wasn't interested. "Ah, I didn't enter the first time," he said. "Even if they didn't think I'd stink the place up, they'd probably say the field was set when the entries first closed."

He turned his head my way. He wanted me to tell him that wasn't a problem, that the change in the schedule meant that there'd be some dropouts, especially along the Europeans, so he could claim his place. I didn't.

"It'll be a tougher course than the one in Myrtle Beach," I said. "I hear they have some bunkers there, you can hear people speaking Chinese down toward the bottom of 'em."

Now Bobby could play the picked-on role. "You're trying to discourage me," Bobby said. "Haven't you ever heard people are supposed to encourage the blind?"

"I'll encourage you not to drive GoKarts anymore."

I drew a breath, ready to go on with a long list of things I'd encourage Bobby about, but he interrupted me.

"I'm sorry about that stuff," he said. "It's in the past."

"Right," I said, sarcastic as hell. "Bobby, it's in you."

Bobby looked pained. "Don't you believe a person can change?"

I thought of Clayton Mote. "Yeah," I said. "But only for the worse."

Angela looked wounded when I said that, and I was sorry I'd hurt her feelings. But, really—if it was easy to change, we'd all have flat bellies and straight As on our report cards and Bobby probably would've won the PGA and a lot of other tournaments.

Bobby sipped at his beer. He was thinking so hard I could almost hear gears grinding in his skull.

I had an idea.

"You want to play in it, don't you?" I asked him.

He nodded. "What the hell else am I going to do for a living? Photography?"

"Tell you what," I said. "I'll make you a bet."

Bobby perked up. He'd never heard of a bar bet he couldn't win. "Okay," he said. "What is it?"

"Let's play a little night golf, just like Jack Nicklaus and Stevie Wonder," I said. "Sudden death at Eadon Branch. You and me. You win, I'll caddie for you if the PGA lets you in the tournament. I win, you never mention it again."

Bobby half got out of his stool, then sat down again. "How're you going to play?" he asked me. "You can't see in the dark."

"I got a sleeve of those fluorescent, glow-in-the-dark balls some-where in the shop."

"Glow in the dark?" Bobby asked.

"Yeah. They got some kind of insert in them that glows for an hour or so. Chemicals," I said, as if I knew something about chemicals.

Bobby thought some more. "You got a conflict of interest," he said. "How'm I going to know you're lining me up straight? You could make me miss, just so's you'd win the bet."

I shrugged my shoulders. "You gotta trust me," I said.

He nodded. "And you don't get any strokes?"

"That's right."

Slowly, a smile spread over his face. "All right, Coach," he said. "I trust you. You're on."

"Hey," Angela intervened. "What about me? Don't I get to play? I could be on your team, Henry."

I looked at her. She looked innocent. Of course, she could look innocent robbing a bank. It occurred to me that she was figuring that with her
on my side, I'd lose, and then Bobby could make me caddie for him.

"Yeah," Bobby said. "Alternate shot."

I looked at Angela. "You'll play hard?" I asked her. I knew she'd been
hitting golf balls fairly regularly while Bobby and I practiced. I didn't
think she could actually hit the ball well, but I didn't want her batting it
sideways.

She didn't blink. "Of course," she said.

"We need two strokes a hole," I said to Bobby.

"One," he offered.

"It's a deal," Angela said quickly.

I snorted. I wouldn't have agreed to it except for two things. One was
that I didn't think the PGA was going to let Bobby play, not if Cade
Benton had anything to say about it. And two is that I wanted to be partners with Angela, even if it was for something as goofy as this.

We all have our ulterior motives.

"Two strokes would be stealing from him," Angela said sweetly.

"Damn straight, Partner," I said.

So we bought a six-pack to go and bid good night to Gully's, leaving
Rebecca Pollard smoldering at the other end of the bar, with her transient
trucker still working hard.

It had turned into a beautiful night. The moon was three-quarters
full and the sky was cloudless; that thunderstorm had pushed a mass of
clean air into the Gaulor Valley. It smelled as soft and sweet outside as the
first kiss I got from Peggy Shiflett.

I got the strangest feeling driving over to the course in the truck, Angela
flush against me and Bobby riding shotgun, the wind rushing in through the
open windows. Every muscle in my body seemed to be primed, almost tin-
gling. I had a hollow feeling in my gut, but I didn't feel nauseous or frightened. It was like I was readier than I'd ever been in my life.

I figured it was Angela's proximity. Of course, it might've just been
the beers, because we were all three stumbling and giggling a little when
we got out of the truck and walked around to the front side of the clubhouse. Bobby was whistling something and it took me a minute to pick
up on the tune. It was "Georgia on My Mind," and I knew why that song

was rattling around in his head when he got to the bit about moonlight in the pines.

Angela and I could see it, see the way the moon cast deep, dark shadows on the golf course and turned the bunkers into spectral apparitions. He had to imagine it, and that's what he was doing for himself. Any other time, it would've saddened me and probably Angela, too. But on this particular evening, It didn't. It just made me appreciate what I was seeing more than I would ever have done before.

I opened up the shop and found the night balls and my golf bag. We stepped out onto the first tee and looked down at the fairway spread out before us, at the way the starlight glinted off Eadon Branch and turned it a dappled silver, like the underside of a rainbow trout.

"Oh, God, it's so gorgeous," she said and then she couldn't say anything else for a minute. She just had to contemplate it.

"Bobby," she went on, "the pines look like church spires in the darkness. The night sky is almost purple and there are a zillion stars. Some of them are big and bright and some of them are just like clouds of sugar way out there. The moon is big and white and hanging over Eadon Mountain. And the fairways look ghostly and gray."

Bobby stood there for a moment, as if he, too, was seeing what Angela and I were seeing. "Angela M. Murphy," he said. "Don't go getting poetic on me."

"That's right," I chimed in. I didn't want to have to try to match her in the poetic descriptions category for fear I'd reveal how poor and barren my mind was. So I changed the subject. "What are the rules here?"

"You and Angela alternate shots, against me," Bobby said. "You get one stroke. Rules of golf."

"All right!" Angela yelled. "Who's the honor?"

I decided not to correct her golfing syntax. Instead, I pulled out the golf balls and pushed in the fluorescent inserts. It must've been the same stuff they used for the kryptonite props in the *Superman* movies. The balls glowed green like very sick, very bloated fireflies. They were oddly cool to the touch.

"You're the honor," I told Bobby. He was fingering the club I'd given him, the TaylorMade demo driver I used. I got him lined up and, just to be fair, I pointed him down the middle. Without warming up or anything, after about six beers, he was pretty badly impaired. He only hit it about 260 down the fairway. Of course, it might've been that glow-in-the-dark golf balls don't travel quite as far as your average Titleist.

"Damn," he said. "Feels like I'm hitting a wooden ball. Sounds weird, too."

"But, you know, it sure looked good. Like a UFO," I said. "We're gonna get ink in the *National Enquirer*. 'Little green spaceships sighted over Virginia mountains.'" I told him where the ball had gone. I could see it, vaguely, down in the fairway, glowing faintly.

Now it was our turn to hit, and I explained the options to Angela. I wanted her to say right away that I should tee off, but damned if she didn't take a minute of cogitation to come to that conclusion.

I teed up the second ball. I'd calmed down a little bit while I focused on getting those inserts in, but I still had some of that feeling of being primed that I'd had coming over in the truck. Then I had a premonition that I was going to dribble the ball off the tee, just foozle it as Clayton Mote had liked to say, and that Angela would laugh at me. It was so real that I shuddered. But I reminded myself that I didn't need a perfect swing and I wasn't hitting into Clayton's little woodland alley. This was a big target.

So I relaxed a little and made a good, strong turn and stayed balanced. That green ball did feel like wood. And it looked weird, going up over the tree line for a moment, hanging in the air like a strange new star, then falling to earth. It was thirty yards short of Bobby's, but it was out there and in the fairway.

"Whoo!" Angela yelled. "All right, Partner!"

She high-fived me. I tried to act nonchalant. I was floating, though. There's nothing like hitting a good first tee shot in front of a woman you want to impress. And Angela was making me feel like she really was my partner, that she was rooting for us.

She had that knack.

I shouldered the bag and we set out. The rain had left the grass damp and soft, but there hadn't been enough to make the footing muddy. It was just the kind of rain you want for a golf course every evening, and you could almost smell the turf growing underneath us. But it was a little slippery, so I moved slowly as we went down the hill in front of the tee, Bobby with his right hand on the butt of the bag. Angela walking beside me, skidded a little, and reached out for my free shoulder. She kept her hand there the rest of the way down. I didn't mind. I felt like a balloon. Even if I slipped, I'd just float. They'd float with me.

Bobby was still whistling "Georgia on My Mind."

We got clear of the branches of the elm over the tee and we could see the holes to our left. "Look at the moon on the pond," Angela said. She pointed. The water looked still and deep and the moon's reflection was a single, glistening, wavy column of pale white, the color of an eggshell.

"No wonder people park there," she said, and she was right.

"Let's not talk about parking," Bobby said. "I'm trying to concentrate on golf."

Angela looked at me. "See?" she asked. "People can change."

I laughed and was about to say something sarcastic, something nasty. But I didn't. Even I couldn't be but so cynical with a woman like Angela on a moonlit night like that.

"'Course," Bobby said, "I don't really know if I can hit the ball without thinking about sex. Never having tried it and all."

Angela cut him off, not happy with the drift his mind was taking. "Are we here to yack, or are we here to play golf?" she demanded.

"Hey, this is what guys do on the golf course," Bobby said, feigning offense. "They bare their souls."

"Do it when it's your turn to hit," Angela said.

"Women are so insensitive," I said.

"Got that right," Angela said. We were approaching our ball. "All right, Partner," she said. "Whatta we got here?"

"About two-fifty to the middle," I said.

"What club are you figuring? Smooth seven?"

I didn't know whether she was serious or whether she really thought she could hit a seven-iron that far.

"Might be too much," I said. "Wouldn't want to Blue Angel this one."

"Damn," Angela said. "Every time I think I've got the slang down, you throw a new one at me. What does 'Blue Angel' mean?"

"Fly over," I told her. "As in fly over the green."

"Oh." She nodded.

"Whyn't you take an eight and just try to make good contact," I suggested.

"Yeah, Angela, I don't think you'll fly the green with an eight," Bobby said.

I gave it to her and she hefted it. Put it in her hands with a baseball grip. I figured this was not the time to give her a lesson.

The jeans and black polo shirt she wore seemed to make the middle of her body disappear in the darkness. She was all pale arms and face, glowing in the moonlight. Under a black cap, her hair looked dark and shining. She stepped up to the ball and her naturally inward turning knees got a little more knocked until she looked like a kid on ice skates. But then it got apparent that she'd picked a few things up watching Bobby. She didn't look like a total novice. She waggled the club a few times and then stopped.

"If I swing, it counts, right?" she asked.

Bobby was standing there, hands on hips, facing in her direction as if he could see her. Now he smiled benevolently. "Of course it counts," he told her. "Try to hit it as hard as you can."

"No, Partner," I said. "That'd be doing it the way Bobby does in the last round of a major. Swing easy. You don't have to hit it perfect."

Bobby laughed.

She looked at us both and winked at me. She took a nice slow back-swing, kind of shifting her shoulders instead of turning, but she kept some balance and rhythm and came down and made contact. It was a thin little shot that took off like a mad bee about three feet off the ground, flew for about ninety yards and rolled twenty more.

She turned and looked at me for a reaction.

"All right, partner," I cheered. "That's our wedge shot."

She whooped. We high-fived again. I was starting to like this game.

"How far out are you now?" Bobby asked.

"It'll be about one-fifty," I guessed.

He nodded. "Okay. That'll mean one more for Greyhound that'll be fat and short, then Angela chips up, two putts and you might make six with a stroke handicap. Looks like I need a birdie."

I ignored the insult. "Looks like," I said.

We walked up to Bobby's ball. I checked the yardage against a dogwood tree off to the right side of the fairway.

"Two-thirty," I told him.

"Gotta go for it," Bobby said. "Two-iron."

I set him up behind his real ball. I didn't have to describe the hole, we'd played it so often. Now, though, he didn't trust me. "Angela, where's he got me pointed?" he demanded.

Angela stood behind me and sighted down the line between the clubface and the ball. "Right at it," she said.

He still didn't believe it. "I bet you got me lined up a little right, figuring I'll fade it into that bunker."

With that, he turned himself about six degrees left. "You're a smart one, Bobby," I said.

And, of course, he turned it over a little bit, still thinking we were trying to sucker him into the right bunker. It was a good shot, ending up pin high. But it was in the weeds to the left of the green.

"Oh, too bad, Bobby," Angela giggled. "Looks like you're going to need a machete."

We didn't high-five this time. I gave her the clenched fist and we tapped knuckles. I didn't care. I just wanted to keep having a reason to touch her. I pulled three beers out of the bag and passed them around.

"You really had me lined up straight?" Bobby asked as we walked toward my ball.

"Right at it," I confirmed.

"Durn," he muttered in mock dudgeon. "Just when you least expect it, an honest caddie."

I ignored that. Our little green orb was glowing coolly on the damp grass, even with the boxwood shrub in the rough that marked 150 yards. I put the clubs down and Angela guided Bobby to a stop.

"Smooth eight, Partner?" she asked me.

She was really into it.

"A seven," I replied. "These balls don't go as far as the regular ones."

She nodded wisely. "That must be why I didn't reach the green."

"Must be," I agreed with her.

I couldn't see the flag, but I had an advantage. I remembered where I'd put the hole when I'd mowed the greens at dawn that morning. It was just a little left of center, maybe ten paces in from the front edge. So I picked out one of the tree silhouettes on the horizon and aimed at it. And I hit it good. The little green ball stayed right on my target tree with that

crisp forty-five-degree arc you get from a properly struck seven-iron. It's
the best-looking shot in golf, in my opinion—a seven-iron tracking right
at the flag.

In fact, I'd hit this one too good. I could tell it was going to be long.
Angela didn't know that, though, and she whooped it up like the ball had
gone in the hole. Her smile sort of infected me, and I started singing
about peaceful dreams and Georgia roads as we walked up the fairway.
Angela and Bobby joined in. We sounded like three cats in a fight. It
didn't matter. We loved hearing our voices in the night air, sensing a little
echo off the face of Eadon Mountain. We caterwauled all the louder.

It turned out that Angela and I were about twenty-five feet past.
Bobby was away and his lie wasn't good. The ball looked like a buried
ember sitting down in the grass—if embers were green. I took Bobby's
hand and placed it in the grass behind the ball. Then we walked up onto
the green and along the rough path to the hole. He'd have to find a way to
hack it out of the grass, play it a little above the hole, and stop it quickly
because the green sloped away from him.

"And you're in two-putt range?" he asked.

"I don't know," I said. "I'm going to have to hit one of them."

"So you three-putt," he said. "I still need birdie to win."

He asked for the sand wedge and took a few practice swings, to get a
feel for how resistant the grass was. Being wet, the lie was a little heavier
than it would've been during the day. Then he set up behind the ball, got
the line from me, and swung.

It was a marvelous shot.

He blasted the grass under the ball like it was a sand shot. The ball
floated onto the green, lit gently, and rolled slowly toward the hole. I
thought it was going in. Angela started to shout. But it hit the flagstick
and lipped out, stopping about six inches below the cup.

"Oooh," she said. "Great shot."

I described it for him, still amazed at what he could do under circumstances like these. The man had a gift. I picked up his ball. "We'll give
you that one. Nice four."

Bobby strode onto the green like Chi Chi Rodriguez, smiling, doffing
his cap to an imaginary crowd.

"Take that, PGA!" he shouted to the moon.

He swirled his wedge in the air in front of him like a sword, then jammed it into an imaginary scabbard.

"Uh, I'd leave that to Chi Chi," I said. "You might poke someone's eye out."

Now it was our turn. Angela was softly whistling as I handed her the putter. She hunkered down behind the ball and stared over it toward the cup. I stood behind her, put my hands on my knees, and bent over her head. I could smell the soap she'd used in her hair that morning, mingled with the evening dew and the smell of the grass. The moonlight shone in her hair. I took a deep breath.

She moved her hands to her face, cupping them around her eyes, making a visual tunnel.

"I never understood why Tiger Woods does this when he putts," she said. "I still don't."

"Keeps the moonlight out of his eyes," I suggested.

"Yeah," she murmured. "We gotta make this, don't we?"

"If we want to win the hole," I said.

"Oh, we want to win," she told me.

We stared down to the hole some more, and something unusual happened. I could see the line of the putt. It wasn't one of those stupid things you see in a movie sometimes where a neon light guides the way to the hole. This was real life. There was no neon. I could just tell where the ball had to roll to go into the hole. The line started out about a foot right of the hole. And it curled gradually toward the dark cup, like the curve of a bow when an arrow is nocked, a gentle bend that got a little sharper at the end. I was as sure of that line as I was of the path between my bed and the bathroom.

"Whattaya think?" she whispered.

I figured she didn't see it. So I described the line to her, not telling her that I could actually sense it, and I helped her line up the putter till it was aimed exactly right.

"How hard do I hit it?" she whispered.

It was a downhill putt and I figured that the risk was she'd hit it too hard.

"Just hard enough so it sneaks in the side door as it dies," I said.

"That's what 'die it in the hole' means?" she asked.

"Yep."

She stroked the putt. Somehow, she started it out right on the line, though she hit it a little harder than I'd wanted. But that little green bugger hugged that line like it was a railroad track, took the curve, and headed for the hole. It was one of those putts where you know halfway that it's got a chance and then you have a second or so of excruciating suspense, watching it make for home.

"Get in the hole!" I yelled.

It did, just like a rabbit scooting into its burrow, like it knew where it had to go. It clunked in the cup.

"Yes!" I hollered.

Angela, in front of me, leaped in the air, hands upthrust like a ref signaling touchdown, her shoulders up around her ears. Her hat came off. "It went in," she shouted.

And she leaped right into my arms, threw her hands around my back, and hugged me, she was so delighted.

I couldn't help myself. I kissed her.

It was like diving into the clear, cool water of the old granite quarry on the other side of Allegheny Gap at the end of a long summer day of work—sweet, delicious, and bracing all at the same time. It felt like seeing your home after a long time lost.

And then she kissed me back.

She squeezed just a little with the arms she'd wrapped around me, and her lips kind of worked against mine. They tasted like honey, but warm, firm, live honey.

Then I felt her stiffen. I opened my eyes in time to see her pull away. I tried to read what I saw on her face.

Surprise, for sure. Maybe shock.

She took another step back and grinned at me a little, kind of crooked. I couldn't tell if she was telling me she liked it or she was just embarrassed.

"Nice putt," I said.

She grinned wider, with her whole mouth.

"I think I'm starting to like this game," she said.

"I can't believe it," Bobby grumbled.

"Who is that?" a voice called out. "Henry, is that you?"

It was Eudora. I looked in the direction of the sound and saw the white light of a flashlight coming up toward the first green from the direction of the cart shed. I heard the whine of an electric cart motor.

"Put away the shotgun, Mrs. Mote!" Bobby yelled. "We'll surrender!"

"Hi, Eudora," Angela called. She sounded like she was welcoming her to a party. I noticed that she stayed a little closer to me than normal. We weren't touching, but she was in my space, or I was in hers. It was nice.

If Eudora noticed anything, she didn't show it. As she drew closer, the moonlight started to outshine the flashlight and illuminate her a little. She was wearing jeans and an old flannel shirt that she generally wore when she had chores to do. Underneath that, I could see a bit of her night-shirt, so I guessed she'd gotten out of bed. And she didn't look too festive. Actually, she looked grim.

"I swear, I almost called the sheriff," she said after she'd scanned the light over the three of us and satisfied herself we weren't vandals. "I could hear you people up to the house."

"Hi, Eudora," I said. "We drove past the house when we got back into town and there were no lights on, so we figured you'd gone to bed."

"You got that right," she said.

I realized, suddenly, that this probably wasn't the first time she'd come down to this golf course late at night after hearing someone being too noisy, not the first time she'd had to defend the place by herself, as it were, and I felt a little ashamed for all those years I spent on Tour, not really caring about the burden she was carrying. I stepped forward and kissed her on the cheek.

"Sorry to wake you up," I said.

"We're celebrating," Angela said.

"What do you mean, we?" Bobby said. "I just lost a chance to enter the PGA."

The words came out of my mouth before I had a chance to think much about them. "Hell, Bobby," I said. "Go ahead and enter. I'll caddie for you."

I don't normally let someone off like that if they've lost a bet. I knew right away why I did it. It was because I thought it was what Angela wanted to hear. I wanted her to think of me as magnanimous and generous.

She grinned. Bobby looked surprised.

"You sure you want to do that, Coach?" he asked me.

"Go ahead and enter," I said. "Before I change my mind."

"All right!" Angela exclaimed. She clapped her hands together.

I wondered at that moment whether Angela hadn't been pulling a little reverse psychology of her own. I looked at her. Her blue eyes were gleaming in the moonlight. She looked as innocent as fresh grass in April.

THE NEXT MORNING, BOBBY FAXED HIS ENTRY DOWN TO THE PGA HEAD-quarters in Florida. That was Friday, the beginning of the Labor Day weekend. We practiced all day Saturday, all day Sunday, half the day Monday. Bobby was hitting the ball well. His putting was shading toward good. But by Monday afternoon, we couldn't concentrate anymore. We had to know. Bobby said the PGA office had a weekend crew, and he would call them. He placed the call from the pay phone by the men's room door. I went back behind the counter with Eudora and Angela to wait for the news.

We didn't have any chance to brood about what might happen. Labor Day was the day of the annual Allegheny Gap Headlight Tournament, which J. R. Neill organized. The rule was you had to have a miner's hard hat with a headlight on it to play. We had a couple of dozen miners in the shop, drinking beer, adding up scores, and arguing about handicaps. They were scarfing down hot dogs and cheese sandwiches like they were potato chips. Their orange and yellow hard hats, streaked black with coal grime, bobbed up and down around their tables as they ate and drank. It was one of our busiest days of the year.

"Eudora, where do you keep the hot dogs?" Angela called out.

"Should be another box in the back of the freezer," Eudora replied from the cheese sandwich station. "I bought extra."

I was grabbing a fresh six-pack from the bottom of the refrigerator, so I opened the top side and got the hot dogs. I gave them to Angela without saying anything or even making eye contact. It wasn't just that we were busy. To tell the truth about it, I was afraid if I talked to her very much she'd say something to let me know that that kiss on the first green was just something caused by the beer and the moonlight.

"Thanks, Henry," she said.

"You're welcome," I replied.

That's the way we were being—polite. She was back in her own space and I was in mine.

Bobby came back from the pay phone, trailing a hand lightly over the corners of the tables and the backs of the chairs to orient himself. When he got close to the counter, J. R. Neill, who was sitting there having his lunch, reached out and guided him to the last available stool. Bobby sat down.

It was hard to tell exactly what he'd heard. His face reflected nothing. His lips were set in a straight line, but he didn't look mad or anything. Just like he was thinking about something.

"What'd they say?" I asked him.

"Well, Coach," he said. "It's not good news."

"They won't let you play?"

He shook his head.

"Why not?"

I wasn't totally surprised. I'd seen enough rulings from the people who ran golf to know they were capable of almost anything. It wasn't that they meant to be harebrained. They didn't. They just were. Put a blazer on some guys and their minds get a little flinty.

But I'd figured that even the blazers wouldn't make them forget the P.R. pounding they'd taken in the Casey Martin case. I saw Bobby in the same category—a golfer with a disability that had to be accommodated.

I'd figured wrong.

"They say it's because I entered late, although they have had some cancellations from the Europeans. And they say they don't think the rules changes I need are fair to the rest of the field."

"Not fair?" Angela had been listening, and now she jumped in. "What do they mean, 'not fair'? How else are you supposed to play?"

"They said Casey Martin riding in a cart didn't directly affect striking the ball. Blind rules do."

"Why? Henry doesn't swing for you. He just helps you get set up."

Bobby shrugged. "They don't see it that way."

"Bastards," J. R. Neill said.

"Did they say anything about your playing ability?" I asked.

He shook his head. "Nope. They just talked about my entry being late and the rules. I'm sure they know about that damn eighty-nine. They said

I hoped I realized that if they gave a spot to me, they'd be taking it away from someone on the alternate list who could take the spot and maybe play well and win some money to keep his card."

"You got a lawyer?" I asked Bobby.

"You should sue!" J. R. said, excited.

Bobby shook his head again. "Nope. I do have a lawyer. But it would cost me thousands of dollars just to get started on a suit, file papers, and whatnot. Maybe fifteen grand."

"So?" I asked him.

He shook his head. "I don't have enough money to risk it. That's a lot just to try to get into a tournament where I might not win any money."

I wished like hell he wasn't wearing those Oakleys, so I could get a look in his eyes. "You said you thought you could play."

He smiled, but it was a weak smile. "I do, Coach," he began. "But—"

I cut him off. "Shut up," I told him.

I went to the drawer under the register where Eudora kept the checkbook we used to pay the Eadon Branch bills. I found a pen. I wrote a check. I could see Bobby listening to the sound of the pen on the paper, wondering what I was doing.

I put it in his hand.

"What's this?" he asked.

"It's a check for my half of fifteen thou," I said. "If we're in this, we're in it fifty-fifty."

Eudora looked like she was going to burst—and not with pride.

"My money, Eudora," I said to her. "I'll cover it."

Covering it would take about two-thirds of the Henry Mote personal fortune, but somehow it seemed to me to be worth it. I didn't have a wife or kids to worry about. And the mines were hiring. Besides, the only way I could think of to come up with a quarter million dollars to pay off the note on Eadon Branch was to get half the $750,000 winner's purse that F. Rockwell Peddy was putting up.

Bobby just held the check in his hands, running a finger up and down its edge, not saying anything.

"I want a piece of that," J. R. Neill said. He reached in his pocket and pulled out his wallet. He opened it up and fished a couple of hundred-dollar bills out. He stuffed them into Bobby's hand.

"I wanna be able to tell people that I got hustled by a future PGA champ," he said. "Pay me back out of your winnings."

"I can't let you—" Bobby started to object.

But Conrad was, as usual, right next to J. R. And, as usual, Conrad followed J. R.'s example. He pulled a couple of hundred from his wallet—in tens and twenties.

"Pay me back from your winnings," he repeated.

I was amazed at the walking-around money J. R. and Conrad were carrying. Maybe we hadn't been charging a high enough green fee.

Bobby didn't say anything for a moment, just kept running his fingers up and down over the check and the cash like he was trying to read the print on them with his fingers. He didn't shed any tears, but he did grope around for a paper napkin and blow his nose.

"You guys shouldn't do this and I can't accept it," he said, extending his hand and proffering the money.

No one took any. Eudora, in fact, reached into the cash register and pulled out the day's green fees, a short stack of tens and twenties. She pressed the money into Bobby's hand. He held it there, uncertain, then let his hand drop slowly to the countertop.

"You're the playing pro out of Eadon Branch Golf Club," she said. "We're sponsoring you."

"Better odds than Powerball, Eudora," J. R. said.

She nodded in agreement.

The room had gotten quiet as the rest of the miners heard what was going on. Then Conrad took his hard hat off, turned it upside down, and dropped another twenty dollars into it. He passed it around the room.

Angela's eyes were glistening. She leaned over to Bobby and whispered in his ear, explaining, I guess, what was happening and why the noise from the miners had changed from the previous raucous cacophony to a purposeful murmur.

The hard hat came back. There must've been another thousand dollars in it, wrinkled old green bills nestled inside the gray plastic lining, worn shiny from use. I just took Bobby's hand and pressed it inside, let him feel the money.

"Well . . . ," he said. His voice was cracking a little.

"Bobby, shut up and go practice," J. R. growled.

"Kick some butt, Bobby," Conrad said.

"Yeah," one of the miners chimed in. There was a round of applause.

Fortunately, no one said, "You da man," or I'd've lost my lunch. It was a damn sight too sentimental for me as it was.

We did practice, till dark that day. But only after we made two phone calls. Bobby called his lawyer in Georgia and instructed him to file a suit to force the PGA to let him play.

And I called the Associated Press and had them patch me through to Ken Alyda. I figured a little publicity mightn't hurt our chances.

WHAT I HADN'T COUNTED ON WAS A WHOLE LOT OF PUBLICITY. BUT ONCE Alyda's story hit the wires, our phone started ringing and it didn't let up. Bobby talked to CNN, ESPN, MSNBC, NBC, CBS, ABC, and UPI. The only abbreviation that didn't call was NASA. Then he and Angela ducked out to McDonald's to get some food. I fielded calls from the *New York Times* and the *Atlanta Constitution*. By ten o'clock, calls were starting to come in from overseas, and we were both fed up with it, and so we let Angela be our spokeswoman to a reporter from *Yomiuri Shimbun* out of Tokyo.

"That's correct," she said after listening to what must've been one of the longest interrogative sentences on record. "*Arigato* to you, too."

These reporters all had a tendency to tell you what they wanted to write and ask you if you agreed with it. If you did, it was a short interview. If you didn't, they might argue, or they might ignore you. But what they never did was call with an open mind and just try to get information.

But from the tone of the questions, I could tell that they were biased in our favor. Bobby was the little guy, the underdog in this story. The guy from the Atlanta paper asked me if I thought the "suits" at the PGA were prejudiced or just stupid. It wasn't hard to guess how his story would read.

Finally, at around ten-thirty, with the phone still ringing, Bobby said, "Let it ring. You think they can find us at Gully's?"

"You'd have to be pretty stupid not to figure we'd be out at a bar," I said.

"Some of the guys I've talked to sure qualify," Bobby said.

"Let's go," Angela said. "Film at eleven."

So we got a vantage point in the bar at Gully's and watched TV. The film, unfortunately, was not likely to be in any keepsake video Bobby would pass down to his descendants. First there was some tape from the previous year's PGA and the disastrous sixteenth hole. Then there was some footage of Bobby playing in the Cooters tournament down in Myrtle Beach. Neither one was flattering.

The stories themselves tended to emphasize Bobby's rights under the Americans with Disabilities Act, but that wasn't flattering, either. The underlying message was "Here's a guy who can't really play golf anymore, but he's got a legal right to try, except that those bozos who run golf are too bigoted to let him."

ESPN, at least, tried to be balanced. They'd managed to track down Little Dickie Reynolds, and they put him on to make the case for barring Bobby from the tournament.

Little Dickie Reynolds was one of those pro golfers who just can't seem to understand how privileged he is. He was always one of the first to whine if there was something wrong with the greens, or the rough was too high, as if playing for someone else's money on a course with bumpy greens was the equivalent of doing three years in a Mexican jail.

He seemed absolutely clueless about the lives of people who somehow got by on less than the two or three million a year he earned for playing golf. He'd made a well-publicized move from California, where he was from, to Florida. Said he couldn't stand paying all that tax money to a liberal, big-spending state government. When he was on the Ryder Cup team, he refused to meet with the president at the White House on the grounds that the president had dodged the draft back during Vietnam. Of course, Little Dickie had been about six years old during Vietnam, but he was absolutely certain that if the war had gone on another fifteen or twenty years and *he'd* been drafted, he'd've gone. And whenever someone raised a fuss about women or blacks not being, shall we say, on an equal footing in some of the clubs where tournaments were played, the reporters could always count on Little Dickie to say what did sports have to do with politics, anyway?

Despite, or maybe because of, those things, Little Dickie was a revered figure in the golf world. For one thing, he was a traditionalist. He still used wooden clubs. He occasionally wore plus fours and he always wore a white linen cap with no advertising on it, just like Hogan. Beyond that, he was good. He'd won a Masters and a British Open.

"It's not that I wouldn't like to see Bobby Jobe have a chance," Little Dickie was saying. "He's a nice guy and he was a fine player. But there are some larger issues involved than just the misfortunes of one individual."

And what, the reporter asked, might those be?

"The integrity of the game," Little Dickie said. "Golf competitions have always been about a single individual. No one blocks for you. No one passes the ball to you. It's just you. A blind golfer—and we all feel sorry for Bobby Jobe, don't get me wrong—can't play by himself. He needs his caddie to set up his club, pick out his line, and do all the things that a sighted golfer is expected to do. He's playing a different game and it's not golf."

"Why do they call him Little Dickie?" Angela wanted to know. "He looks just as big as the guy who was interviewing him."

"Well, he says it's because his father's name was Richard," Bobby said. "But if his father's name was Jack, people who see him in the locker room might still call him Little Dickie, if you get my drift."

Angela grinned.

Surely, the reporter asked, Little Dickie didn't think blindness was an advantage.

"Of course not," Little Dickie said, clearly miffed by the question. "And no one is more sympathetic to the plight of the blind than I am. But—"

"Oh, please," Angela said to the television.

"But golf has rules. Anyone who wants to play has to play by the rules. Bobby Jobe, unfortunately, can't play by them."

Did Little Dickie think he could still play at all?

"Well, to be honest—and I admire Bobby for trying to make a comeback after his accident—from what I hear he can't. He has trouble breaking 90. Now the PGA Championship is about the best professional golfers in the world competing against one another. If we were to let Bobby enter, he'd be taking a spot away from someone who *is* one of the best professional golfers in the world."

I looked at Bobby. He couldn't see the bland, innocent look on Little Dickie's face, but the words were coming through clearly. Bobby's shoulders were drooping.

"Turn the damn thing off," I asked the bartender. After taking a glance at Bobby, he did.

11

▼

IT WOULD BE NICE IF I COULD TELL YOU COMMON SENSE, JUSTICE, AND kindness persuaded the PGA to let Bobby play.

It would be nice if I could tell you that Bobby's lawyer won a landmark lawsuit helping to establish the rights of the blind.

What happened was the bottom line persuaded the PGA to change its mind.

In golf a big chunk of the bottom line comes from television. Another big chunk comes from corporate promotions departments. CBS Sports would've had to be comatose not to notice the avalanche of publicity that we touched off. And F. Rockwell Peddy has never been shy about attracting attention, either. Before Bobby's lawyer could even have someone type up the papers for our case, CBS and Peddy were both leaning hard on the PGA to reverse itself. That's like having the power company lean on you to pay your electric bill. They had leverage.

We heard all this from Ken Alyda, the AP golf writer. He told me Tuesday morning that it would take about twenty-four hours for the PGA to figure out it had no choice but to knuckle under. And he was right, almost to the minute.

At ten o'clock Wednesday morning, Eudora hustled out of the shop and down to the practice green, where Bobby and I were working on long sand shots. This was an act of faith. Sand Valley Golf Club, we knew, has enough sand to qualify as a beach resort except that it's thirty miles from the ocean. It's got so much sand that they don't even rake it after they hit out of it. I figured that even though we weren't in the tournament yet, we had to act as if we were. And that meant getting ready for a lot of long sand shots.

We were working on a theory of mine that it's best to hover the club just over the ball, without touching it, when you address that shot. It makes it a little easier to make contact with the ball without first hitting sand. In greenside bunkers, Bobby was accustomed to having me lay the sole of the club in the sand behind the ball. That was good for explosions, but not for shots where he needed to pick it clean. Hovering the club over the ball without touching it took a little practice. It wasn't hard for a sighted person to pick up, but the sighted person had that visual feedback to use in orienting the clubhead.

Eudora looked like she'd just gotten a call from the lottery telling her there'd been a mistake in last week's Powerball drawing. She had hold of the folds of her skirt to help her move faster. "Telephone for you, Bobby," she said. She lowered her voice till she was almost whispering, even though Bobby and I were the only people around.

"It's the PGA," she said.

Bobby went ahead and hit the shot he'd been preparing, a seven-iron that he caught clean and sent straight down the practice fairway about 160 yards. I noted the distance. He lost 5 or 6 yards off his normal seven-iron using that technique.

"What do you think, Eudora?" he asked her. "Should I take their call?"

She didn't understand he was kidding.

"You better," she said, in a voice I remembered her using to make sure I did my homework.

"I don't know," he said. "Maybe you better tell 'em I'm out at an art gallery shopping for paintings."

There was a bitter edge to his voice. Bobby hadn't said much about the way being kept out of the tournament made him feel. That was as close as he came. He cracked little jokes with an edge to them.

"I think you better go up to the shop and talk to 'em, Bobby," I advised him, "before Eudora can find the bunker rake and whup your butt with it."

"Oh, well in that case, sure," Bobby said. He oriented himself to the sound he'd heard from Eudora, walked up out of the bunker, and stretched out his hand. She took it, smiling a little, and led him up the hill to the shop, just like he was her boyfriend.

BY THE TIME I FINISHED RAKING THE BUNKER AND FOLLOWED THEM IN, Eudora was absently checking the numbers on a thin sheaf of lottery tickets. The jackpot was up to sixty-two million, but she wasn't really paying much attention at that moment. She was trying too hard to listen to Bobby's conversation without appearing to snoop.

"Uh-huh." Bobby was nodding.

"That's right," he said.

"I understand."

With that, I figured Ken Alyda had gotten it wrong.

"Okay," Bobby finished up. "Thank you. Bye."

He hung up the phone slowly, with a curious kind of expression on his face like he was dazed or shocked. He didn't look happy.

"I'm in," he said.

"In the tournament?" I asked him.

He nodded and sat down. He didn't look jubilant. He looked worried. I could relate to that.

I remembered back to when I played football for the Hilltoppers and wanted worse than anything to be a starter. Finally, at the beginning of senior year, the coach tells me I'm his starting left guard. And instead of being happy about it, all I could think of was embarrassing myself in front of the whole town.

I guessed that Bobby was thinking, suddenly, that playing in a real Tour event meant returning to his peers and being judged by them. It meant cameras on him and millions of people watching if he screwed up. When you're striving to get in, you don't think about those things. You just want in. But once you're there, they're all you can think about. Every year on the Tour, I'd see guys who'd spent ten years of their lives trying to get a playing card and finally did it. And they came out and it took them six months to remember to breathe.

I thought I knew the way to snap Bobby out of this. I walked up to him and clapped him on the shoulder. "Showtime, Bobby," I said.

I figured I'd appeal to his vanity. He was always the kind of player who liked to strut after he hit a good shot.

"Yeah," he said in a flat, tired-sounding voice. "Showtime."

There wasn't any strut in it. If a voice had legs, this one would barely be crawling.

But he drew himself up a little and said, "Well, I guess we better do some practicing, Coach."

"Might be a good idea," I said.

"Got six days before we have to be in Jersey," he said.

"Lot of time," I told him.

"Enough to learn to play Sand Valley," he said.

"Definitely," I agreed.

Our voices were rising, and of course we were showing off for ourselves. But I was pleased anyway. For one thing, Bobby was reacting to pressure by asking to practice. For another, it was like we were talking ourselves into being cocky. And I figured that if we acted cocky, and felt cocky, and played golf like we were cocky, who'd know that we were both scared?

We headed back to the practice green. A breeze was blowing off Eadon Mountain and for the first time in months, it was a cool breeze. I looked up at the elm tree over the lesson tee. Some of its leaves had started to go yellow at the edges.

"We should call Angela, tell her before she hears it on the radio," I said to Bobby. Angela had gone back to Nashville for a couple of days.

"All right," he said. "And I want your father to go with us."

"What?" I'd heard him. I just didn't like what I'd heard.

"He figured out my swing faster'n anybody I ever worked with," Bobby said. "I want him around in case something goes wrong." He paused. "Besides, I can afford him."

"Just do me a favor," I said.

"Sure."

"When they interview you, don't say you're getting swing tips from Hogan."

BOBBY RENTED A CAR, A BIG OLDSMOBILE, FOR THE TRIP TO ATLANTIC CITY. It was just like the courtesy cars we used to get on the Tour, a nearly new, plain-vanilla piece of Detroit iron. Our bags and the clubs fit easily in the trunk. It was early Sunday morning, chilly. Just before we pulled out, J. R. and Conrad drove into the lot in J. R.'s GMC. J. R. was carrying an enve-

lope I recognized. It was the one I'd used to send back the money he'd collected from the miners to help pay for Bobby's lawyer. They got out and
shook hands with Bobby, told him Allegheny Gap was proud of him, and
they'd all be watching and rooting for him.

Then he gave me the money.

"Thanks, but we didn't need it," I said. I assumed they hadn't understood that the lawyers hadn't gotten involved. "We didn't have to sue," I
explained.

J. R. put a big, callused hand over the one I was using to proffer the
money. "We want you to bet it for us," he said. "They got betting in
Atlantic City, right?"

"I believe so," I told him.

"Well, put it on Bobby's nose," he said. "We figure you'll get good odds."

The envelope felt worn and wrinkled and warm in my hands and I
could see J. R. and Conrad and the rest of the miners debating what to do
with it, handling it. I knew it represented pretty much the money they
had left after the union and the government took their pieces of a day's
wage for tearing coal from the earth a half mile underground.

"I will," I said. "We'll get good odds."

Eudora hugged Angela and Bobby and wished him luck. She gave me
a bag of pimento cheese sandwiches and a kiss on the cheek.

"Now don't you go feeding Angela any of that junk you eat on the
road," she warned me.

I looked at Angela, wondering how much she and Eudora talked. But
Angela was looking Raggedy Ann that morning, completely innocent.
She had her hair done in thick, red bunches that flared above her collar.
She looked cheerfully, innocently back at me.

"I won't tell the Doritos people you said that," I answered.

"Do they have Powerball in New Jersey?" Angela asked.

"I don't know," Eudora said. "Probably."

"Well, if they don't, I'll call you and you can buy some tickets for me,"
Angela said.

"What's the jackpot up to?" I asked.

"Seventy-nine million," Eudora replied. "No one's won in weeks."

"Bound to be one of you," I said. I blew her a kiss and we were off.

Once we were on the road, Angela started chattering from the backseat in a way she rarely did, like she was just trying to fill up the silence. It was mostly about the head of her department back at the hospital in Nashville, and how she didn't really agree with this woman's approach to rehabilitating the blind, thought she was too cautious, too conservative. The woman was white canes and Braille. Angela was facial vision and talking computers.

She didn't say right out, but the talk reminded me that her time with Bobby was going to end. I'd been thinking about her a lot, of course, trying to think of a way to talk to her about how much her kiss had meant to me. But the more I thought as I drove along, the more foolish it seemed that saying that would be. I figured she was trying to tell me something— tell me that she was planning on going back to Tennessee after the PGA, that her work was her life, and all that.

When I'm afraid to do something, I can make up all kinds of good reasons not to do it.

DR. MEHTA HAD MADE A HALFWAY SUCCESSFUL EFFORT TO CLEAN UP CLAYTON Mote. He'd taken him to Kmart and bought some new clothes—a couple of pairs of khaki Dockers, some polo shirts, a pair of walking shoes. He'd made sure Clayton's beard was shaved and let his hair grow out enough to make you think this was a man who just liked short hair, not a man whose head once a week passed through the hands of a barber whose major concern was killing lice.

Not that Clayton figured to blend in. Didn't matter how he was dressed. There was still something about him that told you he wasn't right. There was the way he kept focusing his eyes in the wrong places. Normal people'll look you in the eye or they'll look at the ground, or maybe they'll look over your shoulder at something, like a clock or a pretty girl, but you'll still sense that their attention is focused rationally. Clayton didn't focus on anything normal. He'd have his eyes fixed on something like your kneecap, or the end table in the little lounge where we got together with him. Anywhere but your face. It was like looking you in the face for his brain would be like touching a hot burner on a stove for your finger. And, of course, there was the way his ear was always cocked to listen to voices no one else could hear, the way he sometimes mumbled responses to those voices.

I told myself that this was my father and I shouldn't worry what any-one else up there would think of him. But I couldn't help being nervous about it. Being the caddie for a blind golfer, knowing people were looking at him like they'd look at a zoo animal, knowing that my job was so much more than toting clubs, that was distraction enough. When I saw Clayton, I started to wonder whether taking him wasn't unfair to Bobby, even though Bobby'd said he wanted him along.

"Hello, Pro," I said, trying to smile. "Nice outfit."

He ignored all of us for a moment, just sat on that fake leather couch in the waiting room, staring at the end table, listening and mumbling.

Then he turned toward Angela. "Hogan knows the secret," he said, like he was letting her in on some delicious little lover's confidence. "Hogan knows. Hogan hates Snead."

Then he looked down at the floor and resumed mumbling.

Nice to see you, too, Dad.

We walked Clayton and his little plastic satchel out to the car. If he was excited to be leaving, to be heading for a golf tournament again, he didn't show it. Just kept looking at the ground and the trees and the sky like he hadn't seen them for a long time.

Before I got in the car, Dr. Mehta took me aside. He handed me a piece of paper with some telephone numbers. Some were his. Some were for a mental hospital near Atlantic City that I was supposed to call if Clayton got to be more than we could handle.

"I don't think these will be necessary," he said. "But just in case."

I stuffed the paper in my pocket, anxious not to look at it.

"A final word, Mr. Mote," he said. He took me by the arm. "I think this will be beneficial for your father or I wouldn't have permitted it," he said. "But I want to caution you not to expect too much."

"Oh, I don't," I said. And I didn't. I'd gotten off the white-horse thing.

"Sometimes the treatment of a disease is like waves washing against a rock," he said.

"What do you mean?"

"It looks as if the waves do not affect the rock. But then one day you look and the rock is smaller. One day it may even be gone."

I nodded. "Got it," I said. "Waves against a rock."

He was in my rearview mirror, watching the car pass through the hospital gates, before I remembered that it can take waves a million years to wear down a rock.

I drove, with Bobby riding shotgun and Angela in the back seat with Clayton. I mostly passed the time watching them in the rearview mirror and listening to Angela talk to him. She said something about everything we passed, from apple orchards to tollbooths. She'd ask whether Clayton liked apples, whether he saw the horses in the pastures, what he thought of the rapids in the Potomac River, whether he'd seen any televised games from the Orioles' new stadium, what kind of fish he might catch in the Delaware River. It sounds as if she treated him like a child, but she didn't. She was always respectful and her voice always carried the hope and expectation that he'd answer her question intelligently. Sometimes Bobby or I would join in with a comment or two. It didn't matter what she said. Clayton didn't respond to anything. Just piped up with an occasional "Hogan knows" or looked out the window and moved his lips, mumbling something to himself. Angela's patience impressed me.

I started to think about her patience and the sweet core of her soul, and before too long, I was getting careless with my driving. Damn near sideswiped a truck. So I put in a Patsy Cline CD and listened to her sing for a while.

Clayton might've talked, I knew, if Bobby or I had asked him about golf. But neither he nor I wanted to talk about it. Bobby seemed to have checked out most of the time. He had a forlorn, distant look on his face.

When we got to the causeway that links Atlantic City to the mainland, I tried to be jolly. "Looks a little like Oz, doesn't it?" I said.

And it did. The highway into town rolls past your normal low-rise American sprawl of shopping malls and gas stations and fast-food places for a mile or so, then hits a patch of brown, reedy marshland. Across a narrow bay lies Atlantic City. The casino hotels, late in the day, reflect the light from the setting sun and glitter brightly. Of course, at that distance, you can't pick out the surrounding neighborhoods, where the old houses are falling apart. Up close, Atlantic City is obviously an old resort trying to hang on by attracting gamblers. Up close, the Atlantic City hotels look like hookers in satin hot pants walking the street outside a soup kitchen. But from the causeway, everything looks better.

"You remember that movie, *The Wizard of Oz*?" I asked Clayton. "Feels like we're at the end of the yellow brick road, doesn't it?"

I looked in the mirror at Clayton. He was mumbling to himself, staring out the window at a billboard that told him Harrah's was where serious slot players go. If he was thinking about Oz, he didn't let it show in his face.

Another wave, I told myself, washing over the rock.

Il Palazzo wasn't hard to find. It had a neon sign in white, green, and red that must've been six stories high itself. The hotel was basically just a plain glass-and-steel box, but it was overlaid with a lot of plastic intended to suggest it was in Italy. When you drove up, there was actually a canal that led from the valet parking station to the door of the casino, and white gondolas, trimmed in gold paint, would carry you the last two hundred yards if you wanted. Right in front of the casino was a huge fountain, again white, that looked like that Roman fountain with all the statues where tourists throw coins. You see it in all the movies.

There was a big sign over the door that said, "F. Rockwell Peddy presents Il Palazzo."

I wasn't about to shell out whatever they were asking for valet parking, so I pulled a hard right at the gondola station and found the self-parking garage, another hundred yards or so farther from the action, but only fifteen dollars a day.

We walked through the garage and saw a sign that said, "Bus Lobby." A bus had pulled up and what looked like the entire population of a Philadelphia nursing home was getting out. There were women in wheelchairs, men with walkers. Inside the lobby they lined up to turn in their bus ticket stubs for five dollars' worth of slot machine tokens.

The sight of them got Clayton Mote's attention. He stopped mumbling and stared.

It was enough to get anyone's attention. They were like the Ghost of Christmas Yet to Come, a reminder that if you're not careful, you can grow old and find yourself so feeble that the only recreation you're capable of is sitting in front of a slot machine pulling levers and feeding quarters. And so bored that you're glad to do it.

I wasn't sure if Clayton saw them the same way, but something about them put him off. He turned away from them after a minute like you'd turn away from the gory part in a bad movie. He resumed his conversation with the inside of his brain.

They cured me of any desire to pass some time at the tables. I wanted to get out to the golf course five minutes ago.

So we checked in, got our small rooms without ocean views at the special tournament rate, and found out where the transportation desk was. I hadn't had a chance to unpack before the phone rang. It was Bobby.

"Let's go, Coach. I figure we can get out there and walk it before dark."

I looked at my watch. It was five-thirty. Bobby had never gone with me on one of my course inspection walks before. He'd never wanted to go out to a course this close to happy hour before.

"You know what time it is?" I asked him.

"I know we don't have enough of it," Bobby said. "Get the Pro and Angela. Tell 'em they can come. We can eat late."

"You feel okay, Bobby?"

"Sure, I feel fine. Why d'you ask?"

"Nothing," I said. "No reason."

MOST GOLF TOURNAMENT SITES THESE DAYS LOOK LIKE KING ARTHUR AND the Knights of the Round Table are camping out at a billboard factory. There are more white tents and more advertising signs than Jack Nicklaus has trophies. There are signs to tell you that so-and-so is the official mustard of the tournament and tents to hold all the wholesale mustard buyers that so-and-so wants to entertain. The players actually like seeing all this stuff. They know that's where all the dollars come from.

But that wasn't the kind of PGA Championship that Sand Valley Golf Club was going to put on. There were no tents, no sponsor signs. With F. Rockwell Peddy putting up the purse, there didn't have to be. In fact it would've been hard to know there was a tournament going on except for the television towers that carpenters were nailing together behind the greens and the yellow ropes along the fairways. They had a gate cut in the fence along the seventh hole to let spectators in, but they had to park far away and ride up in buses. Sand Valley looked much as it would on any other day.

That look was quiet. Sand Valley is not the sort of club to advertise itself. It's hidden away in a little New Jersey town with a couple of pizza parlors, a Core States Bank, and a Mobil station. I might've driven right by the entrance if I hadn't had a map.

Years ago, when the course was built, there was nothing in that part of New Jersey except sandy, hilly land that was no good for farming. A few guys from Philadelphia recognized the land's potential, though. They bought it cheap, put together a club from among the best golfers they knew, and designed a course to test those golfers—severely.

It was never a country club. No tennis courts. No swimming pool. No wedding receptions on Saturday afternoons. The golfers at Sand Valley had other clubs for those purposes. Sand Valley was just golf.

I started to get a feel for the place about a quarter mile after you make the turn from the little town. It's a private road. There's a guardhouse where you show your pass. You see a little clearing by the side of the road where, I suspected, the caddies had to park. TV trucks were in it. Then you go left around a curve and you're right below the eighteenth green.

You can see a fairway of crosshatched green, surrounded by sand and scrub. The whole thing is lined by woods that look darker than the forest around Sleeping Beauty's castle. You have to hit up from that fairway to the green, carrying the ball over bunkers that are big enough to hide the Eadon Branch pro shop in. Above them, you can see the top of a little red flag, flapping gently.

You get just that glimpse and then you're in the players' parking lot. Beyond it, you can see the clubhouse and a dormitory the club maintains for out-of-town members. They're just plain little frame buildings and at first—knowing that the membership at Sand Valley could afford to build a marble palace with champagne fountains—you think that these buildings must be maintenance sheds.

It was Angela who helped me figure out what I was seeing. "Somehow it reminds me of a monastery," she said.

I wondered when she'd seen a monastery. But the comparison wasn't bad. Of course, there was no chapel. But you had the sense that this was a place of retreat, a place of simplicity, a place where people examined their souls. The services and meditation just took place on the golf course.

It was around six by then, and the late sunlight was coming in bright white shafts through the chinks in the pines that soared all around us. Where it hit the grass, the green of it all but exploded in your eyes. In the shadows of the trees, though, the grass looked cool, dark, almost black. The sky above was a bright, clear blue.

There were lots of people around, but no one I knew. I'd been wondering what it would feel like to rejoin the Tour at long last. I felt disoriented, actually—like if you came back to a neighborhood you used to live in and found it full of strangers. It wasn't what I had imagined all those months back in Allegheny Gap.

I didn't let on about any of this to Bobby, or Clayton or Angela. I just let them trail along beside me, taking in the bits and pieces of the golf course you could see from the clubhouse area. Bobby's hand lay lightly on my shoulder. There was a tee on our left with a ravine and a pond in front of it and a green that looked to be about 240 yards out, all carry. There was a big green on the other side of the building, a green that sat lower than the fairway that led to it. Pine trees cast their shadows over it, shadows that seemed almost to wiggle in the undulations of the ground.

Bobby sniffed and turned slowly as if he could see it. "Some golf course, eh, Pro?" he said to Clayton. Clayton didn't reply, but he was looking, taking it all in.

"Let's go to eighteen green," Bobby said. I blinked. I hadn't known he knew I walked courses backward when I was checking them out. We headed across the lot toward the final hole.

"Young man!" a voice called out.

I turned and looked. It was Jello McKay.

We hadn't been close when I was on the Tour. I mean, we got along fine if we were both looping in the same group, but I'd never hung with Jello off the course. It wasn't a black versus white thing. It was more an old versus young thing, a soul versus country thing. But I greeted him then like my best friend come back from the dead. I gave him a quick hug, told him I was glad to see him. I really was. Jello was looking a little older, a little heavier, a little more grizzled around the edges. But he was looking good to me.

Bobby stuck out his hand. Jello looked at him coolly, then took it.

"Nice to have you back," Jello said. "Guess you won't be making any more remarks about skin color."

Bobby reddened. Angela looked curious.

But Bobby had the grace to apologize, which I had almost never heard him do. "Lot of things I won't be making remarks about anymore, Jello," he said. "Sorry if I pissed you off. Sorry I said it."

Jello looked as surprised as I did to hear it. There was a moment of awkward silence.

"Who you with?" I asked Jello.

"Some lucky unknown," he said.

"Who?"

"Don't know yet," he said. "That's why he's unknown."

Jello was looking for work.

"But he will be lucky, that unknown man," Jello said. He had that bravado in his voice that you usually hear from guys who are looking for a loop and maybe two weeks away from either finding a job or sleeping under a bridge. I thought Jello had a pension, but sometimes guys sell their pensions, or their ex-wives get 'em. "See, I've caddied here before. Sand Valley is a track you gotta know. Yardage book's no good."

"When'd you work here?" Bobby asked.

"Back when I was with the fire department in Camden, I'd come down here weekends. "

"So how come the yardage book's no good?"

Jello looked at us like we'd let our brains drip out our ears while we were off the Tour.

"Yardage book ain't gonna read greens for you, young man," he said. "Greens here're very subtle, quick in most places, not so quick in a few, harder to read than a blue-eyed woman."

"Help us out, then," Bobby said.

"We need all the local knowledge we can get, Jello," I said.

Jello, I guess, was feeling benevolent about Bobby's apology. He agreed. So we all walked together. I introduced Clayton and Angela as friends of Bobby's and let it go at that.

Just as soon as we took a good look at the last green, I started to get an idea of what the course was about. Eighteen wasn't a green protected by a bunker and a water hazard. It was a huge hazard with a grass island in the middle of it. A neck of the pond behind the clubhouse snaked out in front of the green area. Then the ground sloped sharply upward, pocked by those gaping bunkers. They looked almost like a necklace draped on the hillside in front of the green. What grass there was was shaggy and dense. The green itself sloped away from the fairway.

Bobby took my arm and walked slowly along the fringes of the green, scuffing his feet in the rough, getting an idea of how tight it was.

"Sunday pin'll be on the front," Jello said. "Always is. You don't wanna go for it. Get in those bunkers and you can't get up and down to a front pin."

I nodded. There was a sandy waste behind the green, too. You couldn't be aggressive with a pin cut on the back side, either.

"Make you a bet," Jello said. He walked onto the green and took a golf ball out of his pocket. He squatted down by the pin, his big butt almost scraping the ground. He flipped the ball to me.

"Bet you five you can't roll it to the hole and tell me which way it's going to break," he said. I looked at the green. It was subtle, but I thought it looked like the ball would break about one cup to the right.

"Bet it goes left," I said. I rolled the ball to him. It broke a little left at the end, away from the hole. I got the break right, but not the speed. The ball drifted about four feet past the hole, like it was scudding on ice. Quick.

"Not many guys see that," Jello said.

I laughed. "I didn't either," I admitted. "Just figured you wouldn't bet me on a putt that broke the way it looked like it would."

Jello laughed. "Main thing," he said, "is not to get greedy here. Hit the fairway, play maybe a seven-iron to the middle, and be happy to make four."

That was standard advice for almost any hard par four. But as we walked down the fairway, I could see why it wasn't easy to follow.

What Sand Valley did was try to intimidate a golfer. When you stood on the tee, what you saw looked like the road out of Palm Springs—acres and acres of sand and brush. The fairway looked like a distant oasis. Not only that, but the trees pinched in just where the fairway began, making it look tighter than it really was. If you could ignore all this and hit a decent tee shot, you found that the fairway was actually quite generous. But standing on the tee, you thought you had to hit the best shot of your life just to keep it in play. It was the same thing with the second shot. You couldn't see the green—just a bit of the flag flapping over those enormous bunkers. You saw all the trouble very clearly, from the pond to the sand. You didn't see your target. You had to have faith to hit the ball where it needed to go.

The pattern repeated itself as we walked along. In front of every tee box, Sand Valley had a couple of hundred yards of sand and scrub. Every green looked like it was an island in a heaving sea of trouble. I was worried right away about all the sand. It was loose and fine, the kind of sand that cupped a ball in a little crater. Then there was that local rule that you didn't rake up after you walked through some or hit out of it. You just tried to smooth your footprints a little bit. Between footprints and fried-egg lies, the sand was going to be tough for Bobby to handle.

So was everything else. It was a nasty, brutal, beautiful golf course.

Bobby didn't say much as we walked along, Jello explaining and me making little notes on a scorecard. And Clayton was still lost in his diseased brain. We got to the fourteenth tee, which is on what feels like a cliff. The green is 160 or so yards away, across a pond that was gleaming gold in the evening sun. Towering trees surrounded it, and at the very tops of those trees, the leaves had started to turn, going yellow and orange. The breeze had died down to nothing, and the air was still and fragrant. As long as you didn't have to thread a golf ball through the trees and over the pond and down to that little island of grass with a hole in it, it was one of the more beautiful spots on this planet.

"It's very numinous," Angela said.

"What-in-ous?" Jello asked her.

"Numinous," she said, and then she looked at her shoes, realizing she'd embarrassed us by using a word we didn't know.

"What's 'numinous' mean?" Bobby asked. Clayton mumbled something incoherent.

"If a place has a sacred spirit, it's numinous," she said. She blushed fiercely.

"In Africa," she explained, "the people have sacred places in the desert. That's where I heard the word used."

"A sacred spirit." Bobby smiled. "I sorta like that. I get a feeling here, too. Something in the grass, the trees, the sand."

I looked out over the fourteenth green again. The sun was going down and the light was oblique, casting the shadows of the tree trunks across the green, deep and black. They fell at regular intervals, like the columns in a temple.

There was something to what Angela felt, I thought. It was one sacred, spiritual, frightening son-of-a-bitch golf course. And it occurred to me that all of that might help Bobby Jobe. A lot of players would look at it and be intimidated. Bobby might play it better because he couldn't see it.

12

▼

INSPIRATION CAN BE DANGEROUS, ESPECIALLY IN A GAMBLING TOWN. IT certainly was that night. The sense I had that Bobby Jobe was going to play well at Sand Valley overwhelmed my other senses—especially my common sense.

That night, after dinner, when everyone else was in their rooms, I went down to the casino level. I had that money from J. R. and Conrad and the rest of the guys at Eadon Branch, with instructions to put it on Bobby's nose. I walked through the casino, looking for a sports book. Finally, I asked a blackjack pit boss where to find it. He was a friendly guy with a yellow tie and a pompadour haircut that looked like it had been preserved in some kind of oil back in 1959.

"They don't have that in New Jersey," he said. "That's what the computer in your room is for. It's there for youse if youse want it."

"I didn't see a computer," I said.

"Look on your TV zapper," he advised me.

So I went back upstairs. The TV remote, sure enough, was just slightly less complicated than the cockpit of an airliner. I found a button marked "computer" and pressed it. The screen switched from ESPN to a blue-sky background with a button to click on for "Internet." So I clicked on it.

And then, without doing anything else, I'm connected to this Internet sports book operating off of some island in the Caribbean. It was a Peddy operation.

I probably wouldn't have gone any farther, but I liked finally using a computer. I'd never had one. I kept seeing stories on the TV news about computer this and Internet that and I'd always felt like it was one more way the smart people in the world were getting ahead of me.

So I punched a couple of yes buttons and the next thing I know it's asking me if I want to use my Visa card to open my wagering account. I was impressed that the computer even knew I had a Visa card, though I guess I shouldn't have been. It was the only credit card I had and I'd used it to check into the hotel.

So I said yes to that, and the computer asked me what event I wanted to bet on. I pressed the button next to "PGA Championship."

And right away, I got a list of all the players. It was so easy I should have known better than to keep going but, like I said, I had the money from the guys back at Eadon Branch.

So I pressed the button next to Bobby's name, and the screen said:

BOBBY JOBE 800–1

I never was too good at math, so I used the little HBO booklet to write the multiplication on. If Bobby won the tournament, J. R. and the boys would be collecting $320,000 in return for the $400 they'd given me.

And that started me thinking. I could add to their money. If I kicked in another $500 off my Visa card, the payoff to me would be $400,000. That'd be enough to get the course back in the black and buy my ticket out of Allegheny Gap in a new car.

That was stupid, I thought. It was the kind of fantasizing that Eudora did with her lottery tickets. I didn't take after her, I told myself.

I clicked the buttons. The screen asked me how much I wanted to bet. I clicked till it read $400. Then I got crazy. I clicked some more till it said $1,000 and let it go. I figured what the hell. As long as I was going to pay off the note and buy a new car, I might want to ask Angela to go out dancing.

I DREAMED I WAS THIRTEEN AGAIN AND CLAYTON MOTE WAS SHAKING ME awake before dawn because he wanted to go practice. I was drowsy in the dream, sleeping like I was drugged, and it took a long time for me to wake up. It was like I was riding the elevator to the top floor of a skyscraper, ascending toward consciousness, with bony fingers prodding me. Then the elevator doors opened. I was awake. I opened my eyes.

And Clayton Mote was in fact prodding me. It was not the Clayton Mote of my dream, the father with the angry brow and the bushy black hair. This was the older Clayton Mote, with the shaved gray head and the blank gray space where his eyes were supposed to be.

"No, Daddy," I said before I remembered I didn't call him Daddy anymore.

If the word registered with him, he didn't show it. He kept prodding me, a little more gently now that my eyes were open. His lips were moving and murmuring noises came from his throat, but I couldn't make out the words. There was enough light in the room for me to make out that he wasn't dressed. He was in his hospital skivvies with bare feet. I looked at the red numerals of the clock-radio beside the bed. It was 5:43 in the morning.

"Clayton, how'd you get in here?"

He didn't answer me. He had his ear cocked the way he did when he was listening to voices, so I suppose he hadn't heard. I guess I must've left the door unlocked. Or maybe he knew how to pick locks. Who knew? I reached up, grabbed his hand, and stopped it in midprod.

"It's too early," I said. "Go back to sleep."

"Practice," he said. "Beach."

I shook my head. "Too early," I told him, pronouncing it very distinctly, as if he were a foreigner who might understand if I spoke clearly enough.

Then it seemed that I did have his attention. His face got hard the way it used to when he was angry, and he shouted suddenly. "Have to practice on the beach!"

I hushed him, the way you'd hush a little kid getting started on a tantrum. I told him everyone was asleep and the sun wasn't up and Bobby didn't practice this early in the morning.

"I gotta practice," Clayton said, whining now. He'd gone from angry to needy in the space of a second. "You've got clubs."

"Does Hogan want you to practice?" I asked him quietly.

He looked away like he had a guilty secret. I could tell from that that he was hearing the voice in his head he thought was Hogan. But he wasn't so crazy that he didn't know that other people didn't hear the voices he heard. So he just repeated that he had to practice and I had clubs.

I looked up and saw Angela in the doorway. She was dressed in a long

Vanderbilt T-shirt that ended somewhere right above her knees. Her hair was rumpled and her knees were knocked and her feet were bare and I suddenly so desperately wanted to see her that way every morning of my life that I almost forgot Clayton was there. How long she'd been standing there, watching, I didn't know.

When she caught my eye, she stepped into the room. "I heard noise," she said. "I thought you might need some help."

I remembered, then, that I was sleeping in some dingy old Jockey shorts that had a few holes in them. And my own hair was rumpled and my gut felt big. I didn't move. I kept the sheet up around my chest. "We're all right," I said.

Clayton looked anxiously at Angela. He was hunched a little, kind of cowering. He reminded me of a dog that knows he's peed on the rug, knows he deserves a whipping, and yet knows that his master is kind and may let him off with a scolding. I remembered when he'd lowered his head to no one, and I suddenly felt so damn sorry for him.

I had two choices. I could argue with him and maybe wind up wrestling him back into his bed. Or I could go along with him. Going along seemed the lesser evil.

"It's okay, Pro," I said. "Let's go practice."

I turned to Angela. "This is going to require me getting out of bed, and you might be overcome with desire if you see me with no clothes on," I said.

She smiled, nodded, and left. I got out of bed feeling quite pleased with myself. That'd been damn witty, I thought. I started throwing some clothes on, but before I could zip my pants, I heard a sound in the hallway, the sound of something scraping against the wall outside, and then Bobby appeared in the doorway. He was dressed in his underwear and his Oakleys. His hair was rumpled and he didn't look happy.

"What's all the ruckus?" he demanded.

"The pro wants to hit some balls down on the beach," I said.

"What time is it?"

"About dawn," I replied. "Sorry to wake you up."

I expected Bobby to chew me out, but he didn't.

"I wasn't sleeping anyway" was all he said.

"This won't take long," I promised.

I zipped up my pants and scooped up a box of Titleists and grabbed a couple of spare wedges that I kept separate from the golf bag so there wasn't any chance I'd carry them onto the course by accident and cost Bobby a penalty.

"Let's get you dressed, Pro," I said.

"What the hell," Bobby said. "I'll go with you."

"Bobby," I objected. "It's too early."

He shook his head. "I want some air."

"So do I." Angela's voice, hushed, came in from the hallway. She'd thrown on some clothes, too. A few minutes later, the four of us were walking through the Il Palazzo casino, carrying golf clubs and golf balls, looking for the exit to the boardwalk. A couple of the blackjack players, their faces sallow and haggard, noticed us and stared for a second, but they were between hands. The slot players were oblivious. It was like every morning at dawn a blind guy, a caddie, a crazy man, and a redheaded woman walked through the casino with golf equipment, looking for the beach. Nothing unusual.

It took us a while to find the door—casinos not being in the habit of making it easy for customers to find a way out. The air outside was damp and tired, just a little chilly. The sun, coming up over the ocean, had only just streaked a line of low clouds purple and orange. The waves trundled without energy to the shore, spilling their white foam on an empty beach.

I handed a pitching wedge to Clayton and dropped a few golf balls by his feet, wondering what he was planning to do with them. He lined himself up to hit parallel to the water line. Without stretching, without so much as a practice swing, he addressed the ball, swung, and clipped it cleanly off the sand. The ball popped up high, until you could see some sky between it and the roof of the shopping pier a couple of hundred yards away. Then it fell, with a slight, educated fade, and plopped into the sand.

"That's one," Clayton murmured.

"You gonna hit a hundred, Pro?" Bobby asked.

Clayton nodded without looking up. "Gotta hit a hundred," he said. "Perfect contact."

"We only have twelve balls," I said.

But if Clayton heard that, he said nothing. Instead, he took a second ball, swung, and produced an identical shot that looked like it might have come down in the little sand crater made by the first.

"Two," he said.

"I heard Gary Player used to practice on the beach," Bobby told him.

Clayton didn't respond till he'd hit two more balls, each of them clipped nicely off the sand.

"Hogan told him," he said suddenly, turning to Bobby. "Hogan."

Bobby's policy was to play along with whatever Clayton said. "You're getting good contact, Pro," he said. "I can hear it."

That must have thrown Clayton's concentration off, because he caught the next ball a little heavy. It landed twenty yards short of the first four. Clayton didn't react, just set up another ball. He hit that one well.

"One," he said.

"Whatta you think of when you're hitting those shots, Pro?" Bobby asked.

I looked at Bobby, mildly surprised that he was showing this much interest.

"Cup the left wrist just a little bit at the top," Clayton replied immediately.

Bobby stretched his hands behind him like he was making a backswing and asked, "Like this?"

But Clayton didn't bother to look up. "Cup the left wrist at the top," he repeated. "Hogan knows."

Bobby tried again to duplicate the move at the top of his imaginary backswing. "The secret, eh, Pro?" he said.

Clayton actually smiled. He shook his head no, not that Bobby could see it. "Hogan knows," he said. There was a trace of smugness in his voice, like he knew the secret, too.

Bobby caught the slight difference in Clayton's voice. "That's not the secret?" he asked Clayton.

Clayton looked at the sand by his feet. "Hogan knows," he repeated.

I didn't like that. I didn't want Bobby thinking of his wrist position on the eve of his last chance on the Tour. Better he started thinking about chasing pussy again.

I waited till Clayton had hit a couple more and sidled up next to him. I put a hand gently on the shaft of the club.

"Breakfast, Pro," I said softly. "Time for breakfast."

And just as he had back in Staunton, Clayton responded docilely to the prospect of food. He gave me the club and waited to be led to his meal.

I felt lousy about doing it. It reminded me of those dogs, Pakovsky's dogs. The look on her face told me Angela felt lousy about the situation too. I almost asked her what else I could do. But I didn't.

We went to a cafeteria called the Doge's Table which the casino kept open twenty-four hours a day. Half the people in the place were wearing sunglasses to protect their bloodshot eyes and the other half were looking like they could use another hour or two of sleep. Anyone who'd be in a casino at that hour had to be not quite right in the head, so we fit right in.

I dumped about four sugars into a mug of black coffee and asked Bobby when he wanted to go to the course.

"Right now," he said. "I want to do it before the media gets there."

Angela said she'd like to stay at the hotel till a more normal hour and wouldn't mind looking after Clayton. So Bobby and I finished eating and drove out there. Bobby didn't say much on the way. It was like we were going to a funeral instead of a golf course. That wasn't good. You want your player to be taking things too lightly, if anything, on the first day of practice. The pressure of a tournament is a cumulative thing. It wears a man's mind down. That's why so few guys go wire-to-wire. The pressure builds up on them each night they have the lead until they crack.

The ideal attitude is loose and casual right up to the starting bell, fairly serious after that. But you don't want to get too serious ever. The best way for anyone not named Tiger to win, I've noticed, is to be two or three shots off the lead going into Sunday. Then you start off thinking that you've got very little to lose. No one expects you to win and you already know you're going to make a nice check. You might as well do the best you can and see what happens. That's the state of mind that leads to a man's best golf.

Bobby looked like he had the lead after the third round and the final round had been held up a couple of days by rain. He was already a little wrinkled around the edges.

But one thing I remembered from the old days was that Bobby couldn't be pushed out of a bad mood. If you tried, he just got worse. He was smart enough to figure out what you were trying to do but not smart enough to let you do it.

So I shut up and we drove to the course in silence. The players' lot was

empty. The sun was halfway over the trees on the eastern horizon, looking bloody red. Mist was rising from the fairways as the dew started to
burn off. The only sounds were the whirring of mowers as the grounds
crew started making the course a little faster, a little trickier.

"Let's get going before it gets too numinous," Bobby said. I felt hurt
for Angela's sake by his sarcasm.

"Like you could even spell 'numinous,'" I said to him. Bobby turned
his face toward me and if I hadn't known better, I'd've thought he was
looking at me, looking for something in my eyes he hadn't noticed before,
some clue about why I was defending Angela.

"Let's get going," he said again, suspiciously.

Then he seemed to forget it, turning his attention to what surrounded him. He stood by the car door while I got the clubs out of the
trunk. He reminded me of a bear just out of its den, scratching his belly a
little bit, sniffing the air, listening.

"Smells like a lot of sand," he said.

"Not where you're going to be hitting it," I said.

He changed his shoes by the car and we walked to the first tee. The
starter wasn't there yet, though there was a little sign that said the course
opened for practice rounds at 7 A.M. That was still a few minutes off.

I told Bobby about the sign.

"The hell with that," he said. "I can't see it."

"I can," I pointed out.

"We'll just tell 'em you can't read," he said with a little of his old arrogance. "What are we looking at?"

I glanced at the yardage book. "Four-forty, par four, dogleg right, big
fairway, sand in front of the tee. Carry about two-ten to the fairway left,
two-thirty fairway right. Don't want to cut it much. The corner's tight."

That was what I told him. I didn't say that the view from the first tee
at Sand Valley was like looking off your front porch if you lived in Death
Valley. There was nothing in front of the tee but scrubby sand and little
bushes. The fairway was just a promise over the horizon. Only reason I
knew it was there was because I'd walked it the night before.

"Sounds numinous," Bobby said. He never could leave a bad joke to
die, but I decided not to argue with him this time. I wanted him focused
on the round. "Driver?"

"Let's try three-wood," I said. "You might hit driver through the fairway."

He took the club and laid it over his shoulders, stretching his back a little. He didn't have to do it much. He was born limber.

He cracked that three-wood pretty good with a nice little fade on it to set up the approach and we set out. Ten paces from the tee markers we hit sand. We walked through it for fifty yards or so before Bobby said anything.

"Boy, there's a lot of sand," he said. "Feels like we're on the beach."

Fifty yards later, he said, "How many yards of this stuff did you say there was?"

"Not enough for you to worry about," I said.

But he was worrying about it. I guess he had a sense of what a golf course should feel like underfoot. He was used to feeling grass of varying lengths, maybe asphalt or gravel on the cart paths, and sand in bunkers only. Walking over so much sand made him edgy.

"Why're we weaving around?" he asked me.

"We're just avoiding some bushes," I said. "Scrubby little things."

We walked a little farther.

"You sure this is a golf course, Coach?"

"No," I said. "It isn't. I actually kidnapped you and took you to Arabia. You're going to work the rest of your life picking up camel dung."

I was glad when we emerged from the sand onto the fairway. Just to make sure he got a full picture, I walked him over to the left side of the fairway, had him touch the pine that defined the rough. Then we walked to the right side of the fairway. It was nearly forty paces, which is a lot for a championship golf course. "See?" I said. "Nice and wide."

He nodded, but I could tell his mind was still back on the sand we'd trekked through. I was afraid he was seeing it in his mind as a Sahara Desert he had to crank the ball over on every tee shot. That would make him tight, make him overswing. He'd be just as intimidated as the sighted golfers would be.

"It's no different than hitting over the water to the 16th at Cypress," he said. "I do that with a three-iron."

Bobby had loved that course and that hole. Whenever we played the AT&T, we always snuck over to Cypress to get in a few holes. He'd never rinsed one on No. 16.

"Yeah," I said. "Use that."

It was the first thing he'd said all morning that was even vaguely positive. I started to feel better.

He played well till we got to the seventh. It's a par five that must look, from the air, like some heavenly butcher took a cleaver to it and dismembered it. There's a tee box and the usual expanse of sand. Then there's a fairway. But it's cut off by another expanse of sand and scrub they call Hell's Half Acre. Then there's another island of fairway, more sand, and finally, 570 yards from the tee, an island of putting green. All that's missing are a few bleached skulls.

But it wasn't as tough as it looked, Jello had told me. You just had to be conservative. He recommended a three-wood to the first fairway, then a two-iron, and finally a wedge.

But when I laid out this strategy to Bobby, he balked. "I hate to give away a birdie chance on a par five," he said. "How far's it to the end of the first fairway?"

"Three-ten," I told him.

"Let's try driver and see what happens," he said. "That's what practice rounds are for."

I checked the wind. There wasn't much, but what there was was behind us. I checked my thoughts. I didn't want him to hit into the sand right away. I wanted to find an obscure corner of the course where we could go and practice recovery shots.

"No," I said. "Three-wood. Let's play it like we mean it."

So he took a three-wood and hit it, but his heart wasn't in it. He blocked it high and right, and it came down on the edge of the rough.

"It's okay," I said. "You're safe."

But he wasn't, really. The weak tee shot had made Hell's Half Acre a long, sandy carry. When we got to the ball, I checked the yardage book, paced it off, and told him, "Two-thirty to carry the hazard." I showed him the lie—first cut of rough. Bobby didn't like to hit woods out of the rough.

"Two-iron," I said.

He took the club and we addressed the ball, and I felt suddenly as if a tube had opened between his brain and mine and I knew what he was thinking. He was thinking of the long two-iron on the sixteenth at Oak

Valley in the last PGA, the one he'd duck-hooked into the creek. I told myself that it was just me, that there was no tube between our brains, but I couldn't shake the feeling. It wasn't what you want to be thinking about before you execute a shot.

Sure enough, he snapped it. It was just a practice round, so you couldn't say it was pressure. Most likely, it was a case of the longish grass in the rough closing the clubhead as it contacted the ball. Whatever it was, the ball started low and left and then dove into the sand well short of the second stretch of fairway. Bobby didn't need me to tell him what had happened. He could tell well enough.

"Shit," he cursed. "The hook!"

He slammed the club into the turf and snapped the head off at the hosel. He looked ready to take the jagged end of the shaft and use it to rip his guts open. Then his shoulders slumped. He tossed the shaft to me and said, "Souvenir for you."

I tossed the shaft into the woods.

"It was the grass," I said. "Turned the clubhead over."

"No it wasn't. It was my swing," he replied. "We in the gunch?"

"Yep."

"Let's go find it," he sighed. It was like he had a toothache and knew he needed to go to the dentist. He was that enthusiastic.

We walked quietly down the fairway toward the sand. The sun was up over the treetops by that time, and the dew had all burned off. Two blue jays darted in front of us, on one another like pilots in a dogfight. Their heads were the color of the sky, a gray-blue. For a moment it seemed like it was just me and Bobby playing at Eadon Branch again.

Then reality intervened. For five minutes, I couldn't find the ball. Bobby stood around like a guy waiting for a late bus while I looked. Finally, I spotted it, hiding under the gnarly lower branches of a shrub.

"Unplayable lie," I said.

"Lemme see," Bobby replied.

So I had him squat down and I put his hand on the ball, let him explore the situation manually. He pricked his finger on a thorn and sucked a little blood out of it.

"Okay," he said. "Unplayable."

We didn't get much help dropping two club lengths, no nearer the hole.

The bush was still in the way of a shot that had any chance of being long enough to get out of the hazard. I was starting to understand how Hell's Half Acre got its name. If this had happened in competition, it might've been that the best option was to chip out backward. But I gave him a five-iron and let him hit it. He caught it heavy and it flew weakly into the bush.

We dropped again. This time, I arbitrarily dropped it out of range of the bush, something I couldn't have done in competition. It fell into one of the footprints we'd made looking for the ball. Since Sand Valley had no rakes, there was nothing to be done about them.

All I wanted was to get out to some grass again. I gave him an eight-iron.

"Cup the left wrist at the top," he muttered, parroting what Clayton had said on the beach that morning.

He swung, but he couldn't get the club on the ball without hitting some sand first. The shot died like a plane out of fuel and settled in the front expanse of Hell's Half Acre, still twenty yards short of the second segment of the fairway. By my count, if this had been a tournament, Bobby'd've been lying 5 there. Nine would've been a good score to shoot for.

He dusted some sand off his shirt front and said, "Let's go in."

"Go in?"

"Yeah, " he said. "Gotta work on my swing, my sand game, get rid of this hook."

"But we haven't even finished nine holes," I said.

He scowled at me. "Look, Greyhound," he said. "What the fuck difference does it make if I play the course? I can't see the holes, anyway. You scout it and I'll work on my swing."

Even though it was a cool morning, he was sweating and I could hear a panicky edge in his voice. I imagine he was seeing himself in this same spot, flailing around in Hell's Half Acre during the tournament, with the TV crews and everyone else watching and him afflicted with a snap hook. He had to be panicking if he thought he could work on his swing while I scouted the course.

I thought about cussing him out, maybe even slapping him in the butt, forcing him to go on. If the tournament had started, I would have—not slapped him, but chewed him out. But it was still early in the week. It was too soon for trying that stuff. Like I said, caddying is like being a jockey. You don't whip your horse while you're in the paddock. You soothe him, settle him down. So I just picked up the bag and turned toward the clubhouse. He latched on and followed.

Unfortunately, the media had eaten their breakfasts and gotten to the course. No sooner had we got close to the locker room than there was a pack of about sixty of them.

"Bobby, why'd you practice so early?"

"Bobby, is it true your caddie makes all the decisions?"

"Are you really like Iron Byron, Bobby?"

"Bobby, are you going to sue the PGA?"

Bobby could only guess at how many there were and how close they were standing. I could imagine what it must be like for him to have these voices jump on him out of the dark, like bandits in an ambush. Not soothing. I tried to start shoving through the pack, but even I could see that Bobby was going to have to say something. The problem was, there was no way for him to answer when everyone was shouting questions at the same time. Normally, the Tour had press conferences in a media center and a Tour official acted as a monitor. But the Tour wasn't going to help us, so I figured I'd have to play that role.

I jumped up on a bench. I waved my hands. The questions kept coming.

"Shut up!" I yelled.

That lowered the clamor down to a loud murmur.

"Bobby can't see whose hand is up and call on you. So I'll do it one at a time," I said. "Ask your question when you're called on, you'll get an answer. Otherwise, we're moving on."

Where we would've gone I had no idea.

I pointed to the woman who'd raised her hand first. She asked an idiotic question. "Bobby, is it true you started your round before dawn?"

"Well, I sometimes have a little trouble telling day from night," Bobby drawled.

There was a little laughter. Bobby relaxed and smiled.

Someone else asked Bobby how he hit the ball at all. "I guess we better show you."

So we moved over to a practice green and gave a little demonstration of how he got lined up, how he got the clubhead positioned, and so on. The golf course gates were open now and some galleryites, standing at the back of the gang of reporters, clapped when the first shot, a little lob, flew softly over a bunker and stopped about ten feet from the pin.

"I'm a professional golfer," Bobby turned and said. "What'd you expect? Ground balls?"

A guy in a Channel 5 polo shirt pushed a mike forward and asked the next question. "What would you say to Mike Richardson, who'd be in the tournament if you hadn't entered?"

Bobby flushed. I was afraid he'd say something nasty. But he got control of himself. "I'd say the same thing he'd say to the guy behind him on the qualifying list: 'Better luck next year.'"

But the guy from Channel 5 wasn't finished. "Isn't this really a publicity stunt?" he demanded. "Aren't you looking for a career as a speaker?"

Bobby grinned. "Well, yes," he said. "I'm interested in publicity. But I want to get it by winning the tournament. And if I'm gonna do that, I've gotta practice."

I figured that was my cue.

I shoved through the crowd of reporters and got between the ropes at a practice station. The reporters trailed after us. This wasn't what I'd planned to do, but the ropes were the only shelter I could see from the media horde. Bobby latched on and followed.

David Frost, the South African, was watching our progress, standing there with a pitching wedge in his hand. He was hard to miss. He's one of the players who rarely wears a hat, and he has a head of coal-black, wavy hair. Bobby'd been paired with him a couple of times, the last being the Kemper in Washington.

When we were fifteen yards away, Frost strode forward until he was in Bobby's path.

"Bobby Jobe," he said. "Welcome back." He stuck out his hand.

He pronounced it "Bawbby Jowb." Bobby stopped dead still.

"Frosty?" he said, recognizing the voice and the accent.

Frost stepped up and clapped him on the back, seeking out his right hand and pumping it.

"That's right," he said. "Good to have you out here again."

Then he stuck his face close to Bobby's ear, still gripping his hand, and said softly, "I just want you to know how much I admire you for trying this. Little Dickie is full of shit."

I was the only one besides Bobby who could hear it. I could've kissed him.

Bobby almost did. Instead, he just stood there, pumping Frost's hand and grinning.

There's a saying on the Tour that if you go into the locker room complaining about the 8 you made on the last hole, half the people don't care and the other half wish it'd been a 9. It sometimes seems that way.

But there's another side to professional golf. The majority—not all, but a majority—of the guys who play are good people. They help one another out. They suffer in their fellow players' misfortunes and they rejoice in their victories.

It's not that they don't want to beat you. They do. But they want you to play well. The smartest of them realize that half the fun in golf is finding out what you're capable of, and you won't find out unless the competition forces you to.

That's one of the things about golf. It's not like football or basketball or boxing or tennis where someone is facing you and trying to stop you. You and everyone else in the tournament are on the same side, basically. Everyone is playing the course. Everyone's trying to get the best out of himself.

Some guys never get that, of course. They never get friendly with the people they compete against, thinking that this will give them an edge. Some people succeed this way. Hogan was like that, I've heard. But in my experience, it doesn't help most people. It isolates them and winds up making it harder for them to succeed.

Bobby had been halfway like that himself. Maybe Clayton Mote was, too.

But other guys understand this part of golf, and Frost was one of them. He did his best to make Bobby feel at home as we set up and started hitting shots, chatting about the wine he was starting to produce on a farm he and his brother owned back in South Africa, griping about the customs regulations he had to cope with to sell it in the States. When Bobby hit his first shot, a nervous little wedge that fell ten yards short of the target flag, Frosty watched carefully. He didn't say anything, just watched, till Bobby hit another wedge that he caught crisply and sent right to the target flag.

"Amazing," Frost said. "Well done."

Then he went back to his own practice.

I hoped it was just what Bobby needed to forget about what had happened at Hell's Half Acre and have a good, relaxed practice session. It wasn't. After a couple of wedges, he asked for the three-iron, which was the closest we'd have to a two-iron till I could get the Callaway people to fix us a replacement. Then he started trying to fix his hook.

It just got worse and worse. He was cupping his left wrist so hard you could've drunk coffee from it. His rhythm and timing got all screwed up. He hit snap hooks. He hit high cuts. And with every bad swing, he got more self-conscious. He couldn't see the way guys were looking at him from the corners of their eyes, couldn't see the way they were shaking their heads about the shots he hit. But he could imagine it. And he could hear the murmurs of the spectators gathered behind the ropes to watch him.

I had to stop it before he forgot how to swing entirely.

I looked at my watch. It was a quarter to ten.

"Lunchtime," I said.

Bobby stuck the three-iron in the ground like a cane and leaned on it. "What time is it?" he asked me.

"Time to eat," I said.

He got it. He knew he wasn't making progress, that if he kept hitting balls the way he was going, he wouldn't be able to hit the course with his hat.

"Okay," he said. "Might as well."

I EXPECTED TO FIND THE PRO AND ANGELA IN HIS ROOM, WATCHING TELE-vision. Dr. Mehta had told us that my father could always be pacified by daytime television. He liked soaps. But they weren't there.

We went looking for them. Or, rather, I did and Bobby came along, his hand on my shoulder.

We found them at a five-dollar blackjack table. That time of day, the tables were half shut down. The one they were at had only four players: a couple of old guys from off a bus, a fat guy with three gold chains around his neck, and Clayton Mote. The weird part was that Clayton didn't look any odder than the others—just another guy trying to kill time faster than he killed five-dollar bills. Angela was standing behind a railing, a long arm's length away, but she wasn't controlling him. She was just watching. Clayton, in his new slacks and shirt, looked like a normal person. As I came up, he took a hit with a 4 showing, pulled a jack, and flipped over his cards, busted. Angela smiled like he'd just broken the bank.

"The pro is doing great!" she whispered as we approached.

I turned and watched with her. Clayton stood with a 15 and then watched the dealer turn over a jack and a queen.

"Looks to me like he's losing," I whispered back.

"The point is he's playing," she said.

That was Angela. She couldn't accept the idea that all Clayton could do was watch TV or practice golf or give lessons. She was going to show him he was able to do more, even if more was playing blackjack in a casino. The woman was born to rehab. It crossed my mind that maybe what I needed to attract Angela was a broken lip. She'd instinctively want to prove to me I could kiss again.

Damn, I was getting stupid over her.

"Whose money?" I asked her.

"Dr. Mehta gave him a little pocket money," she said.

"You add to it?" I asked her, reaching for my wallet.

She didn't answer, unwilling to discuss the issue.

"He's playing blackjack?" Bobby whispered from behind me. He, of course, couldn't see Clayton, but he could hear enough to figure out what was going on.

"Yeah," I said. At the table, Clayton took a card with a 12, pulled a 5, and stood on it. The dealer busted. His expression didn't change. He just waited intensely for the next pair of cards.

We could hear the bells of the slots, the murmur of the dealers, the squeals of the winners, and the groans of the losers. As far as sound went, it was an interesting place. I figured Bobby might like it, might want to stay for a while, maybe long enough for us to cadge some free food. But he wasn't interested.

"Can you ask him to cash his chips so he can watch me practice?" Bobby asked, impatient.

"Wait a minute, Bobby," I said. "I think we ought to give it a rest."

The last thing Bobby needed was a lesson. He just needed to relax and start trusting his swing again.

"Can't, Coach," Bobby said. "Only got a couple of days left till the tournament starts."

"Yeah, but . . ." I started.

Bobby wasn't listening.

"Pro," he whispered again, louder.

Clayton took a hit on a 3 and pulled a 6. If he heard Bobby, he didn't react.

"Pro," Bobby tried again, louder still.

Still no response. The dealer flipped a 19 and Clayton's bet was pushed.

"Pro!" Bobby just about shouted.

People looked around, but Clayton Mote didn't. Angela, looking embarrassed, went around the rail and plucked Clayton on the sleeve, whispered in his ear. Clayton's expression never changed. But he got up from his seat and handed his chips to her.

"I need a lesson," Bobby said to him. "I want to hit balls on the beach. I want you to help me stop hooking the ball."

The teacher part of Clayton Mote's sick brain switched on. He nodded. "Lesson on the beach," he said. He nodded again. "Stop hooking. Hogan knows."

I couldn't stand it anymore. I pulled Bobby aside and whispered in his ear. "Bobby, this is ridiculous," I said. "You can't go taking a lesson from him two days before the PGA! He could mess you up."

Bobby put a hand out and found my shoulder. "He can't mess me up much worse than I am now," he said. "I'm scared to death of the hook. And besides, I think he knows what he's talking about."

"What?" I snorted. "What Hogan's ghost tells him?"

He squeezed my shoulder softly. "I just have a feeling this is what I need, Coach," he said. "Let's do it."

One thing I know is that in the end, the caddie doesn't know squat. We did it Bobby's way. We got in the car and drove up the coast past Brigantine to a wildlife refuge. Apart from seagulls and sandpipers, it was deserted.

I pulled the shag bag and the clubs out of the trunk while Bobby changed shoes. Clayton and Angela waited. Clayton, now that we were there, seemed disengaged or shy. It was a breezy, sunny day and it made me think of kites for some reason. I wanted to send a kite up into the air and watch it get small against the sky, then make it dive like a pelican over the glittering waves. I never got to do that when I was a boy, but I saw a kid do it on *Baywatch* once.

But we were there to work.

Bobby latched on and we walked to a level spot on the beach, one where the sand was packed down by the last high tide. I didn't want to start off in the really loose, fluffy stuff. He hit a few wedges that way. The first one was fat. So was the second. The third he clipped, but it was a pull hook. Seeing it curve was like seeing a fresh zit the morning before the senior prom.

We tried one more, hoping that it would get better. But it didn't. In the state of mind he was in, he couldn't have hit the ocean with spit. Each swing got uglier until finally he hit a nasty, hooked top that veered about twenty yards left into the surf. The club went in after it, turning like a helicopter rotor.

"Damn!" Bobby yelled to the sky. "I can't hit the damn ball!"

I got the club, walking slow so he'd have time to cool off and compose himself. When I got back, I patted him on the shoulders, trying to soothe him like you'd soothe a kid.

"Tempo, Bobby. Slow tempo," I said. Tempo was something safe to think about just before a tournament. Nobody ever hurt his golf game by taking the club back a little slower.

But Bobby wasn't buying. He turned toward the dunes and said, "Pro?"

Clayton didn't say anything. He was squinting in the sunlight, staring at a spot in the sand where Bobby's club had left a little crater.

"Pro, whattaya think?" Bobby asked again.

"Hogan," Clayton said. Nothing else. Just the name. His lips kept moving, but no sound came out.

"Hogan, yeah. What'd Hogan know?" Bobby said, trying to draw him out.

"Hogan hates Snead," Clayton said.

"I know that," Bobby said, like you'd talk to someone who said there was a dinosaur under the bed. "But what'd Hogan know about the hook? I'm cupping the left wrist. What else did he know?"

"Hogan knows," Clayton said. He was like one of those dolls with the string in the back that say the same things no matter what question you ask them.

"Bobby," I interrupted. I wanted to tell him how stupid he was being, asking swing advice from a lunatic on the eve of a big tournament. I wanted to say that the people who said he had a million-dollar swing and a ten-cent head were wrong; it was a five-cent head. But I couldn't say that. His mind was too fragile. "Let's try one more," I said. "Nice and easy."

So we hit another wedge and this one wasn't as bad as the previous one. But it still wasn't right and Bobby could feel it.

"It turned over?" he demanded.

I said, yes, it had.

"Damn," he moaned. He turned toward Clayton again, "Pro, whattaya see?" he pleaded.

Clayton, as it happened, had reached down and plucked a broken shard of a clamshell from the beach and was examining the ridges in it, turning it over in his hand. Bobby couldn't know that, though.

"Hogan knows the secret," Clayton said. It was like he was teasing Bobby, sucking him in. Maybe he was.

Bobby stepped toward the voice and got in Clayton's face. "What secret? What is it?"

Clayton's eyes widened and he stepped backward, reestablishing distance. That was one of the things about him. He felt more than naturally uncomfortable when someone got physically close to him.

Bobby persisted. "What's the secret, Pro? What does Hogan know?"

Clayton took a step back, but the teacher in him was engaged again. "Legs," he mumbled.

"What?" Bobby was nearly panting.

"Come on," I broke in. "Everyone knows Hogan's secret was in the grip and the wrist action."

"Legs," Clayton repeated.

"What about the legs?" Bobby asked.

Clayton looked at him and suddenly smiled like he was getting ready for the Miss America contest. It was the biggest, kindest smile I'd ever seen from him. It was odd, like you'd flipped a quarter and old George Washington had come up with a grin on his face.

"Right knee," Clayton said. "Drive the right knee."

Bobby took a stance and pantomimed hitting a ball, but on the downswing he pushed off hard from his right foot and drove his right knee toward his left.

"That's it?" Bobby demanded. "That's Hogan's secret?"

Clayton nodded, almost shyly, like a twelve-year-old confessing that, yeah, girls weren't entirely bad. "Hogan's secret," he said.

"Wait a minute," I butted in. "That's exactly the wrong thing to be doing hitting off sand. You want quiet legs. Besides, Hogan believed in starting the downswing with the left hip. That couldn't be Hogan's secret."

I looked around for someone to agree with me. But Clayton was glowering at me like he wanted to smack my sassy little mouth but he'd forgotten how—the old father I remembered, but dazed. Angela didn't know a cupped wrist from a cup of sugar. She was looking at me like she expected something from me, but couldn't tell me what. That left Bobby, and Bobby, much as I wished he might, wasn't about to tell Clayton he was full of shit and go back to serious practice. Bobby at that stage was so afraid of hooking the ball that I was just lucky some gypsy didn't come along and offer hypnosis as a sure cure for the snapper. Bobby was ready to do anything, listen to anyone.

"Couldn't hurt to try it," he said.

I shrugged a disgusted, it's-your-funeral shrug. Then I remembered that shrugs don't mean anything to a blind man.

"Let's go," Bobby said, just a bit of the old boss's voice in his tone.

I gave in. I put another ball in the sand, expecting Bobby either to hit it fat or to hook it damn near to England. Of course, he didn't. Golf swings are peculiar that way. Sometimes, making a change that shouldn't help does help, just because it changes the attitude of the player from pessimistic to optimistic. I think that's what happened. All I know is that Bobby hit a sweet, crisp wedge off the sand that took off right where it was aimed and faded about three inches before it fell gently to the beach like it knew where it was going.

"How was that?" Bobby asked. But he knew. He was just rubbing my nose in it.

"That was a useful shot," I said. "Try it again."

Clayton nodded emphatically. I thought he was grinning at me. My face reddened. If Angela hadn't been there, I might've told them both to shove it and walked off. But she was there.

Bobby tried it again. I couldn't see much difference in his leg action. But to him, it probably felt like a huge change. A golfer's body is sensitive that way. Change his swing plane by an inch, and he'll tell you it feels like a foot.

Damned if it wasn't another perfect shot. This time, Bobby didn't bother to ask me how it was.

"Hogan's secret, Pro!" he yelped. "Hogan's secret!"

Clayton looked at the sand. "Hogan," he nodded.

Bobby's confidence, nonexistent a few minutes earlier, soared like a bottle rocket. He hit a few more wedges, then seven-irons, then three-irons, and finally even a couple of three-woods off the sand, a shot that I'd've never even thought of trying. They were all damn near perfect, power fades.

"Drive the leg," he kept saying before each swing. And when the ball was in the air, he held his follow-through position, knowing the shot was excellent. "Hogan's secret," he murmured each time.

It's a weird game.

Even I started to wonder whether Clayton might somehow have figured out something from Hogan. I kept trying to remember when Hogan retired. It was sometime in the sixties. And Clayton Mote had been in Vietnam in the sixties. But that didn't completely rule out the possibility that he'd seen him somewhere, learned something. Maybe he had a memory of Hogan swinging, and he kept playing that memory in his head like a videotape during his years in the hospital, over and over again until finally something jumped out at him, something about Hogan's swing that no one else had ever understood.

Hogan's secret.

Then I thought, No way.

"Good-bye, quacker!" Bobby shouted at the ocean. "I know Hogan's secret."

He sounded giddy to me. You want a player to be confident, but Bobby's mood was like a balloon that was pumped up too much. Any little pressure would be enough to burst it. I realized I had to do something about it. I thought about telling him, "Look, Bobby, you know there's no way in hell Clayton Mote knows Ben Hogan's secret. There's no way in hell he's really hearing Hogan's voice. He's a lunatic. You're hitting it good because you've got your confidence back." And when we were finished and heading for the car, I started to do it.

"Bobby," I said as we walked, "you know that there's no way . . ."

I never finished the sentence, because Clayton Mote started glaring at me again. It was like he knew what I was going to say. And this time there was no confusion in his face. His glare had all the baleful power I remembered from when I was a boy. It had frozen me when I lost that club shaft. It froze me now. I stopped talking, intimidated by those angry eyes.

"No way what, Coach?" Bobby finally said.

I kept my opinion to myself. I told myself it was because Bobby was hitting the ball good. I told myself Bobby'd probably laugh and say of course he knew Clayton couldn't have Hogan's secret, but what harm was there in it if it worked? I told myself, Why mess with his head?

The truth was that Clayton Mote still scared me.

"No way you're not going to play great," I said.

We drove back to the hotel. A couple of hours later, Bobby suggested we go back to Sand Valley. So we went back out there and walked around the course in the twilight, stopping at every green, putting dozens of balls. We got a feel for the speed and figured out some of the breaks. We putted around all the places where Jello McKay had told me he figured they'd cut the pins during the tournament.

We repeated that schedule the next day: out on the beach at the wildlife refuge, then out to Sand Valley to putt in the twilight. When Bobby was resting, I walked the course, planning the shots we'd have to play. On the beach, Bobby's ball striking kept getting sharper. His focus got a little tighter. By Wednesday night, the night before the tournament began, I was half ready to believe that Clayton Mote actually knew Ben Hogan's secret.

13

▼

Rain moved in just after dawn Thursday, a squall line from up in the mountains, up in the direction of Allegheny Gap. It wasn't supposed to last long—an hour or two, they kept saying. But at nine that morning, the sky over Sand Valley was still heavy and gray and it was still raining. Once in a while some lightning would glimmer over the horizon and thunder would roll overhead, and that was enough to keep the players off the course.

A lot of the rain was blowing into my face. I was waiting in the caddie tent, another one of those graveside jobs that they rent from a funeral home, without sides. Maybe a hundred caddies were huddled together in a space big enough for fifty. The lucky ones had gotten folding chairs and spots in the middle. I was on the edge and when the wind blew from the direction of the eighteenth green, it blew the rain all over me. I had a rain slicker, but it was draped over the top of the bag to keep the clubs dry. I was wet and cold and worried. I hadn't seen Bobby around a thunderstorm yet. I didn't know how it would affect him, but I didn't figure it would help his composure any.

That wasn't all I was worried about. Bobby'd drawn an early starting time, 7:12. He was in with a couple of club pros, Doug Hurt and Mike Kitay. I hadn't heard of either one of them.

There was a message in that tee time. The Tour didn't give stars such early times. It didn't pair established players with club pros who got into the field by winning some PGA sectional event. The Tour generally paired established players with other established players, tournament winners with other tournament winners. The Tour was telling Bobby he belonged with the nobodies.

That was all right. We could use that as an incentive. But I hated having to wait. When you're playing a golf tournament, you get mentally geared up to tee off at a certain time. You get physically ready for that time. You go to bed at a certain hour. You eat breakfast a certain number of hours before you start. You arrive at the course a precise interval before you tee off. If you then have to wait, it's like taking your girl to her door, puckering up, and getting a handshake. You feel a certain letdown.

In the meantime, I had to sit around and listen to the jawing in the caddie tent. It was nice to see the guys again. But the circumstances were different. Guys'd walk up to me and shake my hand and say they were glad to see me, and I'd shake and say I was glad to see them. But we'd both be thinking that the guy never called me after what'd happened the previous year, never checked in to see how I was doing, never offered to help me find another loop. No one wants to be reminded of how quickly life on the Tour can end.

And the other thing was that I was out of practice talking with them. Caddies'll surprise you. Some of them read Tolstoy and Dickens and guys like that. Some of them play the market and make more money that way than they do on the bag. Some of them are communists and some of them keep watch for black helicopters full of people trying to put fluoride in their drinking water. But a lot of them just know cheap motels, ESPN, and titty bars. Seemed like I was surrounded by that type that Thursday morning. And after about fifteen minutes of talking about which Atlantic City blackjack tables had the prettiest dealers, I got tired of it.

Finally, when the rain had diminished to a few spritzes, the word came down. Play would start at 9:45. And because there was less daylight in September than August, they were going to have to start half the field on the tenth tee. That's a way of getting a few more groups around the course than by starting everyone off on No. 1, the way they usually do at a major championship. We were going off No. 10.

Our tee time would be 9:57. It was already 9:25. I grabbed the clubs and hustled over to the locker room and cadged a dozen clean towels from the attendant there in return for a ten-dollar tip. I pride myself on being a good mudder, a caddie who can help his player around in wet weather.

That requires towels. I checked for the umbrella, the extra gloves. By the time I had everything tucked away, the bag looked pregnant. But it felt good to be going over a checklist again in the hour before a major championship. I had my usual stomach churning, and even that felt good.

Bobby was sitting quietly in front of his locker, his rain pullover on. He was hunched over his feet, lacing and unlacing his shoes, like he had to get the knot just right. That was another nervous habit he had, like going to sleep on airplanes. It meant he was tight and anxious. Of course, I'd've been worried if he hadn't been, considering what he was about to do.

The best thing I could do was try to slow Bobby down a little bit. I said no thanks to the guy with a golf cart offering to ride us over to the practice tee. Instead, I told Bobby we'd better walk. And I set a very slow pace. It cost us about half of the warm-up time they were giving us, but I figured Bobby didn't need much physical warm-up anyway. He did need to get his head in the right place. He needed to get into the right rhythm.

I remembered, for some weird reason, a round we played with Ernie Els at the Heritage when Ernie was on top of the game. Ernie had an intestinal bug that day, and he must've stopped in every Port-o-let on the front nine. But what impressed me was the way he walked on the way back from the Port-o-let to the tee. Everyone was waiting on him because he usually had the honor. But he strolled up to those tees so slowly it was like he was checking out whether the grounds crew had done a good job weeding and picking up scraps of paper. He wouldn't be rushed.

I tried to imitate that pace, that feeling, as we walked. "Okay, Bobby," I said. "We're starting out on No. 10. That's good. Means we just have to hit a little iron off the first tee."

"Shit," Bobby replied. "I liked Number One for starters."

He was right. No. 1 was a good opening hole for him. It called for a fade, his favorite shot. It called for a three-wood, which was a little easier to get going with than a driver. No. 10 was, in comparison, a vicious little starting hole. It was a hole where you could make birdie or you could take six.

But it did him no good to think that way.

"Nope," I said. "No. 10 is best. We got a chance for a fast start."

"Chance to go in the Devil's Asshole, too," Bobby said.

I was surprised. I hadn't told him about the Devil's Asshole. I'd just told him that No. 10 had a pit bunker front right. He must've heard about it in the locker room. Or maybe he'd just heard about it. The Devil's Asshole was maybe the meanest, most unfair pit bunker in America. I've heard there are worse ones in Scotland, but I hadn't seen any.

"It wasn't built there," Jello had told me. "The ground just caved in and filled with sand years ago. Like the devil did it." He'd grinned, but then he'd said, "Lots of time, you get into that bunker, the best thing to do is go back to the tee and hit your third."

"It's a birdie hole," I told Bobby.

I tried to keep chattering to him that way while he warmed up, hitting his wedges and irons, a few drivers. I kept talking about the way we were going to play each hole, the drives he'd hit, the putts he'd make. I wanted good pictures in his head.

But his face didn't suggest it was working. He didn't fight me. It was more like he discounted it, knowing that I was trying to get him into the right frame of mind. His face stayed tight.

The good thing was he was hitting the ball real well on the range. Every shot went just where I aimed him. Contact was crisp. Whatever he was doing with his right leg was by now looking natural to me, and all I noticed was his timing, his balance, and his rhythm. They were all spot on, as Steve Elkington likes to say.

We took a few practice putts and headed for the tenth tee. There weren't many spectators. The rain, I guess, had held the crowd down, and it was Thursday morning in any case. The big names weren't scheduled to go off until later in the day. There might've been a couple of hundred people gathered at the first tee. Angela and Clayton Mote had gotten some dark green plastic garbage bags and punched head holes in them. Clayton looked homeless and befuddled and I imagined he wondered what he was doing out in the rain.

Then, of course, there was the television crew from ESPN, which was doing the early rounds and seemed intent on recording every step Bobby took. And half a dozen print reporters, including Ken Alyda. I nodded to him and he did something I'd never seen a reporter do. He clenched his fist and gave me a "Let's go" sign.

We drew lots for the honor and Bobby finished third. Kitay, a stocky, gray-haired pro from a club in upstate New York, took an iron and managed to get the ball in the center of the green, twenty-five feet from the hole, which was cut back right. Hurt, a redheaded kid from Maryland, hit much the same shot. I checked in his bag to see what was missing. He'd hit a nine-iron.

"Now on the tee," the announcer said, and he paused. "From Dalton, Georgia." Someone whooped. "Bobby Jobe."

I was relieved. I thought he was going to say something about the accident, or being the first blind golfer, or something. He didn't. He was like the Sand Valley club itself. Elegantly simple.

The applause came, and it was more than the polite applause that always greets a player on the first tee. It went on for a while and there was whistling. Bobby stepped forward and tipped his cap. I pulled his nine-iron and stepped up close to his right ear.

"Okay," I said to him. "You know this hole. Pin's back right a little. Eric Dickerson front. Richard Petty to the hole. Lawrence Taylor to the back."

"Coach," he hissed. "I don't know squadoosh about stock-car racing! What the hell number is Richard Petty?"

Live and learn. I figured everyone from Georgia loved racing. "Forty-three," I said. "You got one-forty-three to the hole. The sky is crappy gray, there's no wind, there are evergreen trees all around, and there's nothing but sand and bushes between us and the green."

In truth, the green was starting to look like a little island receding in the distance. But I didn't tell him that.

"How much to clear the Devil's Asshole?"

I looked at my pin sheet. "One-thirty-five to be safe," I said.

"Whattaya think?"

"Solid nine," I said.

"And drive the legs," he said, with just a little grin. "Hogan's secret."

I couldn't tell if he was kidding me or not with the talk about Hogan's secret. I didn't want to argue with him about it. So I just clapped him on the back and squatted down behind the ball to line him up. The left side of the green was framed by the crease at his waist and the shaft of his club as he took control. A little gust of wind kicked the flag into motion. It was an austere, stern hole, but beautiful in its way, and I remember thinking just before Bobby swung how unlikely and how lucky it was that I was there.

The shaft flashed before me. The click was pure and so was the shot. It rose high over the trees, headed straight for the flag. As it reached its high point, a pillar of sunlight broke through the clouds and lit up the green. I'm not making that up. It's on the ESPN tape, just like the rainbow that filled the sky over Winged Foot as Davis Love III played the last hole of the PGA he won in 1997. It was like someone had turned the lights on. The green shone. The air got warmer. Bobby's ball landed three feet beyond the pin and stopped dead. It lay there, gleaming in the brightness.

Of course, the place erupted, at least to the extent that a couple of hundred soggy members of a golf gallery can erupt.

Bobby was still posing in his follow-through. He knew he'd hit it good. I exhaled. There's nothing quite like hitting it pure on the first shot of a major.

"Where?" was all he said when he turned to me.

"You're putting," I told him. I handed him the putter.

It was better than just on the green, but sometimes your depth perception can fool you and make a ball that's really ten feet away look two feet. Then you get to the green expecting a tap-in and you're disappointed. Bobby didn't need any disappointment. I think he knew it was closer, but I think he also knew why I didn't tell him that. He just nodded and waited till he heard the clank of the clubs as I shouldered the bag, then put his hand out a little and waited for me to butt the bottom end against his fingers. We took off.

Since the green was built like a pedestal, I could read it pretty well as we walked up toward it. The overall slope was a little to my right. When I got behind the ball, I thought I could see that it was going to break in that direction. But fortunately for us, Kitay putted well past the hole and had to make a four-footer for par on almost the same line as Bobby's putt. He played for about two balls of break and didn't get it.

So I aimed Bobby inside the right edge and told him four feet, firm. He hit it exactly that way, and the ball dove right in the hole. We'd birdied the first hole. The crowd erupted again. Of course, probably none of them had ever seen a blind man play golf, much less beat par on a hole like No. 10 at Sand Valley.

Bobby tipped his hat.

"Sun come out?" he asked me.

"Yep," I told him. "Just when you hit that nine-iron."

"Feels good," he said.

I liked hearing that. It told me he wasn't concerned with the crowd. He was aware of things like the warmth of the sun on his head, things that had to do with his body. That was good. I wanted him to be feeling that way when he was swinging well.

We got a par at No. 11, a nice, steady par: drive in the fairway, wedge below the hole, lag putt, tap-in. It was what we needed to establish a rhythm. The weather was getting better and I could see our gallery was starting to swell as people got to the golf course and heard that the blind golfer was not only on the course but hitting some pretty good shots.

We jazzed that crowd up pretty good on No. 12, which was the softest hole on the course, a short par four, dogleg left. Bobby hit a four-iron and sand wedge to ten feet and the putt went down like it was on tracks to the hole. We were two under par.

"I feel kinda strange," he said as we walked toward the tee at No. 13.

"How do you mean, 'strange'?" I asked him. I was afraid he might be feeling sick at his stomach or something. But it wasn't that.

"I feel like I'm watching myself," Bobby said. He lowered his voice, so I could barely hear him over the hubbub around us. "It's like I'm sitting on a TV tower and I see myself playing. I see you. I hear what you tell me to do. I watch myself do it."

I didn't care what he thought he saw as long as he kept hitting it stiff. "Okay," I said.

It was only later that I understood what Bobby was trying to tell me. There's a spot golfers try to get their minds to. Sometimes you hear people call it the zone. Or they say they're in a groove. What it means is you're playing so well and so confidently that you don't need to think about how to do it. You just need to think about what to do. Your body and mind then do it. It's like being detached, except that you're completely engrossed in the game. It's hard to explain, but finding that spot is one of the big reasons people keep playing golf. It feels so good.

And that's where Bobby had got himself to. Or fallen into. If he had said, "Okay, now I'm going to get into the groove," it wouldn't have happened. It's not something you can cause by force of will. You have to prepare yourself as best you can, have the best attitude you can, and hope that it happens. Ninety-nine times out of a hundred, it doesn't. But this felt like that one-in-a-hundred day.

I started to feel it myself on No. 13, which is where the back nine at Sand Valley starts getting truly difficult. It's a long hole in two segments that looks like it ought to be a par five because it's a double dogleg. But it's a par four. Bobby hit a great three-wood off the tee and then drew a three-iron into the green. He caught a bad break. It kicked off a little slope and rolled forty feet from the hole. At that, he was doing fine. Neither Kitay nor Hurt could even reach the green, and Kitay had to take an unplayable lie from the waste area down the left side.

The putt broke three different ways. It went uphill and downhill, broke left and right and left again, and finally, about four feet from the cup, started to look like it was magnetized. I knew it was going in a split second before the crowd did and I yelled, "Yes!"

All Bobby could hear was the "Ye—," because of the roar that went up. I looked around. Our gallery had grown to a couple of thousand or more, and they were clapping and whistling like we'd just outlawed downturns in the stock market. Old men with gray hair and paunches were punching the sky. Little old ladies were beaming at us. I looked around, just for a second, trying to find Angela. I couldn't. If she was there, she and Clayton had been swallowed up in the crowd. I wanted to know that she was sharing this, that maybe someone else in this place was thinking about those first days at Eadon Branch and how far we'd come.

Bobby was three under. I reminded myself not to look for a scoreboard. If Bobby asked me, I wanted to be able to say I didn't know.

"What's the wind doing on fourteen?" he leaned over and asked me.

I looked at the tops of the trees over by the fourteenth tee.

"Right to left," I whispered. "Not much."

He nodded and fell silent again, and I knew what he was doing. He was visualizing the fourteenth hole. He was thinking about the tee shot he was going to hit. The odd thing was that I started thinking the same way. I could see the fourteenth hole in my mind's eye, see the shot Bobby would want to hit, a little fade that held against the breeze. And I kept that thought in my mind as we walked over to the tee, kept it even though people were slapping us on the back, telling us "Way to go," telling us to birdie the next one.

We didn't, but it didn't bother me. We got our par, solid. And as soon as the second putt rattled into the cup, I started thinking about the tee shot we'd have to hit at No. 15, across a pond to a long, narrow fairway. And we hit that shot.

And that's the way the round went, like we were in a tunnel or something where the only thing we could see, the only thing we could pay attention to, was the shot immediately ahead of us. Nothing miraculous happened. Bobby didn't hit any four-hundred-yard drives or hole out from any fairways. He just played golf the way it can be played. Fairway. Green. Hole. Only one more birdie putt fell for us, and one par putt lipped out, but that was all right. Pars were good scores at Sand Valley. I sometimes had the feeling he was a machine, a ball-hitting machine, and all I had to do was aim it right to get the shot we needed.

It wasn't until he lagged up to a foot on No. 9, our last hole, that I looked at a scoreboard and realized what was happening. Bobby was still three under. If he sank that little putt, he'd have shot 67 and he'd be leading the tournament, at least temporarily. I looked around a little, trying to catch sight of Angela. I couldn't see her, but I started to notice the photographers, the writers, the TV cameramen, the thickening horde of spectators.

I felt a little like you do when you dive into the flooded quarry at Allegheny Gap on a summer day. You go under the water and the world changes. It gets quiet and dim, and you can hear the sound of your own heartbeat. You make your way upward in that state and then your head breaks the surface and suddenly, light and sound are restored—the sun is shining, kids are yelling, birds are chirping. I felt like I was breaking the surface there on that ninth green, except that what I'd been immersed in was a golf game.

I realized that it had turned into a sunny, warm afternoon, an Indian summer day. And that people were literally hanging out of pine trees to see Bobby putt out. That I was sweating a little and my sneakers were coated with mud about an inch thick that I'd picked up walking through the sand wastes between the tees and the fairways.

I could sense that Bobby was breaking the surface in some way, too, because he was looking around, listening to the little sounds coming from the crowd as Kitay and Hurt putted out. Their scores would be in the upper 70s. When we lined up for the last putt, our rhythm was gone. There'd been a sureness to every stroke that round and now it was again as if we were feeling our way through the routine, just as we had that first day of practice at Eadon Branch. And the putt slid by the left side of the hole. Bogey.

The noise that came from the crowd was a quiet, perfunctory sort of moan. It was like the people were disappointed that they couldn't begin an ovation.

The ovation started a moment later after Bobby tapped in the bogey putt. It was loud, and there was yelling, but it was more deliberate than that. It was long, sustained applause, what you hear, I'd always assumed, when you walk up the last fairway in the last round of a tournament you've won.

Bobby responded to it by tipping his cap and then turning around and trying to high-five me. It happened that I was holding the pin, which the caddie for the last player to putt out on any green has to stick back in the cup. He damn near impaled himself on it. But I managed to slide it out of his way. And that was the picture the papers all carried the next day, Bobby giving me an awkward high-five with the flagstick jutting out from beside his shoulder.

Behind him, over his shoulder, the scoreboard display was changing. Bobby was at two under with an 18 next to it, for a completed round. Steve Jones was at four under after 15. Tom Lehman, Vijay Singh, and Lee Janzen were at three under out on the course. There wasn't anyone at five under.

"Looks like you're tied for fifth, Bobby," I said. "But it's early yet. Lot of guys out on the course."

I didn't say it, but I was thinking that the course was only going to get harder if the sun stayed out and dried the greens. We'd caught a break with our early tee time. I didn't think anyone was going to shoot much better than 68, even though I hoped someone would. It would take some pressure off to be shy of the lead.

Bobby seemed more surprised than I was by what had happened. He smiled, but it was a smile like he might have if little Robby had sat down, at the age of two, and read him something out of the newspaper. It was a smile that was as much bewildered as pleased.

"That was the best round of golf I ever played," he said, shaking his head a little. "The best round I ever played. Who'd've thought—Hogan's secret from your father?"

Before I could say anything, Kitay and Hurt and their caddies were on us. Kitay shook his head like he couldn't accept what he'd seen. "Great round," he told me. "Incredible."

I wanted to tell Bobby it wasn't incredible and it had nothing to do with Ben Hogan's secret or Clayton Mote. It was just what Bobby was capable of. But I kept my mouth shut. Bobby put his hand on my shoulder and we walked off to the collar, where I bent down and picked up the bag. "Give balls to the score ladies and the sign kid," he reminded me. I'd always done that anyway. The scorekeeping ladies asked him to sign their hats. He did.

They needed three marshals to help us squeeze through the crowd pressing against the ropes that defined the path to the scorer's tent. I looked for Angela and Clayton. I couldn't see them. I figured they'd been blocked by the growing horde.

Inside the tent, it was suddenly cool, dim, and oddly quiet. A fan turned slowly in the corner. I added up the numbers again and put Bobby's hand in the right spot on the scorecard. He signed. We were official.

Cade Benton walked in, acting as if he'd never met the guy who'd told us to forget about it after the first round of the Captain Dick Classic. He was acting like having us enter the tournament and put it on front pages all around the world was his idea all along.

"Well done, gentlemen," he said. "The press is rather anxious to speak with you, Bobby."

Bobby nodded like this was some kind of burden he'd take only because he had to. But I knew better. And I knew better than to hang around.

"I got to find me a hot dog stand." I hoped Benton would take note that there was no free food for the caddies like there was for the players. If he did, he didn't say anything.

Bobby shrugged and accepted my reluctance to talk to the writers.

"Just let me hold on to your right shoulder, Cade," Bobby prompted him.

I was hungry, in fact, but I didn't plan on going after food right away.

I wanted to find Angela. I wanted to find my father. I kept scanning the crowd, looking, thinking that if I had known how good Bobby was going to play, I'd've told them where to meet me after the round. I hadn't figured on shooting 68. But I wanted someone to tell me how well I'd done.

I finally saw them, still wearing those garbage bags. They were sitting on the top row of the bleachers by the practice tee, watching the late players warm up. Angela's hair was slick and wet. Clayton Mote was hunched over, looking down at the ground under the bleachers, rocking slowly back and forth. I climbed up to see them.

"How did it go?" Angela asked. My father didn't even look up.

"You didn't see?" I asked.

She shook her head. "The pro wanted to be here," she said. "Watching the golfers swing."

I felt lousy about that. I looked at my father. He'd seen something he found interesting in one of the players out on the practice tee, because he was staring out there like it was Jesus Christ teaching Jack Nicklaus a new way to cut a six-iron. If he even knew I was there, he didn't show it.

"Did you do well?" Angela asked.

"Not bad," I told her. I felt deflated.

They'd already had lunch and Clayton didn't seem to want to be dislodged, so I told them I'd meet them in an hour at the car and went off in search of that hot dog, feeling like Bobby'd shot 86 instead of 68. I was wiping mustard off my mouth when a woman who worked for Cade Benton came up to me and asked, "Mr. Greyhound?"

I laughed. "Yeah."

"Mr. Benton asked me to find you and bring you to the media center."

"The media is Bobby's job."

"Well, they want to talk to you, too."

Truth be told, I was ready to be talked into it. Even if Clayton Mote was too crazy to watch what we'd done and Angela didn't really know enough to appreciate it, all the people back in Allegheny Gap that might've been laughing behind our backs were going to be sitting in front of their TV sets with their mouths open. I kind of wanted them to be thinking of me, too. People like Jimmy Edmisten.

So I said yes and walked into the media center. It was set up in the Sand Valley maintenance barn, except that they'd laid out carpets and long tables and chairs and turned it into a room like an auditorium for the press to work in. They had a second room partitioned off for interviews and reporters were spilling out of that room. Bobby was talking into a microphone and I could hear him.

"No," he was saying, "I can't tell you the secret or who taught it to me."

Oh, Jesus, I thought. Not the secret. I turned the corner into the room. Bobby was sitting up on a little stage behind a table draped in white with Cade Benton beside him and a couple of dozen microphones and tape recorders in front of him. I stopped at the back for a second. The lights in the room were very bright. There was almost no space. Every journalist at the tournament was jammed in there. I started to realize that the world was going to see what Bobby'd done different than I did. I saw it as just Bobby and I playing up to our abilities. The world saw it as damn near the Second Coming.

Benton noticed me and beckoned me up to the platform. I suddenly didn't want to go again. The horde of writers intimidated me. More than that, I could see on Bobby's face how much he was enjoying this moment. It was undoubtedly something he'd dreamed about for a long time, the moment when he could walk into a room full of guys who'd written, or at least thought, that he had a ten-cent head and make them say they were wrong, or at least think it.

Besides, I was afraid I still had mustard on my mouth. I was wiping it off with my sleeve when Ken Alyda noticed me.

"Greyhound," he said, "glad you could join us. Are you the one who taught Bobby Ben Hogan's secret?"

"Yeah, and if you were, what is it?" someone else called out.

I looked toward Bobby, trying to figure out how seriously he was taking this Hogan's secret stuff and how annoyed he was that a question was being directed at me instead of him. He wasn't smiling.

"Well," I said, "I think Hogan's secret was that if you hit the ball in the fairway and close to the hole, golf gets a lot easier."

There was a little laughter.

"No, seriously, what's the secret?" some guy called out.

"Lots of practice," I said. "And Bobby has sure done that."

Alyda nodded. "Greyhound," he said, "it sure does seem like you do more for Bobby than a regular caddie and that you deserve a lot of the credit for what happened out there today."

Alyda was being nice, and I appreciated it. I looked toward the platform. Bobby didn't look happy. I didn't think he'd look any happier if I accepted any more credit for what he'd shot.

I had an inspiration.

"Well, I wish that was true," I said. "But actually, the person who deserves the credit is Bobby's rehab counselor, Angela Murphy. Without her, we wouldn't be here."

I said a little prayer that she would watch the news and see me say that. And I waited for Bobby to add something. I waited for about five seconds. So did all the reporters.

It dawned on Bobby that this was his chance to thank us. He leaned toward the microphone. "Yeah," he said. "I'm very grateful to Henry and Angela. They've worked very hard and it's obvious that without them, I wouldn't be here."

I could tell he was sincere and I understood how a year earlier, it wouldn't have occurred to him to thank anyone, except maybe the Lord if he thought the cameras were rolling. But his thank-you came out so slowly that it almost sounded worse than saying nothing at all. Some people might've thought that Bobby had to be hit over the head to recognize that he owed anything to anybody. My own view was a little different. I think people with rare talent—like Ali, like Babe Ruth—are always self-centered. It's part of their talent. They couldn't do what they do unless they were arrogant. Some of them learn to mask it. Some of them gradually grow up and recognize the importance of other people in their lives. Some never do either. I wasn't sure which group Bobby belonged in, but he was closer to the grown-up group than he had been a year ago.

I didn't care that much, to be honest. You forgive a lot from a guy who shoots 68 in a major championship.

14

▼

I T TOOK A LONG TIME TO GET AWAY THAT DAY. BOBBY WANTED TO PRACTICE at Sand Valley instead of out at the beach. I understood. He wanted to wallow in it a little more, to stand out on the range and hear his peers tell him how well he played. He deserved that. And he enjoyed it. Hell, I enjoyed it, too. When someone like Tom Lehman walks up and shakes your hand and tells you you did a great job for your player, it means a lot. Tom Lehman did that. So did a lot of other guys.

It was past five o'clock before Bobby finally said he'd had enough and we got into the car for the drive back to Atlantic City. The sun was low behind us when we swung onto the causeway and crossed the bay to Atlantic City. The reflection off the hotel towers along the boardwalk was bright enough to hurt.

That was when Bobby kind of casually asked, "So did you tell Angela and the pro where to meet us?"

I damn near swerved off the road. Bobby felt the car jerk around and inhaled sharply. He thrust his foot at the floor like he was hitting a brake pedal.

"What's the matter?" he asked. "Dog in the road?"

"No," I told him. "I told Angela we'd meet them and drive them back to the hotel around two hours ago. I forgot about it."

Bobby didn't seem concerned. "Don't worry about it," he said, breezily. "There's lots of ways for them to get back. Someone gave 'em a ride. Or they took the caddie bus."

I worried about it. I punched the accelerator and must've come close to the record for running the causeway into Atlantic City.

But you can't move as fast when you're a celebrity. When we got to the hotel a doorman was stationed at the entrance to the cheap garage. He jumped in front of me when I showed the attendant my pass. We had to get out of the car, which he took. Another doorman escorted us to one of those goofy gondolas that Peddy had paddling down the canal.

"You want us to ride in this?" I asked.

"It's a service for our VIP guests, Mr. Mote," the doorman answered.

"I'm not feeling very VIP," I said, starting to decline, but Bobby squeezed my shoulder and stopped me.

"Henry," he said, "one thing I've learned over the years is that when the world wants to kiss your feet, you take your shoes off." I rolled my eyes. But I could tell it would take longer to explain why I wanted to walk than it would to ride in their little fake gondola.

So we floated up to the door, where a couple of photographers took our picture. The doorman was a Vietnamese or Thai kid from Absecon, New Jersey, according to the ID badge he had clipped to his striped T-shirt. His name was Ricky.

"Congratulations, Mr. Jobe, Mr. Mote," he said. "Great round. Welcome back to Il Palazzo."

And it was like that all the way through the lobby and into the elevator. People were tripping over themselves to open doors for us and congratulate us. I looked around for any sign of Angela or Clayton but I didn't see them.

When I got to my room, there were more changes. There was a bouquet of flowers and a basket of fruit on the desk, compliments of F. Rockwell Peddy. And there was an envelope. Mr. Peddy requested the pleasure of Mr. Mote's company at a dinner that night honoring past PGA champions. I put that aside. I wasn't sure how I wanted to react to an invitation that was so obviously related to how well Bobby had played. If he'd shot 86, I didn't think Mr. Peddy would've thought Mr. Mote's company would be such a pleasure.

I picked up the phone and dialed Angela's room. No answer. I tried Clayton Mote's. She picked up the phone.

"It's all right," she said after I'd apologized. "We rode back in the caddie bus."

"You're sure you didn't mind?" I asked.

"Not at all," she replied. The way she said it, it was hard to tell whether she meant she really hadn't minded, which I doubted, or whether she meant that my company was so unimportant to her that she'd just as soon take the bus.

"Uh, good," I said. Then I fell silent. Sometimes my own eloquence astounded me. But I was not eager to press her to clarify herself. "How's the pro?" I finally asked.

"He's discovered the Golf Channel," she said. "Right now he's watching someone give a lesson."

She didn't say anything, but I felt suddenly ashamed of myself. He was my father and my responsibility, and here I'd gone and left her to baby-sit him.

"He been talking much?"

"No."

"Didn't say anything about the round we played?"

"No. He did seem to like watching the players on the driving range."

"Well, hey, I'm sorry you had to look after him so long," I said. "I'll come down and take over. And, what do you say we go out somewhere for dinner tonight, celebrate? Bobby and I are invited to this past champions dinner, but I was thinking I didn't want to go."

I scowled at my reflection in the mirror over the dresser. That was a stupid thing to say. Why hadn't I told her I wanted to be with her?

"No place fancy," she said. "I haven't got the clothes for it, and neither does the pro."

"That makes three of us," I said. I was ridiculously relieved she was willing to have dinner with me.

So I went down the hall to Clayton's room and knocked on the door. She opened it. Her hair was frizzy from the rain that day, and I could still see the imprint of her baseball hat in the red strands. I grinned at her, goofily, wondering how to be with her.

She didn't grin back. She was polite, but no more than that, and I apologized again for not meeting them at the course when I'd said I would. She just nodded.

I would have liked to tell her about everything that had happened that day, from the press conference to the practice tee, tell her about Tom Lehman speaking to me and about all the attention Bobby was getting and the attention I was getting, too. About the whole celebrity thing. But I didn't. I figured it would just dig the hole I was in a little deeper. I was hoping she'd mention what I'd said about her at the media center. But she didn't. We agreed to meet in an hour and she left and that was it.

Clayton barely reacted when I came in. David Leadbetter was on the screen, and some hacker was making a swinging motion with a beachball pressed between his elbows. Leadbetter was talking about triangles. Clayton looked like he was in love with geometry. His mouth was shut and he was staring intently at the screen. I sat down on the bed next to him. He didn't move away or move closer. Just stiffened a little, I thought.

"So, didn't see much of our round today, huh?" I asked him.

He kept staring at Leadbetter and the triangle like it was Julia Roberts getting undressed.

"Did you, uh, like what you did see?" I tried again.

He sort of rocked on the bed. I couldn't tell if he was nodding or not.

I was still feeling hyped, so I decided to violate one of my rules of the road. I opened the minibar and pulled out a couple of Millers. I don't have a rule against Millers, of course. It's the minibars. But I broke the rule, cracked them both, and handed him one.

On the television, Leadbetter's pupil was by this time actually hitting balls with the beachball between his elbows. Leadbetter was saying something in that African accent of his that sounds like a British version of redneck. His floppy Panama hat was covering his eyes, but I thought he was close to laughing at the idea that he could get paid big bucks for teaching people to swing with beachballs between their elbows. Who'd've thought that thirty years ago in Zimbabwe? But Clayton kept staring at it. I figured maybe I could get his attention when there was a commercial, but then I realized—this already was a commercial.

I clicked my can against his can. "To more 68s," I said.

He didn't respond, but he did take a sip of beer. Seemed to like it. He tilted the can back and downed half of it in one smooth swallow. He smiled at me like we were partners in crime, and I realized they probably didn't let him drink in the hospital.

"Tastes pretty good, huh?" I asked him.

He nodded and finished off the can, then resumed staring at the television.

I figured he'd ask me if he wanted another one, which was good. Force him to communicate. Another wave washing against the rock, as Dr. Mehta would say, though he probably wouldn't approve of a wave made of beer.

The Leadbetter infomercial ended and Golf Center came on and suddenly, there was Bobby on the screen. I turned it up and listened to him talk. He was explaining how "the secret" had helped him swing better, then telling the reporters he wouldn't say where he learned it. I looked at Clayton. If he understood that he was involved in this whole thing, he didn't let on.

Then I came on the screen, and I said those words about Angela. I thought I looked a little heavy around the jowls.

"Have they showed this already?" I asked Clayton. "Did Angela see it?"

"Hogan," he croaked at the screen. "Hogan's secret."

It took me a second to realize he was responding to what he'd heard Bobby say about ten seconds earlier. It was like Clayton's brain was on tape delay, like those sports call-in shows where they leave time to bleep out cusswords.

"Did Angela see it?" I repeated, not very hopefully.

"Hogan," he replied. "Hogan taught him the secret."

The score, I thought, must be something like Rock 100, Waves 0.

I SHOULD'VE HAD THE SENSE TO LEAVE WELL ENOUGH ALONE WITH CLAYTON. He wasn't really hurting me with his silence. Why should I care if the only thing he wanted to talk about was the golf swing? I should've been satisfied with it. At dinner, I could've let him have a nice, quiet conversation with Hogan while I talked to Angela and tried to see if she was still mad about being forgotten that afternoon.

But I wasn't smart enough to do that. I cleaned myself up and changed clothes while Clayton sat docile in front of the television. We went down to meet Angela in the Doge's Table. She was at one of the best tables—smack by a window that had an expansive view of the white plastic facade of Il Palazzo's parking garage.

Angela had no makeup on. Her face was scrubbed clean and pale. She didn't have the sunburned tinge she got on sunny days no matter how much sunblock she put on. Her hair was pulled back in a ponytail and she was dressed in fresh jeans and a white shirt with a Vanderbilt University logo. I wished she'd been wearing her Eadon Branch shirt. I'd've taken that as a good sign. As it was, I sensed she was still ticked off. She smiled at the pro and put a hand on his shoulder. She just nodded at me. Polite. But that was all. I felt like asking her if she'd caught the film of Bobby's press conference on TV. I didn't. You ruin something like that by calling attention to it.

We immediately separated. Angela liked salads and vegetables and went to get some. But Clayton was a meat man. So was I. The place was crowded and we moved slowly through the line Clayton had picked out, toward the guy carving roast beef. Clayton held his plate like a shield in front of him.

I started picking at him. "So you still haven't told me what you thought of the golf you saw us play this morning," I said.

He didn't say anything. He seemed to be fascinated with the view of the parking garage.

"I thought we played well, too, thanks," I said. "Your tip about practicing on the beach really helped, you know. He was hitting it very crisp this morning."

Clayton turned, avoiding my eyes, or so it seemed to me, and surveyed the tables behind us. It seemed like he was trying to orient himself.

"You're not at the hospital," I said. "You're in Atlantic City. "

He blinked, mumbled something I couldn't make out.

"Excuse me?" I said. "Are you talking to me?"

His eyes got wider, as if he felt threatened. I paid no attention.

"Do you ever think about your family?" I asked.

I said it in a low voice so no one else could hear it. Clayton reacted as if my words were slapping him across the head. He turned away, hunched over, and shuffled up to the front of the roast beef line, which we'd finally reached. He handed his plate to the carver.

"Do you wonder what's happening with them?" I asked him from behind. "Where they are, how they're doing, whether they're thinking about you?"

I didn't care that he was turning away. I wanted him to. I sensed that on some level my words were reaching him. I wanted them to. I wanted him to feel them. I don't know why it happened that way, that evening.

Maybe it was because of people doing things like giving me a ride on the VIP gondola, but I don't think so. I guess I was still angry with myself for forgetting about him and Angela that afternoon. I don't know. I just suddenly couldn't think of rocks and waves anymore.

Clayton didn't say anything. He seemed to shrink within himself, like he was reacting to a cold wind. The carver had heard my last question. He looked up warily from the side of beef he was working on and checked me out quickly. I wanted to tell him I wasn't the odd one, it was the guy in front of me.

Clayton took his plate, half full of roast beef, and silently walked away from me toward the potatoes. Instead of calming down, I chased after him.

"You want to run off, huh?" I hissed at him. "Just like you ran off before?"

He picked up his pace a little like he was an old, lame horse and my words were lashing him and he wanted to bolt but his body just didn't work that way anymore. He shuffled past the fish and vegetables toward the pasta section.

"You gotta face me, Clayton," I said, raising my voice enough for other people to start to look at me.

Then I saw where he was going—straight toward Angela. She was getting some of that corkscrew pasta with the vegetables and olives and stuff in it. He pulled up next to her and just stood there. I stopped in my tracks, afraid she'd think I'd been harassing a poor mental patient—which, of course, I had been.

I didn't know how he figured out that I wouldn't bother him when Angela was around, but he'd found safety just as sure as a kid can hide behind his teacher's skirts if some kindergarten bully is picking on him.

I didn't know how much Angela had seen. She made out as if nothing was going on.

"Would you like some pasta, Pro?" she asked sweetly. He held out his plate and she heaped some of that corkscrew stuff on it. She didn't ask me.

"Come on, let's sit down," she said to him. "Looks good, doesn't it?"

I walked beside her. "That doesn't help, Henry," she whispered to me.

I blushed. I wanted to argue with her, tell her she didn't understand why I'd done it. But I didn't. She was right—it didn't help.

We sat down. Suddenly, the place felt unbearably cold to me. It wasn't the air-conditioning. It was the plastic fork on my tray, the Formica tables, the fluorescent lights overhead. I would've given anything to be sitting down at a table with a plain white cloth, candles, a wool rug, real stuff. I wasn't sure the food on my plate wasn't plastic.

I looked at each of the people around me as I sat down. They looked no different than they had five minutes ago. It seemed unbelievable to me that they weren't feeling as cold and uncomfortable as I was. Then I thought that maybe I was catching Clayton's disease, that this must be, in a small way, how he felt all the time—alone with his strange and troubling thoughts and puzzled about why the world didn't share them. I felt ashamed.

Clayton, I could see, was still agitated. He normally ate like he hadn't seen food in a month, pushing it into his mouth as fast as he could chew it. But he wasn't eating. He had his utensils in his hand and the food was in front of him, but he was just staring at it. If you looked carefully at him, you could see he was bobbing up and down in his seat a little, squirming, and his lips were trembling.

Angela tried to soothe us both, I think. She was talking about how what we see is not as important as what we perceive and how we respond to what we see, and how Bobby and I were showing that perception and response can actually replace sight in some circumstances. Or some such stuff. I was watching her lips move, and the sound was hitting my ears, but it wasn't sinking in.

I was trying to think of something to say in reply when Clayton suddenly stood straight up like he'd been electrocuted. His thighs bumped the table. Angela's minestrone soup sloshed out of its bowl and into her lap. I stopped eating in midbite. Even though you know someone you're with is mentally ill, it's still a shock when he starts acting like it.

Clayton's eyes were fixed on the hallway outside the cafeteria.

"Snead!" he said in an urgent sort of voice. And he took off toward the exit, his plastic knife and fork still clutched in his fingers.

I recovered in time to look in that direction and see a Panama hat in the center of a cluster of people in suits. Then the hat disappeared down the hallway, in the direction of the banquet room. Clayton was going after it in a weirdly long stride, like a kid in school who wants to get somewhere fast but doesn't want to break the rule against running in the halls.

I realized that Sam Snead might actually be in the hotel. He was a past champion of the PGA. I felt stupid for not thinking of it before. Then I thought of the plastic knife. I bolted after Clayton.

Clayton was faster than I anticipated. He was out of the Doge's Table and into the corridor before I got clear of a busboy in the aisle.

By the time I got out there, Clayton was already standing in a position to do some damage. Sam Snead had paused outside the door to the banquet room. He was leaning on the arm of a pretty young woman I assumed was a relative of his, a granddaughter maybe. They had stopped in front of a row of blown-up old black-and-white newspaper pictures of PGA winners, mounted on easels. His was one of them. The picture showed him hoisting the Wanamaker Trophy, a big smile on his face.

The face under the hat now looked like it belonged to the grandfather of the man in the picture. His head was like an old walnut, brown and shriveled. The hat rested closer to his ears instead of sitting jaunty on top of his head the way it did in the picture next to him. The hair under the hat was wispy and dry and nearly white. He stood on his heels, like his toes hurt. Snead, I figured, had to be well into his eighties.

But his voice was still clear and loud and I could hear a snatch of what he was saying as I hustled down the corridor toward him, hoping I'd get there before Clayton did something.

"Jimmy Turnesa was a damn fine player," he said. "Won the medal that year. Beat Dutch Harrison, Ben Hogan, and Byron Nelson to get to me. And one other guy . . . oh, yeah, Jug McSpaden."

I almost shouted at him not to mention Hogan again. But as I got closer, I could see that Clayton was just standing there with his mouth open, like a fan who comes into the visual range of a golfer and lingers there, hoping to be recognized but aware that it would be wrong to move closer into the circle of space reserved for the golfer's actual acquaintances.

I grabbed Clayton's hand and took the plastic knife and fork out of it.

Snead looked at us expectantly. I think he was wondering why we didn't just hand him something to sign and get it over with. There was a moment of awkward silence.

"Won that trophy right here in Atlantic City," he said, as if he thought we needed some kind of prompting or explanation. "On the Seaview course in 1942. Went into the navy the next day."

Clayton was breathing hard, like he'd just run the length of the building to catch Snead. He seemed to gather himself, catching his breath and clearing his throat. I tightened my grip on his hand, thinking that maybe I should grab him in both arms and hustle him away before anything happened.

"You're *old*," Clayton said. He said it in the way a little kid says something that seems to him a profound discovery but is painfully obvious to adults.

Angela arrived at a trot just as he said it. She was still trying to brush the remnants of her minestrone off her jeans.

Snead looked at us for a moment, and I could see some recognition in his eyes. They were watery, and the flesh around them was drooping and wrinkled, like the eyes of a manatee I saw once in Florida. But they still focused.

"Yeah," he said sadly. "I'm old."

Angela seemed to know just what to do. She put an arm around Clayton, comforting him and restraining him at the same time.

"I think we'd better finish dinner, Pro," she said. She started to lead Clayton away. Clayton went docilely, as he usually did to food. But he looked back. I could hear him say "old" to her, a little quieter this time.

"Jimmy Turnesa was in the army already," Snead said. But he was starting to sound a little disoriented himself, because everyone else was thinking about what Clayton had said. Snead seemed intent on finishing his recollection before he lost it.

"He had a whole bunch of soldiers from Fort Dix in the gallery rooting for him."

He paused, and I could sense that he was seeing that fairway and those soldiers again, fresh in his mind's eye. Most of them, I imagined, were dead now, killed by age if they hadn't been killed in the war.

"Fort Dix still around here?" he asked me.

"I don't know," I said.

"Closed it down years ago," one of the men with Snead said. He must've been one of the hotel's greeters.

Snead nodded vaguely, still looking at me.

"You're the caddie for that blind kid, aren't you?" he asked me.

I nodded.

"You handled him good today," Snead said. "I saw that, I thought, Boy can't be too smart to be looping for a blind guy, but he's not stupid, either."

I didn't know whether he was complimenting me or teasing me. I was thinking about Clayton, and about Angela, and it was only later, thinking about all this, that I understood how remarkable it was that Sam Snead, the guy whose picture had hung on the wall in the Eadon Branch pro shop forever, recognized Henry Mote.

I think I thanked him. I'm not sure.

One of the men escorting Snead looked at his watch. "It's dinner-time," he said. But Snead didn't move. He did things at his own pace, as someone his age, I guess, is entitled to do.

"That Clayton Mote?" Snead asked, gesturing with his head up the corridor in the direction Angela had taken him.

I nodded again.

"He's still not right in the head, is he?" Snead said.

"No," I said. "He's not."

"A shame," Snead said.

"I know he once tried to hurt you," I said, beginning an apology.

Snead shook his head. "Nah. Took a swipe at me with a five-iron once, but he telegraphed it. I got out of the way. Just grazed me."

"I heard it was a four-iron," I said.

Snead laughed. "Might've been."

He paused and then went on. "I tried to help him out a little when he came out on the Tour, being as how he was from the mountains. Introduced him to some people. Somehow he got the idea I was trying to sabotage him. He said I had my caddie kick his ball into the rough."

"It was the disease he has," I said.

Snead nodded. "I know." Then he chuckled back in his throat. "Been guys told caddies to kick their balls out of the rough," he said. "Never known one to tell his caddie to kick someone else's in."

I couldn't bring myself to laugh, but I was in no position to tell Snead off. Maybe to win as much as he did for as long as he did you have to limit the amount of sympathy you can feel for a competitor.

"He kin to you?" Snead asked me.

"My father," I said.

Snead nodded slowly.

"How'd you . . . ?" He started to ask me something. But he must have thought again, because he stifled the question. I thought I knew what it was, and I was glad he hadn't asked me.

"Well, good luck with him," Snead finally said. "And good luck in the tournament. Helluva round you had today."

"Time to go, Uncle Sam," the woman with him prodded him. "We're late already."

Snead nodded and seemed to lean on her a little more as they turned and walked into the banquet. Through the door, I could see the explosions of flashbulbs as he entered. Then I heard the way applause started, beginning in a scattered way at the back of the room and then swelling as everyone got the news that Sam Snead had arrived.

I walked back to the Doge's Table, giving some thought to the question I had seen in Snead's eyes. How, he'd wanted to know, had being Clayton Mote's son led me to being the caddie for Bobby Jobe?

WHEN BOBBY CAME BACK FROM THE DINNER, HE CALLED ME. CLAYTON AND I were in my room, watching the Golf Channel again. They were showing some film of the 1961 PGA, when Jerry Barber knocked in a 55-foot putt on the final green to catch Don January. I was just thankful neither Snead nor Hogan were in contention that year.

"Hey, Coach," he said. "Come on up. I need you to tell me about these clothes they gave me."

"The pro's with me," I said.

"Bring him, too," Bobby told me.

So I switched the TV off, got Clayton by the elbow, and went to Bobby's room on the ocean side of the hotel. Bobby opened the door before I could knock a second time. He was wearing a blue blazer with a yellow tie—silk I think. He seemed keyed up, nervous.

"So whattaya think of these clothes?" he asked me when I was three steps inside the door. Clayton, behind me, hung in the doorway, hesitating. "They gave 'em to me for the dinner tonight. Should I keep 'em?"

I pulled Clayton into the room, sat him down in front of the TV, and handed him the remote. He started clicking until he'd found the Golf Channel again.

"I don't think they have cable in the hospital," I told Bobby. "The pro can't get enough of the Golf Channel."

"So whattaya think of the clothes?" Bobby asked again.

"They look fine to me," I told him. "But what do I know? I buy my good clothes at Wal-Mart." I couldn't figure out why Bobby would care what I thought about his new threads. He'd never asked my opinion about clothes before.

"Guess I'll keep 'em then," he said. "Guess who I sat with at dinner tonight?"

I shrugged. Then I remembered he didn't see shrugs. "Damned if I know," I said. I lowered my voice so Clayton wouldn't hear. "Hogan?" I was needling him.

But Bobby grinned like a pleased little boy. "Better than him," he said. "Who?"

"Jack Nicklaus," he told me.

I was impressed. "Fast company," I said.

"I was at a table with F. Rockwell Peddy, some babe named Marina he's dating, Nicklaus, Barbara Nicklaus, and Paul Runyan," Bobby reported. "Runyan—God, he must be nearly a hundred. He was telling us stories about playing with Bobby Jones."

"Sounds great," I said.

Bobby stepped over to the minibar and groped till he found the door and opened it. He pulled out a bag of chips, ripped it open, and started eating.

"Trouble was, I was too nervous to eat," he said between mouthfuls. "Wished you or Angela was there."

I could imagine him, hungry, but unwilling to embarrass himself by pawing at his food, too proud to ask someone to help him.

He started telling me a story about Runyan at the first Masters, back in 1934. It was a long story, involving Jones and Walter Hagen, and I was only half listening, feeling restless. Bobby's room had a sliding glass door which led to a balcony and from the balcony, you could see the ocean, dark and endless. I opened the door a foot or two and let the sea air wash over me.

Down on the beach, I saw a woman walking. I looked harder. She had a mess of wild hair under a baseball cap. When she passed through a band of moonlight reflecting off the ocean, I could see her profile. It was Angela. She was barefoot. A wave washed over her feet.

I stopped Bobby just as Runyan, Jones, and Hagen were about to tee off on No. 10 at Augusta. "Bobby, there's something I gotta do," I said. "Tell me the rest tomorrow."

And I bolted out the door.

I ran down the hallway to catch the elevator. After I mashed the down button, I waited for about ten seconds, then ran down the stairs five flights to the casino. And I jogged through that, damn near running over a couple of old ladies carrying quarters in buckets.

All the while I was telling myself that in golf, the worst time to hit a shot is when you absolutely can't wait to hit it, when you want it so bad that you're ready to push aside everyone in your group so you can poke your tee in the ground, set a ball on it, rear back, and crush it. Nine times out of ten, when you do that, you better be carrying a chain saw in the side pocket of your golf bag, because you're probably going to have to take down some trees and clear some brush to hit your second shot.

I was thinking that it's the same way with women. When you want them too bad, it never turns out right.

But I kept running, out the door of the casino and onto the boardwalk, like I was afraid some shark was going to jump out of the surf and drag Angela in. I dodged around a guy selling Italian ice in a pushcart and ran along the boards, my eyes on the beach. People must've thought I was trying to get away after a botched robbery in the Taj Mahal.

I kept running because even though I knew I wanted it too much, I also knew that all my life I'd hesitated when I should have acted. I was tired of hesitating. I knew that somehow my life had changed when Bobby shot that 68, that things were going to be different. I wanted them to be different with her.

I ran past a pier with a ride called the Wild Mouse. I thought I saw her up ahead, ducking through the support pilings for another pier. This one looked like a derelict ship, wrecked on the beach. It was empty and ghostly. The beach at Atlantic City is never going to be mistaken for the beach in Hawaii where they have the Tournament of Champions every year. No palm trees, no long, empty stretches of sand. Instead of the murmur of the surf, you hear the tinkling and ringing of slot machines when someone opens a casino door, punctuated by occasional sirens.

But damned if I didn't feel romantic as I jumped the rail and landed in the sand. I ran after her, huffing and puffing. She was ahead of me, on the other side of the empty pier. I ran a little faster and called out to her: "Hey, Angela!"

She stopped and turned around. I stopped running and started trying to casually stroll along. She waved at me.

The neon from the casinos was bathing her face in garish colors— blue and hot red. The breeze off the ocean was tossing tendrils of hair in front of her face. She had rolled up the legs of her jeans so she could walk in the surf, and she was standing a little splayfooted as I walked up.

I thought she looked good. Great, even.

"What brings you out here, Henry?" she asked.

"Oh, just taking a walk," I told her.

Her eyebrows twitched when she heard that, and I realized how stupid it sounded, since I was still puffing from running after her.

"Okay, well, I saw you out here and I thought I'd like to take a walk with you," I acknowledged.

I hoped she'd smile when she heard that. Women generally like it when a man confesses something. But her face didn't give me anything.

"Where's the pro?" she asked.

"Bobby's watching him," I said. "Or, at least, Bobby's with him."

That made her smile. We started walking along the beach. The water broke over my sneakers, but I pretended I didn't notice. I was afraid if I stopped to take them off, she'd have time to decide she wanted to be somewhere else.

"You remember that day you came to Eadon Branch the first time to ask me to work with Bobby?" I said.

"Very well," she said. Her voice was so soft it was hard to hear her over the sound of the surf hitting the sand.

"You were right, you know, and I was wrong. I mean, I never thought it was possible for Bobby to come back and shoot 68 in the PGA."

She didn't say anything. I think I was embarrassing her, because I peeked at her from the corner of my eye, and she was walking with her head down, watching the water wash over her feet. She didn't look like she minded hearing it, though, so I plunged ahead.

"Anyway, I'm grateful to you," I said.

"You and Bobby have done the work," she said.

"Yeah, but we wouldn't've without you," I told her.

She turned toward me, stopped walking. And damned if the moon didn't choose that instant to duck behind a cloud. Whatever light there was in her eyes was muted. But they were wide-open, and I thought they were glistening.

"Thank you, Henry," she said.

I kissed her.

She put her arms around me and pressed me close, and I inhaled the scent of her hair and tasted her. It felt like I was coming home, except it was a home I'd never been to before.

I could have kissed her forever like that, but after a moment she pressed gently against my shoulders and separated us a little, like she'd gotten control of herself. She didn't pull away, though. She stayed there, I in her arms and she in mine.

"You're welcome," I said.

"Let's walk some more," she invited me.

I felt drunk, suddenly, like the sea air was beer. I kept my arm around her as we walked.

"You know," I said. "This round changes everything."

"How do you mean?" she asked.

"Bobby's gonna be big," I said. "We're going to be back on Tour. We're going to be doing exhibitions. There's going to be money, finally."

"Um," she said. I should've listened to her more carefully. I would have sensed that it wasn't an encouraging "um."

I pulled her a little closer to me. She was maybe an inch taller than I was, but I was on the high side of the beach. "So, anyway, what I want to say is that I don't want you to go back to Nashville. I want you to come out on Tour."

I was afraid to look at her when I said that. I don't know how her face reacted. If it hadn't been for the way she'd kissed me, I wouldn't've ever had the nerve to ask her.

"As what?" she said.

"Well, you could still help Bobby, of course," I said. "But mainly, uh, with me."

She stopped walking, and I did look at her. Her face didn't show any of what I feared. She was smiling one of those smiles that's very close to tears. But then she pulled away.

"So whattaya say?" I asked her, even though I could already see the answer on her face.

"No, Henry," she said.

I didn't really hear her. I wanted her so much, it was like the only word I was going to hear was "yes."

I kissed her again, but this time it was a big mistake. She didn't slap me. She just stood there a second, passive. Then she pulled her head back, the way Muhammad Ali used to lean back away from a punch.

But my gonads were doing the thinking for me by this time, and I still didn't get it.

"C'mon," I said. "We'd have fun. We could have fun tonight."

She shook her head.

I tried to pull her closer to me. "Didn't you watch the round today? We shot sixty-eight. We're hot shit!"

"Calm down, Henry," she said.

I still didn't get it. I reached out and caressed her cheek, moving my hand back toward her ear. She stood there and let me do it, but it was like my hands stank of onions.

"C'mon," I said. "Cut loose. Forget what they told you in that school."

I am Mr. Smooth.

She shook her head, emphatically. "Sorry, Greyhound," she said. "It's not for me."

"But why?"

"It's not you," she began. Then she shook her head. "That's what people always say, isn't it?"

"So it is me?"

She looked pained. It reminded me of the way people look when they're about to put down a dog they really like.

"No, it's not." She shook her head, but she didn't convince me.

"What is it, then?"

She stepped back. "Let's not get into this now, okay? You guys have a tournament to play. After it's over . . ."

Now I felt she was telling me I wasn't man enough to handle being shot down and carrying a golf bag in the same week. It pissed me off.

"Yeah, sure," I said, sarcastic as hell.

She looked like she was struggling to not cry. She drew herself up and said she was going back to the hotel. She didn't ask me to go with her. I just stood there, watching her walk away.

"Why not?" I yelled after her. "Why not?"

Angela turned around. "It just wouldn't work," she said.

That was all. I couldn't figure out what she meant. Couldn't think of anything to say, couldn't remember what she'd told me once about being betrayed by a man who was on the road all the time. All I could think of was how embarrassed I felt and how I wouldn't ever let her see that. I watched as she climbed the stairs to the boardwalk and disappeared into the hotel, ready to turn my back at the first sign she was having second thoughts about rejecting me.

I went in then, took all the money I had in my wallet, and cashed it for chips. It came to seventy-three dollars. I sat down at a blackjack table and put it all out there. I pulled a 10 and a 3, took a hit, got a jack, and walked up to my room. I flicked the remote control till I had the sports book at Peddy's Internet casino.

The odds on Bobby, I saw, had dropped from 800–1 to 100–1.

15

▼

I WANTED TO SLEEP LATE THE NEXT MORNING, BUT KATIE COURIC WOKE me up.

Actually, it wasn't Katie Couric herself. It was her producer, a woman named Laura, and she was calling at six in the morning to see if I'd go on *The Today Show* at eight o'clock.

"Talk to Bobby," I said.

"Well, he's already doing *Good Morning America*," the woman said. "And besides, we think you have a better perspective."

It ticked me off that they'd been calling him already. He needed to rest, since we had a late tee time. I told her I preferred to sleep. I'd have done it if they offered me some money or if I thought the guys back in Allegheny Gap would be watching, but they figured to be either down in the mines or fast asleep when *The Today Show* was on.

But after she hung up, I couldn't get back to sleep. It's hard enough to sleep during a tournament, harder still when you're in contention. But when television programs start calling you up and asking you to go on, it's unsettling. Finally, I got up and took a walk on the boardwalk.

At that hour, there wasn't anything going on. The sun was barely over the ocean, already white and burning, promising a hot day. Scraps of litter and old newspapers blew in the breeze. A few gamblers, with the dazed look of losers, were standing against the railing, facing the ocean. It seemed to me they were considering wading in and not turning around. I looked on the beach, tried to pick out the footprints Angela and I had made the night before. The tide had washed them away, of course.

I walked for a couple of hours, trying to think about the round we had to play. I had breakfast at a McDonald's. We were the front-page picture in the copies of *USA Today* they were handing out with the Egg McMuffins—that shot of Bobby high-fiving me on the green at the last hole. I tried to remember the way I'd felt at that moment, but it seemed like a long time ago. When I'd scarfed down the sandwich, I went to the pay phone at the back of the restaurant and called Bobby's room. The phone was busy. I had some coffee and tried again ten minutes later. Still busy.

I could guess why. If *The Today Show* thought it was worth putting Bobby's caddie on TV, then half the world must want to talk to him. I hung up the phone, walked back to the hotel and went up to Bobby's room.

He answered the door wearing boxer shorts, Oakleys, and a phone in his ear. He beckoned me in, listening to someone and occasionally grunting. He turned in my direction and mouthed a couple of words: "It's GMA."

I thought for minute he meant *Good Morning America*, but then I realized that this GMA was Global Management Associates, the people who lined up exhibitions and endorsements for him. I could hear parts of the conversation. It was about motivational speeches and exhibition appearances. Bobby was mostly agreeing.

Finally, he hung up.

"Amazing how a little sixty-eight can move the marketplace," he said as he opened one of the drawers of the dresser and extracted an outfit. Bobby had had me sort his clothes by the day, putting each outfit in a separate drawer. In the Friday drawer, he had khaki slacks, a blue Callaway shirt, and black socks.

"And a little eighty-six can move it in the other direction," I said.

He frowned at me for a second, like a widow being told that Publishers Clearing House hadn't really sent her a check for ten million bucks.

"They're offering thirty thousand for a one-hour talk in Orlando next month," he said.

"Need someone to carry your microphone?" I asked him.

WE GATHERED UP ANGELA AND CLAYTON. SHE DIDN'T SAY ANYTHING SPECIAL to me, or touch me, or otherwise give me any reason to think she regretted what had happened the night before. She just smiled like she did when she first met me and said good morning. I said good morning back, same neutral voice. I was going to handle this with class. We got in the car and left. It had clouded up since my morning walk, and I was glad. When you carry a bag for a living, bright, hot sun doesn't exactly cheer you up.

Clayton was the only one letting on that the previous night had changed anything. He had something new to talk about with the voices in his head. I half listened to him mumbling as we rolled along, and it sounded like he was reporting to Hogan about his encounter with Snead the night before. "Snead's *old*," I heard him say a couple of times.

When we got to Sand Valley, I did something Clayton used to do to me when he wanted me to hush in front of strangers. I grabbed his arm just above the elbow and squeezed it—hard. I didn't want the cameras and the tape recorders to catch Clayton explaining how Hogan was telling Bobby how to win. That would've made an amusing little item for *SportsCenter*. Clayton seemed to understand the signal. He shut up.

The press was on Bobby like crows on a sick squirrel as we walked to the clubhouse. A few writers were in the locker room, interviewing other players. They drifted over and watched him change shoes, as if they were going to report which laces he did up first, the right shoe or the left.

When we got to the range, Bobby tried hard to ignore everything. But his rhythm was off. I could see him getting frustrated as he worked his way from the wedges down through the mid-irons and started hitting woods. His shots weren't off much. A spectator wouldn't have noticed. But they were all missing by five yards or so. That much right, that much left, that much short. His face got the shade of a half-ripe tomato and a sweat stain started seeping through the back of his shirt.

"I can't find the ball with the clubface," he half moaned, half whispered to me.

"Don't worry about it," I said. "You always play your best when you don't warm up great."

But he wasn't buying that. "Can you see the pro?" he asked.

"Now's not the time . . . ," I started.

"Dammit," he hissed. "I didn't ask you what fuckin' time it is! I asked if you can see the pro!"

I looked back toward the bleachers behind the practice tee and I spotted Clayton and Angela. Clayton appeared to be watching Little Dickie Reynolds hit two-irons halfway down the range from us.

"Yeah," I said.

"Get him," Bobby ordered.

I didn't like the idea, but it wasn't the spot to argue with him. We had maybe half an hour till our tee time. So I walked over to the bleachers, caught Angela's eye, and, by hand signals, communicated that Bobby wanted them out on the tee with him.

A marshal, one of those old Sand Valley guys, stopped them at the rope. They didn't have the right credentials. I nodded to him. "Bobby Jobe's swing teacher," I said. "And his sports psychologist." The old guy nodded appreciatively. It made sense. Stars have entourages. He let them through.

Clayton, for once, appeared to be paying attention as he walked over the turf toward Bobby. The grass was as tight and as green as emeralds. It was nothing like the field he practiced on at the hospital. In fact, we'd've been happy to have it for putting greens at Eadon Branch.

The breeze freshened then and swung around into our faces. It was getting strong enough to ruffle the trousers against your legs. We didn't need that. Bobby had always been a shaky wind player. He tended to get quick with a breeze in his face, like he was trying to swing harder to compensate for it. I was going to have to work to slow him down.

"Hey, Pro. Watch my action, wouldya?" Bobby said as we walked up. He was already in something close to a stance. He had his three-wood in his hands.

We got set and he hit a shot that was supposed to fade, but instead drew sharply left—almost a duck hook. Bobby didn't even wait till the ball was on the ground before he was taking the club back to where he set it at the top, cocking his head back toward his hands.

"Wrists okay?" he asked Clayton.

Clayton mumbled for a second.

"What?" Bobby pressed him.

"Yes." Clayton nodded, his head bobbing up and down emphatically. "Wrists okay."

I teed another ball. "Watch the legs this time," Bobby instructed. "Am I driving 'em okay?"

He hit again and the ball behaved better. It still curved the wrong way, but it was a decent miss.

"Again," Clayton said.

He stood directly behind Bobby and cocked his forearm at about a sixty-degree angle to the horizon. He watched the ball fly. The forearm, I knew, was a way teachers used to gauge a player's backswing before they all got video cameras and computers.

"You're off plane," Clayton said. "Stay on plane."

"I thought the secret was in the leg drive," I told him.

"It's all connected, Greyhound," Bobby said, impatient. He hit another ball. It was close to good. He turned back toward Clayton. "That feels better," he said.

Clayton nodded. "Hogan knows." He smiled as he said it. The smile looked evil to me.

But Bobby was happy. "What time is it?"

I checked my watch. "Time to go."

"Let's do it." Bobby nodded. He turned in Clayton's direction. "Thanks, Pro."

Clayton didn't respond. He wasn't listening anymore.

"Good-bye, Pro," I said.

"Snead's *old*," Clayton reported.

Then Bobby put his hand on the back of the bag and a New Jersey state trooper helped the marshals part the crowd enough for us to get through. It was like running a gauntlet. They kept clapping us on the back, touching us, reaching for my left hand to shake it.

I saw a few blind people in the crowd, the first blind people I'd ever seen in a golf gallery. They were carrying those white canes, some of them, and they were being escorted by sighted people. There may've been a dozen of them. I guessed their escorts were going to be describing the action to them.

The wind picked up even more as we got to the first tee. Bobby could feel it, could hear it rustling the pines that lined the right side of the hole. Kitay and Hurt were already there. Hurt sidled up to us. "I always knew I'd play golf in front of a huge crowd someday," he said to Bobby. "I just didn't think it would happen in quite this way."

"Big, huh?" Bobby asked him.

"Unbelievable," Hurt said.

And it was a big crowd. It seemed like everyone at the golf course had gathered to watch Bobby play. People ten deep lined the restraining ropes all the way down to the bend in the first fairway and, as far as I knew, past that.

I didn't take any pleasure in the crowd's attention as I waited for the group ahead of us to clear the fairway. I was thinking back to the day before and to that special feeling Bobby and I'd both had, that feeling of immersion in the waters of the old quarry. I wanted to get that feeling back, but all I could feel was that nasty, unpleasant sensation like you want to throw up but can't, the sensation that accompanies a nervous, jittery day. I covered up by being busy, wiping off golf balls, cleaning clubs, tossing tufts of grass into the air, watching the wind sweep them into the crowd to the right. I set Bobby up for a three-wood off the tee, telling myself the only thing we could do was to follow our routine on each swing exactly as we had the day before. So I got him aimed with the club shaft and set up behind the ball and then I reviewed the shot we wanted. "Okay, Bobby, dogleg right, nice little slider out there, smooth and solid, not too high, let it run. If you draw it a little, that's fine, too. It'll hold it against the wind. You're aimed at the fourth tree from the right edge of the short grass. Got exactly the right club. Just like yesterday."

He hesitated. "What do the trees look like?" he asked me.

"Wind's left to right," I said. "Not too strong. Don't worry about it."

I thought he wanted to know what the wind was doing to the tops of the trees, which is usually a better gauge than how it feels on the tee.

He didn't. "No, what do they *look* like?"

On another morning, I would've been patient with him, would've told him the color of the pines, the shape and the height and the way brown needles carpeted the ground beneath them. That was what Angela would've done. Which was why I wouldn't do it.

"For crissake, Bobby, they're trees," I snapped. "You remember them? Dogleg right. Three-wood. Let's go."

I was sorry the instant the words left my big, ornery mouth.

He didn't say anything. He just nodded and got set. He swung almost exactly as he had the day before. The gallery erupted again, and this time the noise was so loud you'd have thought he'd made birdie to win the tournament. People were still getting used to the fact that a blind guy could actually hit the ball. They'd clap as long as he didn't whiff it.

But this shot wasn't really worth clapping for. He'd lost something very small but very essential in his swing—a certain peace, a certain comfort, a certain arrogance, maybe. Guarding against the hook, I guess, he cut it too much and the wind pushed it into the right rough.

"Damn wind," Bobby said.

As if in answer, a gust came up and blew sand against our pants legs, down around the shin. You could feel it down there like it was being sprayed by something. The weather forecast hadn't predicted this wind. It seemed like it had sprung up from nowhere.

"Gotta slow your tempo down in the wind," I said. "We'll take an extra club, be solid. It's what Hogan would do."

I hoped the last might get a chuckle out of him, loosen him up. It didn't. He was oblivious. I turned toward the gallery and caught sight of Angela and Clayton, sitting in the bleachers on the side of the tee. She looked pained, like she'd heard what I'd said to Bobby and been hurt by it. Clayton looked preoccupied. I told myself to forget about it, to focus on the next shot. I told myself Bobby'd hit much worse shots off the first tee by his own self, without my help. This one was on the golf course, at least. We'd recover. But it was hard to shake the feeling that I'd spoiled this round.

The wind picked up even stronger as we approached the ball. You could hear it. The trees moaned and rustled. If you turned into it, the wind blew around in your ears. But it was hard to stay turned into it, because the direction kept shifting. It seemed to be blowing in circles. In the big waste bunker along the right side of the hole, I saw something I'd never seen before on a golf course. The wind whirled around in the lee side of a grassy hummock and kicked up a tight little mist of sand that spun around like a top before it drifted away. It was a God-awful thing to see when you were trying to figure out what club to hit for an approach to a green that was hard to hold on a calm day.

The lie we had didn't help, either. The ball was nestled halfway down in the rough. It seemed likely to jump.

The wind kept gusting and dropping off. I tossed grass in the air three times and got three different readings. Bobby kept turning, trying to face the wind so he could figure it out. Finally, I figured we'd better choose a club and get on with it. He was getting too nervous. I gave Bobby a nine-iron.

"Lawrence Taylor," I said. "The wind's swirling, kicking up little dust twisters in the bunker. The trees are swaying gently. Sky is cloudy. Thick, gray clouds."

He smiled, but without any laughter in it. Then, damned if he didn't go through the entire Clayton Mote–Ben Hogan secret checklist on his practice swing, carefully cupping his wrist and driving his legs and checking his plane.

"Just see the shot," I told him. "Hit it."

He hit it pretty well. But on a windy day, Sand Valley plays like an Alabama trooper with a ticket quota to fill on the last day of the month. It doesn't forgive even the smallest mistake. This ball was pulled a little left and long. The wind came up harder as it flew. Instead of hitting the front of the green in the center, it hit the back left, took a big bounce, and disappeared. The crowd's silence told Bobby it wasn't a good shot.

"Long and left?" he asked me while he was still holding his follow-through.

"Yeah," I said.

"Oh, God," he said. He took his stance again and repeated the same drill he'd tried during the practice swing. He was trying to find Hogan's secret and use it like Scotch tape to hold himself together.

He could barely get the ball back on the green from where it had settled, on a sandy path under a pine tree. He made bogey there and bogeyed the fifth as well. He bogeyed the seventh when the wind suddenly gusted in our faces and knocked his wedge approach into the sand. By the time we made the turn, I had gone from thinking about taking the lead to thinking about making the cut. The course and the wind were picking at Bobby's game, uncovering every weakness. The only comfort I could find was the certainty that it wasn't going to be easy for anyone else.

There was a delay on the tenth as the group ahead of us finished up. Bobby stood off to the side of the tee box and kept trying to rediscover whatever it was he thought he'd learned from Clayton Mote. I looked out toward the green. The wind was swirling again, kicking up those little sand tornadoes in front of the tee. The trees on the left side of the hole looked like they were blowing one way and the trees on the other side were bending in the opposite direction. The Devil's Asshole just sat there in the midst of all this, like the unblinking eye of a snake.

The electronic scoreboard by the tee clicked as the names of this threesome came up. We were now plus one for the tournament, plus three for the day, and no longer on the list of leaders. Bobby heard the clicking, sensed that I was watching.

"How far back are we?" he asked.

"Don't know," I said. "Not far. It's a tough day."

"I gotta get started," Bobby said.

"Just play your game," I told him.

Cliché No. 114 in the *Book of Useless Caddie Expressions*. Who the hell else's game was he going to play?

We had the honor, since both Kitay and Hurt had bogeyed the ninth. Bobby turned around like a lost boy, trying to catch the wind in his ears. "What's the wind doing?" he asked me, almost whining.

I looked out and saw three of those sand tornadoes kicking around in the gulf of sand and scrub between us and the green. "Swirling," I said. "But helping. We're just going to hit a solid nine to the middle of the green. Fat target."

"How much to clear the Devil's Asshole?"

It was the same question he'd asked the day before. This time the tees were set three yards farther back. I looked at my pin sheet anyway. "One-thirty-eight to be safe," I said.

I wanted him to nod and take the nine-iron as if no other thought had ever entered his mind. He didn't.

"I don't want to hit it in that bunker," he said. "I think a smooth eight."

I'd've rather heard him say he wanted to try playing left-handed. Something in your head doesn't understand the word "don't." If your last thought is "don't hit it in the water," or "don't say something stupid to this girl," you'll hit it in the water or say something stupid nine times out of ten.

But I'd messed up his mind enough already with what I'd said on the first tee. I just wanted to encourage him.

"Yeah," I said, like he'd suggested an option I hadn't thought of. "Smooth eight."

I gave him the club.

I should've argued with him.

Trying to take a little off the shot changed his rhythm and balance. Worse, the wind died away just as he was taking the club back. He sensed that and decided he needed to swing a little harder. It was no surprise, with all that stuff rattling around in his head, that he caught the ball a trifle heavy. I could tell by the sound at impact it wasn't hit right, and so could Bobby. The click of ball against club was sludgy, muffled by the chunk of turf he caught first. "Damn," he said, almost before he finished his swing.

Still, for a moment I thought we were going to get away with it. The ball took off right on the line I'd aimed him on and it actually lit on the green. But the green at No. 10 has a false front, and as smooth and fast as that green was, there was no way the shot was going to stay up.

The gallery didn't understand that, though. They saw it hit the green and there were a few quick claps, the beginnings of applause. But they died away as the ball started to trickle backward. It rolled real slow and every second I thought maybe an old pitch mark or a blade of grass the mower missed would grab it and hold it on the green. The crowd started to moan.

"What happened?" Bobby demanded.

"You hit the false front," I said. "It's rolling back."

The moans got louder as the ball picked up a little speed on the front edge of the green and then hit the collar. If the rough had grown up between the green and the bunker, it might have caught the ball and held it up the way Fred Couples's shot to No. 12 at Augusta held up above the water at the 1992 Masters. But Sand Valley wasn't as charitable as Augusta. The grass slowed the ball down just a tick, and then it disappeared into the Devil's Asshole.

Kitay and Hurt looked away. The moan from the spectators died off like a pricked balloon.

I waited for Bobby to get pissed, to blame me, somehow, for not talking him into hitting a full nine-iron. He didn't, though. Just set his lips in a tight line and took a deep breath, trying to pull himself together.

The walk to the bunker felt like a slog across the Sahara. The wind started to mock us, picking up again, blowing hard behind our backs. His ball was lying about a foot from the base of a six-foot wall of sand. If it'd been dry, coarse sand, I could see where maybe the best bunker player in the world, maybe Irwin or Player, might feather a wedge underneath it and pop it up onto the green. Nine players out of ten, though, even pros, were going to leave it in the bunker.

He could try to go backward to a little spit of grass in front of the bunker. But there was no room for me to squat and get the club lined up. Even if it worked, he'd be trying to play a long sand shot to the pin for his third.

That left the option of declaring an unplayable lie and going backward as far as we wanted on the line between the ball and the hole, the option Jello McKay had mentioned. We could go back to the tee, take a stroke penalty, and start over, hitting three.

The rules official with us was a man named Rod Thompson from the PGA. I put the bag down next to him so there was no question of where our clubs were. I walked Bobby into the bunker, putting his hand on my shoulder. It felt like we were going down into a mine or a grave. The sand smelled musty.

I could feel Thompson peering over my shoulder, checking to make sure we didn't break any rules. Behind him, I could hear the gallery talking, wondering what we were going to do.

"Got a nasty lie here," I said, hoping that the way the sound echoed off the walls of the bunker would start telling him what he needed to know.

I guided him around the position of the ball and then placed his hand on the grass at the top of the lip, so he'd know how high it was and how much space he had to work with.

"Can I get it out?" he asked me.

"No," I said. "I don't think so."

"What are you saying, Greyhound?"

"I think we gotta go back to the tee."

I might as well have told him he had cancer.

"No," he said.

"Yeah," I told him, "you don't want to make a big number here . . ."

"Yeah, but going back to the tee? I've never done that in my life! Are you sure?"

I thought about it for a second. I couldn't think of any other choices.

I looked around. Thompson was looking at his watch, and I realized he was timing us for slow play. The ESPN crew was grimly filming everything.

"Yeah," I said.

He sighed heavily. I don't want to say he was giving up, because who knows what goes on in someone else's head? But if he'd had to arm-wrestle Michael Jackson at that moment, I'd've bet on Michael.

I picked up the ball and let him tell Thompson what we were going to do.

The walk back to the tee seemed to take forever. The murmur in the gallery turned to a buzz as people tried to figure out what was going on. Kitay and Hurt waited on the side of the green, and the players in the next group, standing on the tee, looked curiously as we approached. I felt like I had no clothes on and the whole world was poking fun at my ugly little runt's body. My face was hot.

The bag felt like a telephone pole as we walked onto the little promontory that contained the tee box. Jello McKay was there, on the bag of some club pro I didn't recognize. He nodded at me, sadly, but I took that to be an affirmation that I'd made the right choice, and it gave me some encouragement.

Then Bobby started that damn practice routine again, checking his wrists and his legs and his swing plane. I grabbed the club and stopped him.

"Forget that shit," I whispered to him. "Just see the pin and fire at it."

Bobby kind of snorted at me, and his mouth wrinkled into a sneer.

"Try to remember, Greyhound, you idiot. I used to see. I can't see anymore. I can't see the fucking pin!"

He was halfway between screaming at me and crying.

I knew what he meant, but I thought he was wrong, too. I lay the nine-iron against his legs and tried to look like I was talking to him about the shot I wanted him to hit.

"Bobby, you used to see, but you didn't have vision," I said, my voice low. "You used to be able to spot the difference between a C-cup and a D-cup from two-hundred yards, but you couldn't see what you were doing to your life. Now you can't see, but you can have vision. True vision. And you can see that pin and see the shot you can hit to it."

He looked at me like I'd just puked up a toad.

"True vision," I said again, weaker.

Then he laughed. "Henry," he said. "That's the biggest pile of shit I ever heard in my life."

"No," I answered. "Clayton Mote talking about Hogan's secret is."

He laughed again, and I started to grin, too. I don't know why. Looking back on it, it felt odd. I'd never seen Bobby laugh at himself before.

"Neither one of us knows what he's doin', does he?" Bobby asked me.

"Nope," I said.

"Okay," he said. "Let's do it."

THIS TIME, THE SWING WAS LOOSE AND LONG AND POWERFUL, AND THE click was like a light switch. The shot homed in on the flag, the wind stayed constant, and the ball hit and spun back, stopping fifteen feet in front of the hole. The crowd applauded, but it was relieved, polite applause. They'd probably been thinking Bobby might hit it backward.

"How is it?" Bobby asked.

I told him.

He shook his head and shrugged like he was saying he might as well give up trying to figure out golf. He flipped the club toward me, but gently.

"True vision," he said. And he laughed again.

I tried like hell to read the putt we had for a bogey four, but I missed a little break right by the hole. The ball slid by.

"Guess my vision was untrue," I said.

Bobby grinned again and tapped in for five. We were that far over par, but it was the only time I'd ever seen him smile as he finished a double-bogey.

"Where do we stand?" Bobby asked.

"We're five over," I said.

"I know that," Bobby said. "Where do we stand in the tournament? What's the cut going to be?"

"Don't know," I said. "Can't see a scoreboard right now."

I lined him up on the eleventh tee. "True vision," he said, just before he swung. He put the ball in the fairway.

So I kept using the true vision thing. He was taking it as a joke, of course. So was I. But the good thing was, it relaxed him. It got his mind off the wind and Hogan's secret and he started to play decent golf again. He racked up four solid pars in a row.

I didn't tell him this, but I was watching the scoreboard all the time. With the greens firming up and the wind blowing, no one was shooting a very good score. Lehman, at one under, had the lead. If we could hold it at five over, we'd make the cut easily.

As we walked to the fifteenth tee I decided to violate my own rule against telling Bobby where he stood. I didn't want him pressing to make birdies, thinking he had to get lower to make the cut.

"Cut's going to be plus eight or nine," I told him. "Just keep doing what you're doing."

He nodded and drove the ball into a bunker.

"Forgot about true vision," he said as he gave the club back to me. And he cackled.

We bogeyed that hole, but he parred the last three and finished at six over for the day, four over for the tournament.

"That's our bad round for the tournament," I whispered to him as we waited for Kitay and Hurt to putt out on No. 18.

Bobby turned in a tight circle, listening for something.

"The wind's gone," he said. He shook his head. "Amazing."

He was right. The air had gone dead calm as we walked to the eighteenth green.

"Doesn't matter," I said. "We're one of the last groups in. Everybody had to play in it."

I looked at the leaderboard behind the green:

Lehman 139

Reynolds 140

Love III 141

Woods 142

Duval 142

We were five back. Not close, but still in it. Barely.

I shouldn't have been, by that time, but I was surprised when Benton's assistant showed up in the scorer's tent and told us the media wanted us in the press room. If you shoot 76 in the second round and fall five shots back, you don't expect a lot of interview requests. I should have figured by the number of photographers and TV cameras following us during the round that as long as Bobby couldn't see, the press was going to pay attention.

And I should have anticipated the first question once we got to the press conference. It came from a fat guy in a golf shirt who said he was from New Jersey's News Channel 33.

"Bobby," he asked, "what did you mean by true vision?"

Bobby was even less prepared than I was for the question.

"How'd you know about that?" he asked.

I saw a couple of reporters smile and shake their heads.

"ESPN's got good microphones, Bobby," someone called out.

"What did you mean by true vision?" the first guy persisted.

Bobby gave 'em that bashful good ole' boy smile and for a second I was afraid he was going to say something about the Lord. He didn't.

"Oh, Greyhound and I were just kidding around," he said. "Didn't mean anything."

16

▼

As soon as he finished his steak, Bobby got it into his head that he needed more work on Hogan's secret.

We were eating supper in a high roller's suite. The hotel manager had tried to pretend it was something they'd intended to put Bobby in the first day but overlooked. I found one of Greg Norman's straw hats in the closet, so I knew that Greg would've still been in the suite if he hadn't missed the cut.

Bobby turned toward Clayton, who was carefully devouring the last bits of some cheesecake. If they had a Clean Plate Club at that hospital, I was sure Clayton was the president. He never ate unless he was fed. But he always ate every scrap he was given.

"Pro, I think I need a lesson," Bobby said.

Clayton scooped the last bit of dessert into his mouth and mumbled, "On the beach."

"Good idea," Bobby said. "Let's go, Greyhound."

"Bobby, you don't want to do this," I protested, but weakly.

He nodded vigorously. "This is my competitive advantage. I can practice at night."

"You and Stevie Wonder," I said. I thought about telling him to shove it. But I was still his caddie and a caddie practiced when his player wanted to practice. That was one of the first rules.

I looked at Angela, hoping she'd take my side and talk Bobby out of it. Angela had been more pleasant to me at dinner. She smiled at me and laughed at one of my jokes. I figured she was trying to get things back to the way they'd been between us before that disastrous walk on the beach—to being friends. But she just arched her eyebrows a little bit and said nothing, as if to say she didn't have a dog in this fight.

So I scooped up a few of Bobby's spare clubs and some balls and we all went. It was bracing outside. The sea air was somehow fresher than it felt on the balcony. I don't know why—maybe it was because I was moving. I took deep breaths and my head started to clear.

The air around us, at the same time, was getting misty. A light evening fog wafted in from the ocean. It gave the neon signs around the boardwalk a hazy glow. We cast no shadows as we walked down the steps to the sand.

I felt Angela's hand tugging gently on my arm. She slowed me. Bobby and Clayton got far enough ahead of us so the sound of the surf made it hard to hear them.

"I felt like I wasn't squaring the clubface somehow today, Pro," Bobby said. "I want to check and see if I'm pronated right at the top."

"Henry," Angela said, her voice low.

"Yes," I said. I tried to make my voice cold, businesslike. I must've thought that would keep her from knowing how much I was hurting.

"Someone from the hospital called and told me they saw you at Bobby's press conference yesterday."

"Mmm?" I said, articulate to a fault.

"They told me what you said."

"Oh?" I said. I wouldn't look at her.

"Thank you, Henry. It was sweet of you."

"It was just the truth," I said, gruff as hell. But classy, I figured.

Up ahead of us, Bobby was standing on the beach and Clayton had circled around behind us. He was dragging a couple of wire trash cans. I watched him place them into position on the beach. The distance between them roughly equaled the width of Clayton's practice alley back at the hospital.

I didn't feel good about watching him position the baskets so precisely. It was like walking into the toilet in high school and catching some guy playing with himself.

"Henry," Angela said. "I'm sorry . . ." She stopped. I did look at her then. Her face looked grave and pained.

"Sorry for what?" I snapped.

She flinched a little at my tone. "Sorry that things happened the way they did last night. I—"

"It's all right," I cut her off. "I shouldn't have made a pass at you."

She looked like she wanted to say more, but I could tell my eyes and my face weren't inviting her to say anything. She looked out at the ocean, sighed, and said nothing. So did I.

Clayton finished and came back down the beach toward us. Bobby took a couple of practice swings with a wedge. I left Angela and walked over to Bobby.

"Your swing looks great. I wouldn't mess with it," I said.

"Doesn't feel quite right," he insisted.

Clayton came walking up the beach to us, mumbling, head down. Angela hung back, ten yards away, her head silhouetted against the neon from the Il Palazzo casino sign.

Bobby could hear Clayton coming. He took another swing. "How's it look, Pro?" he asked. Without waiting for an answer, he went on: "Gotta hook-proof this swing."

"You got in trouble today slicing the ball," I pointed out.

"Yeah," Bobby said, "but that was because I was worried about the hook and overcooked it."

"Gotta hit a hundred," Clayton said.

"Let's get started." Bobby nodded.

Reluctantly I set up a ball for him. I was barely paying attention. I was thinking about why I'd been so hard on Angela when she tried to apologize. Bobby swung the wedge and hit a high soft shot that I lost for a minute in the lights from a Ferris wheel on a pier down the beach. It faded slightly and fell just outside the right-hand trash can.

"Missed right," Clayton said. "Gotta start again."

Bobby nodded. "What'd I do wrong, Pro?"

"Legs," Clayton said. "Hogan knows."

"Drive the legs, huh?"

"Gotta hit a hundred," Clayton said.

"Gotta get hook-proof," Bobby told him.

He hit another ball, and this one was perfect, right between the two waste baskets.

"That's one," Clayton said. "Gotta hit a hundred."

Suddenly, I had had enough. I'd messed up with Angela. I wasn't going to mess this up.

As Bobby waited for me to place another ball in front of him, I stood up. I took the club out of his hands. I felt weird. My hand was trembling, but I knew I wasn't drunk.

"No," I said. "You're not gonna do this."

Bobby turned toward me, groping for the club. "Whattaya mean?" he said, irritated. "Give me my club."

"This is not what you need," I said to him.

Before Bobby could answer, Clayton Mote stepped up and tried to grab the club from me. "Gotta hit a hundred!" he yelled.

He was strong, and his eyes were bright with passion. He almost tore the club from my hands. But I tightened my own grip, and for a second, we were locked together, toe to toe, four hands on the shaft of the club, struggling.

"No," I said. I forced myself not to yell back at him, but it was a struggle. The cords of my neck were so taut they were sore the next day. "You're sick, Dad. You're not going to make him sick."

Maybe it was hearing his mind described like a virus. Clayton Mote sagged away. He let go of the club. He seemed to shrink from me, to turn tail like a whipped dog.

I was breathing raggedly, hunched over. My whole body was shaking. I straightened up. I took a breath.

"Not going to let you do it," I said.

Clayton lowered his eyes to the sand and said nothing.

"I'm damned if it's sick," Bobby objected. "He's got me hitting it great. I think he does know Hogan's secret."

I turned on Bobby.

"Hogan's secret," I said. "You know what Hogan's secret was? It wasn't his hand action or his knees. It was his head. He just wanted it more than anyone else. He didn't let anything stop him from getting it."

Bobby didn't say anything.

"Now you can stay out here with this crazy man and pretend there's some secret leg move or wrist cock you can learn that'll make you win," I went on. "But if you do, you're going to fuck up this tournament just like you fucked up the last one. I just wish you could do it without me. I just wish the pro could coach you tomorrow."

It was a nasty thing to say to him. Bobby scowled. Clayton crossed his arms in front of him and stuck his chin in his chest like he was freezing to death. His lips started moving, but whatever he was saying he was saying only to himself.

"All right," Bobby finally said. "We'll do it your way, Henry."

I listened for the tone of voice that promised I was going to be fired when it suited Bobby. I didn't hear it. I started to hope he might accept what I was saying.

"Good," I said. "Let's get some rest."

I picked up the bag of shag balls and gave Bobby my elbow. I put a hand on Clayton's shoulder and nudged him back toward the hotel. Angela was still standing where she'd been throughout this whole thing, ten yards away. I nodded to her as I walked past, very polite. She didn't come with us. She said she wanted to take a walk along the beach, and she disappeared into the mist drifting in from the ocean.

I PUT CLAYTON TO BED FEELING LIKE ONE OF THE ORDERLIES IN THE HOSPITAL who moved him through his routine. He was submissive and docile, but he wasn't there. When I offered him one of the red sleeping pills Dr. Mehta had sent along, he took it from my hand like a baby takes food from his mother, without question. I watched to see if he might fake swallowing it like Jack Nicholson did in that movie about an insane asylum. But he didn't have that much guile in him. I could see the pill ripple its way down his gullet.

He was gone, mentally, and I felt like it was my fault. Giving golf swing lessons to Bobby had been maybe the one link he had with reality, the one way he could interact with another human being. I'd taken it away from him.

"We'll find someone else you can give lessons to, Dad," I said.

He didn't respond. He just went to the bed, got in, and closed his eyes. Eventually, so did I. I even fell asleep.

I dreamed that Bobby was leading the tournament by two strokes going into the last hole. The dream was so vivid that I could see the scoreboard in my mind, and I remember who was in second place: Sam Snead.

But a young Snead, the way he was in that photograph, the way I guess he was in Clayton's mind. I could see the pond and the bunkers in front of the eighteenth green at Sand Valley, see the trees, see the sky above them. It was a clear blue sky without a trace of clouds. I could smell the grass. It was dry, a little withered, the way it gets late on a warm afternoon in September.

In the dream, I lined Bobby up perfectly for the second shot on the hole and he hit it perfectly. It took off like a rifle shot, hung in the air the same way Michael Jordan used to seem to hang in the air for a second, then dropped gently to the green, ten feet away from the hole. And then Clayton—but the younger Clayton, the bushy-haired father I remembered—ran onto the green and stole the ball. He disappeared into the woods. I started looking for witnesses—spectators, officials, the score ladies. But they had all vanished.

"Where's the ball, Coach?" Bobby kept asking. "Where's the ball?"

The bell in the cupola over the clubhouse—I know, there isn't one at Sand Valley—started ringing. Bong. Bong. Above its din I could hear Clayton Mote somewhere screeching, "Snead's old. *Old!*"

I woke up. The phone was ringing. I picked it up. It was Dr. Mehta.

"We're okay, Doc, I think," I told him after I'd blinked a few times. "Waves breaking against a rock, you know."

He laughed. He sounded very close. "Where are you?" I asked him.

"I am in the casino at Il Palazzo," he said.

He couldn't have surprised me more if he'd said he was calling from the moon. But I could vaguely hear the sound of slot machines in the background.

"Why?"

"I was watching television yesterday evening and I saw a report on you and Mr. Jobe," he said in that odd accent of his that at first sounds English, but isn't. "It was very exciting. To think that one of our patients is involved in such a deed! I am off this weekend, so I decided to drive up here and see if I could be of service to you."

I looked at the clock. It was six-thirty. "You drove all night?"

"Most of it," he said, but he sounded as if he liked nothing better than spending seven hours in his car.

I invited him up to the room and inside of five minutes, he knocked on the door. He looked like he'd driven all night—his hair was rumpled and his shirt was wrinkled. The shirt was a faded orange color, with the tails hanging out over his baggy jeans. He had sandals on. But I was glad to see him.

I had a sudden urge to tell him everything that had happened with Clayton, Bobby, and me. I finished by telling him about the beach and the way Clayton had seemed to be when I put him to bed. I don't know why I told him all that. I wasn't raised to blab to anyone, let alone some guy from India I barely knew, even if he was a shrink.

"So, I think the rock is bigger than ever," I concluded.

Dr. Mehta didn't chew me out. He didn't tell me I'd been a good guy, either.

"Very interesting," he said, nodding.

"Is he worse?" I asked.

Dr. Mehta didn't pretend he knew the answer. He shrugged and smiled. "We'll see," he said. "I think I'll go wake him and talk to him."

I guess some questions don't get answered. I gave him my key to Clayton's room. To tell the absolute truth, I was relieved he was there and taking over again. It's not a good thing to say, but there it was. Angela, I thought, wouldn't have felt that way.

I looked at the clock. It was eight-thirty. I'd talked for longer than I'd realized. I called Bobby. We'd agreed I'd wake him at eight.

"Sorry," I said. "I got tied up."

I expected him to be mad, partly because I was late calling and mostly because he was still mad about being ordered around on the beach, although I'd apologized to him for doing that when I dropped him off at his room. But when I got to his suite, he wasn't mad. He seemed unconcerned. He was already showered and cleaned up, wearing the clothes I'd put together for Saturday's round—a blue shirt, khaki slacks, a blue Callaway hat.

"My socks match?" he asked me.

They did. They were both black.

He wanted to go out for breakfast, get some air. We walked through the casino, which was as close to empty as it ever got, and out onto the boardwalk. The morning air had a chill. It was cold enough to make you wish you had a sweater but not cold enough to make you go back upstairs and get one. Clouds were coming in from down the coast. On the beach, a lone swimmer was coming out of the water. He was an old man with a big belly and old-fashioned baggy blue swim trunks. A couple of people roller-bladed past us, Spandex and sunglasses in fluorescent colors. Their skates made bumpy, thrumming sounds on the boards. We walked south, past a taffy store that was opening its doors. It smelled sweet.

I saw a Greek place that had thick coffee and some kind of sweet, layered pastry. We sat down at a little booth in the back with a cracked brown Formica table.

Bobby ordered coffee and some of the pastry. I just had coffee. Once the coffee came, he put cream and sugar in it, very carefully, then wrapped both hands around the mug when he drank it.

"I've been thinking about last night," Bobby said.

"I'm sorry," I said. "I shouldn't've lost my temper."

I was going to explain about Clayton and me, about the history of it, but he waved his hand.

"'S all right," he said.

"Good," I replied.

"I've been thinking you were right," he said.

"About what?"

"About what Hogan's real secret was. You know, in his head. Guts."

The waitress came with the pastry and asked if we wanted anything else.

"You got any swing secrets?" he asked her.

"No," she said. "We got donuts, bagels, Danish, toast."

"Good," Bobby told her. "Don't need any swing secrets."

She rolled her eyes like she couldn't figure out why God kept inflicting these obnoxious customers on her.

Bobby scarfed the pastry down in two quick bites. He got the coffee cup in his hands again and finished it off.

"Got a good feeling about this round, Coach," he said.

"Glad to hear it." I was.

"I think you hit on something with that stuff about Hogan's mind."

"Well . . ." I said.

"But forget that true vision stuff, okay? That's just a little too weird, you know?"

"Sure," I said.

Then he stopped talking. He was quiet on the walk back to the hotel. He said nothing on the drive to the golf course for the third round. I'd've thought maybe he was getting too tight, but when I looked at his hands, he wasn't rubbing his thumbs against the backs of his fingers the way he sometimes did when he was getting ready to throw up all over himself. His hands were still, on his knees. His head was up, or I'd've thought maybe he was asleep.

When we got to Sand Valley, you'd've thought Bobby was leading the tournament instead of five strokes back. People were on him from the time we got out of the car. They wanted more than autographs. They wanted to touch him. People even patted me on the back, talked to me.

"True vision, Bobby," a woman said. It was like she was starting a chant. "True vision," people said. "True vision."

It was like walking a gauntlet, but a gentle one.

A cop came up and offered to help clear a path. "You want to ride over there?" he asked Bobby. "We can get you a car or a cart."

"No," Bobby said. He was signing some kid's hat. "We'll walk. Just keep us moving."

He was enjoying it. Then I started to. I started smiling at the people, and thanking them, and they started smiling back. I mean, I didn't say "True vision" back to them or anything stupid like that. But it seemed like they were giving something to us, like we were drawing strength from their hope to see us do well. They seemed to get something in return from being near us.

The practice tee at this stage of a tournament has a different atmosphere than it does on Tuesday morning. There aren't so many guys out there, for one. The equipment reps and the agents and the swing doctors and the psychologists have by and large gone home. So've the guys who missed the cut. It's just a few dozen players warming up. They don't socialize much like they do early in the week. They spread themselves out and go about their business quietly. In front of us, I could see Woods standing with Steve Williams and Butch Harmon, checking his position at the top of the backswing. I took that to be a good sign, that he was fiddling with his swing, maybe trying to adjust it so his back didn't hurt, though with Tiger you never know. He's the only player I ever saw who was clearly superior to Bobby in physical ability. Before his back started bothering him, he could win tournaments while he was trying to fix a swing flaw. Now it was week-to-week for him. Duval was ten yards to their right, hitting wedges at the first flag on the range, maybe fifty or sixty yards. He was dropping every ball within five feet of his target and I thought that if he started putting well, he could be the man to beat. Little Dickie Reynolds was down at the opposite end and Jay Delsing, whom we were paired with, was in the middle. I found a spot between Duval and Delsing where the guys who went off earlier had left a few patches of clean turf.

"Let's hit some golf balls," I said. I was saying it mostly to myself. It was time to get focused. Bobby already was. He went through the bag in precise fashion, hitting shots directly at the flags I aimed him toward. He was hitting the ball so well you could almost feel the clubs vibrating in that tight, powerful way they do when they catch a ball dead in the center. Bobby, I knew, could feel it in his hands. There's a sense you have when you're hitting the ball real well that it stays an extra smidgen of a second on the clubface, flattening there, before it takes off.

"Feels good," he grunted after he launched his last warm-up drive toward the fence at the end of the range. We moved toward the practice green.

Delsing and his caddie saw us leaving and he waved, saying they wanted to go with us. Delsing was an older guy, pushing forty, a long time on the Tour but no wins. He was tall and thin and he usually had a ready grin on his face. But he looked rigid that afternoon. His caddie was a guy who'd been on several bags in my four years on the Tour. His name was Lizard Ziomecki, a name he got because of a habit he had of sitting in bars, tossing peanuts in the air in front of himself, and then sticking out his tongue to catch them. We started off, but it was slow going because of the way the people surged closer to Bobby.

"Amazing," Lizard said to me, "how many fans Jay and I have around here."

I just grunted. I understood why people wanted to see Bobby play, but I was still a little embarrassed about it around Tour people.

I glanced behind me. Despite the ropes that were supposed to hold them back, the fans had surged around Bobby. Some wanted autographs. Some just wanted to touch him. Before I could help, Delsing saw the situation and figured out what to do.

He got Bobby's hand on his shoulder and ran a sort of interference for him as they moved toward the green, grabbing the hats and programs people were thrusting forward and holding them in front of Bobby to sign, then handing them back to the person who'd offered them. At the same time, he kept moving. I even heard him ask one kid what his name was and then pass it to Bobby so he could personalize the autograph. It was only a moment's kindness, but I respected Delsing for it. A lot of guys in his position wouldn't have done it. He was a guy who had to grind every September and October, playing all the last tournaments on the schedule to make enough money to keep his card. He'd never been this close to the lead this late in a major championship. He could've been totally absorbed in grooving his putting stroke. He wasn't. When we'd finished putting and were ready to go to the first tee, he told Bobby to play well and you could tell from his voice that he meant it.

Applause erupted from the bleachers alongside the first tee when we came inside the ropes. It was a strange kind of applause that came in two waves. One was from the people who could see, and then there was a second group that started a few seconds later. I glanced over that way and saw that several hundred blind people had found seats there. You could tell they were blind because a lot of them had those long white sticks. How long they'd been waiting to listen to Bobby tee off, I didn't know. I guess they started applauding later because someone had to tell them it was Bobby coming onto the tee. Once they did, though, they kept it up. It was more than the polite applause you hear at every first tee. They whistled. They stomped. They banged their sticks on the bleachers.

"Blind people?" Bobby whispered to me.

"Yep," I said.

He just nodded, and it struck me that he might be feeling a responsibility to them.

"Take me over there," he said.

So I did. When he was in front of them, he thanked them for coming out and supporting him.

"Go get 'em! True vision, Bobby!" one of them called out. They whistled and stomped some more.

I figured that was the last thing Bobby needed, to be thinking that if he screwed up, he'd be letting blind people down. So I grabbed his arm and led him back to the tee, running down the features of the first hole for him even though he already knew them.

Out in the fairway, Jose Maria Olazabal and Billy Mayfair were walking out of sight around the corner of the dogleg. It was time to play. I could see, in the corner of my eye, the crowd start to swell. People craned their heads to peer down toward the tee and see Bobby. The low murmur of their voices died away and I could hear a lark singing in one of the trees by the tee. But then all that fell away and I saw only the hole.

It lay before us like a winding road and I felt as if all I had to do was drive. When I used to play on the minitour down in Florida, or sometimes when Bobby played, I'd get a twinge of doubt on the first tee. Just for an instant, you think, "What if I've forgotten how to hit the ball? What if I miss it completely?" That's part of the challenge of the game—to put those thoughts out of your mind and hit the ball the way you know you can.

But this afternoon, for some reason, that was no challenge at all, because thoughts like that never entered my mind. Not Bobby's either. His face and his posture were exactly the same as they'd been on the range. The swing was the same. The result was the same. I pointed him, he swung, we heard and felt precise contact, the ball went where we wanted it to go. Down the fairway, onto the green.

He parred the first seven holes just like that. His birdie putts were good efforts. They never finished more than six inches from the hole, but they didn't go in, either. That was all right. At Sand Valley, with the greens as slick as they were and the rough still growing, pars were fine scores.

There was a scoreboard behind the fourth green and I took a look while Delsing putted. Woods had dropped a couple of strokes at the second hole. I could imagine him drilling a wedge over that green and into trouble. The pin was set to tempt him to do that. Lehman had bogeyed the third. Little Dickie Reynolds had the lead. We were still five back, but we'd moved up a few notches just by staying at even par. The rest of the field, except for Reynolds, was struggling.

Bobby, though, was giving me that feeling of being deep in the game, in the zone. I stopped noticing the sandy wastes in front of every tee. I didn't even pay much attention to Hell's Half Acre in the middle of the seventh hole. I was locked into the targets we were aiming at. Bobby was hitting them.

The only distraction came between the seventh green and the eighth tee, where the guys from Allegheny Gap were lined up to watch us pass by. Like Dr. Mehta, they must've driven half the night to get there. "Eadon Branch!" J. R. Neill called out. "Eadon Branch!" Conrad repeated.

Bobby stopped and grabbed the bag so I had to stop, too. He turned in the direction of the voices. "Hey, guys, how are you?" he said. "Nice of you to come up. 'Preciate it."

They beamed, and Bobby nudged the bag a little, telling me to move on.

I liked the way he handled it. He didn't lose his focus, and he made them happy at the same time. It's nothing that Palmer hadn't been doing all his life, but it was something Bobby had never been able to do. He was serene, is the best way I can describe it.

"Beautiful day, isn't it?" he asked me as we walked up the eighth fairway.

I looked at the sky. It had gone almost cloudless in the hour we'd been out on the course. It was still warm, but the air had none of the humidity of earlier in the week. It was autumn air, like football weather in Virginia.

No. 8 at Sand Valley is a tricky little par four, not much more than three hundred yards, but the green shrugs off golf balls and the chipping areas are murderous. I'd given him the three-iron on the tee and set up a wedge second. It was a downhill lie—that was unavoidable. But Bobby handled it, stiffing the wedge and nearly holing it. The green had lots of spectator room behind it and one of the biggest crowds on the course. The roar hurt my ears.

Delsing had to hit next because he hadn't laid up as far back as Bobby had. I can only imagine what Bobby's shot and the crowd reaction did to him, but he went for the pin as well and just thinned it a little. It hit the green and rolled off the back edge. Then he couldn't stop the chip coming back and he was lying four when he finally got his ball inside Bobby's.

Delsing could've marked it, but he was right in Bobby's line. So he stepped up and tapped it in—but it didn't go in. It was one of those invisible little breaks that Jello McKay had warned me about, and his ball caught the left lip and spun out. He made 6 and I thought I could see his wheels start to wobble as he walked to the edge of the green.

With the teach from Delsing, I aimed Bobby's putt a ball to the right of dead center and it curled in. We were one under for the round.

From the way the crowd was yelling, you'd have thought we'd won the Ryder Cup or something. People screamed and yelled. I could only understand fragments of what they were trying to say. "All the way," I heard. "True vision." And the inevitable "You da man." It was like walking through a tunnel of sound. I could only imagine what it was like for Bobby, for whom sound was so important.

He waited till we were standing by the tee and Delsing was getting ready to hit before he said anything. "This true vision is powerful horse-shit," he whispered.

"Whatever you're doing, keep doing it," I whispered back.

Of course, I don't believe in true vision. What I really think is that he kind of hypnotized himself until his attention was focused tightly on his targets and his body was relaxed and loose. Whatever it was, Bobby Jobe started to play golf like I'd never seen before.

He knocked his wedge to three feet and birdied nine. He parred ten when a six-footer broke a few inches more than I'd thought it would, so that was my fault. He birdied eleven and parred twelve. He parred thir-teen, then birdied fourteen. The odd thing was, at first it didn't feel like he was hot, playing over his head. It felt like he was playing golf the way he should always play it. It felt like his normal game, if you could believe that the golf he usually played was something less than normal.

No one else saw it that way. In fact, it started to look like the entire population of southern New Jersey was squeezed around the Sand Valley golf course, howling and yelling and hanging from trees to get a glimpse of us. There's a weird old green-and-white water tower by the twelfth tee and I counted six kids clinging to the beams that held up the cantilevered, bulbous upper half of it. They looked like monkeys. The Goodyear blimp appeared to have parked a thousand feet or so over our heads. We needed a squad of six New Jersey state troopers to move from green to tee. The only place that wasn't full of people was the pond in front of us at the fif-teenth, and I wouldn't have been surprised if people started swimming through that to get a closer look. It was the closest I've ever been to a riot on a golf course, but there was no sense of threat. It was like everyone was on this ride together.

I sneaked a look at the leaderboard as we waited to hit Bobby's tee shot. He was four under for the day, even for the tournament. The only player ahead of him was Little Dickie at two under. Lehman was tied with us. Everyone else except Delsing had fallen back. Jay had been carried along on our momentum and made a couple of birdies himself. He stood tied for fourth at three over.

The leaderboard clicked as the numbers changed, and I could see Bobby heard it. He cocked his head that way. He sidled up to me. "Not going to ask you where we stand," he said. "But we're doing pretty good, huh?"

"Not bad," I told him.

"Yeah," he said, "and that Gates guy has made a little money."

When he said that, I stopped thinking this was normal and realized it was special. It reminded me of a recording Eudora has, a recording Ella made of 'S Wonderful back in the fifties with Nelson Riddle. She sings the first verse, very sweet and melodic. Then the band takes over and picks up the tempo very gradually. It builds and builds and then crests in a chorus of horns. And then Ella comes back in and she's taken the song to a new plane. It's just gorgeous. It swings and it's poetic both.

That was where Bobby's golf game had gotten, to a new plane. It was effortless. It was joyful.

But it wasn't something you could turn on like a television set and leave on. It was as delicate as a spider's web, as fleeting as water in your hands. The wait on the fifteenth tee was enough to cause it to leak away. Olazabal was looking for his tee shot in the woods on the left side of the fairway. I don't know how long they gave him to find it, but it seemed more like ten minutes than the five you're allowed under the rules.

I could see the delay affect Bobby. It started with listening to numbers click in the leaderboard. Then he chatted a little with Delsing. Then he chatted with the sign boy. Then I noticed his thumbs rubbing against his fingers. Pretty soon he was walking in tight little circles around the tee box, talking to himself.

When it was finally clear ahead of us, he tried to do all the right things. He went through the routine just like he'd been doing. He even said "true vision" to me with a sarcastic little smile. But he wasn't where he'd been. He didn't crack up. He just started playing average golf on a harder-than-average golf course. He managed to par the next three, but it wasn't easy. He got up and down from a bunker on sixteen and chipped up close from the right side of the green on seventeen.

On the eighteenth tee, I saw Clayton Mote alone in the crowd. He must've gotten away from Dr. Mehta for a second. He was staring intently in our direction. At first I thought he was watching Bobby's swing to see if he was driving his legs or something. But then I could see right into his eyes and I knew he was staring at me.

He had a terrible, piercing stare, as if once he pushed his mind out of the swamp inside his skull he was endowed with superhuman perception and concentration. I couldn't meet his eyes for more than a fraction of a second. I had to look away. It was too painful.

Maybe I was distracted then and maybe Bobby sensed it, because he hit his sloppiest drive of the day, a push into the rough on the right side. He, of course, had no idea that Clayton was around. The lie was bad. That was all he cared about at the moment. He put his fingers in the grass a foot behind the ball to get a feel for it.

"How deep in it are we?"

"You can see the top of the ball, but that's all," I said.

"Yardage?"

I'd paced it off from the closest sprinkler head.

"One-fifty front, one sixty-one hole." At that moment, I couldn't think of football players with those numbers. My mind was too jumbled.

"How much to clear the water?"

"One twenty-three."

"Gonna jump?" He meant was the ball going to go a little farther because he was hitting it from the rough and wouldn't be putting much backspin on it.

I looked at the lie. If he hit it decently, it was going to jump.

"Most likely," I said.

He turned in a little circle, looking for the sound of wind in his ears. But the air was still.

"Eight?" he asked.

I didn't like the eight-iron because the pin was back right and that meant the major trouble around the green was back right—a nasty bunker. If he left it short, he'd have a semireasonable bunker shot to the hole.

"Nine. 'Cause of the jump," I said.

"Okay," Bobby said.

But I guess I was still distracted by Clayton Mote, because I didn't read that lie right. Bobby swung all right, but the ball didn't jump. Instead, the grass grabbed the club and slowed it down. He hit an ugly little shot that was lucky to clear the pond. It settled into the rough between two of the bunkers guarding the green and disappeared.

The crowd's silence told Bobby everything he hadn't already figured out from the sense he had of his swing and the contact between ball and club.

"Bunker?" he asked.

"Rough," I said. I didn't tell him that the lie was likely to be so bad that he'd wish he was in the sand. I waited for him to chew me out.

"Sorry, Coach," he said. "Didn't put a good swing on that one."

"I'm sorry," I said. "I saw the pro looking at me. I didn't read the lie right. "

Bobby just shrugged. "No accounting for fathers, is there?"

I shook my head. "No," I said. "Sometimes they teach you Hogan's secret—"

"And sometimes they don't know from Victoria's Secret," Bobby finished.

"All you can do is try to get your ball up and down," I said.

"If we got any more philosophical," Bobby said, "they'd have to call us Greeks and cover us with plaster."

Delsing was up and he hit his approach right at the flag. I couldn't tell how close he got because you couldn't see the surface of the green from the fairway. The level of the applause said he was somewhere between a tap-in and a makable birdie putt.

Bobby grabbed the bag again and we started walking toward the little footbridge on the left side of the fairway that spans the water that guards the green. The crowd was thick on both sides of the hole, and the clapping and whistling washed over us on every step. There's a tendency to let your mind wander on the walk up the last fairway anyway; you know within a stroke or two what you're going to shoot. It's better, I know, to keep your focus on the next shot.

And then, in the midst of one of the clusters of blind people in the crowd, I saw a head full of red hair and thought it was Angela. I wasn't sure because she was three or four rows deep in the crowd over on the other side of the fairway. But I thought about her and about the vision she'd had and how it had brought me and Bobby to this place and how she thought what we were doing might encourage other blind people. I knew I was supposed to be mad at her for blowing me off the way she had. I couldn't be. Suddenly, my eyes were watery.

I didn't want to use my ball-wiping towel to wipe them, and I didn't have anything else. So I asked the scorekeeping lady and she produced a tissue.

"Are you all right?" she asked me.

"Allergies," I said. "Must be something around here I'm allergic to."

Just then a huge roar went up from the gallery and I thought for half a second it was about me. But of course, it wasn't. I followed the eyes of the sighted spectators to the scoreboard behind the green. The board showed that Little Dickie Reynolds had taken a 6 on the fifteenth hole. Lehman had already fallen back and Duval and Woods had never mounted any charge. Bobby was just a stroke back.

"What is it?" he asked me, referring to the noise. "Someone make birdie?"

"No, it's Little Dickie," I told him. "Bogeyed No. 15."

"So where does that put us?" he wanted to know.

I thought about telling him I didn't know to try to force him to think about the next shot instead of the score. But I wasn't capable of jerking him around at that moment.

"Second," I said. "Stroke back."

"So if I par this one, I'm gonna play with Little Dickie tomorrow?"

"Looks like it."

Bobby didn't react visibly except for getting a little tighter in the jaw. "All right," he said. "Let's go to work."

And we did. We found the ball, and I held his hand as he felt the height and texture of the rough around it. I described how it lay, down in the grass, but with a fortunate little cushion of turf underneath it. I paced the distance to the edge of the green, to the pin, and to the spot I wanted the ball to land on. I told him the trajectory he needed.

I grabbed his arm behind the triceps as he took the only stance available to him, with his rear foot in the bunker and his left foot in the grass. He choked down on his lob wedge, took a couple of practice strokes and swung.

Somehow, he caught it just right. The ball popped up light as a balloon and floated up to the green, headed right for the flag. I could hear a thunk when it landed, but I couldn't see it. The green was above my head.

The swelling noise from the crowd told me it was a good shot. It got louder and louder as the ball rolled toward the hole. Then there was a moan. When I saw it on *SportsCenter* that night, I saw how the ball stopped on the edge of the hole and refused to fall in.

I stood up, grabbed Bobby's arm, and helped him out of the bunker. We walked slowly up the bank toward the green. The crowd noise died away for a few seconds after the moan. Then it picked up again as we came over the crest of the rise and onto the green.

"Let's tap it in," I said, right in his ear so he could hear me. We did.

That touched off a new wave of cheering. I stepped away from Bobby, leaving him alone by the hole. The applause got louder still. It was coming in thunderous waves. It was Bobby Jones coming up Broadway after winning the Grand Slam. It was Michael Jordan bringing the sixth and last championship trophy back to Chicago. Delsing tucked his putter under his arm and started clapping. Lizard joined in. Finally, I did, too.

Bobby turned slowly in his tracks to hear it from all directions, like a kid standing under the Gaulor River Falls upstream from Allegheny Gap on a hot summer day. The kid will let that cool water wash over him forever. Bobby and the crowd seemed to want the ovation to go on that long. They needed to tell him how they felt about the round he'd played. He needed to hear it.

Finally, it got embarrassing. Delsing still had a birdie putt. I stepped out to Bobby and took his arm. We moved over to the side of the green. The crowd got the idea and settled down. They groaned politely as

Delsing's birdie putt slid by the hole, then clapped politely as he tapped in for his par.

I kept looking for Angela and Clayton in the gallery. But it seemed as if neither one was there. Maybe there were just too many people.

But I couldn't miss the scoreboard. Reynolds was the only one without a black number next to his name, the only one who'd been able to better par at Sand Valley for three rounds. There were lots of guys at ten, twelve, fourteen over par, numbers you don't usually see after the cut in a professional tournament. Sand Valley was justifying its reputation.

Lizard and I got behind our state troopers like Emmitt Smith getting behind the Cowboys line, with Bobby and Jay Delsing trailing us. We started working through the crowd toward the scorer's tent.

Clayton Mote appeared in front of us as suddenly as one of those kids you see jump out from between parked cars in the safe-driving commercials. One moment Bobby and I were surrounded by anonymous fans and our state troopers. The next, he was there in front of me, staring right in my eyes. I jerked to a stop. Bobby bumped into the bag behind me.

"What the hell?" he asked.

One of the troopers made a move to grab Clayton, but I put a hand on his shoulder to let him know I knew the man.

"Hi, Dad," I said quietly.

Clayton started breathing heavily, like steam pressure was building up inside him. He wouldn't look at me. He shifted his stare to the ground. Dr. Mehta appeared then, trying to squeeze through the crowd like a New Yorker pushing onto a subway car. Obviously, Clayton had gotten away from him. He reached out and put a hand on Clayton's arm, seizing control. Just as he did, Clayton looked up at me again.

His mouth opened, but no words came. It was like he had a hot coal in his throat and couldn't spit it out.

Then he stopped, seemed to sag. He looked as if it had been a tremendous effort just to get in front of us and he was exhausted. His eyes rolled back a little so the whites showed under the pupils. He sagged back toward Mehta. He started mumbling to himself.

A buzz started in the crowd as people began asking themselves questions about what they were seeing.

"You'll have to clear a path for the players," one of the troopers said firmly to my father.

"No, it's all right," I said.

Mehta sized up the situation, whispered something in my father's ear. Clayton didn't respond. He mumbled some more, louder. It was as if his real self had struggled to the surface for a minute, then been sucked back under.

"I think I'll take him for some water," Mehta said. He started to lead Clayton away, pushing through the crowd.

17

▼

I GOT BOBBY BACK INTO HIS SUITE. HE SAID HE WANTED TO LIE DOWN before dinner, so I left him alone. I had an urge to call Angela's room. No answer. As I hung up the phone, I decided I was lucky she hadn't been there. I'd had no idea what I would do or say if I actually saw her, and the odds were in that situation that I'd wind up saying something stupid. I wished I'd never asked her to be my girlfriend, because it was clear that her turning me down meant she couldn't be my friend, either. I decided to go for a walk. I had to do something.

J. R. Neill and Conrad Williams from Allegheny Gap intercepted me by a row of quarter slots. They were wearing Eadon Branch golf hats. They were unshaven and red-eyed.

"Glad Bobby had a good round," J. R. said. "When you saw us, you didn't look happy we came up."

I felt guilty for myself and pleased again that Bobby hadn't let them distract him. "Just my game face, J. R.," I told him. "We were both real glad to see some folks from home."

"Home," Conrad echoed. "You bet our four hundred bucks?"

"Got eight hundred-to-one," I told them.

"Hot damn!" J. R. said. He turned to Conrad. "I told you he'd do it."

"Hot damn!" Conrad repeated. "That'd be thirty-two thousand dollars!"

I didn't correct his multiplication. I wouldn't've known he was off if I hadn't done the figuring myself on the back of the HBO schedule.

"Don't go spending that money at the crap tables," I told Conrad. "We're a stroke down and Little Dickie's a tough player. Lot of tough players out there."

"Doesn't matter," J. R. said. "I got a feeling about true vision."

"True vision!" Conrad chimed in. He was all but rubbing his hands together like a miser.

"Not you guys, too," I said. I tried to change the subject. "So you drove straight through?" I asked.

"Damn straight," J. R. said. "And we brought your mother, too."

"Eudora?"

"You got another mother?" J. R. asked.

She was in the casino, playing blackjack with a couple of geezers at a five-dollar table. The dealer was a somnolent Chinese woman with a 9 showing. Eudora had three hands going—a 6, a 4 and a 3 up. The geezer to her left busted as I walked up. It was Eudora's play.

"Stick," I said, walking up behind her. "On all of 'em."

She recognized my voice, turned. I thought she was going to argue with me. Behind her, the dealer waited, both expectant and bored.

"I'm on a roll," I told Eudora. "Stick."

She just nodded and waved her hand over the cards. "I stick."

The dealer's expression never changed. She flipped over a 5, dealt herself a queen, and paid Eudora three rose-colored chips.

"Told you," I said. I kissed her on the top of the head.

Eudora tossed one of her chips to the dealer and put the rest in the purse she was carrying, a white woven purse that matched the white shoes she was wearing. She had on a pale green print dress. It looked like a church outfit, except that the shoes were flats and Eudora rarely went to church.

"How d'you look so fresh after eight hours in a car?" I asked her.

"Well, we checked into a motel outside of town, toward the golf course," she said. "Didn't think we could get a room here."

She closed her purse. "And, of course, I didn't want to check in if it'd upset your father. He's here, isn't he?"

I nodded. "Matter of fact, he was playing blackjack at this table a day or two ago."

She got whiter than the lime we put on the turf in the springtime to balance out the acids in the rain.

"I better go then," she said. "I don't want him to see me."

Seeing her fear ticked me off. I know it was the sickness, not something he could control. But Clayton Mote was still a mean man.

"What a happy reunion for the Mote family," I said. "Under the same roof again for the first time in fifteen years."

"I'm sorry, Henry," she said.

"Not your fault, Eudora," I said, and hugged her. "C'mon. I'll walk you over to the Taj Mahal. Better casino anyway."

We found the boardwalk door and stepped outside. I scanned the surf, looking for a redheaded woman. I couldn't see one.

"How're you two getting along?" Eudora asked.

It took me a second to realize she meant me and Clayton, not me and Angela or me and Bobby.

"You know how he is," I said. "Frustrating. Most of the time, he sits and talks to himself or listens to voices in his head. But he did come out of it once in a while to tell Bobby something about his golf swing."

I didn't tell her about the previous night.

I think she was both sad and relieved. It would've hurt her to hear that I'd established a rapport with him.

"The doctor thinks he might be getting a little better," I said.

"If he's not screaming at you, he is," she affirmed.

I put my arm around her shoulder and gave her a little hug. "I'm glad you're here," I said. "How about dinner tonight with me and Bobby?"

She brightened for just an instant. "Would your father be there?"

I nodded. "He's been eating with us. Dr. Mehta would be there, too."

Again, she looked frightened. "I think I'd rather play blackjack, Henry," she said. "They'll probably comp me for a meal."

I decided I'd done enough prodding. So I kissed her on the cheek at the door to the Taj Mahal. She was inside before I remembered that I hadn't told her how much money we could win if Bobby took first place.

I walked along the beach for a while, but I didn't see Angela. There wasn't even a drunk sleeping under the boardwalk. There was just the sound of the waves in one ear and the sounds of the casino in the other ear and the neon lights glowing in the darkening sky. Another mist was rolling gently in from the water, as if it, too, was forming waves— in and out, higher and lower, lapping at the beach.

•   •   •

IT TURNED OUT TO BE JUST ME AND BOBBY FOR DINNER. DR. MEHTA DECIDED that Clayton needed a quiet meal and an early bed. We still didn't know where Angela was. It was a good enough meal—porterhouse steaks—but there seemed to be empty spots around the table.

Bobby relaxed a little. He started using his fingers to push his food onto his fork, something that made his eating more efficient but which he would only do when eating with me or Angela. With other people, he was too embarrassed. He ordered lemon meringue pie, which is not a great choice for a blind eater, since the meringue gets all over the fingers. They do better with a piece of plain cheesecake.

"Fathers are funny, aren't they?" he asked when the pie was gone, wiping his fingers off in a napkin. "Bad as mine was, I still wished he could've lived long enough to see me play football between the hedges at Georgia. Or play golf tomorrow, for that matter."

He was trying, I knew, to help me feel less lousy about how things were turning out with Clayton. He wasn't doing a hell of a great job of it, but I appreciated the gesture anyway.

Bobby stopped rubbing his fingers but didn't put the napkin down, like he'd been struck by a thought so powerful it paralyzed his brain. "You know, I sure would like to have Robby and Paula watch that round tomorrow," he said.

"I'm sure they've been watching on TV," I said. "Paula, at least. Robby may still like Mickey Mouse better."

"I got an idea," Bobby said. "Let's call the airlines."

So I got out the phone book and called Delta and found out the flight schedule between Nashville and Philadelphia on Sunday morning. There was a flight scheduled to get in at 10:15. We didn't have to be at the course till half past twelve, since we were in the last group. It was doable. We could pick them up at the airport and still make our tee time.

Bobby grabbed the phone from me when he heard that information, laid his hand on the keypad, and punched in a number. I sat back and listened.

"Hey, Paula, it's me . . . Thanks, glad you watched . . . Yeah, it was amazing. Just one of those days. Well . . . hey, I was wondering if you and Robby wouldn't like to come and watch the final round tomorrow. Henry and I checked and there's a flight gets you into Philadelphia on time."

There was a long silence on Bobby's side of the conversation. Paula was explaining something unpleasant, because Bobby sagged like my old Ford truck when it's full of fertilizer bags.

"Well, I know you have plans, and I know they're important," he said. "But this is a special occasion . . ."

Paula was turning him down, and it was painful to witness. I got up and walked to the balcony, but I could still hear his side of the conversation.

"Please, Paula," he said, "not for me, but for Robby. . . . Well, all right. I understand. Maybe the next time. Yeah, I'll tell him."

I thought he might get mad, but he didn't. He just quietly hung up the phone, taking care to make sure that it was resting properly in its cradle.

"Sorry," I said.

He didn't turn toward my voice. "She said to tell you you're doing a great job and keep it up," he said.

"That was nice of her," I said.

"Paula always liked you," he replied.

"And I liked her."

Then he turned toward me. "Do you think I've blown it with her?"

"Well," I said, "you played around with other women, then you divorced her. It's not the way to most women's hearts that I know of. But what do I know?"

He nodded.

"I wouldn't give up on her," I offered.

Bobby bit his lip. "No. I won't. She said she'd be rooting for me."

He seemed shocked by her refusal, and I started to worry about how it might affect his play the next day. I told myself it was a selfish concern, but I still thought about it.

"It's funny," Bobby said. "I feel like I'm different somehow. Like my intentions are better. Like you said, I could tell the difference between a C-cup and a D-cup, but I couldn't tell what I was doing to her? No, I knew what I was doing to her, but I didn't see what I was doing to myself. Now I do see that. But that doesn't mean Paula's going to come back, does it?"

"You're asking me about women?"

"Oh, God," Bobby said. "Has it come to that?"

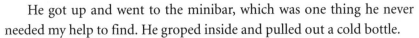

He got up and went to the minibar, which was one thing he never needed my help to find. He groped inside and pulled out a cold bottle.

"What's this?" he asked me. It was root beer.

"Heineken," I said.

He must've picked up something in my voice that tipped him off I was kidding him, because he rubbed his fingers over the bottle a moment and scowled.

"Heineken has an oval label, Greyhound. This one's got no label."

"It's special Heineken," I said.

He sighed, put the bottle back, and pulled a can out of the refrigerator. He opened it, tasted it, and wrinkled his nose. "Bud Light?"

"Miller," I said.

"That's the trouble with being blind. You end up drinking light beer."

"Aw," I said.

At least he wasn't feeling so sorry for himself about Paula, I thought.

He sat down in a chair and swallowed about half the can. "You know," he said, "the really weird thing is that I don't feel any better than I do. I mean, here I am, in the last group in a major and six months ago I didn't think I'd ever play again. So why am I not just thrilled?"

"'Cause you want to win tomorrow," I said.

He nodded and sipped his beer.

THE NEXT MORNING, I WENT UP TO BOBBY'S SUITE FOR BREAKFAST AS USUAL, but neither of us felt like eating much. I read the Sunday morning sports pages to him and we listened to the audio from the morning *SportsCenter*, both wishing the time would pass faster. Then it was time for Bobby to dress. I had held back a black shirt for him, but he rejected it. He told me he wanted to wear the white shirt he'd used on Wednesday for the practice round.

"But you've got khaki pants and white shoes," I said. "You'll look like you ought to be driving a Good Humor truck."

"I don't care," he said.

I didn't argue with him, but I pulled the darkest hat he had from his Callaway collection and gave it to him.

"No," he said. "There's a hat in the closet I want to wear."

I shrugged and went into the closet. On the shelf, I found a beat-up old Eadon Branch hat he'd worn for practice that summer.

"Doesn't Ely Callaway pay you to wear his hats?" I asked him.

"Ely's got enough customers," Bobby said.

Neither one of us seemed to know what to say next. We just stood there like dopes.

"Well, I guess we better get our asses out there," Bobby said. "We can't have the touring pro from Eadon Branch missing his tee time."

We were so tight that if you'd plucked our arms, you could've played "Dueling Banjos." Used to be, I'd've been worried about it. But now I figured that if you didn't feel nervous in a situation like the one we were in, you had something wrong with you. So I just put him in the car and drove.

When we got to the course, we were immediately surrounded. There were the state troopers walking around us, fending people off. There was the CBS crew. There were a couple of people from Cade Benton's office at the PGA Tour. But it was a lonely cocoon. We were surrounded by people we didn't know and had nothing to say to. On the practice range, nobody talked to us. I polished the clubs till you could've eaten with them.

Little Dickie Reynolds stayed on his end of the range. We stayed on ours. I knew his caddie, Albie Miller, a little bit. Albie nodded to me as they passed by us, looking for a patch of turf to warm up on. But not his boss. Little Dickie acted like he was the blind guy and couldn't see us.

Maybe he wasn't thinking only about what he'd said on television before the tournament about Bobby not deserving a chance. Maybe it was just his way. I've heard stories about playing partners in the final rounds of major championships who never said a word, just let the other guy stew in the silence between them. Hogan used to be that way. Generally said no more than two words during a round, and those two words were, "you're away." I've heard that Hale Irwin never said a word to Mike Donald during the Open playoff that he won in 1990. Donald finally cracked on the eighteenth hole. Some guys are like that.

On top of everything else, it was sweltering out. A weather front from the South had pushed up into New Jersey and the air was muggy and close. I started to sweat before we left the range.

Bobby's game face softened for the first time when we got to the tee and the blind people in the gallery heard he was there. They went crazy, whooping and whistling and screaming about true vision. Seemed like there'd been more of them with every round, and on this day I'd guess there must've been nearly a thousand of them, carrying canes, wearing dark glasses, some hanging on to the elbows of sighted companions.

Only when he saw the CBS camera crew that was trailing the group move into position did Little Dickie break his silence. He walked up to Bobby with a broad smile on his face and extended his hand. He grabbed Bobby by the elbow so he'd know he was there and said, "Bobby, best of luck today. Play well."

Bobby shook his hand. "Thanks, Dickie," he said. "I appreciate your kind thoughts. Same to you."

Even Albie Miller had to stifle a snicker. Little Dickie flushed and scowled.

Our official for the day was Cade Benton, wearing a white shirt and a striped tie. You knew it was humid if he decided to go without his blue blazer. He tossed a coin and Dickie called heads and won.

"Ladies and gentlemen, our two o'clock pairing, please welcome, from Orlando, Florida, Dickie Reynolds." The crowd applauded politely, but underneath that sound, I was sure I heard a few hisses from the blind section. So did Little Dickie. He looked like he'd been poked in the rear end with a hot fork. He looked up and glared in their direction. Of course, since they couldn't see it, a glare might not've been the most effective intimidation device.

But Dickie settled over the ball and hit a good, crisp three-wood into the neck of the dogleg. He watched it fly for a moment, then bent over to pick up his tee before it landed. He knew it was good.

I glanced to the right and in the midst of a crowd of people with white canes, I finally saw Angela. She was wearing her golf shoes and her Eadon Branch shirt. I caught her eye, figuring that purely on golf matters, it was okay to be normal with her. She smiled and held up a clenched fist. I'd been pumped up before I saw her. Now I was like the Pillsbury Doughboy.

"And from Dalton, Georgia, please welcome . . ."

The announcer didn't get Bobby's name out before the roar of the spectators drowned him out. The blind gallery's cheer started first this time and lasted longest.

Bobby tipped his Eadon Branch hat and I started forward toward the tee markers, but the noise was still coming. We had to wait an extra five or ten seconds before the last call of "True vision!" echoed off the surrounding pines. I was starting to wonder if I was going to have "true vision" written on my tombstone.

I squatted, took hold of the clubhead, and laid it down behind the ball. For a moment I found it hard to breathe. The trees lining the fairway seemed to inch closer together. The neck that had seemed so broad a target on Tuesday started to look like Clayton Mote's practice alley through the trees at the hospital in Staunton.

I fought to get my mind to create a picture of the shot I wanted, to hear the thwack of the ball against the middle of the clubface, to see it start out low, straight, and strong and get small in a hurry. Slowly, weakly, my brain conjured that picture up.

"Smooth three-wood," I told Bobby. "Big target. You know the shot. See it and hit it."

I was just damn glad I didn't have to hit it. But Bobby swung smoothly and the ball went where it was supposed to go. I exhaled.

Fortunately, there's a lot of routine work involved in caddying and it saves you at times when you feel like wandering off into the woods and throwing up. You automatically pick up the bag, wipe off the clubhead, put it away. You see the path trod through the sand waste in front of you and you set off, thinking about the yardage you'll have to the green.

The crowd from Eadon Branch was waiting down the left side of the fairway—J. R., Conrad, and the rest. And walking with them, under a big straw hat and hiding behind dark glasses, was Eudora. She looked like one of those movie star pictures you see on the front page of *National Enquirer*, the pictures where they're trying not to be recognized. I caught her eye. I smiled at her. She smiled back, quickly, furtively.

Little Dickie's ball was five yards behind us and he hit a seven-iron that he drew, trying to get at a pin cut back left. He drew it too much. It caught the bank on the edge of the green and tumbled down into the surrounding sand. That reminded me not to be too aggressive, especially early. So I gave Bobby an eight-iron and aimed him for the middle of the green. That's where he hit it.

We got to the green and Little Dickie had to wait for quiet before he chipped up. Since we were the last pairing, no one had hung around the first tee after we left. All of them were trying to squeeze into someplace where they could watch us—maybe five thousand people in a space that wasn't built to accommodate more than a few golfers and their caddies. They were crowding around the front edges of the green. Kids were climbing trees behind it. In the back of this mob, the blind spectators were making their way along with us, canes in front of them, clinging to their sighted companions. Then there were the photographers following us—maybe fifty of them, all scrambling for good position inside the ropes. The course was starting to feel like an airport at Thanksgiving.

Little Dickie scowled as he waited. Finally, he stepped away and went through his entire routine again, scuffing his wedge in the sand and kicking up little clouds of grit. The sand he was in was a waste area, not a hazard under the rules. In fact, it was a mean little place to be, like a dirt road that some sand had blown over. There must've been less sand under his ball than he thought, because he caught the ball half-solid and sent it over the green into a bunker on the other side.

As soon as they heard the click of ball meeting club, the crowd started to moan. The moan intensified as the ball landed in the bunker, and then silence fell. For about three seconds. That's how long it took for the blind people in the gallery to get a fill on what'd happened. And when they got it, they started to cheer and whistle.

Little Dickie went from pale to purple in an instant. He climbed onto the green and went directly to Cade Benton. I couldn't hear exactly what he said, but I did hear the word "ejected."

Benton hitched up his trousers and walked over to the edge of the green, facing the blind spectators. He cleared his throat. It got very quiet. The only movement was from the CBS camera crew, maneuvering to get a shot of Benton's face.

"I'm going to have to ask you to please observe the customary decorum among golf galleries," Benton said.

A stubby blind woman, shorter than the white cane she was carrying, had edged her way toward the front of the crowd facing Benton. She had close-cropped gray hair that hung over her forehead in bangs, a denim dress, and black sneakers.

"And what's that?" she demanded of Benton in a loud voice.

Benton looked startled that someone would ask. "Well, um, you applaud only for good shots," he said.

The blind woman considered this for a second. "And what if we don't?" she asked.

A little buzz started in the rest of the gallery.

Benton stiffened, then remembered who and where he was. "Well, I'm sure you will," he said.

Standing behind him, I could see the flush start to spread up from Benton's neck to his ears.

"Maybe I should say something," Bobby whispered to me.

"Don't," I whispered, grabbing his arm. "Benton's paid to handle stuff like this. You don't know her. You're not responsible for her."

Little Dickie caught too much sand with his explosion and barely got it onto the green. Most of the spectators were silent, but a few applauded derisively. They were behind us, though, not in the cluster where the blind spectators were standing.

Little Dickie, from inside the bunker, glared over the lip until the place was as quiet as a church. He was still away, maybe forty-five feet from the hole. Without taking anywhere near his normal time, he putted, and rolled it five feet past the hole. He had a tough putt left to make 6.

Bobby rarely paid much attention to what playing partners were doing. He just wanted to know when it was his turn to hit. But this time he asked me what Little Dickie had done and he made me give it to him in rushed, whispered detail.

"Anyway, let's make this putt," I finished. "Little Dickie isn't your responsibility."

"I know," he said.

I was worried that he didn't believe it, that he thought he was responsible. The blind spectators wouldn't have been there if it weren't for him. I was afraid that subconsciously, Bobby might try to make it up to Little Dickie by blowing a putt or something.

But he didn't. He made a nice lag to two feet, almost on the same line Little Dickie had. I marked the ball without telling Bobby where it was. I wanted to see Little Dickie putt out and get a read from his ball.

"Bobby, would you move the mark a clubhead to the left?" Little Dickie asked. "Er, I'm sorry. Greyhound, would you move it?"

Bobby frowned. I looked at Little Dickie. His face was studied innocence.

"You want me to putt out?" Bobby offered. He was feeling guilty, and he figured that putting first would give Little Dickie a bit of an edge and make it up to him.

"We'd trample your line," I said before Little Dickie could answer. Before Bobby could say anything else, I moved the mark.

Sure enough, Little Dickie's putt broke a couple of inches more than it looked like it would. His ball lipped out and he'd started off with a 7.

I replaced the mark and adjusted Bobby's aim accordingly. He stroked it. It was a weak, tentative jab, and it nearly missed the hole. But it rolled around the top of the cup 180 degrees and fell in.

"Center cut," I told Bobby. "Never a doubt."

"Yeah, right," he said. "Don't be sarcastic."

"Since when," I asked him, "have you recognized sarcasm?"

It was nervous talk, but it settled us down some. We didn't get close to the place we were at in the third round, when the game seemed effortless and automatic. I felt every creak when I squatted down behind Bobby. I couldn't make my eyes zero in on the fairways and greens. I kept seeing bunkers and trees. And Bobby didn't act like the machine he'd been the day before. He was fidgety over the ball, and I could tell he was fighting the urge to try to make himself swing properly instead of letting himself do it. But we managed to par the next five holes. So did Little Dickie.

Up ahead, maybe on the seventh green, we heard a tremendous roar.

"Sounds like an eagle," Bobby said. "Duval?"

"I'm not looking at scoreboards," I said. And it was true. I wasn't.

I was worried, instead, about a line of thunderclouds that was moving into the sky over the western side of the golf course. They were greasy-black and moving fast. The sky had been clear when we started, and now it looked like it might open within half an hour.

Thunder rumbled faintly in the distance.

Bobby's head jerked when he heard it. He turned in the direction of the sound, as if he could look at the storm front.

"Gonna rain?" he asked me.

"Looks like it might," I said.

"Lightning?"

"Could be," I told him. "But you know they'll blow the horn before it gets out of Pennsylvania." The Tour had been careful about clearing courses before Bobby's accident. Since then, it had gotten paranoid about it.

Bobby had his three-wood out. He twirled it around in his hands, then extended it back to me. I took it. Ahead of us, the fairway cleared.

"You're up, Mr. Jobe," Cade Benton said.

"You heard the thunder," Bobby replied.

Around us, the murmurs started. People close to us could overhear the conversation. Farther away, they could see that Bobby had no club in his hands.

Little Dickie spoke up. He was too smart to say something like, "Hit it, Jobe. What're ya afraid of, a little lightning?" Instead, he appeared to take Bobby's side. "Maybe we ought to wait, Cade," he said. "Damn horn could go off on someone's backswing."

That was a great swing thought. Take it back slow and twitch when you hear the horn. Thanks, Dickie.

It was a delicate situation. Technically, any golfer has the right to stop playing if he feels the weather endangers him. In reality, no one does unless the horn blows. Bobby knew better than to walk off on his own. Benton knew better than to let people think he was bullying Bobby to play with thunderclouds on the horizon. He pulled out his walkie-talkie and checked in with someone. He listened for a while, then he passed along what he'd heard.

"Radar says there's no lightning in the area, Bobby, and they can spot a leaky faucet anywhere within twenty miles of this place. There's a storm cell west of Philly, but it's heading north. Won't affect us." Benton's voice sounded like gravel being dragged over sandpaper, and he cleared his throat. "But they say if you're uncomfortable playing, they'll blow the horn and wait."

That was about as sincere an offer as the one I used to hear from the high school football coach back in Allegheny Gap when we were getting pushed around: if you boys don't want to play, I'll take you out and let someone else do it.

"I'm not uncomfortable, Cade," Bobby said. "You know what they say about lightning never striking twice in the same place. I figure I've had mine." He paused. "Of course, as far as the rest of you go, well . . ."

He didn't finish the sentence. He just smiled and said, "Three-wood, Coach?"

I glanced at Little Dickie. He was enjoying our company as much as we enjoyed his.

The wind kicked up some—not like it had been on Friday, but maybe a club's worth.

"Two-iron," I said. I explained why.

"You don't think if we hit a three-wood right up to the edge we could reach the green with the second?"

"Asking for trouble," I replied.

He shrugged. "Okay, Coach. Let's go with the two-iron."

I pulled the club and we started getting set. As he held the shaft against his thighs to align himself, the wind died down to nothing.

He lifted his head and turned toward where the breeze had been, feeling and listening. "Still want two-iron?" he asked.

If we switched now to a three-wood, I figured his swing might be hesitant. So I told him yes.

I figured wrong. He tried to hit the two-iron too hard, to make up for the loss of the wind. His body did all the wrong things, unwinding too fast. He cut the ball, and I watched it fade right, hoping that something, some puff of wind, a passing bird, would knock it down while it was still over the fairway.

"Sit," I said.

It didn't. It lit in the rough, bounced once, and disappeared in grass so long it could've had cucumbers growing in it.

Bobby knew he'd mishit it before it landed. "How bad?" he asked me.

"Not too bad," I said. "We'll know when we get there."

Little Dickie hit his own tee shot, a three-wood, straight down the middle. We trekked to the ball. Just before we got to it, the thunder rumbled again.

"I wish this storm would piss or get off the pot," Bobby said.

I looked back. His thumbs were twitching against his fingers like a squirrel trying to chew through a cage.

Our lie was terrible. If the spectators and marshals hadn't seen the ball land, we'd've had a hard time finding it. It had all but disappeared in the rough, like that last jelly bean hiding deep in the green stuff they use to fill Easter baskets.

I guided Bobby's hand to the grass a foot behind the ball. I described the lie. I told him the yardage—55 to the edge of the hazard, 180 to clear it.

"Think I can get a four-iron on it?" he asked.

I didn't think so, but I was feeling bad about shoving the two-iron down his throat off the tee, so I tried to be subtle about it.

"If it's a great swing," I said. "Safer thing to do would be to chip it out short of the hazard."

"And go for a 6," he said.

"Nah. Five-iron, wedge it close and make par," I suggested.

I waited for him to agree with me, but he didn't. He stood there, arms folded across his chest. He bent down again and ran his fingers through the rough. I saw the back of his shirt. It was stained with sweat. I took that as a bad sign. Bobby didn't normally perspire that much.

Finally, he shook his head. "Not going to win this thing making 6s," he said. "Not when the other guys are making birdies. And we're not here to play for top ten, are we?"

"No," I said.

"Gimme the four," he told me.

But I thought about Palmer in the last round of the 1966 Open, trying to hit a long-iron out of the rough. I thought about Snead doing the same thing in the 1939 Open. It was just the wrong play. If Bobby couldn't see that, I'd have to see it for him.

"No," I said. "You're going to hit a lob wedge back to the fairway."

I thought he'd argue with me. He didn't. He paused, like he was thinking. "Okay, Coach," he said mildly. "Whatever you say."

That brought me up short. It was not the first time Bobby had taken my advice on a club. But it was the first time he'd done it that way. Before, I'd had the sense he was half hoping he'd screw up the shot so he could chew me out for misclubbing him. But this time, it was more like he accepted the fact that I had to be the final judge of strategy. This time he said it with trust.

I wasn't sure I wanted that trust.

I had no more time to think about it. He took the wedge and hacked the ball out into the fairway. There was a groan from the crowd when they saw the club, and the applause after the shot was scattered and hesitant. I could almost hear what was going through people's minds. The thunder, the bad tee shot, the cautious recover—the gallery figured this was where Bobby Jobe started to lose it.

I think Little Dickie thought that way, and when he sensed weakness, he raised his own game to take advantage of it. He drilled a two-iron over Hell's Half Acre and down the fairway for his second shot, stiffed a wedge, and made birdie. Bobby missed a twenty-five-foot par putt and made bogey. Two-shot swing. As best I could figure it going off the seventh green, we were tied.

We had a new rhythm, though. The routine probably looked the same. But it felt like Bobby and I had merged, somehow. We were no longer two people, but a unit. It wasn't like I was handling him as a tool. It wasn't like he was using me as eyes. We just fused.

In that sense, we started playing better, even, than we had on Saturday. The crowd seemed to fall away. The western sky brightened and the rumbles of thunder over Philadelphia fell away. Even Little Dickie and Albie seemed to fall away. I can't tell you whether people kept yelling "True vision!" as we played the next seven or eight holes. I assume they did. But I didn't hear them.

I can tell you other things about that last round, like the gray-green color the leaves in the trees turned when the wind blew them, or the direction the grass was growing in on the ninth green. I can tell you how the fifteenth hole looked like a Coke bottle, wide at the bottom and narrowing at the end till the approach to the green looked no wider than the bottle's neck. I can tell you how much every birdie putt from the eighth through the fifteenth missed by. It wasn't much. Three lipped out. The worst miss was two inches, little more than the width of the golf ball. I can tell you how the shadows, buffeted by the breeze, played in the grass on every fairway. That's because we hit every fairway and I was noticing things like that.

We got to the sixteenth tee and Bobby changed our focus.

"Coach, I think we need to know where we stand," he said.

He was right. The sixteenth is a hole you can play two different ways, depending on the situation. The hole is a slight dogleg right, and the fairway is set at an angle from the tee box, like the angle of an off-ramp on I-81. If you aim straight ahead, you have to clear only a couple of hundred

yards of sand, but you wind up a long way from the green. If you aim farther right and carry about 250 yards' worth of sand, skirting the pines
along the right side, you can make the hole a lot shorter, leaving only a
wedge into the green. And that was important if you wanted to make
birdie, because the pin for the last round was as close to the edge of the
pond on the right side of the hole as the rules allow. You couldn't aim at
it if you were hitting a long-iron—too much chance of running over and
into the water. The first three rounds we'd been conservative.

So I looked at the scoreboard behind the tee. "You're still tied for the
lead with Reynolds," I said quietly.

We heard a roar from down below, at the sixteenth green. The numbers on the board changed, clicking as circuits were opened and shut.

"Delsing's in third, a shot back," I reported. "He just birdied."

Bobby shook his head. "Guess he's hot."

I felt that unity between us start to crack. "Don't start thinking about
Delsing," I said. "Let's think about this hole."

"Doesn't matter what he does," Bobby said. "We need a birdie here if
we're gonna win this thing. Let's play it balls out."

"Let's just play it aggressive," I said.

Little Dickie still had the honor, and when he lined up his shot, I
could see that he was thinking the same way we were. He aimed down the
right side, swung, and hit a tremendous drive that cleared the sand, stayed
five yards right of the trees, and then drew into the fairway. I could see one
big bounce and then it rolled out of sight. The applause for him was not
ever as loud as Bobby's—people weren't warming up to him—but it told
me that the shot was in the fairway, a long way down.

I had an idea. Walter Hagen, who had been great back when a lot of
big tournaments were match play, used to like to make sure he was the
first man to hit his approach to the green on a crucial par four. They say
that Hagen even had a kind of change-up he could hit with his driver,
looking like he was hitting it as hard as he could but taking a little off.
That way, he'd be short of his opponent and he could hit the green first.
Hagen found if he could put his approach close, it jacked up the pressure
on the other guy. He tried to get too fine with his shot, and he frequently
blew it.

"Let's hit three-wood," I said to Bobby.

"I thought you wanted to be aggressive."

"This is," I said. "The way you're hitting it, three-wood is ideal."

He accepted it. I lined him up. It was one of those times when I thought not seeing was an advantage. The view from the tee was like the view you get coming over the mountains from Los Angeles toward Palm Springs—a long stretch of desert. The fairway was only a distant stubble of green that bordered the far end of the sandy waste before it fell away downhill and out of sight. But you could see every juniper bush and scrub pine in the hazard. You could see the taller pines along the right side of the hole, waiting to knock a ball down and throw it in jail. You could see blue slivers of the distant pond through the trunks of the pines. You could see the gallery, massed ten and fifteen deep along the left side of the hole. You just couldn't see a good place to land your tee shot.

"Straight out there, Bobby, nice and smooth."

That's the way he hit it.

"Radar-guided," I whispered to him. "Homing in on the target." The ball landed. "And we have a confirmed hit." It wasn't a 300-yarder like he would've hit with his driver, but it was 275 or 280.

Bobby held his finishing position a second or two longer than he normally did, reveling in it, trying to imprint that feeling on his brain. Then he turned toward me and held out the club.

Suddenly, I was aware of the crowd. The noise was like being out on the Gaulor in a boat during the spring melt, when the whitewater is up over your ears. It just roared all around us, surging and foaming. The ropes held the people back like the frame of a boat holds the water back, but you had the same sense that it was a fragile sort of control, that at any moment, the people could break through and wash over you. For the moment, though, we were riding the wave of their energy. I felt strong.

Neither of us said anything more as we walked up the fairway to the ball. There was no need to. We both knew what had to be done. I paced off the yardage from the nearest sprinkler head. He had 125 to the front of the green and 133 to the hole. Little Dickie was fifteen yards closer.

"Dorsey Levins and Emmitt Smith," I told him. "Pin's five in from the right edge."

"Cut a nine?" Bobby asked.

"That's the play."

"I'm going to hit it one-thirty-eight," Bobby said. "Spin it."

That was his full-swing distance when he cut the ball. He took a couple of practice swings to get a feel for the shape of the shot. Then I set him up and aimed him ten feet left of the pin.

Bobby hit it perfectly. The ball took off low with a lot of spin and curled gently toward the flag. It landed exactly where we had planned, five yards past. It spun back. There's something about the way a well-struck short-iron shot looks, like the ball's got a brain of some kind, so that when it hits the green it takes a hop and seems almost to be sensing the hole. Then it hits the ground and rolls in that direction. It's like watching a good bird dog pause, sniff, get a scent, and take off, which is why some guys, when they're watching that kind of shot, will yell, "Hunt!"

This one hunted. It drew back, brushed the edge of the hole, and stopped three feet away. It was a great shot, the kind of shot that when you hit it on the sixteenth hole in the final round of a major when you're tied for the lead causes you to stand up a little straighter and think, "Damn! I can play this game!"

The noise from the gallery—a steadily accelerating roar followed by a brief sigh, followed by hysterical cheering and applause—told Bobby most of what'd happened.

"Spun back?" he asked me.

"Like a yo-yo," I said.

"Knew I pinched it a tad," he said. "We'll make the putt."

Now Little Dickie had to play. I looked at his face. He looked like a poker player with two pair who's been raised and can't tell if the other guy has pulled an inside straight. He was trying to stay calm and confident, but I thought I could see doubt in the corners of his eyes. He had only a wedge into the green, but now he knew he had to get it very close, had to flirt with the pond. It was the sort of situation Walter Hagen loved to put the other guy in.

Little Dickie didn't botch it completely, but he flinched. He aimed at the flag, but he hit it toward the middle of the green. I knew the feeling. You see the flag, you try to hit it there, but at the last instant your hands turn over a little and you guide the ball away from the water. He knew what he'd done before the ball started coming down. Disgusted, he flipped the club toward Albie. It thunked against the bag.

Bobby heard that thunk and he could gauge the noise that the crowd made. "How far is he?" he asked me.

He was all of thirty feet. "Close enough to make it," I said.

Little Dickie took a long time with his putt. I used it all to try to read Bobby's. I read that putt harder than ever Jimmy Edmisten read his Bible. I looked at it from the back of the hole. I squatted in the sand in front of the green and looked at it from there. I walked Bobby over the line. Every look told me it was going to break an inch and a half to the right just before it got to the hole.

Finally, Little Dickie was ready, and we stood still. He laid a decent stroke on it, but it broke two ways and he missed by three inches, leaving himself a tap-in.

I lined Bobby up and he stroked it exactly on the line I'd selected, at exactly the right speed. It had that smooth roll, like it was following a track. It went in.

The noise from the people echoed off the pines and rolled across the pond. Just when it seemed like everyone had to be hoarse, it got louder.

I clapped Bobby on the back, unwilling to do more in the way of celebrating. We still had two holes to play. But we were a stroke in front. I tried not to think of the $800,000.

"Nice putt," I said, sounding as nonchalant as I could.

"Nice read," he told me. He was about as good as I was at pretending to be calm.

The marshals were waving their hands like deranged traffic cops, trying to get the crowd to hush so Little Dickie could clean up his par. It took a while. Then Dickie got very deliberate. I didn't blame him. There was no one behind us, no reason to rush, and every reason to slow down and gather himself. He read that eighteen-inch putt like it was eighteen feet. Then he carefully rolled it in.

We walked to the seventeenth through a narrow gap in the mob, flanked by troopers protecting us from death by slaps on the back. I was trying not to think that we had a one-stroke lead with two holes to play, that I was caddying for a blind man, and that if we could just made two more lousy pars, we would walk off the course assured of fame and glory, to say nothing of riches. I tried not to think about that first evening when Angela brought Bobby to Eadon Branch and he hit the ball at the airplane.

I tried not to think of all the sweaty, miserable hours of practice since then, or of Bobby getting on a bus to come to Allegheny Gap, or shooting 89 in Myrtle Beach. I tried not to think about what I'd say to Angela if we won, or paying off Eudora's loan for her and telling Jimmy and Junior where to stuff their coal mine, or of calling in experts, Nobel Prize chemists, to come up with a drug to bring back Clayton Mote. I tried not to think of any of that stuff, and of course I failed. It all crowded into my mind. Anyone who tells you that it doesn't run through your mind in that situation is either a liar or hasn't been there, in my opinion.

I was actually grateful for Sand Valley's difficulty at that moment, because on an easier course I might've lost my head completely. But Sand Valley always forces you to think. The seventeenth hole has about six options off the tee, none of them attractive. I managed to drag my mind toward figuring out the shot I wanted Bobby to hit, but it was like trying to drag a dog away from a bone and toward a tub full of soapy water.

Bobby was having the same problem. "Hope Paula saw that one," he said, when he latched on to the bag.

Ahead of us, I could see that Duval had played his second and Delsing was getting ready to hit. I remember thinking that there was something missing in the air. The sound of the birds in the trees, I think it was. They stopped chirping about then.

Delsing swung. The ball got airborne, headed for the flag, dropping toward the green.

The earth moved.

An instant later, Delsing's ball rolled into the hole for an eagle.

I KNOW. BOBBY CLAMPETT SAID HE THOUGHT A GUST OF WIND SHOOK HIS TV tower. I know that in the media center, maybe half a mile away, they didn't feel anything. I know that in Washington the next day, the Department of the Interior or the Geological Survey or someone said their instruments hadn't detected anything. I know a lot of people don't believe there was an earthquake at Sand Valley that day.

But I know what I felt. And I know what five thousand other people around the seventeenth hole did. They yelled and screeched, startled, the way you might be if you came upon a snake in your bare feet.

I remember when Eudora used to set the table for Sunday dinner in the years before Clayton went away. She'd lay a cloth over the table, grab it at one end, and snap it a couple of times. It would billow a little and the wrinkles would smooth out. That's what it felt like. It felt like the seventeenth hole was a tablecloth and it was billowing a little. The entire thing didn't take more than a second.

No sooner did the startled, frightened yelling hit my ear than it was replaced by an astonished, appreciative roar that came from the seventeenth green and spread down the fairway toward us on the tee. I've seen what happened on television replays. Delsing had hit a nine-iron into the green. It lit about ten feet past the hole and started drawing back. Then it broke sharply right and fell into the hole. He'd made a deuce and jumped past Bobby into first place. Out in the fairway, Delsing stood up on his toes, then jumped, trying to see what had happened. When he figured it out, Lizard Ziomecki jumped into his arms and they both fell to their knees on the grass. Bent the hell out of his nine-iron.

Did the earthquake cause the ball to fall in? I don't know. I know two things. One is that I felt the tremor just after Delsing's ball hit the green. And the other is that about three hours later, in the moonlight, after all the interviews and farewells, I went out to the seventeenth green alone and squatted down and rolled a half dozen balls toward the hole along Delsing's line. None of them broke right. But maybe I didn't get the exact spot right. The greens at Sand Valley are very tricky. A putt from one spot can break and a putt from a spot just a foot or two away might not break. It didn't matter. Only thing that mattered was the ball went in.

And I know that Bobby nearly fell over when the ground billowed. He was standing on my right, and he fell against my shoulder then fell away from me. He grabbed my elbow, or he might've gone down. We were standing that way when we heard the noise from the seventeenth green.

"Hey! What the hell?" he demanded. It was like he was annoyed. He tightened his grip on my arm, hanging on and pinching. "What's happening?"

"I'm not sure," I said. "But I think we just had an earthquake and I think Delsing just holed out from the fairway."

"Damn it, Greyhound, be serious," he said.

The sweat rolled down Bobby's face and you'd have thought he'd spent the last few months in a coal mine instead of out in the sun. He got almost as white as the shirt and the Eadon Branch hat he'd chosen that day.

The scene in front of us was approaching chaos. A lot of people ran into the fairway. I guess they were trying to get away from the tremors. Or, maybe, they were running toward the green to see what all the uproar was about. It took ten minutes for the marshals and the security cops to get everyone back behind the ropes. By that time, the scoreboard had changed, showing Delsing in the lead. The shouts and cries had gradually subsided. The crowd was still simmering, ready to erupt again. But it was as close to control as it was going to get.

Bobby had reacted to all of this the way a turtle reacts to a kid poking it with a stick. He withdrew. He was still there, physically. But his head was somewhere else. I could only guess where. He didn't say anything or show much emotion. He just latched onto the bag and hung his head.

When the fairway ahead was clear, Cade Benton spoke to someone over his cell phone—his boss, I guess. He turned to Bobby. "Mr. Jobe, you're up," he said.

Bobby came halfway out of it, but when he spoke, his voice seemed small and tired. "Cade, we just had an earthquake," he said. "You sure it's not going to happen again?"

"I'm not sure what we had," Benton said. "Up at the clubhouse, they say there wasn't anything."

"But it's not safe!" Little Dickie protested. "If it happens again, trees could fall on us!" He was looking around nervously, and he fixed on the TV tower behind the sixteenth green. "The tower could come down while we're putting. They gotta suspend play!"

I wasn't sure if Dickie was genuinely scared or thinking that maybe if the round got suspended, Delsing and Bobby would come back cold, make a couple of bogeys, and give him a chance to win. Probably some of both.

Benton looked uncomfortable at the thought of having to stand up to him. "Sorry, Mr. Reynolds." He turned toward Bobby. "You're up, Mr. Jobe."

Bobby straightened his back and squared his shoulders and turned his head toward the fairway, almost as if he could see the hole and pick out a target.

"I think four," I said. "Same as yesterday."

"What about going for it?" he asked me.

I looked at the green again. Driving the green was one way to get the birdie we needed to catch Delsing. In the last few holes of a tournament Bobby'd be feeling enough adrenaline that I suspected he could've hit a driver that far. But I would have bet you my share of the purse against hitting it that far and straight both. Weird things had been happening, but not that weird. And if you missed, the area around the green was unforgiving—lots of little bunkers and hummocks that forced you into odd stances. Then woods so thick they'd frighten wolves.

"Let's let our brains do the thinking for us," I said. "More than one way to make birdie here."

"Just checking," Bobby said. "Four-iron?"

"Yep."

I pulled the club. A bit of turf clung to the sole from the last time he'd used it. I'd missed it when I wiped off the club and put it back in the bag. I grabbed the wet end of my towel, and for some reason I polished that club, aware of every little scratch and nick in it, polished it till it shone. Then I put it in his hands, and we got set up. I squatted down behind him.

The sun broke completely free of the clouds at that moment, and the light bounced off the polished blade of the club, nearly blinding me. I blinked and wobbled a little on my haunches.

He turned his head back toward me.

"True vision?" he asked.

I was sure that if I could've seen through the Oakleys, he'd've been winking again.

"Don't overdo the sarcasm, now that you've figured out what it is," I said. "Hit the damn ball."

He set, swung, and the clubhead seemed to catch and hold the sun throughout its arc. It left a glinting silver halo along its path for a second.

The click was solid and pure and so was the shot. It took off toward a poplar tree on the horizon, hung there, and then fell gently toward the right, just as we'd envisioned. When it landed, I was surprised. It looked ten or twenty yards closer to the end of the fairway than it should have. Bobby was that pumped up. The crowd, still nervous and jittery after the earth tremor, cheered like he'd just walked out onto the pond by sixteen green and done jumping jacks.

"You hit that about two-thirty," I told him. "Feeling a little strong?"

He came out of his follow-through pose, tipped his cap, and handed me the club.

"If I was any more juiced," he said, "I could get an endorsement deal from Tropicana."

It was Little Dickie's turn. He'd argued himself into a terrible state for hitting golf balls. He'd been saying that it wasn't safe to be out there, that trees and towers could fall on his head. And even though he'd not been absolutely sincere, I could see that the words were rattling around in his mind as he surveyed his shot. He had not one but two strokes to make up on Delsing, so he absolutely had to have a birdie here. He picked the same club Bobby'd thought of, his driver. His face, crowned by that plain white Hogan cap, looked tight and anxious. His mouth was a thin little line and his chin was speckled red and white, his jaw was so taut.

When the spectators saw the club in his hand, they cheered and whistled. It didn't help. Little Dickie put a quick, tight swing on the ball and yanked it. He managed to get it up even with the front edge of the green. But he was way left, and the ball settled on the downslope of a bunker.

We set out toward the green. Oddly enough, the gallery noise didn't drown everything else out. I could hear the clubs clanking together as clearly as I could on a quiet evening at Eadon Branch. I could hear my own breathing, hear the rasping as my sneakers scraped over the sand in front of the tee box, hear the sound change as we reached the fairway.

We had 110 to the hole, a sand wedge. Bobby hit it straight at the flag. But as soon as I heard the clubhead meet the ball, I knew it was going to be long. The crowd started to buzz, not knowing what I knew. The ball flew at the pin and seemed to disappear.

The sound, again, told me and Bobby that something odd had happened. Because I couldn't see it.

"What?" Bobby demanded. He sounded like he could barely get the word out of his throat.

"I thought it was long, but I don't know," I said. "Sounds like it might be close."

I turned around and saw David Feherty from CBS standing fifteen feet away. His cameraman had a little monitor, and he knew what had happened. With my face and shoulders, I let him know that we hadn't seen what happened.

"You hit the flag!" Feherty shouted. "You're two feet!"

I looked at Feherty. He was a comedian, but I didn't think he'd joke at a time like that. I could see he was excited. He was jumping up and down.

That was why I'd lost sight of the ball. It got caught in the folds of the flag while my eyes moved onward, expecting to pick up its flight beyond the hole.

"My God," Bobby said, so low that only I could hear him. "My God."

He was standing there, numb. I took the club out of his hands and stuffed it in the bag, then grabbed him by the elbow and prodded until his feet started moving. I expected him to drop back and take the bag the usual way, but he didn't. He stayed abreast of me and we walked to the green together.

The crowd was frenzied now. The past fifteen minutes had been like being churned up inside a Mixmaster. As the word spread down the fairway about what'd happened to Bobby's shot, they got louder and louder. I saw people crying. That's how intense it was.

"It's going to happen," Bobby said to me. "It's going to happen. We're going to birdie this hole and birdie the next and win the PGA."

"Don't get ahead of yourself," I warned him. "We got a ways to go."

"It's going to happen," he repeated. "I don't know why, but it is."

Truth be told, I thought he was right. I remember thinking that this must be the way Nicklaus used to feel in the last few holes of a major. He didn't know whether he was going to win because he made birdies or because someone else made bogeys. But he knew he was going to win.

We came up the little rise in front of the green and I saw the ball for the first time. It was right behind the pin, and as I got closer, I saw that Feherty had gotten it right. The ball was two feet away. It was just below the hole, a straight putt.

I marked the ball, and then Little Dickie started grinding on his bunker shot. He walked over the green and around the bunker, looked at it up, down, and sideways.

I paid attention to what he was doing for about five seconds, because in the mass of spectators pressing against the ropes my eyes fell on Angela,

Clayton, and Dr. Mehta. They had somehow gotten themselves into the front row.

"'Scuse me," I said to Bobby. And I walked over there without telling him why.

Angela looked cautiously at me as I came up. Dr. Mehta smiled. Clayton's face didn't change. He was staring at me, eyes unblinking. He looked like one of those little wrens that sometimes come up to the window of the pro shop at Eadon Branch, where Eudora has a bird feeder. They peer into the interior, but the glass separates you from them and their eyes don't comprehend anything.

I smiled at Angela. It was surprisingly easy. All I had to do was pretend nothing had happened between us and I was just glad to see her. "Been looking for you guys," I said. "How's it going?" I spoke in a low voice, so Bobby wouldn't hear and get distracted.

"We're fine," Angela whispered. "How're you holding up?"

I felt like the load on my back weighed a ton. But I didn't want her to know that. "No problems," I said. "Although I might drink a beer when this is over."

She smiled at me. I took a deep breath. That hadn't been too hard.

Dr. Mehta looked warm and supportive and somehow detached, so I turned toward him. "You felt an earthquake, didn't you, Doc?"

He nodded vigorously. "I almost fell down."

"Did the earthquake make his ball go in?" asked Angela.

He didn't answer directly. "It doesn't matter," she said.

"But I'd like to know," I whispered.

"It doesn't matter," she repeated. "All that matters is what you do next."

She was right, of course, and I nodded my head.

"True vision, Henry," Angela said. And she smiled again, like it was a sweet secret we shared between us. I smiled back at her. It was purely golf, I told myself.

Little Dickie was grinding his feet into the sand, trying to get firmly planted over his ball. It wasn't easy; the slope he was on was about as steep as a bunker can be if you want to keep sand on the face. He hacked at the ball, but he got the back of it. It took off low and hot, skipped once on the green, and kicked off, settling into a bunker on the other side.

The crowd oohed sympathetically.

I walked back to Bobby's side. In a whisper, I explained to him what Little Dickie had done and told him we'd have to wait to putt. Bobby just nodded. His lips were a single thin line, and he was sweating like this was the Hell Classic on a bad day.

Little Dickie had one chance left to win the tournament, and it depended on holing his next bunker shot. He came close. I'll give him credit for that. But the ball missed the hole by an inch or two and trickled two feet past. He knocked that one in. Finally, it was our turn.

I squatted behind the ball, just checking, unwilling to be careless at this moment. It was dead straight. I got Bobby lined up and told him what to do.

"Two feet, dead straight, firm," I said.

I put the blade down behind the ball and he started shifting his feet, trying to get comfortable. Then I saw the putter blade move, almost imperceptibly. His hands were trembling.

Oh, God, I thought. Not now.

"Nice and smooth," I said. "Back of the cup."

He couldn't bring the clubhead back. He stood there like a statue.

"My hands are shaking," he whispered.

"You've made putts with shaking hands before," I whispered back. "Nice and smooth. Back of the cup."

Around me, I could almost hear the spectators wondering why Bobby didn't hit the putt.

Finally, the club moved. He didn't put the worst stroke on the ball I'd ever seen. But he yipped it. The ball headed for the left corner of the hole and I thought for an instant that he'd gotten away with it.

It caught the left edge, spun around toward the back, dipped toward the bottom of the hole, and then spun back out and hung on the lip. A horseshoe.

The sounds told Bobby what'd happened. There was no plunk as the ball dropped in. There was an anguished, grieving gasp from the gallery, a gasp that was followed by a moan, then a buzz.

"Oh, no," Bobby said. He slumped forward, bent over, his elbows down toward his knees. "Oh, no."

He stayed like that a moment, suffering. Then he straightened up, turned his head toward the sky. The skin on his forehead got bright red, then purplish. The veins on his temples bulged. The cords of his neck stood out.

A sound rumbled from his throat, then burst out, filled the air over the green. It was a single word: "No!"

It echoed off the silent trees.

I stood up then, too, and grabbed him around the shoulders. I wanted to grab him before he did something stupid, like kick the ball or slam his putter into the ground and cause it to move. But it was more than that. I felt sorry for him. Who hasn't blown a putt like that?

"I choked, Greyhound," he said in a low, strained voice. "I choked like a dog."

"You hit a good putt," I told him. "I misread it."

He didn't buy it, didn't even bother to dispute it. "I'm just a choker," he said. "I always find ways to lose."

I looked around his shoulder and my eye caught Angela in the gallery. She looked like she was about to cry. I thought about what she'd said.

"We haven't lost yet," I said. "There's one hole still to play."

EVERYONE ON THE GOLF COURSE WAS AROUND THE EIGHTEENTH HOLE. They were ten and twenty deep all along both sides of the fairway. They were packed in the bleachers behind the green, a quarter mile and a lot of sand and water ahead of us. I looked around for Angela, or Eudora, or Clayton. There was no way. They'd submerged in the crowd. It was just faces, thousands of faces.

"Lot of people out there," I described it to Bobby. "Lot of people."

He didn't say anything. I checked the pin sheet.

"The hole's right where Jello McKay said it would be," I told him. "Right front. We gotta drive down the left side to get at it."

Bobby shook his head. "I can't believe I missed that damn putt."

"Forget that putt," I told him. "It's done."

"That was it! That was the tournament, handed to me. And I blew it."

"It's not over yet," I said. "We can still birdie this hole."

He snorted and spat. "Didn't Jello say not to go at a front pin, to take your four and be happy?"

"You got a good memory," I said.

"I've never been quite as dumb as you figured me, Henry," Bobby said. He didn't say it bitterly or angrily. Just said it, like it was something we'd often discussed.

"Yeah, but Jello didn't anticipate you being where you are," I said. "Forget about that. We got to make three."

He nodded, trying to talk himself into thinking he could do it. Out in the fairway, Delsing and Lizard were watching as Duval fiddled over club selection, no doubt trying to decide what stick would clear the front bunkers and still leave him close to the hole. Duval was five strokes back as far as I knew. But he was still grinding. I liked that.

I was about to point that out to Bobby. And I might've gone on from there to say all the predictable things that coaches have been saying since the first loser was fired. Like when the going gets tough, the tough get going. Like winners never quit and quitters never win. I might've told him he didn't get on that bus in Nashville and make his way alone to Allegheny Gap just so he could give up on himself with a hole to play. I figured I had to say something to hold him together.

But Bobby opened his mouth first. He didn't turn toward me. He kept facing out toward the fairway. He spoke quietly, so only I could hear.

"Wanna hear something weird?"

I couldn't imagine what might seem weird in the context of what had just happened, but I bit anyway. "Sure," I said.

"Well, a couple of nights ago, I had a dream about this situation."

"That *is* weird."

"Not this situation, exactly. Like it, though. We were playing the final round. I was me, except I wasn't me. I could see. And I was, I don't know, smarter, I guess. Knew more things. Just better, you know?"

"Can you always see in your dreams?" I asked him.

"Twenty-twenty," he said.

I looked at the leaderboard. It hadn't changed. I looked back at Bobby. Drops of sweat were dripping off the bill of his cap now. I reached up with my towel and wiped them.

"Anyway, in the dream, I was a stroke down with two to play and I hit it stiff on seventeen."

That caught my attention. "Really?"

"Yeah. But I made the putt. And I birdied eighteen, too. And Paula and Robby were there, and they came out on the green when the ball rolled in."

"Nice dream," I said.

"You sort of figure things will work out that way if you finally get your shit together, you know?"

"Yeah, I know," I said.

"But in real life, even if you think you're getting your shit together, you can still gag on the two-footer."

"It doesn't matter," I said. "The only thing that matters is what you do next."

Ahead of us, Duval hit his shot to the green. The light applause suggested he hadn't gotten it too close.

"We're up," I said.

Whispering, I laid out the fairway for Bobby one more time and told him where I was aiming him. The line was toward a bush ten feet to the right of the footbridge that spanned the water on the left side of the hole.

"Let it out on this one," I said. I was thinking that even if he hit it off line, the odds were that the crowd would stop it before it found much trouble. I gave him the driver and set him up. He took it back slowly, very slowly, then crushed the ball. It blasted out against the sky, hanging in my view somewhere between the roof of the clubhouse and the flagpole behind the green. It was straight and true, a beautiful sight.

"Dinner and a movie," I said to him before the noise from the crowd rolled over us.

I picked up the bag and stuffed the driver back in and waited for Bobby to latch on. Dickie hit and we set off through the sand.

I didn't know, obviously, what it felt like to walk down the last fairway as the winner of a major championship. I couldn't imagine the cheers and applause being any louder. It was as if the sound from the gallery was a wind at our backs, picking us up and gently pushing us along.

"Stop a second, " I heard Bobby say. So I stopped, and I felt his hand work its way up the bag toward me. And then I felt his hand find my shoulder, and in a second he was abreast of me, his arm around me.

"Okay, Coach," he said. "Let's go."

So we walked that way, together, down the wide, green fairway. I closed my eyes for a couple of seconds and just listened and smelled, taking it in the way Bobby was taking it in. The sounds seemed to intensify in the darkness until I could almost see them.

"It ain't winning," Bobby murmured. "But I don't feel too bad."

"Beats the hell out of the Cooters Tour," I agreed. "And you can still win."

We were twenty yards past Little Dickie, so I left Bobby by the bag and found a sprinkler head, then paced off the yardage as Dickie got ready to hit. I watched him swing. His face looked taut and angry. I figured that the only thing he'd like less than blowing the third-round lead in a major would be finishing behind Bobby Jobe, and he was about to have both happen to him. No wonder he looked irritated.

He needed to hole his shot to tie Delsing, but he hit to the safe, left side of the green. I couldn't tell from my angle if he'd yanked it. I don't think he did. I think he'd given up on the tournament and he just wanted to beat Bobby. He figured par might be good enough to do that. Which meant he must be thinking Bobby would go for the pin and somehow screw it up.

It was our turn. I told Bobby what happened to Dickie's shot, but I didn't tell him why I thought he'd hit it that way. I wanted Bobby to stay focused on getting up and down and tying Delsing. Bobby figured it out, I think, because his jaw tightened.

"Fifty-eight to the front, sixty-three to the hole," I told Bobby. "Uphill. No breeze."

"Seven?"

"Eight, I think. Tropicana."

He nodded. "Sounds good."

"Don't overdo it," I warned him. "Nice and smooth."

He seemed like a machine again as he took the club, a smoothly running, oiled machine. I set him up, aimed him straight at the pin.

Bobby made his best swing of the day. From takeaway to follow-through, it was like the drawings in Hogan's book—precise, powerful, graceful.

It was, of course, a little too good. He hit it ten yards farther than he ever hit an eight-iron, farther even than Woods or Daly hit eight-irons. It flew thirty feet past the hole, right over the flag, hit the green, and stopped dead.

"Long?" he asked me.

"Some. Sorry. I misclubbed you."

He shook his head. "Couldn't expect to get a nine there," he said. "If you'd given it to me, I'd've probably swung too hard and pulled it or something."

"Let's make the putt," I said.

We walked the same way, his arm around my shoulder, up the last bit of fairway and over the footbridge that spanned the creek in front of the green. I remember that I tried to stare at everything there was to see—the people, the golf course—as if by staring at it I would burn it into my brain and remember it forever.

As we came off the bridge, I stopped us. "Something I want to tell you," I said to Bobby.

"What's that?"

"The way you pulled yourself together on the tee back there after you missed that putt. The way you hit these last two shots—you did good, Bobby."

He smiled, half chuckled, like he was remembering something very funny and very pleasant that happened a long time ago. "I think that's the first time you've ever told me that, Greyhound."

I suddenly felt very awkward and uncomfortable, like the time my teacher in the second grade, Mrs. Horton, made me recite a poem at the Christmas assembly.

"Well, let's go make this putt," I said.

"Good idea," Bobby said.

When we got to the green, Dickie lagged his putt to a foot. He tapped in. I hunkered down to study Bobby's putt. It looked familiar, and then I remembered why. It was the putt Jello McKay had shown me that first evening when we walked the course together, the putt that seemed to break uphill.

Squatting there, I smiled. The putt looked like it would break a little right but instead it broke a little left.

We walked the line of the putt and I got Bobby set up. "Thirty-two feet," I said to him. "A touch uphill. Putt for thirty-five."

I tried to push everything out of my mind except the line I wanted. I pointed the stripe on the putter blade a couple of inches to the right of the hole. It was just, I thought, a matter of getting it started in the right direction. I double-checked the alignment of the blade. It was perfect. But then I looked at Bobby's hands. They were trembling again.

He stroked the putt. I heard a solid click as the blade met the ball dead in the sweet spot. I watched it leave. Trembling hands or no, this one looked good. I could hear the buzz start to grow in the gallery. "In the hole!" someone yelled.

Halfway to the hole, we were in a playoff. I started trying to remember what hole the playoff started on, to think about what club we'd use off the tee. Ten feet away, and the ball was still hugging the line I'd planned.

It seemed to be rolling in slow motion, so slow that I could almost read the "Titleist" on it as it turned, could see the little black numeral 2, could see the triangular array of pencil dots I put under the numeral to make sure the ball could be identified as Bobby's. It was as if I had turned into some kind of superant, an ant with the ability to slow things down. I could see the ball, see the hole, and I could see the ball start to move ever so gently to the left. Rolling as ponderously and inexorably as a boulder.

And then I could see the spike mark in its path. "Roll over it," I breathed.

"In the hole!" people were screeching. Bobby danced away, as if he could see the ball and will it to turn.

The ball hit the spike mark. It hopped. It wobbled ever so slightly to the right, then resumed its roll. It looked like it could smell the hole, could home in on it.

And then it was at the hole, rolling over the right lip, taking the break at last, and coming to a stop two inches past the cup, straight behind it.

The moan from the crowd let Bobby know. He dropped the putter and stood stock still.

I fell from a squat to my knees. I've seen the pictures of that moment, including the one the next week spread over two pages of *Sports Illustrated*. The picture makes it look like I'd been praying for the putt to go in, and that's what the caption said. "Unanswered prayer: Caddie Greyhound Mote's anguished face reflects the fate of Bobby Jobe's last putt at the PGA."

That's a crock. They didn't ask me about that. If they had, I'd've told them that I don't believe in praying, especially when you pray for something like a putt to go in and you haven't been inside a church in fifteen years. I'll leave that stuff to the Edmisten family.

I was just so shocked when the putt missed that I lost my balance. If I hadn't gone to my knees, I'd've fallen flat on my face.

But I don't deny I was upset. In fact, I was worse than that. I felt like I'd hit a brick wall going a thousand miles an hour. I was like those astronauts up in orbit. They're weightless and they don't even sense how fast they're going. That's how I'd gotten during that tournament. To have it end that way was a shock. It still is. I still have dreams where I see that last putt, or sometimes the one on seventeen. The ball is rolling toward the hole. And it hits that spike mark, or it rolls around the back of the cup. And at that instant, I always wake up. I never see the end of the putt.

It surprised me. I'd been thinking that this was a professional thing, that I was helping Bobby like a doctor helps a patient. It's the patient who's sick, who needs to get well. If the patient dies, well, that's medicine.

But I felt like I'd lost. I wanted to stand up and yell, "Wait! Let's do it over!"

But you can't do it over, of course, and I didn't stand up and yell that.

What I did was stand up and put a hand on Bobby's shoulder.

"Sorry, Henry," Bobby said.

"No, I'm sorry," I told him. "You hit it just right."

"Really?"

I told him about the spike mark.

He grinned. "I thought I hit it good. Thanks for telling me."

I couldn't believe he was smiling.

"You okay?" I asked him.

"Well," he said, "I intend to so some serious damage to the minibar tonight. But, yeah, I'm okay."

I put my arm around his shoulders. He drew back a little.

"Don't hug me, Henry," he said. "If you do I might lose it."

I turned the hug into a slap on the back. "Can't do that. Got a tap-in left," I said.

He nodded and I set him up. The putt hit the bottom of the cup with a clunk.

The next ten minutes are a blur. I remember the crowd, standing and cheering. I remember quick handshakes from Little Dickie and Albie. I remember Delsing coming out onto the green and embracing Bobby so hard that their hats got knocked off. Delsing was crying and in a strange way I was glad to see that. It reminded me to feel good for him and Lizard. They'd been plugging away on the Tour for a long time, and this win meant a lot to them. It changed their lives. They deserved it. Feeling good for them took some of the sting out of finishing second again.

Only after all that had happened did I realize I'd just lost my bet and the $800,000 that would have changed my life.

Then I remember David Feherty jumping in front of us as we left the green on the way to the scorer's tent.

"How do you feel?" he asked Bobby.

"I feel like I'd like to have that putt on seventeen back," Bobby said.

"Yeah," Feherty said. "I'm sure a lot of people would like to give you another shot at it. But don't you feel proud of the way you've played, what you've accomplished?"

Bobby wasn't going to give in to the question. I could tell by the way his jaw tightened. Feherty wanted him to say, "Yeah, I did great for a blind man, didn't I?"

"I had the lead with two holes to play and I finished second," Bobby said. "I don't feel too great about that."

Feherty didn't give up. The network had a story line for this tournament, and he wanted Bobby to help wrap it up.

"Is there anything you've learned from the experience?" Feherty asked.

Bobby nodded. "A few things," he said.

Feherty waited for Bobby to list them, but Bobby just stood there, giving him dead air. Finally, he prompted him. "Can you tell us what they are?"

He expected, I guess, for Bobby to say how a man can accomplish anything, overcome any obstacle, if he refuses to quit, or some garbage like that. Or he might've said what I was thinking, which was that it didn't matter that much that Bobby didn't win, nor even that he'd missed a makable birdie putt on seventeen. You can't control short putts, just like you can't control earthquakes or thunderbolts. You can only control your effort. And on that, Bobby had done pretty good. Of course, Bobby didn't say any of that.

What he said was "Yeah. Golf is a very hard game."

Then Bobby grinned. "But you knew that, didn't you, David?"

Feherty let us go.

I took Bobby to the scorer's tent and then to the media center. But I didn't go in with him. I was already thinking of locating the people I wanted to see and I didn't want to waste any time. So I turned Bobby over to one of Cade Benton's girls and told him I'd meet him at the car.

I found Angela, Dr. Mehta, and Clayton Mote standing in the players' parking lot. The sun was getting low in the sky over the golf course, and the shadows of the pines were long and dark. Light fell in warm, golden sheets between the trunks. They were a strange trio—the redheaded woman in the Mets hat and the Eadon Branch golf shirt, the Indian doctor with a body like a bowling pin, and the old man, his head cocked to one side, talking to himself.

"No gimmes," I could hear him mumble as I approached. He was talking, I guessed, about the seventeenth hole. But who knew? Maybe he was talking about some putt he'd missed sometime.

Angela solved the problem I had of figuring out exactly how I should greet her. She gave me a hug. She smelled of soap and perspiration in about equal measure.

"Well done, Henry," she whispered. "I'm proud of you."

"What?" I said. I stepped back from her arms—not being angry with her, just letting her know I could take her hugs or leave them, since they were just between friends. "We lost the tournament."

She didn't bother to argue with me. We both knew I was only pretending not to know what she meant.

"No gimmes," Clayton said loudly.

"I know, Dad," I said. I stepped toward him wanting a hug, a touch, some kind of physical contact. He shrank away like I had leprosy.

"No gimmes," he said, a little panicky. "No gimmes."

Dr. Mehta stepped toward him and put a reassuring hand on his elbow. Clayton calmed down. He was still talking to himself, because his lips were moving. But the conversation seemed more serene.

"So," I said. "Where would you all like to eat dinner? I think Bobby ought to be done with the media in fifteen minutes or so."

Mehta shook his head.

"We cannot," he said. "I promised the hospital we would return tonight. And we must drop Angela at the airport in Philadelphia. We need to depart."

That caught my attention. I looked at Angela. "You're leaving right away?"

"I have to be at work tomorrow," she said. "It's only you golf stars who can take Mondays off."

I thought fleetingly about telling her I needed her to stay, but I couldn't quite bring myself to do it. Couldn't quite believe it would do any good. I figured one more friendly hug would be the classy thing to do, so I stepped toward her. She put her hands on my shoulders and then hugged me, hard. I could feel the bones in her back. She kissed me on the cheek.

"Have a good celebration, Henry," she said.

Somewhere in my mind I was thinking that I had to be forceful, that I had to take her in my arms and tell her I loved her and that whatever it took, I would do. But that was somewhere deep in the back of my mind. In the front of my mind, I was still taking rejection with class.

"We'll miss you," I said. I was truthful, at least.

She pushed a little tendril of red hair off her forehead, smiled again. She blinked a couple of times, and I flattered myself into thinking she might be trying to hold back tears.

"I appreciate that, Henry," she said. "More than you know."

I couldn't think of anything to say to that.

I have always hated good-byes. So I shook Dr. Mehta's hand and thanked him very quickly. And I gave Angela one last brief hug, trying to force myself to remember exactly how she felt, exactly how she smelled.

I turned to Clayton. He looked like he was trying to say something but couldn't, because something was caught in his throat. He seemed about to burst.

"D-d-d" was the sound he made.

I waited a second for him to spit it out, but he couldn't. It was painful to watch him.

Finally I stuck out my hand. He didn't take it. So I pulled him toward me and hugged him. I could feel his body stiffen and try to pull away from me.

Then, for just a few seconds, he changed. He pulled closer to me, and his head was against my shoulder and it seemed like he smelled familiar. He was still trying to say something, and his lips were very close to my ear.

"Don't," he whispered, and I thought he was saying he didn't want to be hugged. I let him go, let my arms drop to my sides. But he clung to me, his fingers digging hard into my shoulders. He was still trying to get words out.

"Don't let her go," he said, looking at the ground.

His voice had been so low only I could hear it.

I blinked, unsure I'd actually heard him say those words. I pulled back a step and half squatted and looked at his face. Whatever grasp on reality he had dredged up to make it possible to speak to me like that was gone. He looked exhausted. His shoulders sagged, he averted his eyes. In a second, he was staring at the pavement, mumbling to himself again.

He couldn't have shocked me more if he'd cut down a power line and stuck it in my ear. I couldn't think, couldn't respond. I just moved on autopilot, took his arm, and opened the back door of the car. I made sure he fastened his seat belt. I waved as they drove away.

I HEADED BACK TO THE MEDIA CENTER TO FIND BOBBY. I REMEMBER THINK-ing that I shouldn't have been feeling so good. I'd lost the tournament. I'd lost Angela. I'd lost the bet that would have saved Eadon Branch for Eudora. Not only that, but I was very tired. My legs were weary and my back ached. It had been a long week.

Truth be told, I was feeling very good. If there'd been enough light, I might've wanted to play another round.

Bobby came out of the media center before I could get there, hanging on to the arm of one of Cade Benton's helpers, a woman named Debbie. Debbie, I noticed, was a good-looking blonde, maybe twenty-eight, with a short skirt and a helluva body. Her fingernails precisely matched her lip-stick. She was holding on to Bobby like she meant to do more than just guide him. What the hell, I thought. Paula wasn't around. Bobby was still Bobby.

"Mr. Mote!" Debbie called out. Then she turned to Bobby. "He's right over there," she said.

We met halfway across the parking lot. Inside the media center, I could hear a bit of what Jay Delsing was saying. It sounded like he was describing what he'd felt on the seventeenth hole.

I took a look at Debbie. The weird thing was that she looked just like the sort of women Bobby used to chase in the old days. But of course, Bobby couldn't have known what she looked like. Maybe it was the perfume she wore. Maybe it was some hormone.

"Uh, Henry, I got something for you," Bobby said. He thrust the piece of paper toward me, and I took it. I didn't unfold it. I almost didn't want to know what he'd written on it. Was it the usual 7 percent caddie fee for a top ten finish? Or was it the maybe the 50 percent I'd mentioned when I gave him the check to pay for the lawyer to sue the PGA? I was afraid it was the 7 percent and I'd have to say something or walk away disappointed. I might've stood there, hesitating, for a long time. But Bobby was waiting and Debbie was watching. I unfolded it.

It was a check made out to Henry Mote, drawn on the PGA Championship's prize account, for $400,000.

"That's second-place money," Bobby said. "I'm not much good at saying thanks. But thanks."

I blinked. Debbie was smiling, even though she didn't really understand what was happening. Hell, I wasn't sure what was happening. I had an idea, but I needed to be certain.

"Uh, Bobby, that's too much," I said, leaving open the possibility he wanted to change his mind.

"No, it isn't," Bobby replied. "They made it out the way I told 'em."

Now Bobby was smiling.

"But you need the money," I said, pushing the check back toward him—but not letting go of it, either.

"Nah," Bobby said. "Ely Callaway's already been on the phone talking about a new contract. GMA's left messages. Only money problems I'm going to have are tax problems. I want you to have that."

"Well, thanks," I said. "It's a helluva lot for caddying."

"You're welcome," Bobby said. "You did a lot more than caddy for me."

I nodded, but I couldn't say anything. I was suddenly overcome with the knowledge that I would not be doing it for him much longer.

Bobby, I guess, found the silence awkward, just as I might find it awkward to walk around with my eyes closed. But it was the awkwardness of the moment, too. We weren't used to being nice to one another.

"Well, don't spend it all in one place."

"Sorry, Bobby," I said. "But that's exactly what I'm going to do."

18

▼

I T WAS APRIL AGAIN AT EADON BRANCH. THE MAGNOLIA BY THE FOURTH fairway had bloomed. The stream was running high and clear and the ground was moist. We had to mow the fairways every day and the grass was lush and fragrant. The purple martins were building a nest on the lintel over the door to the cart barn. I was watching the third round of the Masters on television in the clubhouse. I was drinking a beer. Things change, though. This was draft beer, in a cup.

On the screen above the counter, Bobby Jobe stood over a birdie putt on the eighteenth green. Jello McKay squatted behind him, looking like a vanilla sundae in his white Augusta National coverall. Jello aligned the putter, whispering something about the break or the distance that the television mikes couldn't pick up.

"Too low, Jello," I whispered. The pin was where it generally is on No. 18 for the third round at the Masters, on the shelf toward the back of the green. That shelf looks flat, but that's because the ground around it runs down toward the tee, away from the clubhouse. There was always a tendency to read a little less break into a sidehill putt than you actually got.

Bobby stroked the putt; his action looked smooth and buttery. The ball rolled toward the hole without the slightest bump or twitch, hugging that gorgeous Augusta grass. They had a great camera angle, low, behind the hole, looking over it toward Bobby and Jello.

"Get in the jar!" J. R. Neill yelled.

"In the jar!" Conrad urged.

Halfway there, the ball seemed to have a chance. But as it slowed, it broke across the front of the hole. It died a foot away on the low side. The crowd at Augusta moaned. So did the crowd at Eadon Branch, maybe fifty people packed into the clubhouse, all dirty, tired, and sweating.

"Jobe will have a tap-in for a round of seventy and a total of 208, three strokes off the pace going into tomorrow's final round," Jim Nantz said.

"You were right. Too low. If you'd been there, he'd've made it," J. R. said.

"I don't know," I said, but I was pleased by the compliment. "Hard to tell on TV. Jello knows how to read greens. He might've lined Bobby up right and Bobby pulled it a bit. Golf's a hard game. Augusta's got tricky greens."

"He would too have made it. Don't be modest, Henry," Eudora said.

"You think he'll win?" Conrad asked me.

I shrugged. "I hope so. If he keeps getting into contention, he's bound to win one of these times. He's doing the right things."

Out by the first tee, the amplified sound of guitars tuning up drowned out the sound of a Cadillac commercial on the television. I grabbed Eudora's remote and turned off the set.

"Okay," I announced. "Clubhouse is closed. Kegs are open. Band's starting up. Party time!"

The crowd streamed outside. The sun was getting low behind Eadon Mountain and shadows were lengthening on the ninth and first fairways. A little breeze flickered at the flags on the greens, cooling the air. The branch glinted gray and gold both in the fading light. The air might've smelled like honeysuckle and grass clippings except for the overpowering scent of roasting pork from the barbecue pit we'd fashioned out of half of an old two-hundred-gallon oil drum.

On a little wooden bandstand we'd built for the evening under the tree by the lesson tee, Midnight Rodeo was ready to play. The lead guitar started in, and then the drummer and the harmonica. It was a song called "Eadon Mountain Hoedown," which never got famous because no one like Patsy Cline ever recorded it. But folks around Allegheny Gap played it all the time:

> *Moonlight gleams on a whiskey still*
> *Way up top of a green-tree'd hill . . .*

When they got to the chorus, I stepped up to the mike and spoke. The music kept going behind me, but much lower, like an engine idling. I had some things to say and most of the people bunched around in front of me, except for Raymond and a couple of others who stayed by the kegs. I didn't mind the guys by the kegs. After the work they'd done that day, they deserved as much beer as they wanted to drink.

I pulled out some notes I'd written.

"I'd like to welcome you all to the First Annual Eadon Branch Golf Club Stump Pull and Pig Pickin'," I said. "And I'd like to thank all of you who helped out today clearing the land for the tenth hole. I hope you'll be back tomorrow to help with No. 11."

"We're all gonna be hung over!" Raymond yelled.

"That's all right, Raymond," I said. "We weren't going to let you operate any machinery anyway."

People laughed. I felt somehow taller and better looking.

"Anyway," I concluded, "Eudora and I thought this was the best way to thank everyone. We want you to know that if things go according to plan, by the time we have the Fifth Annual Stump Pull and Pig Pickin', we expect to be clearing land for the eighteenth hole. In the meantime, if the branch doesn't rise and the sun shines, we ought to have the best damn eleven-hole golf course in the country by this time next year! So drink up and eat up, 'cause we have lots to celebrate!"

There was a cheer then, and the band picked it up. I hung around on the bandstand and sang the chorus with them.

> *Grab that girl with the blue dress on.*
> *She looks like she could dance till dawn.*
> *Knows how to step and knows how to twirl.*
> *Don't you know she's an Eadon Mountain girl.*

Something strange happened to me right at that moment. It was like the band suddenly hit a few clinkers or snapped a string. They didn't, of course, But the music, the urge to sing, just blew right out of me like the air going out of a punctured tire. I stepped off the stage and walked alone back into the clubhouse, sipping a beer.

I went to the pay phone and dug around in my wallet till I found the folded scrap of paper that had Angela's phone number on it. It wasn't the first time I'd thought about calling her. I'd thought about it a lot of times. At first I didn't call because I still wanted to show her I was strong or classy or something. Then I didn't call because, damn it, I thought she ought to be the one to pick up the phone first. Then I didn't call because I was so busy with the plans for the new holes. And after that it was because a lot of time had gone by and I didn't have a good explanation for why I hadn't called her.

But I always heard two little voices in the back of my mind. They weren't quite imaginary voices like Clayton Mote hears; they were from live people. One of them was Clayton telling me not to let her go. And the other was just my own, telling me to listen to my old man. But it wasn't until I was out there singing along with the band that the voices got persuasive enough to make me do it.

So I dialed her number. It rang four times. Then the tone of the rings changed a little and I knew I was going to get her machine. Sure enough, I heard her voice, giving her number back and saying leave a message at the tone.

I was sort of relieved actually, not to have to talk to her. The machine couldn't do anything besides take the message. It couldn't say no.

"Um, hi, Angela. It's Henry. Greyhound," I said. I grimaced. If my tongue was any clumsier, it'd trip on my teeth.

"No, it's Henry Mote, I mean. We were having a party here at Eadon Branch because we're breaking ground for a couple of new holes, and I was thinking about you. Kind of wish you were here, truth be told. So, anyway, if you get this message . . ."

I stopped. I wasn't quite sure what I wanted to say.

". . . Just wanted to tell you I wish you were here is all," I finished. I hung up.

I felt kind of stupid, waiting all that time to call her and then not having anything smart to say when I finally did. I went over to the lunch counter, pulled myself another beer, and turned the TV back on. I listened to Ken Venturi talking about who still had a chance to win the Masters. Bobby was on his list.

When the Masters was over, I got up and started to walk outside and rejoin the party. The phone rang.

"Eadon Branch Golf Club," I said. "Soon to be the finest eleven-hole course in Warmerdam County."

"So you wish I was there, huh?"

"Angela?" I knew who it was, but I asked anyway.

"Look out the window, Henry," she said.

I almost yanked the phone out of the wall getting to the window. She was standing there in our parking lot, holding a cell phone to her ear, in the middle of a row of pickup trucks and beat-up old vans. She was wearing her Eadon Branch hat with her red hair spilling out under it and a plaid shirt and jeans. She looked prettier than on that first April afternoon when I saw her a year before. She waved at me. She was only thirty paces away from me, but for some reason, I stood in the clubhouse and waved back at her through the window. I was too surprised to move.

"So," she said, when it became clear that I wasn't going to get my mouth started anytime soon, "are you going to invite me to your party? Sounds like a good band."

I finally was able to say something. "How'd you know to call?"

"This phone tells me when I have messages," she said. "I was driving up here and talking to Bobby in Augusta. When I hung up, I saw you'd called."

I went outside. Her eyes were like a Christmas present.

"Spring has officially arrived at Eadon Branch," I said, smiling at her. "You look beautiful, Angela."

She blinked, looking surprised at the compliment. When she did that, I got a little surprised I'd been smart enough to say it.

"Why thank you, Henry," she said. She blushed enough that it was visible against the fire of the lowering sun.

Without saying anything more, I took a step toward her and she opened her arms and I hugged her. She felt small and light and very good pressed against me. Her hair smelled like daffodils. When I pulled back a little from her, I kept my arm around her.

"What made you decide to come?"

"Partly Bobby," she said. "He told me that as a minority stockholder, he needed someone up here to make sure you did things right."

"Partly Bobby?" I asked her.

"Partly," she said. "He also told me you'd be glad to see me if I came."

"Just shows a man can always be learning," I said, grinning.

She smiled back.

"I'm so glad you're here," I said. "I kept thinking I ought to call you, but I kept finding reasons to put it off. Now I think I was basically waiting till I could show you how things are changing around here."

I walked her around the side of the building toward the bandstand, thinking I might ask her to dance. But Gilmore Clevinger from the police department came up and shook Angela's hand, said it was nice to see her back in Allegheny Gap again. So did Michael and Kim, two of my junior golfers, and then Raymond came over with a beer for her, and it became obvious to both of us we wouldn't get a chance to talk as long as we hung around the beer and the food and the music.

"Can you show me what you did today?" she asked me.

I took her hand and walked her over toward the other side of the clubhouse, where we'd spent the day cutting trees for the first hole of the Eadon Branch back nine.

"You trained Jello well," she said.

"He didn't need much help. Long as his knees hold out, he'll be okay."

We came around to where the tenth tee was going to be. I showed her that, then walked her up the hillside toward the green. It didn't look like much, of course. It was just a long brown gash in the woods, stakes with orange ribbons on them, piles of tree trunks stacked here and there and the moldy smell of overturned earth.

"The fairway's going to be like the tenth at Riviera in Los Angeles and the green's going to be like the green on No. 10 at Sand Valley. Short par four. Drivable if you want to risk the bunker in front," I told her.

She pretended she could see it the way I saw it in my mind's eye, all grassed and dark green, white sand in the bunkers, a little breeze playing with the pin, players standing on the tee trying to decide what club to hit.

"The Devil's Asshole bunker?" she asked.

"Like that." I nodded. "If I can get it to drain right."

She sipped from her beer, still holding my hand. "And if you can't?"

"Well, then we'll stock it with bass and hire some kid to stand out here with fishing poles and rent 'em out for fifty cents a cast," I said.

"You're becoming such a businessman," she said, teasing me.

"Gotta protect my investment."

She let go of my hand, gave me her beer, and put an imaginary club in her hands. She made an imaginary swing. It was a good thing it wasn't real, or she'd have shanked it into the woods.

"Nice shot," I said.

If she knew better, she didn't let on. Golf was sometimes a lot more fun if you played it in your mind.

"Is it the hole the pro designed?"

"Not as far as I can tell," I said. "He had a much longer hole laid out if I read his orange ribbons right."

"He'll like this one, I bet," she said.

"I hope so," I told her. "I hope he can get here in the fall when it's grassed in."

"Any word on the new medication?"

"Dr. Mehta says he's hopeful, but it's too soon to tell." That was why I hadn't asked Dr. Mehta if we could bring Clayton down for the stump clearing. He didn't want Clayton to leave the hospital until he could finish testing some new pill on him. That plus the fact that Eudora wasn't entirely comfortable with the idea.

"Waves against a rock," Angela said.

"Yep."

We'd been talking all around the main thing that was on my mind, and finally, I asked her.

"Why else did you come here, besides Bobby?"

"To see you," she said, a little shyly. She didn't exactly look at me when she said it. She was looking toward Eadon Mountain, and the sun was full in her eyes, making her skin pale.

"I should've invited you," I said. "I'm sorry. "

She turned her face and looked straight at me. A little breeze blew down off the mountain and I felt like I could float away.

"Don't apologize," she said. "I didn't treat you very well back in Atlantic City."

"Oh, no, you were fine," I told her.

"I've been thinking a lot since then," she said.

"What about?"

"About appropriate men." She just let that hang there.

I smiled. "I've been thinking a lot, too."

"What about?"

"I've been thinking how much more appropriate I'm feeling."

"Seems like every time I see you, you look more appropriate to me, too," she said. She smiled, and I took that as an invitation. I kissed her, and it felt like that time we kissed on the first green under the moonlight, except more deliberate, more confident. Happier. Like we were younger and older at the same time.

She took my hand. We strolled down by the pond next to the fourth green. The top of the willow tree was still touched by the last rays of the sun, but down by the ground it was all in shadow. The pond was still and dark.

Up by the clubhouse, Midnight Rodeo started playing "Crazy," just the way they had that night at Gully's. Angela came into my arms and we pretended to dance, our feet scraping the dirt back and forth. She hummed along with the song for a few bars, then I sang a few, about crazy for trying and crazy for crying. Angela cocked her head back sideways a little and looked at me.

"Why Henry," she said. "I didn't know you could sing."

Neither, I told her, had I.